Standby Counsel

A Monica Spade Novel

ALEXI VENICE

Published by eBookIt.com

http://www.eBookIt.com

ISBN-13: 978-1-4566-3542-8

Editor: Sarah Branham Editorial

Cover Design: Alexi Venice and Bo Bennett

Books by Alexi Venice

The Monica Spade Series
Conscious Bias, Book 1
Standby Counsel, Book 2

The San Francisco Mystery Series
Bourbon Chase, Book 1
Amanda's Dragonfly, Book 2
Stabscotch, Book 3
Tinted Chapstick, Book 4
Sativa Strain, Book 5
#SandyBottom, Book 6

The Pepper McCallan Series
Ebola Vaccine Wars
Svea's Sins
Victus – Margaret River Winery (Part I)
Margaret River Winery (Part II)

Dedicated to the courageous prosecutors, defense bar, judges and law enforcement who together make our judicial system work.

Table of Contents

1

Monica's breath floated like a lazy summer breeze over Shelby's ear, waking her from an afternoon nap.

Eyes still closed, Shelby leaned into Monica, a sleepy moan issuing from her full lips.

Exhaling low and slow, Monica teased Shelby with feathery light tongue sweeps across her left ear.

Rumbles turned into tiny squeals, and Shelby's hand sought and found Monica's leg, gripping it with intensity.

"You like?" Monica whispered.

"Uh-huh."

Monica showered breathy kisses and swirls along the delicate contours of Shelby's ear. The tip of her tongue glided from the diamond stud at the top to the thin, gold hoop in the lobe, where she nibbled ever so tenderly.

Shelby's hands skated up Monica's thigh in search of the forest of curls she adored.

Eager for more, Monica left Shelby's ear for the warmth of her mouth.

Shelby's hands slid around Monica's hips and, patting her derriere, signaled that she wanted Monica on top.

Monica threw her leg across Shelby and levered herself over her, their bodies colliding in a sweet, hot fusion.

***

Much later, after a second nap to recover from the rush and release of sex, Monica awoke to Shelby thumbing through the feed on her iPhone.

"Hm." Monica stretched, so her hand could touch Shelby's shoulder, her heart blooming with love.

"Hey, sleepyhead," Shelby said, still focusing on her phone screen.

"I didn't think it was physically possible to have sex that many times in a 24-hour period." Monica ran her finger along Shelby's neck, up to her mass of chestnut curls.

"Each time gets better, though, you have to admit."

Monica's eyes grew wide. "I wasn't that bad in the beginning, was I?"

Eyes still on the screen, Shelby let Monica hang for a few seconds before turning and saying, "No. You. Are. Fantastic. Better than fantastic. The best."

Monica relaxed.

Shelby set her phone aside. "I'm going to need food if you want to continue the shagathon."

"Me too. Let's make pasta or, better yet, pizza."

Shelby smiled and gazed so deeply into Monica's emerald eyes that Monica lost track of where she ended, and Shelby began.

They lay in silence for a few minutes, tenderly caressing each other.

"Shiny diamond," Monica said, gently fingering Shelby's cartilage piercing.

Shelby's fingers moved to her ear to feel of the stud, displacing Monica's. "This—"

"Huge rock—"

"Was a gift." Suddenly, the skin around Shelby's lips tightened, accentuating her strong jawline.

Sensing a shift in mood, Monica traced the back of her finger along Shelby's cheekbone. "Did I stumble into a thicket?" Curiosity was Monica's trademark, and had served her well as a lawyer, but sometimes got her in trouble in her personal life.

"It's fine. I'm fine." Shelby's mouth compressed into a thin line that Monica witnessed only when Shelby was lifting weights at CrossFit.

"Do you want to talk about it?" Monica leaned up on her elbow, so she could read Shelby's expression—now guarded. A jolt of panic coursed through her, but she quickly reminded herself that Shelby wasn't angry at *her*.

"I just need to…get rid of this earring…soon." Shelby threw back the sheets and jumped out of bed. Silence entered their intimacy, as Shelby grabbed her ultra-soft robe from a rocking chair and wrapped herself in it. Keeping her eyes angled away from Monica, she left the bedroom before Monica could explore the topic further.

Monica flopped onto her back and studied the crown molding characteristic of Shelby's one-hundred-plus-year-old house. They had been seeing each other for three months, and Monica had turned her heart over to Shelby. She thought they were capable of discussing anything, since they already had shared so much with each other. Wedding bells had even chimed in the back of Monica's mind, but now she wondered if Shelby's reaction to the diamond stud was a warning to slow down.

It was a gift. How naïve of me. Of course she's had other lovers. A 31-year-old woman who looks like Shelby is bound to have broken a few hearts, and maybe had hers broken in the process.

Monica peeled back the covers and got out of bed. Feeling the winter chill through the walls, she shrugged on her favorite Brewers long-sleeve over a tank and slipped into a pair of joggers. She tiptoed in wool socks to the kitchen, where Shelby was scrubbing a pot in the sink, clanging and banging while viciously scouring.

Monica slid her arms around Shelby's waist and rested her chin on her shoulder. "Hey, gorgeous."

Shelby's body went rigid. "I don't like dirty dishes in the sink."

What the what? Monica thought. *It's just one pot, and I've never ever heard you say that.* "Sorry. I meant to clean it earlier today, but someone got frisky. Why don't you grab a glass of wine and watch the news while I finish this?"

Their routine when Shelby cooked was for Monica to do the dishes, which she happily had done after brunch earlier that day, with the exception of a nonstick pot for oatmeal. A snowbank of soap suds brimmed over its edges, any evidence of food long since chased down the drain by Shelby's scrubber.

Shelby's tone slipped toward irritation. "I'm almost done anyway."

Monica released her hands and pushed back. She went to the fridge to assess its contents for dinner, although she wondered if Shelby was too upset to eat. She grabbed a beer, unscrewed the cap, and cautiously sipped while watching Shelby, who ignored her.

"Can I pour you a glass of wine?"

"I'll get my own," Shelby said too quickly.

Monica straightened, then asked in a softer tone, "Are you in the mood for pasta or pizza?"

"I don't know." Shelby turned off the water and hand-dried the pot with a dish rag, her hands working in a dizzying blur.

Monica stared at Shelby until she looked up. "What's bothering you?"

Shelby's usually warm, hazel eyes held a blistering glare. "Nothing."

Monica attempted a smile. "Let me get out of your way, so you can pour yourself some wine."

Shelby watched with cool detachment, as Monica brushed past her to the living room, where she opened the top hatch of a wood-burning stove and stirred what was left of the coals from that morning. With temps well below zero, and threatening to plunge deeper that night, Monica decided to rejuvenate the fire. She set her beer on the coffee table and added a few logs and some crumpled newspaper. The flames sprang to life, providing a blue glow that Monica hoped would thaw Shelby's frosty attitude.

Satisfied the fire would take hold, Monica adjusted the screen on the front and sat on the sofa with her beer and iPhone. She stared at the news feed until Shelby came into the room with a magazine in one hand and a glass of wine in the other. She surveyed the seating options and selected an overstuffed chair with a quilt thrown over the back— as far away from Monica as possible.

Should I pretend that nothing is wrong? Monica wondered.

Shelby sighed, rose, tossed her magazine on the cushion, and set her wine on a nearby bookshelf. She grabbed the fireplace utensils, making a big fuss over sweeping up a smattering of ashes that she tossed into the stove. "I usually sweep up after I start a fire."

Monica's heart sank. "I'm sorry. In fact, I'm sorry for whatever I said, or did, that pissed you off. I can see I'm no longer welcome here, so I'll show myself out."

Shelby curled into her chair, her forehead crinkling with little dimples above her eyebrows, radiating a mix of guilt and anger, shredding Monica's heart.

"Maybe that's best," Shelby said, her voice a study in deadpan.

Monica shoved off from the sofa, grabbed car keys, and unceremoniously walked to the kitchen door. "I'm going out to start my truck. I'll be back in a few seconds while it warms up."

If Monica was getting kicked out of Shelby's house on a bitter Saturday night, then she refused to sit on a cold seat all the way home. She pulled on her boots and stomped out to the white Ford pickup that she had bought from her grandfather. It started easily, but the windshield was covered in snow, so she turned on the wipers along with the heat and returned to the kitchen.

Either Shelby didn't hear Monica or was intentionally ignoring her, her face buried in a magazine, her wine still resting on the bookshelf.

Monica looked at the microwave clock, 7:20 p.m., and told herself she would wait five minutes for her truck to warm up. She took a drink of beer and decided to make one last effort at trying to understand why the only woman with whom she had fallen in love was being so cruel. Fear bubbling in her chest, she tiptoed back into the living room.

Perching on an ottoman a few feet from Shelby, Monica cleared her throat. "I respect your space, and I understand you want me to leave, but I don't like being tossed to the curb when I don't know what I said or did to warrant it. I've been nothing but loving and *in love* with you. You obviously have something going on that was triggered by my inquiry into the diamond stud in your ear. I'm sorry, but I think it's unfair of you to shut me out." She rubbed her hands together, waiting.

Shelby's sultry eyes flashed then reset to feigned disinterest.

Now in disbelief, Monica said, "I love you, but I'm leaving. Let me know when you can talk like an adult."

Shelby lowered her head to her magazine.

Monica rose and returned to the kitchen, where she polished off her beer, struggled into her thick down coat, and pulled on her dark blue "Love Your Melon" hat that Shelby had given her for Christmas. She grabbed her bag and gloves and left in her little white truck.

As her tires crunched over the snowpack on the winter streets, she wondered, *Why is Shelby so psycho about that fucking stud?*

2

Her Saturday night now a flop, Monica turned into her snow-covered driveway. She had helped Shelby shovel hers earlier that day with the promise of a return favor, but that had disappeared into thin air along with Shelby's warmth. Jilted and still reeling, Monica looked forward to throwing her frustration into each thrust of the shovel.

Shelby had seemed so mature, able to talk through anything, and, above all, sweet. That was the first quality Monica had been attracted to—Shelby's sweetness. Okay, maybe it was her round ass in those workout tights, but the sweetness was a close second.

Monica had never experienced such abrupt rejection by a lover—cut off like the head of an enemy. Her imagination flirted with the extreme, as she pictured a young Shelby with friends at a tattoo and piercing parlor. *Was there a special woman in Shelby's life with a matching diamond stud? If so, is Shelby still in love with her? Why are women so fucking secretive?*

Monica parked, got out of her truck, and removed a shovel from a peg on the garage wall. *Such an irrational response. Sweeping up nothing.*

She scraped the yellow blade on the driveway and scooped up some snow, tossing the shovelful onto the waist-high bank that flanked the driveway. Up and over. The hardest part of shoveling was clearing the mid-winter bank.

I just didn't expect the silent treatment from someone as pulled together as Shelby. Monica pushed the blade down the middle of the single-car driveway, tossing the snow as she went.

I mean, normal people don't get pissed, clam up, and throw you out. Taking satisfaction in the outdoor physical activity, Monica glanced around to appreciate the fresh snow on the pines and the silence of a clear, still night. An owl hooted in the distance, reminding her that there was still outdoor life in the frozen tundra.

With renewed vigor, she shoveled on. *There was nothing I could have said or done differently, was there?*

She quickly cleared another lane from the garage to the city sidewalk. Scrape. Scoop. Toss. *I mean, I was totally awesome in bed…*

She turned before she reached the street, knowing the plow would come by later and deposit more snow at the entrance to her driveway.

Making love to me one minute then turning on me the next! Scrape. Scoop. Toss.

She shoveled her way back to the garage, removed the snow around the concrete apron, then forged a new path back down to the street.

When she reached the bottom, she looked up briefly and waved to her neighbor, as he shoveled his way to the end of his driveway too. They turned at the same time like a choreographed dance, tossing snow over the banks, pushing their blades back up the driveways.

If she can't communicate, then to hell with her, Monica thought, as she took her last swipe at Shelby as well as the edges of the driveway. She glanced around her tree-lined yard, the expanse now a silver glow in the moonlight.

Maybe we've been spending too much time together. Maybe we need a break. The calm, frigid air served as a sobering tonic to her lovelorn, muddled brain.

The owl's next hoot was eclipsed by the city plow truck rumbling down the street, its blade scraping the pavement through patches of snow. Without hesitation, the truck left a foot of packed snow at the end of each driveway. Surprised that the trucks were out so soon after the snow had stopped, Monica cursed and returned to the curb to clear away the side effect of a clear street.

She stabbed her shovel into the crud, which was much heavier than the snow on the driveway. She worked up her heart rate again, tossing each shovelful with the anger she wanted to unleash on Shelby.

When she was finished, she made a final pass along the edges of the driveway and returned the shovel to its peg in the garage.

She entered her small house and hung up her jacket, then sat on a kitchen chair and methodically loosened the laces on her boots, kicking them at the built-in cubbies in her entryway.

Alone in the darkness, she stared blankly into the cubbies, not seeing the mittens, hats or neck warmers stored in them. Into the expanding silence, she moaned, covered her face with her hands, and dropped her head. Giving herself permission to cry, she hoped the release of tears would remedy the heartbreak over Shelby.

After a time, she mumbled some phrases about life being unfair and never falling in love again, as she moped to the bathroom. Refusing to look at the sad, young woman in the mirror, she decided to wash away all thoughts, smells, and sensations of Shelby in the shower. The hot spray was a relief. She stood under it for an eternity, letting the water soothe her broken heart and jumbled emotions, hoping her misery would flow down the drain.

Feeling marginally better when she emerged, she put on fresh clothes and turned on the oven to bake a frozen pizza. While she waited for the oven to preheat, she opened her laptop to catch up on work emails. If the remainder of her weekend was destined for solitude, the least she could do was attack legal documents with a vengeance.

Out of habit, she glanced at her cell phone. No texts or calls from Shelby.

Later, a few bites into her pizza, she felt her cell phone vibrate on the table. Expecting it to be Shelby, she peeked at the screen. Not Shelby, but she recognized the number as the Community Memorial Hospital switchboard, so she answered. "This is Attorney Monica Spade."

"This is the hospital switchboard. I have a SANE nurse in the Emergency Department on hold who wants to talk to the attorney on call."

"I'll take it." Monica searched her memory but couldn't recall the last time the Sexual Assault Nurse Examiner had paged her.

The operator connected them, and Monica said, "Hello, this is Monica Spade."

"This is Julia Brown, the SANE nurse in the ED." Her voice was raised over loud, beeping machines. "We have a 32-year-old female here who isn't saying much other than she was sexually assaulted. I asked her if I could conduct an exam, and she just nodded. Is that good enough for consent?"

"Is she impaired?"

"No. Her drug screen is negative, but the screen doesn't detect all illicit drugs."

"How much time did you spend talking to her?"

"I've been in the room with her for a couple of hours. She's cooperative but silent. Not even crying. I pretty much did all I can do short of a pelvic exam."

"Did she come in alone? Does she have any family with her?" Monica asked.

"The police brought her in. They said she was out in the country and knocked on a farmer's door. He called the police. Her feet are muddy, and she has several lacerations."

"Did she tell you what happened?"

"Not really. She won't say who attacked her, when, or where," Julia said. "She says she was with her boyfriend one minute, and the next thing she remembers is waking up in our ED."

"Did she give you her boyfriend's name?"

"No."

"Is she protecting him? Is he the one who sexually assaulted her?"

"She won't say. I'm not sure he was with her when the assault took place."

"Do sexual assault victims usually suffer from amnesia like this?" Monica asked.

"Occasionally, they can't remember bits and pieces of the story, but they aren't usually a blank slate. I just wonder if she's under the influence of a drug we can't detect, like Rohypnol."

Monica searched her memory. "Is that a Roofie?"

"Yes. A tranquilizer."

"That might explain her reticence or outright inability to recall."

"She just isn't the typical presentation." Julia paused a moment, then asked, "So, back to the pelvic part of the exam. I explained it to her, and she nodded silently. Is that good enough for consent?"

"I think so," Monica said. "Go ahead and start the exam, talking her through each step as you perform the evidence collection. Be sure to emphasize that you'll stop immediately if she asks."

"I always do anyway." Monica heard the rustle of papers in the background, then Julia said, "Something isn't quite right about her, though. I can't describe what it is, but something is...off."

"Maybe make a note of that in the record," Monica said.

"Okay."

"Call me if you need anything else."

"I will. Thanks."

Monica was grateful for the call, a welcome distraction from overanalyzing Shelby's hurtful behavior. She returned to her laptop and opened an employment agreement that the hospital administrator had sent to her. The logic center of her brain read and revised the clauses, while the emotional side replayed various threads of conversation with Shelby over the last few months. On legal autopilot, Monica slogged through the agreement, making the necessary edits.

Several minutes later, her phone screen lit up with a text from Shelby. Monica's heart skipped, but she ignored the message, telling herself she had important legal work to finish. The words in the agreement soon turned into alphabet soup, though, and Monica realized she wasn't comprehending what her eyes traveled over.

A minute passed, and her phone vibrated again with the text.

Is she breaking up with me by text? Monica wondered.

She promised herself she would read Shelby's text after she finished the agreement, so she read on. "Either party may terminate this agreement by giving ninety (90) days' prior written notice to the other party..."

Fuck it. Monica picked up her phone and read Shelby's text.

I'm so sorry. I behaved horribly. Forgive me?

Overcome with relief, Monica considered what to type. She deplored the idea of setting a precedent that rude behavior could be excused by texting an apology.

She pushed back from her desk and agonized over how to play this. *Should I hold Shelby accountable or pretend like everything is okay?* Not a spiteful person by nature, Monica just didn't want this to turn into a routine. She felt anger seeping into the space that confusion and heartbreak had occupied only a few minutes earlier. She tossed her phone on the sofa, so she wouldn't reply impetuously, and paced around the kitchen. While processing, she packaged the uneaten pizza in a plastic container and stowed it in the fridge. *It's good to let Shelby wonder—*

Her kitchen doorbell rang, startling her. Unable to see who it was from the fridge, she walked to the entryway. When she saw Shelby through the small window, her body ignored her mind, responding with a surge of excitement.

Shelby's blotchy, tear-stained face broke into a tremulous smile, unraveling Monica's resolve to play it cool.

She swung the door wide open.

Without pause or preamble, Shelby leaped into Monica's arms, curling her legs around Monica's waist. Unwelcome cold rushed in behind her, but Monica only felt Shelby's hot body hanging on, as if her life depended on it.

"I'm so sorry. I'm so sorry," Shelby said in rush, and, continuing at the same frenetic pace, "Please forgive me. I'm such a witch. I can't believe I lashed out at you in anger. So irrational. I don't know what came over me. Maybe it was the full moon. It won't happen again. I promise."

Monica kicked the door shut and pushed Shelby up against a tiny space of wall above the cubbies, resting Shelby's butt on the shelf. She leaned back and looked at Shelby's bloodshot eyes. "I love you, but I won't be a doormat."

Shelby gulped. "I know. I don't want to lose you, Mon. Maybe someday, but not today, I can tell you about the diamond stud. It just came up so unexpectedly that I overreacted."

Shelby dropped her face into Monica's neck and cried, her legs again coiling around Monica's waist.

Monica felt out of her depth, patting the back of Shelby's head and soothing her untamable curls. "It's okay. I forgive you."

Still in Monica's arms, Shelby pushed off from the shelf, her feet landing on the floor, and her heart landing in Monica's hands. They held each other until Shelby whispered through a jagged breath, "Thank you."

"I love you." Monica kissed Shelby's eyelids. Then her nose. Then her full lips. Then, Monica carried Shelby to her bedroom.

3

Folded in an overstuffed chair next to the fireplace in her four-season porch, Monica sipped at her strong coffee. She had a full view of her front yard, and beyond, the tree-lined street.

She silently congratulated herself on remodeling the space a year prior. She Chip-and-Joanna-Gaines'd the old porch with gray shiplap walls, a corner fireplace, and vinyl plank flooring in a weathered gray. A few throw rugs added warmth and accented the wine hues of the sofa and comfy chairs. In the afternoon, the sun poured through the windows creating the warmest, coziest room in the house.

Returning her attention to her laptop, Monica answered work emails at a brisk pace. She already had showered and dressed for work to free up the bathroom for Shelby, who had stayed the remainder of the weekend and now needed to get ready for school.

If there was one predictable behavior Monica had learned about Shelby—aside from the magical combination that made her scream to a deity in pleasure—it was that Shelby took a solid 45 minutes in the bathroom to get ready for school and was not to be disturbed while doing so. At all. By anyone. For anything. There was a demi-diva living inside that CrossFit body, and she needed uninterrupted shower, hair, makeup and wardrobe time.

Earlier, Monica had laid out some clothes that Shelby could borrow for teaching art class. Even though Shelby was a size or two smaller, Monica was confident that she could find something suitable. Monica didn't mind that her clothes likely would be splattered with paint or clay. As a high school art teacher, Shelby wore the materials of her medium like a badge of honor.

The ringing of Monica's cell phone interrupted her thoughts.

She recognized the number as the hospital switchboard, so she assumed it would be a call from the Surgical Prep area. Early morning weekday questions usually centered around surgical consent paperwork. The last one she had received was about a Somali father who had wanted to be present in the Operating Room to observe his son's surgery. The answer had been an emphatic "no," so he had packed up his son and left, foregoing the surgery.

"Hello. This is Monica Spade."

"This is the Operator for Community Memorial Hospital. I have the Director of the Behavioral Health Unit on hold. Can you take the call?"

"Of course," Monica said.

The operator connected them. "Hi. This is Rory Reese, Director of Behavioral Health."

"This is Monica Spade. What can I do for you?"

"We have a patient named Stela Reiter here. She was brought to the ED Saturday evening by the police as a sexual assault victim, then admitted to Behavioral Health."

"Yes. I spoke to the SANE nurse Saturday night," Monica said.

"Then you know that she has self-inflicted cutting on her too, right?"

"The SANE nurse mentioned lacerations, but she didn't say they were self-inflicted."

"Ms. Reiter said yesterday that her boyfriend cut her while trying to assault her, but the marks don't look like she was playing defense," Rory said.

"Why?" Monica asked.

"They're superficial and placed next to each other in parallel lines. They appear in her groin area, on the outside aspect of her right thigh, and on her left palm," Rory said. "We see self-cutting like this all the time. She probably used her right hand to cut into her left palm. If she were standing, the leg cuts are consistent with her reaching down with her right hand and cutting upward."

"Does she admit to any self-cutting?"

"No. She insists the attacker did it."

"Is she a voluntary or involuntary admit to the Unit?" Monica asked.

"She's voluntary. The ED physician got a psych consult, and she agreed to further treatment on the Unit."

"How can I help?"

"The police are here to interview her again, which seems strange to me."

"Again?" Monica asked. "They interviewed her a first time?"

"Yeah. The same two detectives—Matt Breuer and Brock Curfman—visited Sunday morning, and she agreed to see them, but that interview lasted only a few minutes."

"That's short."

"She wasn't very talkative."

"Interesting," Monica said. "I'm sure they want to investigate the sexual assault thoroughly. I know Matt, and he's a good guy."

"I think she's still asleep. Should I wake her?"

"Maybe you could ask them to come back later."

"They said it's urgent, which doesn't make sense to me for a sexual assault investigation."

"Maybe they arrested her attacker and need information," Monica said. "My advice is to wake Ms. Reiter, and ask her if she wants to talk to them. It's totally up to her. If she does, then they can interview her on the Unit. If she doesn't, then they'll have to wait until she's discharged."

"Okay...I think I can do that."

"You sound unsure."

"It's just that..." He hesitated. "...the detectives are acting sort of...evasive."

"Maybe time is of the essence."

"Um...maybe," he said in a voice heavy with the fatigue of an all-night shift.

She waited a beat then said, "If you need anything else, feel free to call me."

"Will do. Thanks."

They hung up, and Monica gazed out the window at the pinkish hues of dawn illuminating the oak tree in her front yard. *Alleged rape victim. Ran to a farmer's house. Supposed amnesia. The police aren't sharing info, but they're hot to trot. Both the SANE nurse and Rory indicate something doesn't feel right. Curious.*

Monica heard Shelby in the kitchen stirring her mixture of cream and sugar into a mug of coffee.

"I'm out here," Monica said through the open door.

"I'm on my way." A few minutes later, Shelby appeared with a mug of coffee and a container of Icelandic yogurt. She spread out on the sofa in one of Monica's robes, her leg bent, so Monica could see her shapely knee and inner thigh. Not moving her eyes from that glorious view, Monica asked, "Sleep well?"

"Like a baby," Shelby said. "Nothing like a weekend of sex to help me fall into serious REM sleep. My complexion even feels better." Shelby absent-mindedly ran her fingers from her forehead, along her temple, and down her cheek.

The gesture lured Monica's gaze from Shelby's thighs. "You look beautiful."

A spoonful of yogurt stopped in midair, as Shelby's coral-colored lips drew back in a broad smile that radiated playfulness.

As Monica watched Shelby guide the spoon into her sexy mouth, she felt dumbstruck yet again. She considered tossing her laptop to the floor and bowing before Shelby, having her for breakfast.

Shelby's eyes sparkled. "I think I know what you're thinking."

"That obvious, huh?"

"It is to me." Shelby ate more yogurt, removing the spoon from her mouth in a deliberate swish.

"Let's be late for work and go back to bed," Monica surprised herself into saying. Her new law firm needed her, but she was willing to risk missing its morning routine for the pleasure of Shelby.

Shelby laughed, but Monica could tell it was more at the suggestion than in conspiratorial agreement. "I'd love that, but my work isn't as flexible as yours. How about you come over to my place for dinner tonight and stay?" She punctuated her invitation with raised eyebrows and a lick of the spoon.

"What can I bring?"

"Wine?" Shelby asked.

"Done." Monica paused a minute, then ventured, "You aren't going to kick me out again, are you?"

The air seized with tension until Shelby cleared her throat. "Um. No. I'm so sorry for the way I acted. If we can just avoid the topic of my diamond stud —"

Monica held up her hand as if taking an oath. "I won't ask again, but I hope you can trust me enough to tell me someday."

"Someday." Shelby finished her yogurt and sipped her coffee in silence.

Monica was relieved that Shelby hadn't run from the room, but she felt like she was watching Shelby through a keyhole, seeing only glimpses of her.

After Shelby left for school, Monica reoccupied her bathroom and was flat-ironing her long, black hair when her phone rang.

"Hi, Monica. It's Rory Reese again."

She set down the iron. "What's up?"

"The detectives interviewed Ms. Reiter and left."

"That didn't take long."

"Ten minutes, tops. Detective Matt told me on his way out that she didn't say much, but—and this is big news—she's a suspect in a homicide investigation, so they're sending a uniform over to guard her."

"Come again?" Monica asked.

"No kidding." He snorted sarcastically. "Matt said we should consider her dangerous, so now I'm concerned about staff safety."

"Has she acted out in any way?"

"Not yet, but you never know."

"At least they're being proactive," Monica said.

"They should've sent the guard yesterday," Rory said.

"Why?"

"A male by the name of Yuri visited her yesterday, and they sat on her bed and talked for quite a while. Now, I'm concerned they're both dangerous."

"Is he family?"

"I doubt it. They were holding hands and stuff, so I'd guess a boyfriend."

"Is he the one who allegedly assaulted her, or is he a second boyfriend?"

"No clue, but I'm not leaving until the officer gets here."

"Did you ask the detectives about this guy, Yuri?"

"Didn't get the chance. They seemed in a hurry when they left."

"Do you want me to call Matt and see what I can find out?"

"Sure. Any info would be welcome, so we can put a safety plan in place."

"I'll call Matt then call you back," Monica said.

She found Matt Breuer's name in her contacts and called him.

"This is Matt."

"Hi, Matt. It's Monica."

"Hey, Mon. Can't talk right now. At work."

"That's why I'm calling," she said quickly. "The Director of the Behavioral Health Unit is a little freaked out. He told me that you said Stela Reiter is a suspect in a homicide investigation. He's concerned about staff safety."

"We're sending a uniform over right now to guard her. He should be there shortly."

"That means you consider her dangerous."

"She's a suspect, and we're concerned she might try to run."

"Who's the guy named Yuri who visited her yesterday?"

"A guy named Yuri visited her?" Matt asked.

"Yes, for quite a while."

"Family?"

"Looked like a boyfriend to Rory."

She heard some muffled talking then he came back on the line. "Do you have a last name?"

"No. Rory referred to him only as Yuri. What murder are you investigating?"

"Can't talk about it," Matt said.

"Has it hit the news yet?"

"Nope."

She heard other people talking in the background and could tell he was preoccupied. "Okay. I'll let you go. Any information you could share would be helpful."

"I'll keep that in mind," he said.

They rang off.

She called Rory back. "Sorry. I couldn't get any more info out of Matt than you did."

"I'm not surprised," Rory said on a tired sigh. "The uniformed officer just got here, so I'm going home. I gave the staff your number if anything comes up."

"Happy to help."

As Monica finished getting ready for work, she considered the drama of her weekend. She had struck a raw nerve with Shelby by asking about the diamond stud but doubted Shelby would be ready to confide in her anytime soon. *Give her some space...*

The hospital had a potential killer on the Behavioral Health Unit who was being coy with both staff and police. Monica suspected that situation would come to a head sooner rather than later, but she hoped to hell no one would get hurt in the process. *Give her some space...*

She stuffed her laptop in her attaché and left the house to begin another exciting day at Spade, Daniels & Taylor.

4

Later that day, Monica entered the kitchen of her law firm to find Janet, Kathy and Sandie eating lunch at the oval-shaped dining table. A game show played on the television in the corner, serving as background noise to their banter.

"Hi, everyone. It smells delicious in here. What are you eating?" Monica asked.

"Kathy brought in tater tot casserole," Janet said, her mouth full. "It just came out of the oven."

"Help yourself," Kathy motioned to the stovetop with her fork. "Just be careful. It's still really hot."

"Are you sure there's enough?" Monica moved closer and gazed longingly at the bubbling pan of perfectly browned tater tots, melted white cheese, ground beef and creamed corn spilling from the middle. She was instantly transported back to her childhood when her mother used to make the classic midwestern dish. She inhaled the comforting aroma.

"There's plenty," Kathy said while shoveling a large bite into her mouth. "I brought it for the whole office. You better eat some before Jim and Nathan smell it and hoover it up." Kathy's official title was receptionist, but she was the firm mother hen, constantly feeding and tending to her brood.

"Good point," Monica said. "Did Cheryl get a piece? Where is she?"

"She's covering reception while I'm on break," Kathy said. "And, yes, I brought her a generous portion even though she insisted she's 'on a diet.'" Kathy used air quotes to accent her sarcastic tone.

"Cheryl is on a diet every Monday," said Janet, the office manager and Jim's loyal assistant.

"I usually am too." Monica used the serving spoon to heap a small portion onto a plate. "The curse of overdoing it on the weekend." She leaned against the counter and cautiously popped a steaming hot tater tot in her mouth.

"Did you have a good weekend?" Kathy asked, looking at Monica over her leopard-print half-glasses, her black bangs dipping over her eyebrows.

Monica fanned her burning mouth with her hand, attempting to blame her blush on a mouthful of molten hotdish. She drank some water, avoiding answering.

"How's Shelby?" Kathy persisted in her sing-song tone that conjured love.

Monica quickly swallowed. "She's great. Busy with high school activities these days."

"Did you two do anything fun this weekend?" asked Sandie, Nathan's paralegal.

Incapable of hiding her emotion, Monica's face dove a deeper shade of crimson. "Not really...unless you call shoveling driveways fun." She cleared her throat. "We made a lasagna together yesterday while we watched the Packers."

"That was an awesome game," Jim said as he entered the kitchen. "What smells so good?"

"Kathy made tater tot hotdish," Monica said, grateful for his entrance to deflect attention from her love life.

"Eat up while it's hot," Kathy said.

Jim pulled up his waistband, adjusting it for the occasion, and grabbed a plate from a stack. He took a serving size worthy of a football player and joined the women at the table, between bites muttering, "This is the best."

Monica was amazed at his ability to eat something so hot so quickly.

Their communal hotdish bliss was interrupted by the TV beeping, the screen switching to WQOD News, and a deep, masculine voice announcing, "Breaking news." Kathy pointed the remote at the screen and turned up the volume.

A few seconds later, Tiffany Rose, the reporter who had covered the Saudi student murder trial in which Monica's physician clients had testified, was on the air in front of the courthouse, her doe-like eyes seducing the camera. "We apologize for interrupting your regularly-scheduled program with this breaking news. The Apple Grove Police Department just issued a statement that they recovered a man's body in a car late Sunday afternoon. The car was parked in a farmer's field about eight miles west of town. The man was stabbed thirteen times, including in the head, chest, back and groin. His name has not yet been released. The police reported that late this morning, they arrested a woman named Stela Reiter for first degree intentional homicide in connection with the man's death. She was just taken into custody after being discharged from Community Memorial Hospital's Behavioral Health Unit. The police stressed that there is no threat to the public at this time. We will now return to your usual program."

The camera focused on Tiffany for a second then the game show resumed. Kathy turned down the volume.

"That's pretty troubling," Monica said. "I got a few pages from the hospital about that Reiter woman."

"Oh really?" Jim asked. "What were they?"

"Saturday night from the SANE nurse, then early this morning from Rory, the Behavioral Health Unit Director. Both felt something was off about her story."

"No kidding!" Jim said. "She stabbed a guy then came to the hospital. That sounds like a stupid getaway plan."

Monica shook her head. "Not quite accurate. She supposedly went to a farmer's house for help, and he called the police. She told the police that she'd been assaulted, so they brought her to the hospital. Ms. Reiter also told the SANE nurse that she'd been assaulted but couldn't remember by whom, when or where."

"Suspicious," Jim said through a huge bite.

"I don't know," Kathy said. "Some victims are so traumatized that they can't talk about the details right away."

"The SANE nurse said the same thing," Monica said, "but added that something didn't feel right about Ms. Reiter's reticence."

"Why was she admitted to Behavioral Health?" Jim asked.

"Rory told me she had self-inflicted cutting, and apparently said something about killing herself, so the ED physician got a psych consult, and she agreed to be admitted to Behavioral Health." Monica took a bite. "Maybe she was trying to hide from the police."

"The police obviously have some evidence connecting her to the homicide," Jim said.

"Matt Breuer interviewed her twice on the Unit before arresting her," Monica said. "Thirteen stab wounds. Wow. Talk about the definition of overkill."

"I wonder if she cut off his you-know-what!" Kathy asked.

"Stop!" Janet said, holding up her hand. "I'm still eating!"

Nathan chose that moment to enter the kitchen. "Hey, what's up?"

"We're eating hotdish and talking about a murder over the weekend," Jim said. "Help yourself."

He eyed the pan on the counter. "Looks fabulous. Did you make this, Kathy?"

"Yes. It's tater tot. Eat."

Nathan scooped some hotdish onto a plate and stood next to Monica.

"So, Matt was busy with the murder investigation this weekend?" Monica asked Nathan, who was Matt's boyfriend.

"Yeah. Gone since Saturday night."

"Did he tell you any details?"

"Not one. Everything is hush, hush."

"A new mystery for the Apple Grove Police to solve," Monica said, then sang the three-beat tone of the cinematic sting, "Dun, dun, duuun."

"And, on the heels of the Saudi student murder trial," Kathy said, imitating her.

"Don't remind me," Monica said.

"That trial acted as a catalyst for positive change in your career," Jim said.

Monica tilted her head. "How silly of me to forget my good fortune. I learned a little about court while prepping my clients to testify in a racially and ethnically-charged murder trial that brought out true hatred at our former firm. So grateful."

"In spades," Nathan said.

"And against Spade," Monica said, poking herself in the chest.

"My point exactly," Jim said. "After Charles and Richard revealed their true colors, your settlement allowed you to start this firm, and if it makes you feel any better, a few of Charles and Richard's clients have contacted me to do work for them."

Nathan pumped his fist into the air. "Nicely done! Who? Anyone with active litigation files?"

"First National Bank, for one," Jim said. "I can teach you how to do bankruptcies and foreclosures, if you're interested."

Nathan's face fell. "Woohoo. Can't wait."

"Pays really well."

"I'm all in," Nathan said enthusiastically.

"If Charles' practice dries up, then Richard's will surely follow," Monica said. "Karma for the way they treated all of us. I can't believe I worked there for three years, staying in the closet, trying to fit into their elitist, narrow-minded view of life." She shivered. "Glad that's over."

"You emerged with Community Memorial Hospital as a client, though," Jim said. "Al Bowman really respects you."

Monica smiled. "I love doing hospital work, so we're a good match."

"Speaking of Monica's last criminal trial," Kathy said, "I've been scouring the news reports—both here and in the Cayman Islands. They still haven't found Trevor McKnight, the rich kid with a wicked right hook."

"He's at the bottom of the ocean," Jim said, making a slicing motion across his throat.

"On that lovely note," Nathan said, "I'm returning to my office before Jim goes into his conspiracy theories. Great hotdish, Kathy. Thanks."

"You're welcome," she said, then turned to Jim. "What are your conspiracy theories?"

Before Jim could begin, Monica said, "Thanks for the hotdish, Kathy. I have to get back to work."

5

Monica was immersed in the acquisition of a radiology clinic for the hospital, so she had all but forgotten about the violent murder and subsequent arrest of the woman known as Stela Reiter. The police released the name of the male victim, but Monica hadn't recognized him, so, like most of the community, she had carried on with her busy life. That is, until she received a phone call late one afternoon.

She didn't recognize the number that appeared on her iPhone screen, but answered anyway. "This is Monica Spade."

"Hello, Ms. Spade. This is Ruth Gobrecht, Judge O'Brien's judicial assistant."

Monica's body stilled. She didn't have any matters pending before Judge O'Brien so was confused as to why his office would be calling her. "What can I do for you, Ruth?"

"Your name came up in the rotation to serve as standby counsel for a *pro se* criminal defendant."

Monica sat up a little straighter. "That's curious, Ruth, because I don't practice criminal law, and I don't recall adding my name to a list for representing criminal defendants. Maybe you have the wrong number."

"You're Monica Spade, aren't you?" Ruth asked.

"Yes, but I practice civil, not criminal law, and I don't do litigation. I'm a health care and business lawyer," Monica said. "Honestly, I have no idea how my name got on your list."

"This is a volunteer list from a bar association lunch," Ruth said. "It's handwritten, and your name and phone number are on it."

"Well, I don't remember writing my name and phone number on a sheet at a bar association lunch. Can I kindly request to be removed?"

"I suppose, but we really need lawyers to volunteer to make the system work, and you're the only lawyer on the list who hasn't been assigned a case, or multiple cases, for that matter."

Monica held the phone away from her ear while she sighed, picturing Nathan adding her name to the list as a practical joke. "Well, that's a good thing, Ruth, because I'm not a criminal defense lawyer. I don't know the first thing about defending someone accused of a crime."

"That isn't true," Ruth said, "I saw you in court during the Saudi student murder trial.

Oh good, she was there, Monica thought. "That's because my physicians were testifying. I was there only to support them. Big difference."

"That's all the experience you need. You'll be perfect for this case."

Monica pictured herself stammering in court, the TV cameras rolling, and Tiffany Rose reporting on Monica's gaffes. "Ruth, I'm guessing that one of my partners wrote my name on the list to prank me. Can you remove my name and call the next defense lawyer? Someone who actually knows what they're doing in court?"

Ruth laughed briefly. "I don't think so, Ms. Spade. After the defendant fired two public defenders, and insisted on proceeding *pro se*, Judge O'Brien asked me to bypass the usual defense attorneys because they're busy preparing cases. This is a perfect opportunity for someone who doesn't practice criminal law to learn about it, so you can serve as defense counsel in the future."

Monica's heart jumped. "I'm never going to serve as defense counsel in criminal cases. I have no talent or desire for that work."

"Well, Judge O'Brien is appointing you to serve as standby counsel in this case," Ruth said in a definitive tone.

Monica's stomach squeezed, causing a little burn at the apex of her ribs. "Um...I don't even know what 'standby counsel' is. I'm so not qualified for this —"

Ruth sighed loudly then said, "Let me educate you. The American Bar Association has defined the role of 'standby counsel' as: 'Defense counsel whose duty is to actively assist a *pro se* accused. Standby counsel should: (a) permit the accused to make the final decisions on all matters, including strategic and tactical matters relating to the conduct of the case; and (b) only when the accused requests assistance, bring to the attention of the accused matters beneficial to him or her. Standby counsel should not actively participate in the conduct of the defense unless requested by the accused or as directed by the court.'"

"Thank you for reading that compelling advertisement, Ruth. As attractive as it sounds, I still need to pass. Can you tell Judge O'Brien that I'm not a trial lawyer, and I don't know anything about criminal law, so I cannot in good conscience represent a criminal defendant, even as standby counsel."

Ruth was relentless. "You aren't really *representing* the defendant. You're appointed by the court to *assist* the defendant. She wants to represent herself, but Judge O'Brien needs a lawyer to sit with her and explain court procedure, his rulings, and simple stuff like that."

Monica's initial panic turned into annoyance that she was still on this call with this woman. This wasn't her jam, and she wasn't about to get bogged down in some criminal matter for free. She had just opened her new law firm, and she had real clients to represent, lights to turn on, and employees to pay. "Again, Ruth, I don't feel qualified to serve in this role, and I have a busy law practice to manage."

"Okay, Ms. Spade. I'll relay your denial to Judge O'Brien," Ruth said in a cautionary tone.

Silence filled the line while Monica processed, balancing the pros and cons of disappointing Judge O'Brien. "Thank you, Ruth. If he has any questions, please tell him to call me."

"You can expect that he will." Ruth hung up.

Monica set down her phone and stared out the window, wondering what the hell had just happened. *Nathan. That little shit.* She rose from her chair to go ring his neck, but her desk phone rang, pulling her gaze back to its display. She recognized the number as Al Bowman's, the CEO of Community Memorial Hospital, a client for whom she actually felt qualified to provide competent advice.

She picked it up. "Hello. This is Monica."

"Hi, Monica. Al here."

"What's new?"

"I was just served with a lawsuit."

"Who's suing you?"

"That crazy monkey owner, Darcy Lemon."

Monica's mind switched gears. "You've got to be kidding me!"

"I wish I were. This woman and her blasted monkey keep turning up like a bad penny."

"What could she possibly be suing you for?" Monica asked.

She heard him rustle some papers. "It says here that Count One is for the false imprisonment of Marcus."

Monica balked with a sniff.

"Count Two is for emotional distress inflicted upon Marcus."

"That's ridiculous. Monkeys don't have standing to sue for emotional distress. More importantly, I personally returned him to her, and he was in a good mood. I think he liked living in the hospital storeroom better than living with her."

"The storeroom certainly smelled like he enjoyed himself. Yuck," Al grunted, then said, "Count Three is for animal cruelty, thereby causing emotional distress to Darcy Lemon."

"She caused *us* emotional distress!" Monica exclaimed.

"No kidding."

"What's she asking for in damages?" Monica asked.

"Where do I find that?"

"At the end of the complaint."

She waited while he flipped through the pages. "It says that she's demanding a jury trial, and that she's entitled to lost time from work in addition to $500,000 for the pain and suffering inflicted on Marcus and her. Five hundred thousand dollars?" She heard him crumple the papers.

"She's shooting for the moon," Monica said. "Don't let it get to you. It's a frivolous suit, and we'll get it dismissed. Who's the lawyer who signed the pleading?"

She heard him uncrumple and smooth out the papers. "Miltrude Leib."

"You've got to be kidding me! Wally brought this suit?" Monica's voice rang with incredulity.

"You need to get rid of this case, Monica. I will not have our time and resources wasted on this nonsense."

"I understand. Have your assistant scan and email it over. My partner, Nathan, will file a motion to dismiss the suit. He can work miracles."

"What about Jim?" Al asked. "He used to do all of our litigation work."

"Jim does mostly business transactions and construction litigation now. Nathan Taylor is our third partner, and he does insurance defense work and litigation like this. You'll like him. Plus, his rate is lower than Jim's."

"Even better," Al said. "Have him give me a call if he needs anything."

"I will. We'll try our best to get rid of this case, Al."

They said goodbye, and she shook her head. She had half a mind to call Wally Leib herself but thought better of it. If Monica was assigning the file to Nathan, then it would be better if he called Wally. He probably had some tactics he could employ out of the gate, like threatening to move for sanctions and costs against Wally and Darcy for alleging emotional distress by a monkey. What world was that allowed in? Monica reflected back on Marcus' adventures while living at the hospital and the security video of him traipsing through the hallways. *Maybe the video surveillance might convince Wally that Marcus was happy and enjoying himself at the hospital.*

Monica rose from her chair and walked the short distance to Nathan's office. His door was open, so she entered, going right up to his desk and glowering at him.

He looked up from typing on his laptop. "What? You're looking at me like my mother used to when I did something wrong, except your green eyes look like magically-powered gems, scaring me a little."

"You should be scared, you dinglefritz!"

"Dinglefritz?" He repeated. "Now you *sound* like my mother too. What did I do?"

"You signed my name to a volunteer sheet to represent criminal defendants!"

He squinted and frowned, trying to resurrect the memory.

"At a bar association luncheon!"

A smile spread across his face. "Maybe I did do that. Genius move. Did you get a call from the court?"

"Yes! Not funny! Judge O'Brien's assistant called to assign me as standby counsel for a criminal defendant," she said.

He scratched his clean-shaven chin. "I've heard of that. Never done it myself. Did you accept the assignment?"

"Are you nuts?" she asked. "Of course not. I'm not qualified to explain court procedure and rulings to a criminal defendant. And, even if I were, I have this place to run. I can't take time out for *pro bono* work right now."

"I'm pretty sure it's compensated," he said. "Actually, I think it pays more than serving as a public defender."

"Really?" Her ears perked up. "Well, I'm sure it's not close to my usual hourly rate, so the answer is still no."

"You'd be good at it, but I understand why you wouldn't want to do it."

"No more signing me up for stuff, okay?"

"Can't promise that," he said.

"I'll give you a lawsuit if you promise."

"What lawsuit?"

"Al Bowman just called me. Darcy-the-nutjob-monkey-owner is suing the hospital."

"No kidding."

"I'll email you the complaint as soon as I get it from Al."

"That sounds like fun. Who's Darcy's lawyer?"

"Wally Leib."

"Wally Leib?" he asked incredulously. "That batty old woman who shows up at every protest, trying to get on the news?"

"Yes. She's a real treat. Won't listen to reason and screeches threats over the phone."

"When was the last time *she* was in a courtroom?"

"I have no idea."

"I can't wait to see her in front of a jury."

"We don't want this lawsuit to get that far," Monica said. "Al wants the case dismissed as soon as possible."

"Gotcha. Let me read the pleading first. I'll move for dismissal, but it all depends on the judge we draw."

They were interrupted by Kathy knocking on Nathan's door. "Sorry to interrupt, but Judge O'Brien is calling for Monica. Can you talk to him?"

Monica spun around. "Judge O'Brien?"

"Yes. He's on hold. He says he needs to speak to you right away."

"See what you got me into?" Monica glared at Nathan and turned to leave.

"I wouldn't say no to Judge O'Brien," he said after her. "I'm sure it won't be that much work, and you'll get paid for it."

"Suck it, nerd!" she threw over her shoulder.

As soon as Monica returned to her desk, Kathy transferred Judge O'Brien's call.

"Hello. This is Monica Spade."

"Ms. Spade, this is Judge O'Brien. How are you today?"

"I'm fine, Judge. I assume your judicial assistant relayed our conversation?"

"Yes. Ruth told me you declined the opportunity to serve as standby counsel. You know it pays $70 per hour, right?"

"I didn't know that, but I just don't feel qualified, Judge. I'm not a trial attorney, and I don't know the first thing about criminal defense work."

"You don't have to be a trial attorney. Your law school education should be enough, as long as you refresh yourself on the rules of evidence. Remember, you're not actually *representing* the defendant. While you would have an attorney-client relationship with her, you wouldn't do any of the work. She fired two public defenders and insists on representing herself, so I'm appointing you to explain my rulings and court procedure to her. I don't have time to explain everything I do and say from the bench, so we need you for this role, Ms. Spade."

Monica hesitated, maybe for too long, actually considering the idea. She just felt so ill-prepared to explain courtroom procedure. "Who is the defendant?"

He cleared his throat. "Her name is Stela Reiter."

Monica almost fell out of her chair. *The woman arrested for stabbing the young man thirteen times? No way. Nooooo fucking waaaay am I going to become involved in this case.*

After a suitable silence, Judge O'Brien asked, "Are you still there?"

Monica was so shocked by the notorious case that she forgot it was her turn to talk. "Listen, Judge, I can't...I'm sorry. I cannot represent a woman who stabbed someone 13 times."

"Again, I'm not asking you to represent her," he repeated. "Just answer her questions about process. For starters, let's remember that she's presumed innocent until proven guilty."

"I can't even do that!" Monica said. "She was at Community Memorial Hospital, and I took pages from the SANE nurse and Behavioral Health Unit Director regarding her. They're my clients, and they were suspicious of her. Their testimony might be adverse to her—incriminating in some way. I'd be in a conflict, because my first legal duty is to my hospital client and its nurses and physicians."

"Aren't you partners with Jim Daniels?" Judge O'Brien asked.

"Yes."

"He's done hospital work for years. He can prep the doctors and nurses to testify if they're subpoenaed. The hospital doesn't need you to do that."

"They're my clients! I can't be sitting at counsel table beside this Stela Reiter woman while she's questioning—or worse, cross-examining—the SANE nurse or providers on Behavioral Health. I gave them legal advice regarding her."

"That advice wouldn't have any bearing on the trial, so you wouldn't be violating any ethical rules."

"How do you know that?"

The judge laughed. Actually laughed at her. "I'm sure you and Jim can figure out something. He can prep the witnesses, and you don't have to tell Ms. Reiter what your legal advice was while you were on call. Since you're not helping Ms. Reiter cross-examine them, you won't be in a conflict."

"What about the optics?" she asked, mortified at the spectacle.

"You can explain to Al Bowman that you're not representing Ms. Reiter. You're simply court-appointed counsel to explain my rulings and such."

"Al might view me as disloyal. He'll probably fire me as hospital counsel."

"I doubt that," Judge O'Brien said in a dismissive tone. "I've known Al for years. I'll see him later this week at the Rotary luncheon. Don't worry, I'll smooth it over."

"I haven't agreed to do this."

"Oh, you're going to do this, Ms. Spade."

"Isn't that for me to decide?"

"Listen, aside from your service as a member of the bar in this county, you'll be paid $70 per hour, and the publicity will be good for your new law firm. Potential clients will be watching the trial on TV and call you to represent them. Your phones will light up."

"What's the point?" she asked, her voice near breaking point. "I don't want those clients. I don't have a criminal practice! I represent the hospital and other businesses."

"I'm sure your other partner, Nathan Taylor, would be grateful for some increased visibility and more work. He's a trial attorney, isn't he?"

"Yes. Why don't you ask him to do this?"

"He's on our list, but we're saving the trial attorneys for real defense work. We're statutorily prohibited from asking the public defenders to serve in the role, so that just leaves you. Since you'll be compensated, I think you need to do this—for the system, the bar association, and your future law firm."

He was leveraging her with professional guilt, practically ordering her to do it. She had no desire to piss him off, so against her better judgment, she capitulated. "Fine, but you owe me."

He chortled, cleared his throat, and lowered his voice. "I'm a judge, Ms. Spade, I don't owe you a thing for reminding you to fulfill your civic duty as a member of the bar. The State owes you, and will pay you at the rate of $70 per hour, but don't mistake serving in this role as some favor to me. Am I clear?"

Heat flooded her face. "I'm sorry, Your Honor. I didn't mean it that way. It was just an automatic comeback."

"You would do well to break the habit of automatic comebacks in the courtroom for this case."

"I'll make a note."

"Thank you for your service," he said.

"My pleasure," she said, banging her phone down in its cradle.

Well, fuck me. Fuck me. Fuck me. I'm already in trouble with the judge, and I haven't even appeared in court yet. A burning sensation ran from the pit of her stomach to the back of her throat.

6

Monica sank lower in her chair and googled the phrase "standby counsel." A few Bar Association articles described criminal defendants who had ignored their standby counsel's input and were convicted by juries. More troubling, however, were the numerous accounts of contentious relations between the violent defendants and their standby counsel. When convicted, the defendants blamed their standby counsel, even though counsel technically hadn't represented them.

She rubbed her sore eyes. *Yay me.*

In desperate need of advice, she looked at Jim Daniels' electronic calendar and saw that he was available. If anyone could guide her through this unchartered territory, Jim could. He had been practicing law for so long that he'd seen everything. The senior attorney of their firm by at least 20 years, he was a font of knowledge and experience.

In addition, he had supported her at their old firm in her quest to stand up to the good ole boys who told her she had to stay in the closet or be fired. Jim had helped her bring, then settle, a claim for discrimination based on gender and sexual orientation. She was eternally grateful to him.

She knocked on Jim's open door.

He looked up from one of his screens. "Hey, Monica. Come in."

She entered a den of tan tones and dark leather that instantly calmed her. The largest of the three lawyers' offices, Jim's had a bank of windows overlooking wooded hills. He and his real estate developing buddies owned the building, so Spade,

Daniels & Taylor got a break on the rent, and he got the biggest office. A reasonable trade-off.

"How's it going?" he asked, motioning her to the club chairs before his massive desk on top of which sat three flat screens glowing at him. He used one for emails, one for drafting documents, and the other for construction designs while he was on interminably long conference calls.

"I need your advice about something."

"Happy to help." He removed his half-glasses, their absence shaving a few years off his fifty-six-year-old appearance. The hands of time had been kind to Jim's skin, only a few wrinkles around his eyes and between his thick, gray eyebrows. He wore his winter beard, a radiant gray that was neatly trimmed. Ever since he had started dating Dominique Bisset, the District Attorney and many years his junior, his personal hygiene had stepped up its game, not a nose hair in sight. He was dressed casually in a black mock turtleneck and brown corduroy slacks.

"I have strange and troubling news," she said. "Which do you want to hear first?"

"I prefer strange. I try to put off trouble for as long as possible, but it always seems to find me."

She smiled. "Okay. The nutjob monkey owner is suing Community Memorial Hospital for emotional distress."

He closed his eyes and pinched the bridge of his nose. "Please tell me Richard-fucking-Smart isn't representing her."

Monica laughed at the thought of that disaster. "No. Wally Leib represents Ms. Darcy Lemon."

"Leib? She hasn't been in a courtroom in a hundred years."

"I know, right?"

He barked with laughter. "She'll be surprised that trial lawyers don't wear wigs any longer. God help us all."

She joined him in a laugh, grateful to take the edge off her own stress.

"You're not in here to ask me to take the case, are you?" Jim asked.

"Of course not. Nathan happily took it."

"He'll make quick work of her." He allowed a comfortable silence then asked, "And, the troubling news?"

She covered her face with her hands and said through her splayed fingers. "Judge O'Brien just called me and ordered me to serve as standby counsel for the woman who stabbed her boyfriend 13 times."

He blanched. "The woman on the news? The one the hospital paged you about? You? Her standby counsel?"

"I'm as shocked as you are. I told his judicial assistant, Ruth Gobrecht, 'no,' then Judge O'Brien called me himself."

A look of recognition crossed Jim's face at the mention of Ruth's name. "I've known Ruth for 20 years. We taught Sunday school together when our children were little."

"Oh, that's nice," Monica said, picturing Jim at a table with young children, the vision warming her. "Ruth wasn't exactly in Sunday-school-teacher mode on the phone with me."

"I could've told you that she speaks for Judge O'Brien, so never to say 'no' to her."

"Uh-huh. Well, I didn't know that earlier today, so I got a call from the judge himself. He told me that I didn't have a choice. I was the last person on the list and the only one qualified to do nothing, which is how he described standby counsel's role."

"You're on the criminal defense counsel list?"

"Yes, our esteemed partner, Nathan, wrote my name down as a prank, but I'm not laughing."

Jim slapped his leg. "Good one." When he saw the look on Monica's face he erased all joviality from his expression and voice. "No worries. I'll help you get revenge."

"That's not why I'm here." *Men and their games.* "I need to ask you to help Al Bowman with a radiology clinic acquisition while I run this fool's errand for Judge O'Brien."

Jim rubbed his beard. "No problem. I'll take the acquisition."

"Thanks. Now, what do I do about this new role?"

"I've never served as standby counsel, but I know a few people who have." He gazed out the window for help, then clicked his fingers when memory provided the answer. "Kari Kuhl. She was standby counsel for a *pro se* drug dealer a few years back. Helluva trial but a funny story. You should give her a call."

"Kari Kuhl, huh? Cool name. Never heard of her."

"You wouldn't. She runs in different circles. Does mostly criminal defense work."

"I'll call her. What can *you* tell me about the daunting role I'm about to undertake?"

"Did Judge O'Brien tell you he was going to issue an order setting forth your duties and responsibilities?"

"He did not mention that." She already felt clueless.

He recklessly jammed his half-glasses onto his face and turned to a flat screen. After a few keystrokes, he read: "The court issues an order defining the boundaries of your role based on the type of case, like whether you assist in the investigation of the case, help the defendant focus on the relevant issues, familiarize yourself with the prosecution's reports and other evidence, attend all the pre-trial conferences and hearings—"

"Oh, I know he expects me to attend all the hearings," she said. "He flat out told me that I was expected to explain his rulings and procedures to Ms. Reiter in court."

He regarded her over his glasses. "He wants you to sit side-by-side with her at counsel table?"

"That's what I took from our conversation."

"That's pretty front and center. I think Kari sat behind her defendant, so as not to give the impression to the jury that she was his lawyer. Her defendant also wanted it made clear that he was representing himself. He didn't trust lawyers because she was part of the establishment."

"I suppose if I were a drug dealer or violent killer, I wouldn't trust lawyers either—all part of the evil judicial system. I guess I'll have to ask Stela-the-stabber where she wants me to sit." She thought about that for a moment. "Should I be afraid of her?"

He gave her question serious consideration. "I don't think so. I would expect her to be grateful for your assistance, and there will be a guard a few feet away at all times."

"Being thrust into a situation that necessitates a guard close by doesn't reassure me."

"You'll be fine." He returned his gaze to his flat screen and continued reading, "Back to the judge's order. It should indicate whether you're required to research the law and give advice on legal issues to the defendant—"

"Well, that sounds an awful lot like actual lawyering to me," she interrupted. "That would require tons of time for me to get up to speed on criminal law, something I've never practiced. Put it this way—I have no desire to research, write, or argue legal points for her in court. That's waaay outside my comfort zone."

He gazed at her over his glasses. "I'm just reading what it says the court order should address, but I don't blame you for not wanting to become a criminal lawyer overnight." He turned his focus back to the flat screen. "Continuing, you should know whether you're supposed to help interview witnesses or retain expert witnesses that might be helpful to the case—"

"What?!" she exclaimed. "That's a major league problem. Witnesses to Ms. Reiter's care at the hospital, especially physicians and nurses, would place me in the middle of an ethical conflict. She was admitted to and treated at the hospital. The prosecution—your better half, Dominique—will probably call the SANE nurse, the Emergency Department physician, and the psychiatrist who treated Stela on the Behavioral Health Unit. Those people are my clients, but now they might testify adversely to Ms. Reiter, forcing me to strategize with her about how best to cross-examine them. I told you that I answered pages from the SANE nurse and the Behavioral Unit Director while Ms. Reiter was admitted there."

As he listened, he removed his glasses and held them by the bows between his thumb and forefinger. "What were their questions again?"

"They were suspicious of her, because she told them she had been sexually assaulted, but she couldn't remember by whom, when, or where. Then, she had some cuts on her—"

"From fighting off the assailant?"

"No. The providers didn't think the cuts looked like they were from defending herself. They looked self-inflicted."

He raised his eyebrows. "Like she cut up herself to make it look like she was fighting off an attack?"

"Precisely," Monica said. "That's why I think Dominique will call the physician and nurses if Ms. Reiter claims she killed the victim in self-defense."

"Yep." He twirled his glasses by the bow. "I can see how that would place you in a conflict if, and this is a big if, you were actually cross-examining the nurse and physicians. Fortunately, Ms. Reiter thinks she can do a better job of that herself, so you won't be in a conflict, technically speaking."

"I might not be in a technical conflict, but I'll be sitting next to her while she's giving the SANE nurse and physician a hard time. They'll wonder what the heck I'm doing and probably tell Al Bowman about it."

He let her words sink a few seconds before saying, "I seriously doubt it will play out like that, but you should call Al and explain what's happened, so he doesn't think you willingly took this case. Then, in court, just be sure to be neutral while this genius, Stela, makes an ass out of herself."

Monica ran her fingers through her hair. "I can't imagine sitting through this trial next to a killer. She stabbed him over and over and over—13 times. What a monster!"

"It's a homicide case, so yes. Expect gruesome details."

"Have you spoken to Dominique about it? What does she have to say?"

He looked genuinely thoughtful, the glasses twirling at a slower clip. "We haven't talked about it yet. She has so much on her plate that this is just one of many—"

"Oh, come on," Monica cut in. "This is huge."

"That may be true, but she has it under control. We try not to talk about work when we're together." His eyes twinkled with mischief. "That might change, though, as the trial gets closer."

Monica tried not to envision what he was implying. "I wonder if Dominique knows that Judge O'Brien asked me to hold Stela Reiter's hand."

"If she does, she hasn't said anything, and knowing that you and I are partners, I'm sure she'll be quite cautious from here on out." He paused momentarily before saying, "She's a woman who knows how to be discreet, that's for sure."

Monica didn't dare ask what he meant by that. "Well, what do I do next?"

"Here's my advice." He jabbed his glasses into the air with each point. "You should send Judge O'Brien a letter requesting a court order that outlines your duties and responsibilities. Be sure to tell Al Bowman about the case, so he isn't surprised. Call Kari Kuhl and ask her about her experience as standby counsel. And, lastly, you should go visit Reiter in jail to find out what her plan is."

Monica's face fell. "Visit her in jail?"

Jim smiled. "Yeah. That's what lawyers do. We visit our clients in jail to confer."

"She isn't my client."

"You still have a duty to go talk to her and find out what her *pro se* plan is. She might be thinking up crazy antics for kangaroo court, so you'll have to set her straight."

"Of course she's thinking up crazy antics! She's a psychopathic killer!"

"I'd advise you to tone down the labels while you're in jail."

"Will we be separated by glass?"

"Probably not. They usually give you a room with a conference table, so you can talk confidentially and take notes. Have a regular client meeting, you know?"

"Again, not my client," she said. "Is there a guard in there?"

"Of course not. It's a confidential meeting."

"Should I be afraid of her? Is she going to stab me with a pen?"

"Of course not."

"Am I locked in there with her?"

"Yes."

"This is making me really uncomfortable."

"It's not that bad. I've been there several times. You just knock on the door when you're ready to leave."

"What if the guard is on break or something?"

"He won't be. Trust me."

"I really have to meet with her?"

"Yes."

She let that sink in for a moment. "Will you review my letter to Judge O'Brien before I send it?"

"Be happy to."

She pushed up from her chair and stood tall, throwing back her shoulders. "Well, if I'm being forced to do this, I might as well give it my all."

"That's the spirit," he said. "Trust the process. You might actually learn something that will help you grow as a lawyer…maybe add some perspective and nuance to your practice."

"That's what they say—representing a psychopathic killer adds nuance to one's practice."

His laughter chased her from his office.

7

Monica composed a short letter to Judge O'Brien. While she agreed with Jim that requesting the judge to clarify her role was a good idea, she had a sinking suspicion that O'Brien wouldn't provide her the guidance she sought. From the brusque tone of their telephone call, he seemed like he had little patience for newbie litigators, and Monica was all of that and more. She emailed the draft to Jim for his review.

She next turned her attention to googling "Kari Kuhl," the criminal defense attorney who had a story to tell. Ms. Kuhl had a cool website, advertising herself as one of Wisconsin's "Super Lawyers," and posing in a red cape with "Super Lawyer" printed on the back.

Monica almost laughed out loud at the schmaltzy profile picture. *Why are trial lawyers so theatrical and full of themselves?* Below the caped photo was another large photo featuring a slicked-up man in a dark suit being handcuffed by a police officer while a plainclothes officer dropped a large baggie of white powder into an evidence collection bag. The caption under the photo asked, "Have you been unfairly charged with a crime?"

Monica rolled her eyes and called Kuhl's phone number, which was advertised as available 24 hours a day, seven days per week. After explaining who she was, Monica was transferred to Kuhl by the receptionist.

"Kari Kuhl," said a confident female voice on the other end.

"Hi, Kari. This is Monica Spade. I work with Jim Daniels, and he suggested I call you to find out about your role as standby counsel for a criminal defendant a few years ago."

There was silence then Kuhl said, "What a fuckin' disaster. Worst case of my life. Who are you again?"

"I'm a lawyer. Monica Spade. My firm is Spade, Daniels & Taylor. Jim Daniels and I are partners. I've been appointed standby counsel by Judge O'Brien, so Jim suggested I call you. Can you give me any tips?"

Kuhl took a deep breath and blew it out. "Sure. First, though, I need to ask about Jim. It's been forever since I've seen him. How is he?"

"He's doing well. He seems energized by starting a new firm with me, and I'm so grateful to him."

"Right. I might have heard that DSW had a dust up. Did you work there?"

"I think the firm is just Smart & Whitworth now. And, yes, I worked there for three years until I discovered how sexist and homophobic they are, so I left and brought Jim and Nathan Taylor with me."

"Good for you. Charles and Richard Smart have a terrible reputation."

"Apparently, I was the last to learn that. I worked mostly with Jim while there, and he was very good to me."

"Jim is awesome. We've all had a little bit of Jim in our lives."

Monica's ears perked up. "How do you know Jim?"

A snigger of disappointment bubbled up from Kuhl. "Um…a long time ago…when we were still young and foolish…Jim and I were a thing for a short while."

"Oh!" Monica was completely knocked off balance. *Why didn't Jim warn me? What am I supposed to say in response to that?*

"He didn't tell you, did he?" Kuhl asked in a whiskey voice.

"Ah, no. Sorry. I was just a bit surprised for a second."

"I understand. Unfortunately for me, Jim was married to his second wife when he and I were hot and heavy, so it ended kind of badly when she discovered us..." Her voice dragged to a stop, then there was a sharp intake of breath. "Never mind that hot mess. Too much information. Just tell him hello from me, will you?"

"Of course," Monica said. *He's such a shuttlecock. Has he slept with every woman in town?*

"So, you're calling me about my gig as standby counsel?" Kuhl asked.

"Yes. I'm curious about a lot of things, but first, did the judge issue an order defining the scope of your role?"

"Absolutely not," Kuhl said. "He left it to my discretion. He knew I was an experienced attorney, so he trusted me. There are quite a few articles and some caselaw about drawing ethical boundaries between *representing* the accused versus explaining how things work. My case was a cluster-fuck, so I ignored all that stuff."

"Tell me about it."

"Ugh," Kari groaned. "My defendant fired his first three lawyers over the course of six months, all of whom he considered stupid and beneath himself. Even though he didn't have any legal education or training, he insisted he could represent himself better than an actual lawyer. Bear in mind that this guy was an extremely violent individual charged with drug possession, intent to sell, and armed robbery."

"Oh dear." Monica's insides clenched.

"He had a long criminal record, but it gets better. When he issued 102 subpoenas for witnesses to give 'character testimony,' Judge O'Brien appointed me as counsel to explain to the douchebag that the court wouldn't allow witnesses to testify as to his character."

"Did you?" Monica asked.

"Of course. He ignored me, and said he was going to call them anyway."

"I told him he was a dumbass, but he insisted on arguing the point to Judge O'Brien in a pre-trial hearing."

"What did Judge O'Brien do?"

"First, he glared at me. Like it was somehow my fault the asshat didn't listen to me. Second, O'Brien denied every single witness called for that purpose."

"What did your client do?"

"He went on the record as disagreeing with the ruling and threatening an appeal, which was total bullshit."

"Did you help him with his case?"

"I tried, but he didn't listen to a thing I said. I even prepared witness outlines and gave him pointers for his opening and closing."

"Did he use them?"

"Fuck no. He insisted that I sit behind him in the courtroom, and not make any expressions that the jury could interpret as disapproval or disagreement with his idiocy."

"What kind of idiocy?"

"The dumbass didn't know how to address witnesses on cross-examination, so he referred to himself in the third person, confusing the shit out of everyone."

"I don't understand."

"While he was questioning them, he'd say, 'What did the defendant do next?' The witness would sort of look at him and say something like, 'Um...You held a gun to my head and told me to hand over the cocaine or you'd blow my brains out.'"

Monica laughed. "That sounds outrageous."

"It was. I told him multiple times just to refer to himself in the first person, like, 'What did I do next or what did we talk about?'" but he wouldn't. He told me he was afraid of me and kept having nightmares that I was dragging him by a rope tied to the bumper of my car."

Monica's eyes grew wide. "What did you say to that?"

"I told him that was a big hairy coincidence because that would be my fantasy come true." She laughed at her own comeback. "Honestly, Monica, it was the worst experience of my professional career because he didn't listen to a damn thing I said, so I just sat on my hands, frustrated as hell, trying to distance myself from him."

"Oh geez," Monica said.

"I didn't know whether to laugh or cry. He did these extremely long cross-examinations of all the prosecution's witnesses. Judge O'Brien even called him up to a sidebar once and told him he should've stopped his cross 10 minutes ago, because he was just hurting his own case."

"What did the defendant do?"

"Dumbass returned to his chair and continued asking stupid questions for another 10 minutes, basically putting the last nail in his own coffin."

"Did the jury convict him?"

"Yeah. In about 15 minutes. Shortest deliberation I've ever seen."

"What was he convicted of?"

"Felony drug possession, trafficking, extortion and robbery. The whole enchilada. It was a big win for Dominique Bisset, who I think was secretly terrified that she'd lose a case to a *pro se* defendant. It's obviously easier for her to try a case against an experienced defense lawyer because we all agree on what the rules are, and we're bound by ethics. The *pro se* defendant is the equivalent of the wild west, not bound by any ethical rules."

"I hadn't thought of that," Monica said.

"Remember that Dominique has an ethical obligation to protect the rights of the accused while trying to convict him or her. Look up ABA Model Rule 3.08, which has some important language that applies to prosecutors. She has to timely disclose all evidence and information that tends to negate the guilt of the accused or mitigate the offense. Make sure Dominique provides you, or your defendant, information in time for you to analyze it and get an expert witness. She has a reputation for holding onto exculpatory evidence for way too long, then releasing it right before the trial, which leaves you scrambling."

Monica gulped, never having looked at the Rules of Professional Conduct for Prosecutors. She was again reminded that she didn't know what she didn't know. "Thanks for the tip. I'll be on the lookout."

"Give me a call anytime. Who's your defendant?"

"A woman named Stela Reiter. She's the one who stabbed her boyfriend 13 times, claiming she did it in self-defense when he tried to sexually assault her."

"No shit," Kuhl said. "You have your hands full."

"I'm aware, and I'm terrified. I can't imagine stabbing someone 13 times. I mean, wouldn't two or three do?"

Kuhl ignored the rhetorical question. "You should go meet with her as soon as possible. Ask her about the stabbing and the timing. See where she stabbed him first. Why didn't he stop? Did he use a weapon against her? Get the details. I'm sure the police took samples of the blood at the crime scene as well as a boatload of photographs."

"Oh." Monica had no clue what Kuhl was talking about.

"Does the prosecution have the knife?"

"I have no idea."

"Find out whose blood is on the knife."

"Okay."

"Have you ever represented a criminal defendant?"

"No."

There were peals of laughter on the other end of the line. "Baptism by fire, huh?"

"You could say that."

"Maybe the defendant won't want you to do anything."

"I can only hope. And Dominique, what is she like as opposing counsel in court?"

Kari hmphed. "Well, she wasn't sleeping with Jim when I had the standby counsel case, so she was decent and polite to me. Since they started rubbing nasty parts, though, she's been pretty bitchy to me. She won't give me any information, and she won't negotiate any pleas. She won't even make eye contact with me. She just waves her hand in the air, dismissing all my requests and arguments."

"Sorry. I feel like I opened a personal wound. I didn't mean to pry."

"No worries. It's common knowledge that Jim and I had an affair. I don't have any designs on him, so I don't know why Dominique has a broomstick up her ass. So I slept with her lover years ago. Big deal."

"Right."

"By the way, word of advice— Don't sleep with Jim. He makes a better business partner than lover."

"No chance of that. I'm gay."

"Perfect. You're safe then. I'm sure he's a fabulous mentor to you."

"The best."

"Good for you. Listen, I have to run, but it was good chatting with you. Good luck with your case, and if you need anything else, feel free to call me."

"Thank you for your time." Monica replaced the receiver.

She pondered her role and questioned whether she had the tenacity and fortitude for a murder trial. She'd never dream of talking to her clients the way Kuhl described her conversations with her defendant. Was Monica supposed to talk tough? To use profanity and threats and call her defendant a dumbass and douchebag? A chill swept over her body, as she pictured herself arguing with a scary woman who was capable of stabbing a man 13 times. No. She would not engage in that type of name calling. She would approach Stela like she had every other client in her career, starting from a place of respect and civil decorum.

8

Monica swiveled 180 degrees in her chair and looked out the window at the dormant, white scenery. The snowpack averaged at least three feet deep this year, and was deeper where the howling wind had shaped wave-like drifts. She hoped getting lost in the monochromatic snowscape would calm her nerves and clarify the legal implications of this fluke assignment.

She broke out in a sweat over the prospect of visiting Stela in jail, even though Jim and Kari had insisted a face-to-face was part of the gig. Monica dreaded it, but she knew she had to go soon because procrastinating could snowball into rejecting the idea altogether. Best to get it over with, for no other reason than to introduce herself and get a first impression of the killer who would stand trial with Monica sitting by her side. If they tolerated each other, which was a big "if," then Monica could plan a substantive visit later.

She recalled her general rule of thumb— successful people get shit done right away. They don't create pages-long to-do lists where stuff sits and ferments into stinky projects. She had learned that lesson early in her legal career and had put it to good use while running her own law firm. Highly effective people also tackled stuff without fear. *Flush the anxiety, Spade!* She could do this. She needed to be fearless! Judge O'Brien had called her to action, so she would rise to the occasion.

She tossed a yellow notepad, her business cards, and a few pens into a slim attaché case and dropped her car keys into her coat pocket. The only other item she would bring was her cell phone. She sure as hell wasn't going to bring a purse full of objects that potentially could be used as weapons against her. She stopped herself from thinking that way. *Stela has no reason to kill me. Guards are nearby.*

She swung by Jim's office. "Hey. I'm going to the jail to introduce myself to Stela-the-slayer."

His face turned somber. "Good plan. I was just reviewing your letter to O'Brien. I made a few edits, so I'll email it back to you."

"Thanks for taking the time. Should I wait to hear back from him before I introduce myself to her?"

He shook his head. "No. It's just a meet and greet, so keep it short and sweet. See if you two get along. Maybe she'll fire you too, eh?"

"If only I could be so lucky." She jangled her keys in her coat pocket. "By the way, Kari Kuhl swears like a sailor."

He laughed. "You talked to her already?"

"Yes, Romeo. You didn't warn me you had a relationship with her." Monica raised a stern eyebrow at him.

"Sorry. I kind of forgot." He nervously rubbed the back of his neck. "What I thought was a good idea at the time… Anyway, was she helpful?"

"Very. She said I could call her anytime if I run into issues."

"That's Kari. Big heart." His expression softened into a smile.

"Any last words of advice before jail?" Monica asked.

"Remember that you're just a cog in the wheel of justice. Don't make this personal. Stay unmemorable. And…don't turn your back to her. Ever."

Monica swallowed hard. "Thanks for those comforting words. What's not to enjoy about the prospect of serving in this role?"

He squinted at her. "You'll be fine."

"You'll be the first to know if I'm not. I'll call you on my cell."

"Call the guards first."

Her stomach flipflopped, as she turned and left.

When Monica passed Kathy at the reception desk, she was surprised to see Kathy reading a novel, as she usually had her face buried in a *Cosmopolitan* magazine. "Hey Kathy, what are you reading?"

"A Vince Flynn novel. I can't get enough of his Mitch Rapp stories." Kathy splayed the book open with her thumb, as she looked at Monica over her purple cheaters. "Going out?"

"Yes. I'm going to the jail to meet Stela Reiter, my new nonclient, the woman who stabbed her boyfriend 13 times."

Kathy guffawed. "You've got to be kidding me! I heard that she cut off his pecker too."

Monica stopped in her tracks. "I did not hear that." She pictured the psychopathic brutality of that act. "Do you suppose she did that first or after he was dead?"

"That's what I want to know!" Kathy said.

"Wow. If I wasn't terrified before, I certainly am now."

"Tell the guard to stay close."

"I think the guard leaves the room."

"Then sit by the door."

Acid bit the insides of Monica's stomach. "Good advice. If I call here for help, please pick up the phone."

"Oh, I've got my eye on the switchboard at all times."

Monica looked at the book in Kathy's hands. "When you need a break from Vince Flynn, maybe you could offer to help Sandie, Cheryl and Janet get some work done."

"I'll think about it," Kathy said, her eyes glancing back at the book longingly. "Will you be returning?"

"I don't know. Depends on how long this interview takes."

"I'll make a note," Kathy said.

"All right. If I don't see you later this afternoon, I'll see you tomorrow morning."

"Count on it," Kathy said. "This is the only place I can get my reading done." She held up the book and waved goodbye with it.

Monica adopted her best boss face. Her only boss face. "If you don't finish the book tonight, why don't you leave it at home tomorrow?"

"I'll think about it," Kathy said with a smile, then lowered her head to adventure.

"Loved your hotdish for lunch," Monica threw over her shoulder, as she left, satisfied that Kathy got the hint about not reading at work. Managing women who were older had to be done in a "hint and hope" fashion. She had discovered that if she used too heavy of a hand, they dismissed her outright—even got irritated—and Monica couldn't afford to lose them. They were all experienced and good at their jobs—when they decided to be. If her hint-and-hope technique didn't work with Kathy, she'd ask Jim to lay down the law. They always obeyed him. She caught herself wondering if he had slept with any of them, but then cast aside the thought as disrespectful—regarding them; not him.

She drove her little white pickup truck to the jail and checked in at the scuffed up front desk. The place had the utilitarian flare of a white floor, cinderblock walls and metal counters.

She took a few minutes to fill out a form and sign a log book, then she set her phone, keys and attaché on a metal table to be viewed and searched by the guard. As he was doing that, he waved her through a metal detector. She collected her belongings on the other side. She had never felt comforted by men in uniform holding large guns. Quite the opposite, actually.

"Thanks."

"Looks like you'll have your hands full," he said, having snooped over the desk sergeant's shoulder to see who Monica was visiting.

"How so?" she asked.

"Representing Stela Reiter and all."

"I don't represent her. I was appointed by the court to explain things to her."

"I hope you get the story," he said. "No one else has been able to."

Crinkling her forehead, she recalled her failed interrogation of Shelby over the weekend. Prying traumatizing secrets from women wasn't exactly her specialty. "I'm not an expert at getting people to talk."

He shrugged indifferently, but she knew he was curious as hell and anxious to feed the network of gossip that entertained the jail and courthouse personnel.

A burly guard appeared at the large metal door that separated freedom from confinement. He nodded in greeting. She reluctantly followed him, the echo of the door lock bouncing off the cinderblock walls and sending a shiver down her spine.

Several feet down the dim hallway, the guard stopped at a thick metal door with a window at eye level. He scanned his badge, and the door unlocked.

He pushed it inward and walked into the center of the conference room, Monica on his heels.

"Your new lawyer is here," he said to someone Monica couldn't see around his broad back. Monica assumed Stela had been brought to the room, and was impressed at the speed with which they had accomplished that.

The stale room was filled with silence but for the guard's loud breathing. He turned and looked down at Monica. "I'll be right outside. Knock or holler if you need me."

She wanted to follow him out but forced herself to stand her ground. "Will do. Thanks."

He moved swiftly out the door and it slammed shut with a decisive lock, leaving Monica alone with the petite prisoner in an orange jumpsuit.

Monica's legs turned to noodles in the presence of this fey, mousy-looking woman who resembled a school librarian. Stela. In the flesh. Her pale complexion was obscured by brown bangs hanging over her eyes. Ordinary brown eyes were framed by large, horn-rimmed spectacles.

"Mind if I sit?" Monica asked, motioning to the chair across from Stela.

Slouching nonchalantly, Stela gestured with her hand. Monica accepted the limp invitation and sat on the cold metal chair, scraping it on the floor, as she scooted forward. Usually, she would rest her forearms on the table and make herself comfortable, but the dank smell, tantamount to urine, discouraged touching anything. She placed her hands on the attaché in her lap.

Monica was struck by the dissonance of an unimposing appearance on a killer of this caliber. She had expected a scarier-looking woman—perhaps with skull and crossbones sleeves covering her arms. But here sat diminutive Stela, as pure looking as the cold, driven snow.

Monica cleared her throat and didn't recognize her own voice when she said, "I'm Monica Spade. Judge O'Brien appointed me as your standby counsel. I have a card for you." She clumsily unzipped the top of her attaché and fought with the small pocket where her business cards were jammed. Due to her suddenly sweaty fingers, she had a devil of a time removing one. Once she pried the card free, she set it on the table and pushed it across to Stela, who briefly glanced down at it, as if she were trained never to take her eyes off a lawyer sitting across from her. She just sat there, her posture curved like a C, staring in silence at a nervous Monica.

After endless seconds, Stela asked in a saccharine tone, "What's standby counsel?"

"Well, I understand you want to represent yourself, so my role is simply to sit next to you and explain procedure that you might not understand, like the judge's rulings."

"I don't need that," Stela said, her lips compressing into a line and her eyelids following.

"Do you have training as a lawyer?"

Stela didn't respond.

"Did you go to law school?"

Stela remained silent.

"I have to be here," Monica said. "The judge ordered me. You don't have to talk to me. You can do your own thing, and I'll just be available as a resource. In fact, I think I'd prefer if you didn't tell me what happened. Don't even tell me what you plan to do in court, okay?"

Stela broke into a smile and chuckled softly. Just as quickly, her expression grew taut again, as she said, "You can go now."

"What?"

"I don't need you. Goodbye." Stela popped out of her chair and stood stick-straight, facing the door. "Guard!"

Monica jumped at Stela's screech, but quickly gathered herself. "Right. Nice to meet you."

Stela tsked, as she spun her gaze between Monica and the window in the door.

The door opened and the huge guard entered. "Everything all right in here?"

"Yes," Monica said. "Thank you."

Stela turned back and nabbed Monica's business card from the table with her cuffed hands. "I'm ready to go."

The guard looked at Monica, who nodded. He shrugged and stepped back, so Stela could pass in front of him. She was met by another guard in the hallway who escorted her in the opposite direction from whence Monica had come.

Monica and the large guard retraced their route, her anticipation of freedom returning with each step. After she was deposited in the reception area, and the thick, metal door slammed behind her, its lock clicking decisively, she felt her protective veneer slip away. She realized she had been clenching her jaw the entire time she was in the jail, so she opened her mouth and worked her jaw from left to right, stretching it out.

She also realized she was sweating profusely. Even though she had worn her wool coat for the meeting, the temp in the jail hadn't been warm enough to cause her to sweat this much. Her cotton shirt stuck to her back, giving proof that meeting Stela had sent her body into overdrive.

She mumbled thank you to the two guards, as she made her way through the reception area—if one could call the austere anteroom that—and pushed through the double doors into the parking lot. As soon as she exited into the January air, she welcomed the crisp slap of the wind against her face. She forced herself to inhale deeply. Freedom. Despite its subzero sting, the air felt, smelled and tasted of glorious freedom.

She returned to the cab of her truck and started the engine, waiting for the heater to come to life. The cold seat actually felt good against her sweaty body.

Her phone vibrated with a text from Shelby. *Want to come over for dinner?*

Warmth spread through Monica's body. *Sure. What time?*

Whenever…Just let me know

I'm done with work now. I just need to run home and change.

Okay. See you soon, Shelby texted, followed by a heart emoji.

Monica always felt flattered—or perhaps relieved—when Shelby initiated contact. Even though Monica's rose-colored glasses diminished her objectivity, she still had the presence of mind to ask herself if there was a power differential in their relationship. She wondered if she was more into Shelby than Shelby was into her. Probably, but at the moment, she didn't care…

9

Monica carefully guided her truck into Shelby's narrow driveway, walls of snow flanking each side. The little truck was the exact width of the old driveway, which couldn't be widened due to Shelby's house on the left and her neighbor's property line on the right. As Monica bumped along, she concluded that the cracked and buckled concrete needed to be resurfaced, but she doubted that Shelby had the funds on her modest teacher's salary.

She slid to a stop alongside Shelby's charming house, the yellow outdoor light a beacon in the bitter darkness. As Monica got out, she removed an overnight bag from the passenger seat. Conditioned to ice on walkways this time of year, she gingerly stepped over icy patches that spotted the stoop, the light illuminating her breath.

She glanced briefly at a bag of salt resting next to the kitchen door and resisted the temptation to stop her forward movement in order to sprinkle some. That would be a task better suited for the next morning when the salt could work its magic under the winter sunshine.

Accustomed to letting herself in, Monica reached for the door knob and was surprised to discover it was locked. She rang the doorbell for the first time in their relationship.

Light from inside the house poured through curtained windows along with the muffled sound of music. She heard footsteps and the accompanying bustle of Shelby, as she unlocked the door.

"Hey," Shelby said with an inviting smile that accentuated the chevron in the center of her upper lip.

Monica was immediately energized by the flickers of affection in Shelby's hazel eyes, now highlighted by tiny crinkles at the edges. "You're locking your door now?"

"The neighbors said they saw a rando guy walking up and down the street today, so yeah." Shelby held the door wide and motioned for Monica to come into the warmth and smell of dinner.

Monica embraced the aroma, as she stomped her boots on the mat and set her bag on a chair. Something savory was roasting in the oven. "Rando guy, huh? Did anyone get a photo or call the police?"

"I doubt it. No one thinks that fast, you know." Shelby scooped up Monica's bag and left through the kitchen toward the bedrooms, saying over her shoulder, "Make yourself comfortable. We're grilling lamb chops, and the potatoes and Brussel sprouts are roasting in the oven."

"Can't wait," Monica said, flattered that Shelby was chef, hostess and lover, all rolled into a disheveled, sexy package.

She wandered over to the stove in her stocking feet and leaned down to peer into the oven. There were two baking sheets, one filled with halved Brussels sprouts covered in olive oil and onions, the other filled with cubed red potatoes, equally smothered in olive oil and finely chopped bacon bits.

On the counter to the right of the stove sat a white dinner plate with four small lamb chops under a light blanket of plastic wrap that trapped the combination of a dry rub and garlic cloves overlaying the meat. She assumed Shelby had brought them up to room temp and was waiting for Monica to grill them on her back patio. Two glasses of red wine, one less full than the other, sat on a wooden chopping block that served as Shelby's kitchen island. Monica picked up the bigger pour and smelled the fruity blend, eager to take the edge off her frustrating day.

She enjoyed her first sip, as Shelby returned wearing a purple apron with a rainbow-splashed heart in the center. Shelby had designed and painted the symbol herself and sold a variety of apparel and other items bearing it online.

"Yum," Monica said. "Good wine. I just remembered I promised to bring a bottle, didn't I?"

Shelby's eyes flashed with playfulness, signaling that, indeed, Monica had promised. Shelby dismissed the forgetfulness and walked straight into Monica's arms, kissing her softly on the lips. "Maybe. I didn't want to wait anyway, so I opened one of mine. I know where your stash is…I just might help myself next time I'm at your house."

Monica set down her glass and hugged Shelby with strength and purpose, burying her face in Shelby's thick mass of curls and kissing the side of her head. The world suddenly righted itself, no longer seeming so tragic. Monica was simultaneously at peace and filled with desire. "Hm. I love you."

Shelby tightened her arms around Monica's waist. "I love you too."

They remained wrapped in each other's arms for a few exquisite moments, swaying to the sound of soft music.

"Tough day?" Shelby asked, picking up on Monica's tension.

"Mm."

"I'm sorry. I bet you'll feel better after a glass of wine and dinner."

Monica pulled back slightly, so she could see Shelby's face. "I'm sure I will. Thank you for going to all of this work."

Shelby radiated satisfaction, as she looked up into Monica's emerald eyes. "Wait until you see what's for dessert."

A jolt of something hot ran through Monica, making her toes curl. She leaned down and kissed Shelby tentatively, searching for the passion that filled her soul.

Shelby eagerly reciprocated, turning Monica's brush of the lips into a deep kiss, moving her mouth from side-to-side in a sweeping motion.

Monica lost track of time, space and dimension, her stocking feet almost slipping out from underneath her, as they swayed and kissed in the cozy heat of the kitchen, the cruel, harsh realities of the external world fading away. She had never felt more grateful for Shelby's love and affection.

Later, as they dined on the sofa in front of the fire, Monica was oblivious to her own silence.

"You seem preoccupied," Shelby said, sipping her wine.

Monica looked up from cutting a bite of lamb chop. "I guess I am."

"About what?"

"Work. Something strange happened today." Monica ate a bite.

"What's that?"

She finished chewing while deciding how much to share. "Judge O'Brien assigned me as standby counsel for Stela Reiter, the woman who stabbed her boyfriend 13 times."

Shelby dropped her knife and fork with a clash on her plate. She covered her mouth.

"I know, right?" Monica said then described her trip to the jail.

"You met her?"

"Yes." Monica finished her last bite and set her empty plate on the coffee table. She picked up her wine and leaned back into the sofa, admiring the glow and crackle of the fire.

"What is she like?"

"Not what I expected."

"How so?"

"I thought she would be rough-looking and intimidating, but she was just the opposite—demure, withdrawn, quiet, observant as hell, and extremely confident."

"Did she tell you anything?"

Monica puffed. "Not at all. What she told me indirectly, however, is that she's a woman with a plan who doesn't want, or perhaps even need, an attorney."

"Does she have legal training?"

"I asked, but she didn't respond." Monica shrugged. "All I can do is follow Judge O'Brien's orders, but I'm not going to beg Ms. Reiter for information. In fact, I told her she didn't have to tell me anything—that I'd prefer not to know what happened."

Shelby visibly swallowed. "Blech. It's all so gory and surreal. I sure as hell wouldn't want to be in the same room as her, much less hear the details of the murder. We were talking about it in the teachers' lounge, and we couldn't believe that a woman was capable of stabbing a man that many times. I mean, wouldn't he be dead after the first few stabs?"

"Depends on where she stabbed him first, I suppose."

"We just couldn't believe that happened in Apple Grove."

"I know," Monica acknowledged, but secretly thought the teachers were a bit naïve. "We aren't immune from violence here, that's for sure."

Shelby rose and walked her plate into the kitchen, luring Monica to follow with her own. As they did dishes, Monica flipped on the TV to the local news station, WQOD, where Tiffany Rose, the roaming reporter who covered the courthouse, was behind the news desk, subbing for Keith Hoyt, the main anchor.

"This week kicks off the 25th annual ice fishing contest on Half Moon Lake. Anglers have spent the last month setting up their ice fishing shacks over strategic locations on the lake. A fishing village has emerged with more than 100 shacks, the largest number ever."

The camera panned out over Half Moon Lake to capture the charming village on the icy, white tableau, complete with street signs and Christmas lights strung on poles sunk deep into the ice.

Tiffany continued, "We will have daily reporting from the ice village, going door-to-door of the shacks, giving you an inside tour of some of the more elaborate ones, including their modern appliances. I was at Half Moon Village earlier today and interviewed a number of fishermen and women."

The TV imagery switched from Tiffany behind the desk to Tiffany in a designer down coat with a fur-lined hood, her toothpick-slim body at risk of blowing away in the cold wind sweeping over the lake. Fortunately, she was nestled among burly men and woman dressed in camo outerwear. The men answered Tiffany's questions in hushed tones between terse lips that were framed by beards with icicles dangling from them. They were careful not to reveal the secrets of their techniques in bait, lures, or topography of the bottom over which they had chosen to auger a hole. All of that information was guarded and top secret.

"She's gay, you know," Shelby said.

Monica recalled Tiffany hitting on her during the Saudi Arabian student murder trial. "I'm aware."

Shelby narrowed her eyes. "Really?"

Monica raised her shoulders indifferently. "She asked me out for a drink after she interviewed me on the courthouse steps."

"When was this?"

"Before you and I got together."

"Should I be jealous?"

Monica laughed sarcastically.

"Good to know." Shelby rinsed the dish rag, "I've seen Tiffany at the Pink Cave," referring to the only lesbian bar in Apple Grove.

"That's interesting." Monica paused her plate-rinsing. "Are you a regular there?"

"Not lately, but I used to go quite a bit with… ah…never mind." Her voice trailed off, and she muttered something under her breath.

"With whom?" Monica asked, turning from the sink, so she could see Shelby, who was wiping down the counters.

"Ah…just friends, you know?" Her voice rose in pitch. "Why is this suddenly about me? I thought we were talking about Tiffany."

"Please tell me you didn't hook up with Tiffany," Monica said, her heart clenching.

Shelby leveled a look of disapproval at Monica. "God, Mon! Be real."

Monica held up her wet hands in surrender. "I know. You're waaaay out of her league, but I had to ask." She quickly resumed loading the dishwasher, relief flooding her.

Tiffany's TV voice had momentarily faded into the background but now caught Monica's attention. "In the stabbing case by a woman named Stela Reiter, the police reported that the victim, Andy Nelson, worked at *Voila!*, the small appliance manufacturer in Apple Grove. He was employed in the division that makes weapons and guidance systems for the Department of Defense."

Monica shut off the faucet. "*Voila!* makes weapons?"

"Oh yes," Shelby whispered.

Tiffany continued, "I interviewed Dominique Bisset, the District Attorney, earlier today."

The scene switched to Dominique's office at the courthouse.

"Do you think Andy Nelson's employment at *Voila!* has anything to do with his murder?" Tiffany asked.

"We're not ruling it out," Dominique said.

"Did Stela Reiter, the woman who admitted to killing him but insists it was in self-defense, work at *Voila!* too?"

"No," Dominique said.

"Is Ms. Reiter a U.S. citizen?" Tiffany asked. "Our research indicates she has a Romanian passport."

"That's true," Dominique said.

"Is there a tie between Romania and Andy Nelson?"

"We're not ruling anything out," Dominique said, moving the storyline at a glacial pace.

"Is it true that Ms. Reiter fired her Public Defender?"

"Both of them," Dominique said.

"Is she representing herself now?"

"Yes," Dominique said in a monotone. "The court appointed standby counsel today to assist the defendant."

"Who?"

"Monica Spade, a local attorney."

Tiffany's expression lit up. "Have you had cases against Ms. Spade before?"

"No," Dominique said. "She isn't a criminal defense attorney. She's appointed by the court to explain matters to Ms. Reiter, not to represent her."

"That sounds interesting," Tiffany said, her voice filled with mystery.

"Ms. Reiter is representing herself, but Monica Spade will be with her in court to explain the proceedings and judge's rulings."

"Is there a trial date yet?"

"No, but we received word today that Ms. Reiter will request a speedy trial, which is her Constitutional right."

"Are you ready for trial?"

"I'm always ready for trial," Dominique said, patting a three-ring trial binder on the table next to her elbow.

"Do you have evidence that Ms. Reiter wasn't acting in self-defense?"

"Yes," Dominique said.

"Can you share that with our viewers?"

"Not at this time."

"Thank you for your time," Tiffany said. The camera switched back to her in the studio behind the anchor desk.

"Well, there it is," Shelby waved at the TV, "for all the world to see and hear what my girlfriend does for a living."

"Ugh," Monica groaned. "Now everyone will think I want to do criminal work, and nothing could be further from the truth."

"I bet Tiffany will want to interview you next." Shelby poked Monica in the ribs.

"That's the least of my concerns."

Shelby moved closer and grabbed Monica's gaze, placing her hand on Monica's shoulder. "If Tiffany hits on you again, you'd better shut that shit down immediately."

Monica's pulse quickened. "I don't know." She put her index finger to her chin. "Maybe I'll string her along a little for the fun of it."

Without warning, Shelby pinned Monica against the counter and trapped her head between her hands. Only inches from Monica's face, she said, "I love you and want you to myself. I'd like us to be exclusive, if you want, that is...cuz I really want...no fooling around on each other, okay?"

Initially, Monica thought Shelby was teasing, but then she sensed a note of desperation running deeper. "You have nothing to worry about. I'd never dream of fooling around on you."

"I'm glad you agree." Shelby kissed the tip of Monica's nose. "I love you too much to share, but I was afraid to ask...or be the first one to, that is. I'm not making any sense."

Shelby's confession blasted away any lingering doubt that Monica had about the foundation of their relationship. She fingered one of the long curls framing Shelby's face. "You make sense to me. We're exclusive."

Shelby took Monica's mouth in a passionate kiss.

10

Monica sat at her glass desk at the office, daydreaming about kissing Shelby's smooth, taut tummy while they had made love the night prior. Her desk phone rang, rudely jolting her from her reverie.

"Monica Spade."

"Al Bowman here."

"What can I do for you, Al?"

"You're not going to believe this." His strained voice shook with irritation.

"Okay…Try me."

"There's a plane flying over Half Moon Lake trailing a banner that says, 'Boycott CMH for Cruelty to Animals.'" He pounded his fist on his desk so hard that she could hear the rattle of cups and pens.

"Ouch, and the fishing tourney is in full swing," Monica said under her breath, then louder to Al, "Let me guess—Darcy Lemon."

"Darcy and her cracked lawyer, I'm sure," he said. "Can you call the advertising company, or the plane owner, or whomever, and pay whatever it takes to take that banner down?"

"Of course."

"Then sue Darcy for defamation," he said in an ominously-low voice. "People will think we do animal research, which we do not. Moreover, we handled Marcus-the-monkey with kid gloves. You were there. You know firsthand!"

"Let me talk to Nathan about the lawsuit and his discussions with Wally Leib. We'll address it one way or another. In the meantime, I'll contact the aerial advertising company."

"Thanks Monica."

"You're welcome, Al. Hang in there. We're on it."

She replaced the receiver and decided to touch base with Nathan before contacting the aerial advertising company. She rose, her hips a little sore from a CrossFit workout early that morning. Her first few steps to her office door were strained by tight hamstrings, her body cramping from overuse. Shelby had Monica on a merciless schedule called the "21-day challenge" at MoFit, their CrossFit box. The only result she could see thus far was that she walked like an old lady.

"Hey Mon. How's it goin'?" he asked, raising an eyebrow at her gait.

"Sore from CrossFit."

"Shelby's got you on a treadmill, girl!"

"No shit. Listen, I just got a call from Al Bowman." She downloaded the defamatory airplane banner flying over Half Moon Village.

"Wish we could see it from here," he said, looking out the window at the white carpet of snow sparkling under a blue sky. "Darcy Lemon is obviously behind it."

"Precisely. I'm planning to call the aerial advertising company, but I wanted to check with you first to see where you're at in dealing with Wally Leib."

He sighed, his brown, shaggy hair falling across his forehead. "She's such a shitty lawyer, hellbent on election to maintain a lawsuit. She told me they're above settlement talks because Darcy wants 'her day in court' with Marcus. To what end, I have no idea."

"Al won't pay them a dime. He's furious. This suit is so baseless, it's an abuse of process. Have you filed the motion to dismiss?"

"Yes. I included it with the answer to the complaint. The packet was filed with the court yesterday." He waved his hand in the general direction of the courthouse. "I also formally requested Darcy's deposition and demanded that Marcus be seen by an independent veterinarian to assess whether he suffers from emotional distress in any way, shape, or form."

Monica rolled her eyes. "Expensive, but tactically smart."

"If they're going to treat him like a human, then I'm going to apply the standard protocol we use for a human plaintiff. I'm also arranging for an expert witness to testify that Marcus looked happy and healthy while living at the hospital. He was thriving and frolicking."

"Who are you going to retain to say that?"

"Dr. Jane Goodall's grandson, a primatologist with the Washington, D.C. Zoo."

"How will he know if Marcus was happy at the hospital?"

"We called the hospital Security Office and got some fantastic video surveillance clips of Marcus bebopping down the hallways, eating bananas and other cafeteria food, happier than a party animal at a college party. I already emailed the clips to Dr. England Goodall."

"The primatologist's first name is England?"

"Yeah. He's actually England Winston Goodall, III."

"Just rolls off your tongue, doesn't it? People can be so dogmatic about first-born-son naming conventions."

"He isn't even from England." Nathan shoved aside the country with a wave of his hand and first-born naming conventions along with it. "If a fight is what Darcy and Wally are looking for, then a fight is what they'll get."

"Hold on, gunslinger. Al was very specific about making this go away. I don't think he wants to spend a ton of money on defending a frivolous lawsuit—"

"I know. I know," Nathan interrupted. "Hopefully, I'll get it dismissed, but I have to prepare as if we were going to trial. I warned Wally that I'm asking for attorney's fees and costs, because the claims are so beyond the pale."

"Her claims aren't worth a buffalo shit on a nickel."

Nathan smiled. "Niiiice. Alan Arkin from *Argo.*"

"Yep. The fake movie script negotiation."

"Best movie ever. I wonder if Matt has seen it—"

Monica snapped her fingers, calling him back to their conversation. "One more thing. Can you bring a counterclaim against Darcy—defamation for the inflammatory animal cruelty banner currently buzzing overhead?"

He nodded. "I'll amend our answer to include it."

"Thanks Ace."

"That's Ace Ventura to you."

"Alrighty then," she said with a trademark Jim Carrey facial expression, then turned and left.

When Monica returned to her office, she plopped down in her chair with a crash, her quads shredded from being overworked by Shelby's commands: "You go, Girl!" and "It's all you!" while Monica squatted 100 pounds. Monica had to think of an excuse to stop the madness to prevent her body from falling apart.

She scooted up to her desk and googled aerial advertising in Apple Grove, a subsecond search since there was only one company—Apple Aviation Advertising. She dialed the number.

"Triple A, this is Cassidy," a young woman's voice said.

Monica compared the phone number on her flat screen to the one on her telephone display. Same number. "I'm sorry. I thought I called Apple Aviation Advertising."

There was a gum-chewing smack. "Yeah. You got the right number. I abbreviate our name by calling us 'Triple A.'"

"Oh. You know there's a national company called Triple A, right? It's actually three As, and it's a service for roadside assistance."

"Do I know you?" Cassidy asked in millennial indifference.

"This is Monica Spade. I'm calling to speak to someone about advertising."

"Good, because I thought you were calling just to give me a hard time about how I answer the phone," Cassidy whispered as if Monica wasn't on the line, then said in a louder voice. "Monica Spade. Why does that name sound familiar?"

"I'm not sure, but I'd like to talk to someone about advertising."

Another gum-chewing smack. "That's me."

"Wonderful. I noticed your airplane is flying a banner today."

"That's my dad—Oscar. Great day for it. Butt cold but calm, clear and sunny."

"Ahem. Yes. So, how much does Oscar charge for a banner like that?"

"That banner is super long, so a lot. Of course, there's a fuel charge and pilot time."

"I see. Does he have any more availability this week?"

"Only one slot per day right now, due to his limited hours."

"Is that banner booked for any more days?"

"Not yet. She's going day-by-day with this one."

"How much is the daily slot?"

"One thousand dollars."

"I'll tell you what," Monica said. "If Darcy calls to book her banner again, I'll pay you $1,000. Then you tell her the slot is already filled. Deal?"

"How do you know her name, and why would I do that?"

Thanks for confirming her name. "You have my word that you'll get paid."

"Like I've never heard that before. We've never done business with you."

"I'm a lawyer in town. My firm is Spade, Daniels & Taylor."

The line went silent for a second, then Cassidy said, "Now I know you! You were on the news. You're the lawyer for that Stela woman who stabbed her boyfriend 13 times and cut off his pecker."

Monica let the pecker reference slide. "I'm not her lawyer. I was appointed by the court as standby counsel to explain procedure to her."

"Oh," Cassidy said while smacking her gum. "Same difference. Anyway, why do you want to buy the slot if Darcy calls back?"

"I represent the hospital." *A real client,* Monica thought but didn't say.

Monica's clock ticked on the wall while Cassidy processed. "Oh! I get it. You want to block Darcy from flying the banner again!"

"Look at you, connecting the dots," Monica said in a slightly condescending tone to match the snottiness on the other end.

"Yeah. Well. I'm pretty sure Oscar wouldn't let me do that."

"Maybe I should talk to Oscar."

"He's in the air," Cassidy said. "Besides, he doesn't talk to customers."

"Why not?"

"He's got a wicked stutter. That's why I'm here."

Monica wasn't sure she believed Cassidy. "Fair enough. Then you tell Oscar this: I'm going to sue Triple A for flying a false banner that defames Community Memorial Hospital. Instead of making $1,000 per day, you're going to spend $1,000 per day for years to come in attorney's fees and damages."

"What?" Cassidy asked. "You'd sue us?"

"In a heartbeat," Monica said.

"Is the $1,000 per day still on the table?"

"Yes. Just tell Darcy you're booked, then call me for the money."

"Gotcha. Deal," Cassidy said.

"You're a wise businesswoman, Cassidy. Pleasure speaking with you."

"If you're half as good a lawyer for the boyfriend killer as you are for the hospital, Stela will get off scot-free."

"I'm not her lawyer. I have nothing to do with her defense."

"So you say," Cassidy quipped.

"Goodbye." Monica quickly hung up and sent an email to Al Bowman explaining that she could buy out any further advertising for the plane banner. Desperately in need of a chai latte, she was about to get up for a stiff, painful walk to the kitchen when an email arrived in her inbox. The return address was "Stela1034" at "jail.Wis.gov." Monica's hand froze over her mouse.

She wondered how Stela got access to email in jail, but maybe that was a benefit for *pro se* defendants. Monica clicked on it.

"Dear Ms. Spade, I require your assistance as my standby counsel. Please visit me in jail immediately. Stela Reiter."

Monica reflexively pushed back from her desk, an audible puff of disbelief escaping before she muttered, "What the fuck?"

She was tempted to reply, *Sorry. Not today. I'm busy,* but pictured Judge O'Brien rebuking her, or worse, fining her.

As if sensing her ambivalence, another email populated her inbox, this one from Ruth Gobrecht, O'Brien's judicial assistant, with a letter attached to it. He had replied to Monica's inquiry about her precise duties as standby counsel, but his reply was less than satisfactory, capturing a few broad directives and ordering her to: "(1) assist the defendant regarding judicial process and rules; (2) participate, as needed, in the defense; (3) not interfere with tactical decisions; (4) not speak on behalf of the defendant; and (5) refrain from giving the impression to the jury that you represent the defendant."

Additionally, he wrote that the attorney-client privilege of confidentiality attached, so that discussions between Stela and Monica could not be discovered by the prosecution. He copied DA Bisset on the letter, so she, too, would know the parameters of Monica's role.

Monica wondered whether being summoned by Stela to the jail was included among her duties. Probably. At least she was getting paid $70 per hour for the charade. She limped to the kitchen to make a chai tea latte to-go. As she was steeping her tea, Jim Daniels entered.

"Is there any food in here?" His eyes scanned the countertops and conference table. When he didn't see anything to his liking, he went to the fridge and opened it. He removed a white carton of Chinese food with "Nathan" clearly written on it in black Sharpie.

Jim opened the silverware drawer and dove into the carton without remorse.

Monica raised her eyebrow but didn't say anything. She had bigger problems on her mind than Jim eating Nathan's food. "Stela just asked me to come to the jail."

"Oh really?" he asked with a full mouth. "How?"

"She emailed me."

"I didn't know they had access to email," he said through a bite.

"Apparently so. I guess I have to go over there now. Such a pain in the ass."

"I wonder what she wants." A Chinese noodle fell on his beard and clung there.

"Why aren't you doing this instead of me?" she asked.

He swallowed, collecting his thoughts. "Been there; done that. Just go see what her questions are and take care of them."

She shook her head and tossed her tea bag in the trash. "Thanks for your support, bearded man with food on it."

"Chin up, soldier," he said, wiping his beard.

She flipped him off behind her head as she walked out.

11

Buttoned up in her black, wool coat and carrying her warm thermos of tea, Monica breezed through her firm's reception area on a beeline for the glass doors to the parking lot. She once again admired her name stenciled on the door, right below the full name of the firm. Her chest filled with pride, moving the needle up on her self-esteem meter.

"Going out, Ms. Spade?" Kathy asked without looking away from her computer screen.

"You saw me walk by?" Monica asked.

"I see everything."

"I'm beginning to think your half-glasses have secret powers" Monica said. "In answer to your question, yes. I'm going to see Stela at the jail."

Kathy stopped what she was doing and produced a theatrical shiver. "Creepy. I don't know how you do it."

"Go to the jail to chat with a woman who viciously stabbed a man to death?"

"Did you ever find out if she cut off his pecker?"

"You know, she didn't talk much during our last visit, so I didn't really see an opening to explore the details of her personal rage."

"I thought the topic would come up naturally while she was telling you the who, what, where, when, why and how she killed him. If you're going to represent slashers and slayers, shouldn't you get the gory details in your interview?"

"I actually told her I didn't need or want to know the story."

"Just going in blind to court, eh?"

"Since I don't have to address the jury, or question any witnesses, I figured I could just sit back and watch the story unfold."

Kathy adjusted her cheaters. "For some reason, I don't see it playing out that way. You've never been one to sit back and watch anything."

Monica cocked her head. "That's fair. I'll let you know what happens."

"If you need my help with anything, let me know."

For an instant, Monica thought Kathy was joking. She had never before offered to help on a file. "This case has snagged your curiosity, huh?"

"Maybe. Will you be returning today?"

"Don't know. Depends on how long our chat goes." Monica leaned on the door with her shoulder and nodded goodbye.

During her drive to the jail, Monica heard Kathy's voice replaying in her mind, "You've never been one to sit back and watch anything." Kathy had a point.

Once at the courthouse, in which the jail was located, she circled the crowded parking lot looking for a vacant spot. The cars were jam-packed, sometimes at creative angles, since the yellow stall lines weren't visible under the thick snowpack. Skid steers had cleared away the recent snowmageddon, creating gigantic banks at the edges of the lot. She found a spot at the back corner, her truck sitting catawampus next to a 20 foot-high pile of snow.

Despite the late afternoon sun, the air was brittle, crystallizing her breath and freezing her eyelashes, as she walked quickly over the uneven ground into the warm building. She stomped her boots to remove the clumps of snow and sand, and again opted to keep her coat on—perhaps subconsciously seeking a protective layer of armor. She checked in with the sergeant at the glass window then submitted herself to the security inspection by the same guard she had encountered a week prior.

"Cold enough for ya?" He went through the motions of sticking his sausage fingers into her attaché case, which was bare but for a pen, business cards, and an unused legal pad.

"It's a cold one today." She regarded his easy, lived-in smile, twinkling eyes, short stature, and friendly mannerisms, a stark contrast to his work environment. Not fooled, she was sure he could subdue a man twice his size.

"Back to see the Romanian?" he asked.

Her ears perked up. She hadn't confirmed for herself that Stela was Romanian. It was just on the news. "How do we know that?"

"That's what her passport says."

"Oh," she said, as she met him on the other side of the metal detector. "You've seen her passport?"

He handed her the attaché. "Of course. I guess she's a student at the university, or was. She won't see the inside of a classroom for quite a while though, I'd imagine."

"Interesting," Monica said. "What was she studying?"

"Word on the street is chemistry."

"Hmm. Who told you that?"

"Relative of a friend of a dog owner. The usual." His gentle, brown eyes held her own.

"I love small towns," she said. "I'm sure you know more about me than I do."

He laughed. "I wouldn't say that, but probably more than you expect. I'm Bob, by the way."

"Nice to meet you, Bob." She held out her hand, and they shook.

"Do you know what they call a bunch of crows killing each other inside of a tent?" he asked unexpectedly.

Caught off balance, she had to recalibrate her brain to realize he was telling her a joke. "No. What?"

"Murder with intent." He laughed. "Get it?"

Quickly recalling that a flock of crows is called a "murder," she chuckled in spite of herself. "In the tent as in 'intent.' Yeah. Good one."

The hulky guard who had previously accompanied Monica to visit Stela opened the large metal door to the jail. "Ms. Spade?"

"Hello again." She tilted her head back to regard him. "You're a very large man."

He smiled, revealing a chipped tooth. "You should see my brother." He stuck out his bear paw for a shake. "Call me Cliff."

"Okay, Cliff. Please call me Monica. Is Stela in the conference room?"

"The Romanian prisoner is seated and silent, as per usual."

Stela certainly was making an impression on the guards. Monica followed Cliff's broad back down the depressing cinderblock hallway. That disgusting smell she had noticed the first time reappeared—a pungent mix of public restroom and auto mechanic's shop.

He stopped at the same gray metal door of the conference room in which Monica and Stela had met last week.

He unlocked it with a loud click and held it open for her. Her stomach lurched a little at being cooped up in a room with a killer, but she swallowed the butterflies and decided a show of confidence was in order. "Hello, Ms. Reiter."

Stela didn't stand or gesture to shake hands, but she did acknowledge Monica with a polite nod. "Hello, Ms. Spade."

"I'll be outside," Cliff said and closed the door.

The sound of the lock clicking was like a last breath of air for Monica. She briefly calculated the harm Stela could do to her in the time it would take Cliff to reopen the door and come to her rescue. The answer was a lot, but she shoved aside her fears and focused on the woman across the metal table. "I got your email. How can I be of service?"

"I've been preparing the defense of my case, and I need some help with a few matters."

Monica regarded the pale and evenly complected Stela. She was so average and peaceful-appearing that Monica felt even more intimidated, if that was possible. "I'll see what I can do. It depends on what the ask is."

"You think I'm guilty of murder, don't you?" Stela asked in a dull monotone, her eyes sharp. "It was justifiable homicide. There's a difference."

Monica was so thrown off by the accusation that she didn't quite know how to answer. There was neither anger nor hate in Stela's eyes, just intelligence.

"It doesn't matter what I think, and I don't want to know. I'm here to make sure you understand the process, the law, and the judge's rulings to the best of my ability."

Stela slowly moved her long, unwashed hair over her shoulder, a faint oily sheen to the flat brown strands. From the scent, Monica suspected Stela had used some dry shampoo.

"Do you report back to the court and prosecution everything we talk about?" Stela asked.

"No. What you tell me is attorney-client privileged and confidential."

Stela mulled that over for a second. "Do you have a lot of experience in defending criminals?"

"None whatsoever."

An amused smile instantly appeared. "I have enough for both of us."

There it was. Confirmation of prior legal experience. "Were you a lawyer in Romania?"

"How did you know I'm from Romania?"

Monica shrugged. "Passport."

"I've never practiced law."

By the terse, evasive answer, Monica considered the implications of familiarity with the criminal justice system. Stela could also simply be a career criminal. "Very well then. What can I do for you?"

"I need you to contact a certain psychiatrist and ask him to testify on my behalf."

"About what?"

"About the signs and symptoms of PTSD after being sexually assaulted."

Monica had to admit her own curiosity was piqued. "What signs, specifically?"

Stela flicked her hand dismissively. "That will come later. For now, just tell him that I suffered confusion and the inability to recount the details of the attack to the physicians, nurses, and detectives questioning me."

"Okaaay." Monica removed her legal pad and made a note. "Does this psychiatrist have a name and phone number?"

"Dr. Delaney Karpenko." Stela recited the phone number from memory.

"Does he know you?" Monica asked. "Who's going to pay for his services?"

"Tell him that Eugène Ionesco is asking."

"How do you spell that?" Monica asked, pen poised over paper.

Stela spelled both names, even telling Monica to add the accent over the "e" in Eugène.

After Monica jotted it down, she looked up to find Stela studying her. "Who's Mr. Ionesco?"

"Never mind that."

Monica wanted to follow up, but she let it slide. "Is there anything else?"

"Yes. Tell the court I request a speedy trial, which I'm entitled to under the Constitution, no?"

"Uh, okay." Monica made a mental note. "Isn't your preliminary hearing in two days? Can't you tell the judge yourself at the hearing?"

"I can, and I will, but I thought your requesting it might carry more impact."

"Remember, I'm not a spokesperson on your behalf. I don't represent you. If you want a lawyer to represent you, I'm sure we can arrange for that."

Stela waved her off. "Nice try, Ms. Spade. You're stuck with me."

Monica put her hand to her chest. "I'm not trying to leave. I'm just advising you of what I can, and cannot, do. I won't make the request at the hearing, but you can."

"Right," Stela said with finality. "On a separate note, do you know whether the police searched Andy's house?"

Monica flinched at Stela using the victim's name so casually. She redirected her gaze down to her note pad, finding solace in scrawling a random note about searching Andy's house. "I don't, but I can email the DA and ask."

"Do that." Stela's voice held a cool confidence that made the hairs on the back of Monica's neck stand.

When she looked up from writing, Monica trained her eyes on the wall behind Stela, instead of looking directly at her. "Is there anything in particular you're concerned about at Andy's house?"

"Yes. Andy fancied himself quite the philosopher about sex and bondage. He kept a small, spiral notebook of his thoughts, which he encouraged me to read. His entries are quite troubling."

Monica suppressed her shock. *Of course, kinky sex would have to be a part of this case.* "How are they relevant to your defense?"

"He wrote about nonconsensual sex, bondage, cannibalism and cutting. After reading his journal, I was terrified that he was going to do that to me in the back seat of the car that day." Stela's statement would have been more believable if she hadn't delivered it in a rapid-fire monotone that sounded like she was reading from a teleprompter.

Monica studied Stela's tight upper lip and unwavering brown eyes. "Really?"

"He had been building up to that moment for a few weeks, and when he started cutting on me," she motioned to her groin and legs, "I knew my fate would be sealed unless I fought for my own life."

Monica saw a flash of danger in Stela's eyes, so she dropped her gaze back to her pad and returned to notetaking. "Spiral notebook. Got it. Is there a place he usually kept it?"

"Yes. The bedside table or on the coffee table in the living room."

Monica wrote that down.

Stela continued matter-of-factly. "Have you asked the prosecution for any and all the evidence they've gathered, including police reports?"

"No," Monica said. "I didn't know that was my job."

"It is," Stela said with a note of authority.

Monica swallowed. "DA Bisset will be at the prelim. We can ask her there."

"I'd like to study anything they have before the prelim. If there's a chance to beat probable cause for charging me, I'd like to try."

Monica wondered what universe Stela was living in. She admitted to stabbing Andy Nelson to death. The only question was whether it was in self-defense, and that was a question for a jury to decide. "Um, right."

"Will there be TV cameras in court?" Stela asked.

Tiffany's face flashed through Monica's mind. "Probably."

"Do I have to wear this hideous orange jumpsuit?"

"For the prelim? I'm pretty sure you do," Monica said.

"For the trial too?"

"No," Monica said, recalling Trevor McKnight's trial. "You can wear street clothes for a jury trial. They'll put a belt around your waist instead of using shackles."

Stela tilted her head to the side, signaling a need to know more.

"Since you won't be wearing handcuffs or ankle cuffs, they need a way to secure you. The belt is like a shock collar except around your waist. It has a taser built into it."

Stela arrowed her eyes, envisioning the device. After a long second, she said, "It could be worse. In Russia, they'd leave me in this hideous orange jumpsuit and put me in a cage in the courtroom."

Monica wondered why Stela chose to cite Russia as an example. "Right. You'll be treated fairly here."

"Then I need some dress clothes," Stela said, staring off into space. "I'm usually a size six, so I'll need size eight clothes to hide the belt. I'll make a list of what I need and give it to you at the prelim."

Monica was taken aback, confident that her duties didn't include being Stela's personal shopper. "Um. Isn't there someone else who could do that?"

Stela's expression changed from pleasant to diabolical. "No."

"Right. I suppose I could take care of it. Do you have a method of payment?"

"I will by the hearing."

"Okay." Monica heard the strangled sound of her own voice and inwardly chided herself for being such a pushover.

"Now we're making progress," Stela said, her tone changing to friendly again. "I think this standby counsel relationship will work for me." She placed her cuffed hands on the table and pushed up. "That will be all for now, Ms. Spade. Keep an eye on your email in case I need you."

Still seated, Monica looked up at the elfin woman and felt intimidated by her wiry, confident stance.

Out of instinct, Monica quickly rose from her chair too. She was at least eight inches taller than Stela and much broader in stature. Despite being a larger woman, however, she had never felt less safe. "I will. If I don't hear from you, I'll see you at the prelim. Take care."

"Guard!" Stela belted in her soprano.

Monica shivered under her coat, praying that Stela couldn't smell her fear.

12

When Cliff held open the thick door for Monica to exit, he and Bob looked expectantly at her.

"I heard a lot of talking in there," Cliff said, as he leaned against the open door.

"I hope you weren't eavesdropping on a confidential conversation." She moved past Bob toward the doors to the parking lot.

"Wouldn't dream of it," Cliff said. "I kept an ear out for yelling in case she tried to kill you."

Monica turned to him with a genuine smile. "I'm grateful. See you soon."

She pulled on her gloves and pushed through the glass door, again cherishing the fresh air like she was experiencing the beauty and liberation of springtime. The jail was not only scary but also downright suffocating.

As she retraced her path over the frozen tundra in the parking lot, she glanced up to see wisps of clouds obscuring the late afternoon sun. She wondered whether they portended more snow. As she slid in behind the wheel of her truck, she didn't even register the frozen seat, she was so preoccupied with her curious exchange with Stela.

Who is this woman? She isn't just a chemistry student, that's for sure.

Monica replayed Stela's instructions. There was no doubt that Stela had experience in judicial tribunals, if not a formal legal education. She was a woman with a plan and was holding that plan close to her vest. No surprise that she didn't want a public defender. Behind those oversized glasses, Stela wanted to be the star of the courtroom. Having an actual lawyer would mean ceding control, and Monica suspected that Stela was used to being in control.

The clock on Monica's dash told her she could head directly home and get a jump-start on cooking dinner and dessert for Shelby, who was due at Monica's house around 5:30. If Monica was efficient, she could make an apple pie and bake it while they ate dinner. *Shelby is always in a better mood if I feed her dessert.*

As soon as she entered her house, Monica changed into joggers and a ripped long-sleeve she had bought at a Billie Eilish concert. She cranked up the volume to her playlist and took command of her small kitchen, removing five large apples from the fridge. She peeled and sliced bite-sized pieces into a glass bowl, generously spreading brown sugar over them. She sank her fingers into the mix, making sure each slice was thoroughly coated. During the time it would take her to make a pie crust, the brown sugar would marinate the apples, creating a heavenly mixture.

Allowing her brain to process work matters, she followed her family pie crust recipe from memory. Her grandmother had taught her how to make apple pie when visiting their lake cabin up north, where her parents now lived in retirement.

Into a bowl went precise measurements of flour, salt, shortening and water. Next came the handheld dough mixer and a butter knife to cut the stubborn shortening. As Monica rolled the dough between two sheets of wax paper, she pictured the preliminary hearing scheduled in two days, Stela sitting at counsel table arguing her points to the judge, perhaps cross-examining police officers, then demanding evidence from Dominique.

What the hell had gone on in Andy's car and why? If Stela's rape defense isn't true, why did she kill him? He was a local guy who worked at Voila!, famous for manufacturing waffle makers. Can a guy be more boring?

She peeled the wax paper off the top layer of dough and carefully flipped it into a glass pie dish. Next, she dumped in half of her apple and brown sugar mixture, lightly sprinkled a quarter cup of flour over it, followed by white sugar, chased with a generous sprinkling of cinnamon and nutmeg. She added the second layer of apples, flour, sugar and spices then rolled out the top crust. In 40 minutes flat, she had prepped her pie and put it in the oven. Now she could turn to reheating the homemade lasagna she and Shelby had baked and frozen a few weekends ago.

By the time Shelby walked into Monica's entryway, Monica had the table set with a tossed salad, the hot lasagna resting on a cork trivet, and a bottle of red wine between the two place settings.

"God, I missed you today," Shelby said, tossing her dark, down coat onto a chair and removing her knit hat. Her long curls magically sprang back into place.

Monica spread her arms, and Shelby skipped into them. The playful hug turned molten immediately, their curves fitting over and under and under and over in all the right places. Monica rested her cheek against Shelby's ear, thanking her lucky stars for Shelby in her life. She needed this woman as much as she needed air. Her body filled with warmth, as her breasts came to life against Shelby's chest.

"You smell so good," Monica whispered into Shelby's hair.

Shelby's arms tightened around Monica's waist. "Mm."

"Are you hungry?"

"Starved," Shelby said. "It smells delicious in here."

"Lasagna for dinner and a pie in the oven."

"That's what I smell. An apple pie!" Shelby said with the enthusiasm of a child.

"Only for you."

"Homemade crust and all?"

"Of course," Monica said.

"After we eat pie, I have dessert for you too."

"Made from snatch?"

Shelby giggled devilishly. "Always." She arched back enough to look into Monica's eyes. "Thank you for making dinner tonight. I know how busy you are at the firm."

"I wish I could do it more often." Monica kissed Shelby's forehead. "I love making food for you."

"And I love watching you eat," Shelby said.

"Aren't we provocative tonight?"

"A little," Shelby shoved off and removed her scarf, flinging it over her coat. "Good day at work?"

Monica led the way to the table where she poured the wine. "Let's just say it was interesting." She motioned for Shelby to sit. "How about you?"

"Fantastic." Shelby gracefully eased into the bench of the cozy nook off Monica's kitchen. "This cold weather makes me hungry."

"I'm happy to hear it," Monica said. "You're beautiful when you're hungry."

Shelby lifted her glass and rested her elbows on the table. She sipped while she stared at Monica over the rim.

Monica froze, salad tongs in mid-air. "What?"

Shelby smiled. "I don't plan staying hungry for long. I hope you find me equally beautiful when I'm sated."

Monica laughed. "Of course. That was probably a stupid thing to say. I'm flustered whenever I'm near you." She dropped salad into her bowl, but Shelby didn't pick up the tongs. She just sipped some more wine and gazed lovingly at Monica.

"Did I do something?" Monica asked.

"I just want to remember this moment forever," Shelby said. "Being here. Sharing a meal with you. You give me... What's the right word? Hope? No, desire, but that sounds only sexual. Maybe joy is better." She briefly shook her head, clearing her thoughts. "I can't decide, but I want to feel like this forever—just the two of us, reuniting over a meal after a long day at work."

Monica splayed her hand across her heart. "Wow. That's the nicest thing anyone has ever said to me, especially someone as beautiful and sexy as you."

Shelby's eyes glimmered in the candlelight.

Monica picked up her wine and gently clinked the side of Shelby's glass. "To us, and many more home-cooked meals."

"To us," Shelby repeated. She sipped her wine again then set her glass on the table.

Monica used the serving spoon to guide a big piece of lasagna onto her plate while Shelby dished herself a bowl of salad and a small piece of lasagna. Monica remained in awe at Shelby's small appetite, even in the face of an unforgiving winter. Monica's body screamed out for hearty carbs and savory meat.

Shelby's food portions probably accounted for the difference in their body mass too. Monica had toned her body through CrossFit, and wasn't about to apologize for having both a healthy build and a healthy appetite, but she was thicker than Shelby. Shelby had never made a negative comment about Monica's body, though, not even a hint.

Midway through their meal, the timer on the oven beeped, so Monica removed the pie, heaving with steam and golden apple juice. She set it on the stovetop and returned to the warm booth, pouring herself a second glass of wine. She briefly wrestled with the idea of talking about her trip to the jail, but was reluctant to discuss murder, or the person who committed it, in her home. Shelby's company provided a sanctuary from the horrors of her new assignment. God forbid that Monica taint their loving ambiance with evil in its barest form.

"Penny for your thoughts," Shelby said, as she ran the tip of her finger around the rim of her wine glass.

"Just dismissing the thought of talking about work. It isn't important, and I don't want to bring work into my home."

"Does that mean I can't talk about the comedy and tragedy of teaching unpredictable high school students?"

"Not at all," Monica said. "I want to hear about your day at school."

Shelby smiled then described some of the regulars in her classes, their flirtation and heartbreak. Their foolishness and brilliance. Their fears and bravado. And, that was just one afternoon. "Seriously, though, sometimes art class draws something out of a teenager that he or she would never dream of expressing elsewhere—in class, with friends, or at home."

"Art class drawing something out? No pun intended," Monica said.

Shelby smiled patiently.

"I'm sorry," Monica said. "Like what?"

Shelby pondered that question while staring into the dark through Monica's picture window. "Like, this one student, a lovely young girl. I asked the class to do a pencil-drawing of the worst day in their lives."

"That actually sounds difficult," Monica said. "What did you get?"

"More tragic sketches than you'd realize. This girl drew a boy with a handgun to his own head."

"Oh dear," Monica said. "What was that about?"

"I knew that her brother took his life with a gun a few years ago, but I was surprised she had the courage to draw it for everyone to see."

"How did the others react?" Monica asked.

"Almost all of them had known him and remembered the event, and had supported her through it, attending his funeral, then helping her find a new normal high school life. They complimented her on the likeness to her brother and her courage for drawing it. Their shared experience is part of their friendship and history now, but the vivid reminder—there in black and white—was very sobering."

"How is the girl doing?"

"As far as I can tell, really well. She does well academically, has a nice friend group, plays in the band, has a boyfriend. From the outside, everything looks fine."

"You're sure she wasn't drawing the gun to her own head?" Monica's gut clenched, as she asked the question.

"No." Shelby shook her head. "It's definitely of her brother. Very recognizable as a male. I asked her about it after class. She said she's in a good place, two years out from his death. She went to some grief therapy, has loving parents, and regularly goes to church, which is very important to her. I felt reassured after chatting with her."

"So much to process at a young age—for all of them," Monica said.

"We adults can learn a lot from teenagers. We're probably more shocked and thrown off balance to see the raw facts and emotion in a painting than they are, if that makes any sense."

"It does," Monica said. "We take comfort in believing nothing tragic will ever happen to us, that we only see that stuff on the news. Then, life reminds us of death, and that sometimes comes as a surprise to people who have designed their perfect houses in safe neighborhoods."

Shelby's expression grew compassionate. "Is there something I should know?"

Monica blinked. "About me? No. I just want you to know that I don't take moments like this for granted. What we have is unique and special."

Shelby's expression relaxed. "I adore you."

Her attention was like a life-saving drug. "Are you in the mood for pie?"

Shelby cocked a playful eyebrow. "I'd love some." She rose and loaded the dishwasher while Monica cut two pieces of pie, her own slightly larger.

"Want a cup of coffee with dessert?" Monica asked.

"Are you insane? I'd be up all night."

Monica shrugged. "With my Norwegian genes, I could drink caffeine all day and still sleep like a rock. I'm going to because I love the combo."

"You should make some then," Shelby said, running her thumb down Monica's back, then curling her arm around her waist. She stayed close, as Monica poured the water in her small coffee maker and ground some Kona beans. They swayed together in the kitchen to the percolating sound of coffee brewing, love and tenderness filling the air. When the beep signaled the brewing cycle was over, Monica kissed Shelby's cheek.

"I don't want to let go of you," Shelby murmured in a soft voice, "but I really love your apple pie."

"We have all night." Monica's hands fell down Shelby's back and squeezed her small buns. "Do you want a scoop of vanilla ice cream on your pie?"

"No," Shelby said. "I like it plain."

"I'm adding a scoop to mine."

They took their dessert to the loveseat in front of the gas fireplace. Through the bank of porch windows, they could see snowflakes shimmering in the street light.

"More snow," Shelby grumbled, "more shoveling."

"If it's going to be this cold, though, I'd rather have snow than just a brown landscape."

"I agree, but it's just so much. There's nowhere left to pile it."

"I'll help you."

"I plan to retire to a warm climate, that's for sure," Shelby said, as she used the side of her fork to cut her first bite.

Monica watched Shelby carefully, and was relieved at the look of satisfaction on her face, as she savored her first bite. After Shelby swallowed, she looked into Monica's eyes and said, "Love it."

A rush of pleasure hit Monica, as she felt herself blush, which was ridiculous. She'd made pie for Shelby before, but pleasing her, putting that look on her face, completed her world.

"Are you going to eat yours?" Shelby asked.

"Yes." Monica redirected her attention to the plate on her lap. "I was just making sure you didn't die from your piece. Now I know it's safe to continue."

Shelby kicked Monica in the leg.

Monica took a bite and was rewarded with a warmth like summer sunshine. She chased it with a healthy drink of coffee, secretly wondering if life could get any better, cuddling in front of the fire with the love of her life, enjoying her favorite dessert.

Shelby pulled the blanket tighter around her neck. "Brrrrr…"

"Are you cold again? The way you dislike winter, I'd guess you're from the south or something."

"Didn't I tell you? We lived in Georgia when I was little. I went to school through fifth grade there."

"That explains that soft, southern drawl when you're drinking," Monica said.

"I have an accent?"

"Sometimes. It's very sexy."

"Y'all haven't seen anything yet," Monica said in an exaggerated drawl.

"Where did you move to next?"

"Madison. I went to school—through college—there. My family still lives there."

"How did you land in Apple Grove?"

"Positions are scarce for high school art teachers. I initially thought it would be for only a few years, but Apple Grove grew on me, and a few years turned into eight."

"It's no Madison, but I'd say it's pretty progressive for its size," Monica said.

"Having a substantial gay population was key for me. If everyone here were homophobes, then I would've moved back to Madison, but I've always felt comfortable here."

"The Pink Cave always seems packed."

"I'm so over that place!" Shelby scoffed.

Monica angled her head back in surprise. "Did someone get hammered there and make a fool out of herself?"

"Maybe." Shelby suddenly hopped up and disappeared with their empty plates.

Monica heard her put them in the dishwasher, then Shelby returned with her laptop.

"What are we doing now?" Monica asked.

"I have to do some teacher in-service stuff through computer-based training that's due tomorrow, but it should only take about an hour." Shelby opened her laptop and clicked into the school system internet.

"If I'm quiet, can I sit next to you?" Monica asked.

Shelby patted Monica's leg. "As long as you don't bug me."

"Promise," Monica said, "unless I get bored, in which case all bets are off."

"Don't you dare. If I stop in the middle of the module, I have to restart from the beginning."

"Pure torture, but I'll restrain myself." Monica quickly moved an ottoman in front of the loveseat for their feet and grabbed her laptop from the end table. She googled Eugène Ionesco and discovered he was a French-Romanian playwright. *Why would Stela give me his name as a codeword?*

Monica dumped her laptop and grabbed her Kindle from the coffee table. She found a compendium of Ionesco plays, including *Rhinoceros* and *The Leader,* both of which she read while Shelby did her teacher training module.

When Shelby gently closed the lid on her laptop, she asked, "What are you reading?"

"Bizarre stuff that was written in the 1940s and 50s by a French-Romanian playwright."

"I didn't know you liked plays."

Monica grunted in the negative. "This is a one-off, and his plays are bizarre. I can't relate at all."

"Why are you reading them?"

"A client mentioned the writer in a subversive, coded kind of way, so my curiosity got the best of me."

"That's one of the characteristics I admire most about you—your curiosity."

"Really?" Monica looked up from her Kindle screen to find Shelby studying her.

"I admire people who are committed to life-long learning, and with you, it's the reason you're so good at figuring out stuff. Something snags your curiosity, so you follow it like a bird dog until you flush it out."

"If I'm the dog, who's the hunter?"

"Me, silly." Shelby poked Monica in the arm.

"I'm not sure how I feel about you holding a gun while I run ahead of you."

"Don't trust me, huh?" Shelby quickly moved her fingers to Monica's ribs and began tickling.

Monica doubled over, her head resting on Shelby's lap. She resisted laughing, but she moaned until Shelby stopped.

Shelby moved her hands to finger-comb Monica's strands of hair behind her neck and onto her back. "I can't keep my hands off you."

"Likewise," Monica said into Shelby's thigh, then kissed it through her leggings.

"So, what's so bizarre about the plays you just read?"

"They're sort of abstract—which isn't my jam—and they convey some sort of message through odd, very exaggerated behavior.

"Like what?"

"In *The Leader,* the actual leader is walking around with a hedgehog in his arms, stroking it."

"What kind of leader?"

"I get the impression he was an evil politician of a European country, just coming into popularity, like Hitler in Germany."

"Did the writer live through World War II?"

"Yes. He was in the heart of it," Monica said. "Then, the Leader prances around in his underwear while someone presses his trousers, which is like a bad dream. It concludes with either the Leader, or another person, I wasn't sure, as a headless man wearing a hat."

"How does that work?"

"I'm not sure, but it sets up his punchline of: 'What's he need a head for when he's got genius?'"

Shelby groaned. "Sounds like something a drunk teenager would write."

Monica laughed. "I know, right? Like I said, I just can't get into that type of abstract writing. I'm more of a concrete kind of reader."

"Oh yes. Concrete all the way."

When Monica angled her face up from Shelby's lap, Shelby leaned down and kissed her on the lips.

13

The next day, Monica drove to work in an upbeat mood. Despite having to work on Stela's gruesome case, Monica was gooey inside over making love to Shelby. Monica had cherished every touch and sweet nothing in their cozy bedroom, the night wind howling against the house and the snowflakes swirling in the orange streetlamps. She had never dreamed she'd feel this way, yet here she was—in love.

She was tumbling so fast toward wanting to spend the rest of her life with Shelby that she was scared shitless in her new state of vulnerability. She shuddered at the thought. Her heart wanted to lock down Shelby with a ring, but her head said to slow down...slow down...slow down. Monica didn't even know who had given Shelby the diamond stud and the upsetting history behind it. *When is she going to tell me?*

She kicked up fresh snow, as she walked across the empty parking lot. The snow removal service hadn't even cleared her law firm's sidewalks yet. She unlocked the doors and flipped on lights, as she strode to her office. She dumped her gear on her desk and went to the kitchen to make a pot of coffee. As she pushed the power button, Kathy entered, carrying a glass baking dish of something that smelled like a cinnamon orgy.

"Good morning," Monica said, her mouth watering before she even saw what was under the aluminum foil. "What do you have there?"

"Homemade cinnamon rolls." Kathy set them on the counter. "Fresh from the oven. Help yourself."

Monica's tummy turned a somersault and popped up to stand with its arms held high. "I couldn't, but they smell delicious."

"You have to before they get cold. Feel the pan, they're still warm." Kathy motioned for Monica to touch the pan, and when she did, the warmth radiated up her fingers, teasing her taste buds with the promise of a blissed-out sugar blast.

As Kathy peeled off the aluminum foil, the aroma evoked Monica's lustful instinct for cinnamon. "Okay, maybe just half of one."

Kathy handed her a knife and busied herself with making a cup of coffee while Monica carved out a respectable cinnamon roll, carefully transferring it to a plate. A forkful met her mouth. "Oh my God, I'm in heaven, Kathy. Thank you."

"Making you happy makes me happy," Kathy said. "How was your meeting with the pecker pruner?"

Monica smiled and spread a little butter on her roll. "We don't know that she cut his penis, but she did give me a list of stuff to do, which I'm pretty sure standby counsel doesn't have to do…but I'm afraid to say no. I mean, what if she's acquitted and comes after me?" She eagerly stuffed a buttery bite into her mouth, chewing with delight.

Kathy sipped her coffee, grabbed the butter knife, and made a few stabbing motions in the air. "To be honest, I'd worry about that too—the Romanian ripper."

"Terrifying. She said she's going to give me a list of clothes to buy her for the trial."

"Really?"

"You know how much I love to shop," Monica said sarcastically, eating another bite.

"I'll do it." Kathy set down the knife. "I don't mind."

"Seriously?" Monica said around her mouthful of hot, sticky heaven. "You'd do that for me?"

"Of course. I have a good eye, and I love to get out of the office for stuff."

"Cool. I'll take you up on that," Monica said. "By the way, these rolls are to die for."

Kathy laughed. "Thank you, and by the way, I wouldn't use that expression in front of Stela the slayer, or she might take you literally and kill you. On the spot."

Monica scrunched her eyes shut. "I guess I'll have to watch myself around her, won't I?"

"I would," Kathy said.

"Well, I have to confront work." Monica took a step toward her office.

"I'm sure the phones will be ringing off the hook today," Kathy said on her way toward reception.

At first, Monica couldn't tell whether Kathy was being genuine or sarcastic, then concluded she was probably genuinely sarcastic.

Once Monica was settled at her desk, she removed her legal pad from her attaché that had accompanied her to the jail. She looked at Dr. Delaney Karpenko's name and phone number then googled him. He had a psychiatric practice in Cleveland, Ohio, and the photo on his website looked respectable. A tanned man in his fifties, his face had the lines to prove his age as well as a fondness for the sun. His thick head of hair was a deep gray, complementing his outdoorsy complexion.

Monica wondered how Stela knew him. She navigated to his bio page and was surprised to see that he emigrated from Ukraine, not Romania, as Monica had assumed. He attended college at Ohio State and went to medical school at Cleveland Clinic

Lerner College of Medicine and did a residency in psychiatry there. Well credentialed. Very impressive.

Still, the question remained as to where he and Stela had crossed paths. Or had they? As Monica recalled their conversation, Stela had instructed Monica to tell him that "Eugène Ionesco," the cracked French-Romanian playwright, was asking. *Is Karpenko a genius without a head? If so, I'd like to see him testify.*

Whatever the circumstances, Monica had the unpopular task of calling him to see if he would be willing to testify that it would be "normal" for someone who had just stabbed her boyfriend 13 times not to tell her physician or the police that her boyfriend had been trying to rape her.

She dialed the number.

After three rings, a male voice said, "Delaney Karpenko."

"This is Attorney Monica Spade in Apple Grove, Wisconsin. I was asked to call you by Stela Reiter."

There was a pause during which Monica thought he was going to hang up on her, but he asked suspiciously, "Who?"

His answer indicated he either didn't know Stela or knew her by an alias. That answered Monica's first question. "If the name Stela Reiter doesn't mean anything to you, I'm supposed to say Eugène Ionesco is calling."

A sharp intake of breath was followed by a dead-serious tone. "How can I be of service?"

Monica could almost feel him sit up straighter. "Yes. Well, I'm serving as standby counsel for Stela Reiter. You can google her while we talk. One 'L' in Stela, and Reiter is spelled 'R.E.I.T.E.R.'" Monica waited a second.

"Got it," he said, followed by an expletive in a different language.

"Long story short—Ms. Reiter stabbed a young man 13 times, so she's on trial for intentional homicide. Her defense is that he was trying to sexually assault her. She asked me to retain you to testify about the PTSD symptoms she suffered afterward."

"What symptoms, specifically?"

"That she couldn't remember the sequence of events, and couldn't even talk about them, for the first few days. She wouldn't say anything to her doctor or cooperate with the police detectives who questioned her. She says it was from the PTSD. She was on radio silence until the police found his body and placed her under arrest."

"Oh," he said, drawing out the vowel as his mind wrapped itself around Stela's situation. "I could do that. I'd need to interview her, of course. Where are you located? What's the timeline?"

"We're in Apple Grove, Wisconsin, about a two-hour plane ride for you. The timeline is compressed. Stela wants me to request a speedy trial, so whenever the judge can set a date, we'll go to trial. It could be soon."

She heard him curse again, but he said in a business-like tone, "Of course. Email me your contact information and where I can interview Ms. Reiter." He rattled off his email address.

"You can interview her at the jail, where she's currently residing."

"Right." He was a silent a moment, then added, "Send me everything the prosecution has provided to you."

"The prosecution hasn't provided us with anything yet. As soon as they do, I'll forward the materials to you, with Stela's permission, of course."

"Of course."

"I'll let Stela know you're on board."

"Do that right away for her peace of mind."

"I will," Monica said.

When they ended their call, Monica stared at the phone in amazement. Dr. Karpenko, the hired gun, never asked for a retainer or any type of payment. Usually, physicians who were experienced at testifying, which his website advertised, provided their fee structure up front then requested a down payment before they put an ounce of effort into the case. *Sounds like dropping the name Eugène Ionesco is a new form of currency. Bitcoin. Ionesco coin. Hope I don't get paid in that.*

14

Monica began her day by driving to the courthouse for Stela's preliminary hearing. She hadn't heard from Stela by email, and she hadn't seen her since their last jail visit. This would be Monica's first official appearance in court as Stela's standby counsel, and she was a little nervous, although she didn't know why because she didn't have to present anything. Maybe she anticipated how uncomfortable she would feel sitting next to the beguiling butcher.

Fifteen minutes before the hearing, Monica warily entered the courtroom and eyed the familiar surroundings. She had endured Trevor McKnight's felony murder trial in this courtroom, so she had spent some serious time sitting in the uncomfortable pews of the gallery. Her physician clients had been beaten about the head by Trevor's lawyer, who attempted to blame them for the death of a young Saudi student whom Trevor had punched outside a bar. Monica had hoped that would be the last time she was involved in a criminal trial, yet here she was.

The wood-paneled walls were illuminated by the harsh glow of fluorescent lights, reminding her of her dislike for the stale atmosphere. Indicative of 1970's government buildings, the room was boring and average, unlike the grand design and ornate woodwork of courthouses built in the early 1900s. Too old to be considered modern and too new to be considered charming, the courtroom was a sad representation of recession-era architecture.

Nevertheless, here she was, so she'd make the best of it. She passed through the bar and placed her attaché case on the counsel table next to the jury box. She removed her black coat and set it on a chair behind the table. She glanced around nervously, and a smattering of others entered, including Tiffany Rose from WQOD TV. As soon as Tiffany's eyes found Monica's, they intensified in recognition. "Hello, Ms. Spade. Fancy seeing you here."

"Hello," Monica said at a cooler temp than Tiffany's flirtatious tone.

Tiffany removed her coat to reveal a thin, little dress that was so short it made her look like a school girl on her way to a dance. Under the weight of thick makeup, Tiffany batted her fake eyelashes. "The DA told me you're special counsel for the boyfriend killer."

Monica resisted the urge to groan at Tiffany's sensationalistic description of Stela, which Monica was sure would be Tiffany's opening salvo on the news.

"Sort of," Monica said, "I was appointed by the court to be Ms. Reiter's standby counsel."

"Right. Care to go for a drink tonight and explain to me what standby counsel means?" Tiffany subtly swished her hips in a seductive manner that Monica found immature.

"I'd like to, but I promised my girlfriend I'd go to her house for dinner."

"I didn't know you had a girlfriend," Tiffany said. "I guess I shouldn't be surprised, though, being a big shot lawyer with your own firm and all."

"Well, I don't know about that, but my hands are full right now. Thanks for the offer."

The doors swung wide, and Dominique and her entourage entered. Dominique strode down the aisle, followed by Lori, her victim witness coordinator, the victim's family members, and Detectives Matt Breuer and Brock Curfman. Lori seated Andy Nelson's family right behind Dominique's counsel table.

"Good morning, Ms. Spade," Dominique said, extending her hand for a shake. "Welcome to criminal court."

Monica appreciated the courtesy and sincerity of her gesture. Since Dominique and Jim Daniels were still going strong, there was a natural connection between the two women, and they had socialized a fair amount.

"I wish I could say I'm happy to be here," Monica whispered. "Terrified would be more accurate."

"That makes two of us," Dominique said in a low voice. "Everyone expects me to get a conviction against a *pro se* defendant, so anything less will damage my reputation. Since I never know what harebrained ideas *pro se* defendants will come up with during trial, I have to assure that due process is followed."

"Not as easy as it looks on TV, huh?" Monica asked.

"Not even close." Dominique was interrupted by Detective Brock Curfman leaning over and saying something to her. He was one of the detectives who investigated the case, so would testify as to his findings to establish probable cause that a homicide was committed.

Monica moved away, taking her chair at counsel table, removing the blank yellow legal pad and pen from her attaché and setting them neatly before her. Unlike Dominique, Monica had nothing else. No trial binder. No files. No laptop. Just a blank notepad and a pen. She felt a little foolish, but this is what the court had hired her to do.

Signaling the judge's imminent arrival, the court reporter and court secretary came in and settled in their designated boxes. The court reporter sat directly below the judicial bench, so she could hear the judge and see all of the parties clearly. The court secretary sat to the left of the judge's bench, so she could administer the oath to witnesses, put exhibit stickers on evidence, and perform a variety of other tasks to keep the court running smoothly.

A loud creaking and slam of a metal door behind the backdrop to the judge's bench signaled that Judge O'Brien had entered the courtroom. The bailiff hailed, "All rise," so Monica was back on her feet in deference to Judge O'Brien.

"Please be seated," Judge O'Brien said in his pleasant, uncommanding baritone. He was bald but for a neatly trimmed, gray ring of hair that ran from temple to temple like a sweatband. His resting face bore a frown and creased forehead, the result of many years of reading caselaw and presiding over an adversarial forum. His black glasses were square, accentuating his pudgy nose. He glanced at counsel tables and acknowledged the lawyers. "I see we're ready for the defendant to enter. Bailiff, please bring her in."

The bailiff spoke into his lapel microphone, and the side door next to Monica's table opened. In walked Stela in her orange garb with a thick, brown leather belt to which her wrists were chained, but that didn't handicap her from carrying a large, three-ring binder. She quickly glanced around the courtroom, her eyes snagging on the TV camera in the back. She adopted an angelic look for the camera then returned to shuffling to the counsel table next to Monica, who was standing.

Monica could feel the burn of the TV camera on her back.

Before Monica could say anything to Stela, Judge O'Brien said, "Good morning Ms. Reiter. This is a preliminary hearing for the State to show probable cause that a felony was committed. Are you still representing yourself in this matter?"

"Yes, Your Honor," Stela said clearly and loudly enough for the TV camera in the back to pick up. She placed her binder on the table and opened it.

"Very well. Will the State please call the case?"

"Yes, Your Honor," Dominique said. "This is State versus Stela Reiter, case number 2019-CF-000126. The Defendant is charged with First Degree Intentional Homicide. The State appears on behalf of Dominique Bisset and the defendant appears *pro se* with the assistance of court-appointed Standby Counsel Monica Spade."

"Thank you," Judge O'Brien said, "Please be seated." He focused on Monica. "I trust that standby counsel has explained the nature of this hearing to the defendant?"

Monica blushed because she hadn't explained anything to Stela.

Stela spoke for both of them in a clear, feminine voice. "Ms. Spade and I haven't discussed this hearing, but I'm familiar with the process. I hereby waive my right to a preliminary hearing, but I want to go on the record by saying that the prosecution has not provided any exculpatory evidence to me or Attorney Spade."

There was dead silence in the courtroom, as Judge O'Brien and Dominique quickly processed what Stela had just announced.

"Did you just say that you're waiving your right to a preliminary hearing?" Judge O'Brien asked.

"Yes," Stela said. "I admitted in my last interview with Detectives Brock Curfman and Matt Breuer that I stabbed Andy Nelson to death in self-defense. The fact that I killed him isn't an issue. I did. The question for the jury will be whether my being assaulted, almost raped, and terrified that he was going to cut me up—slowly and for his own sexual pleasure— justified my taking his life, no?"

Stela's delivery was so matter-of-fact that Monica almost forgot Stela was talking about herself. Monica could hear crickets chirping but for the sound of journalists' fingers tapping away on their laptops.

"Ahem," Judge O'Brien said, clearing his throat. "Indeed. Does the prosecution have anything to add?"

"The prosecution hereby requests that bail be set at one million dollars. The defendant has admitted to committing a heinous crime so is a danger to the public. She has no ties to the community and holds a Romanian passport, so she's a flight risk."

Judge O'Brien furrowed his brows. "Does the defendant wish to comment?"

"Yes," Stela said. "Setting bail at $250,000 would be sufficient. I surrendered my passport to the Court at my initial appearance, and precedent in this state supports $250,000 for killing someone in self-defense. I would direct the Court's attention to…" She glanced down at her notes in the three-ring binder that lay open before her. "…*State versus Bakowski* at 125 Wisconsin 2d, page 34, a 1994 Wisconsin Supreme Court case."

Citing caselaw like a pro, Stela startled Judge O'Brien into blinking several times before he turned his attention to the computer on his desk. "Yes. Just a minute, let me pull it up. What was the cite again?"

Stela repeated it, and Monica watched both Judge O'Brien and Dominique pull up the case. Silence remained while they glanced through it to check the veracity of Stela's reference.

Dominique spoke first, "If I may, Your Honor?"

"Go ahead," he said while still paging through the case.

"I'm familiar with the case cited by the defendant. It involved a resident of Milwaukee who had lived there for 30 years and owned a convenience store. He was defending himself during a robbery at the convenience store and killed the robber. The defendant in that case owned the convenience store, had ties to the community, no criminal record, presented no threat to the public, and wasn't a flight risk. That's why his bail was set at $250,000. The circumstances were entirely different than Ms. Reiter's case."

Everyone waited while the judge took his time scrolling through the case. Monica was silently betting against Stela on this one. Unless the Clerk of Court accepted Stela's mysterious Eugène Ionesco currency, Monica guessed that Stela would be sitting in jail through trial.

"All right," Judge O'Brien finally said. "The Court has reviewed the case cited by the defendant and considered the arguments by both the prosecution and defense. The court hereby sets bail at one million dollars for the reasons cited by the prosecution."

Monica could feel Stela's body go rigid beside her. There was an eerie quiet about the woman—something more stealthy and sinister than rage. On high alert now, Monica realized that she was clenching her jaw and tensing her body. She made a mental effort to release the tension and find space in her body to relax. She couldn't maintain this level of anxiety throughout the trial, or she'd be a nervous wreck. She had to prepare for an emotional marathon, not a sprint.

"Do the parties have anything else to bring before the Court?" Judge O'Brien asked.

"Yes," Stela said.

"Go on," Judge O'Brien said.

"As I mentioned a minute ago, I haven't received any documents from the prosecutor's office despite requesting them from both standby counsel," Stela tilted her head angrily at Monica, "and DA Bisset. I know there have to be police reports, photos of the scene, lab reports, a pathology report of Andy Nelson, information gathered from a search of my apartment, and information gathered from a search of Andy Nelson's house. Yet they provide me nothing. Nothing," she said, her pitch rising with passion. She leaned forward, peering around Monica to stare at Dominique.

Monica's face turned red. She was guilty as charged because she hadn't emailed Dominique yet for them. She had told Stela they could ask for them at today's hearing.

Dominique shrugged. "The prosecution isn't withholding information. We're happy to provide information today to Ms. Spade. We can make arrangements after the hearing."

"Does that satisfy the defendant?" Judge O'Brien asked.

"Yes and no," Stela said. "I want the documents sent directly to *me*, not to Ms. Spade." When Dominique didn't oppose Stela's request, she continued, "I have a second request that I need to put on the record, Your Honor."

"What's that?"

"I specifically request the prosecutor to order the police to search Andy Nelson's house for his journal of fantasies about bondage, nonconsensual sex, cannibalism and sexual pleasure by cutting women, including torture."

Monica knew this request was coming because Stela had asked her to do the same, which she hadn't done yet.

There was a collective gasp in the courtroom.

Judge O'Brien's face went a deeper shade of pale. "Please explain the relevance, Ms. Reiter."

"Andy wrote several fantasies in a journal that he required me to read. They're about bondage and torture. I told him I wasn't interested, but he insisted, pestering me, then making me read them." Her face contorted briefly, as she gathered her thoughts and continued, "The point is that his desires and sexual fantasies that he shared with me go to my state of mind when he was over me in the back seat of his car, wielding a knife and cutting on me, as he stripped off my clothes and was about to rape me, then God knows do whatever else to me... Probably mutilation."

Monica was astounded at Stela's unwavering delivery, not a tear visible or hitch of the voice audible. Monica pictured Tiffany at the back of the courtroom, hanging on every word. She could see the headline now: *Boyfriend Killer Mentions Kinky Sex.*

15

Monica glanced to her right at Dominique, who was so practiced in the art of maintaining an inscrutable expression that a bomb could have gone off under her table, and she wouldn't have flinched. Despite her poker face, though, Monica detected a subtle twitch of Dominique's left eye, accentuated by a delicate, dark freckle resting high on her cheekbone.

Judge O'Brien looked at Dominique. "I assume the police searched Andy Nelson's house?"

"Yes, Your Honor."

"Was a journal, as described by Ms. Reiter, recovered?"

"I don't think so, Your Honor," Dominique said. "I'll have to speak to the detectives. If it was recovered, we'll provide a complete copy to the defendant. If it wasn't recovered, the detectives will go back and look for it."

Monica glanced at Brock and Matt sitting behind Dominique. Matt removed a pen and notebook from his shirt pocket and scribbled. Monica guessed that they hadn't yet recovered the sex notebook.

"Very well," Judge O'Brien said. "I hereby order the police to recover said notebook, and for the prosecution to copy and share its contents with the defendant."

"Will do," Dominique said.

"Anything else?" Judge O'Brien asked, directing his attention to Stela.

"Yes," Stela said.

"What is it?" Judge O'Brien sounded exhausted, and the trial hadn't even begun yet.

"I hereby request a speedy trial," Stela said.

"We usually address that at the arraignment, but as long as you raised it, we can discuss it now," Judge O'Brien said. "You're Constitutionally entitled to one. How soon did you have in mind?"

"Next week," Stela said with a straight face.

Monica flinched at the sound of a crash. She turned to her right to see Dominique righting her water bottle on her counsel table.

Judge O'Brien's startled gaze landed on Dominique as well.

"Sorry." She quickly smoothed her hands over her blazer. "The prosecution can't be ready for trial in a week, Your Honor. I'll need at least 30 days."

He nodded. "One week is a little fast for the court docket as well. The defendant's request will be taken into consideration."

"With all due respect, Your Honor—" Stela said.

Uh-oh, here we go, Monica thought.

"I'm the one who's sitting in jail with a million-dollar bail that we all know I won't be able to post," Stela said, her voice dipping to a contralto, her Romanian accent awakening. "I came to your country to study, and not only am I beaten, cut, and almost raped by my American boyfriend, but now I'm on trial for defending myself. I've always read about superior American justice with its due process for people like me, but I guess that's only a myth, no?"

Judge O'Brien looked at Dominique for a response.

"I can't imagine starting this trial next week or even the week following," Dominique said. "We will have several *motions in limine* that we have to prepare. We have several witnesses that we need to subpoena, giving them fair notice, and we haven't even concluded our investigation, per the request by the defendant to search the home of the victim to look for his notebook of sexual essays, or whatever." Dominique threw her hands in the air, exasperated by her own to-do list.

Judge O'Brien held up his hands for the arguments to stop. "I understand. As I said, I'll take the request for a speedy trial under advisement. In the meantime, I think we should set a hearing for next week to review the status of the investigation, what's been shared with the defendant, and both parties' preparations for trial."

"You have to be kidding—" Dominique mumbled but stopped when Judge O'Brien glanced sharply at her. She clamped her mouth shut and compressed her lips into a tight grimace.

"Anything else?" Judge O'Brien asked in an uninviting tone, swiveling his gaze between Dominique and Stela.

"Not from me," Stela said, her voice returning to feminine sweet instead of fervent prisoner.

"Nothing from the State," Dominique said.

"We stand adjourned," Judge O'Brien said then slammed his gavel on the sound block resting on his massive desk. He remained seated, however, looking at his computer screen and ignoring the parties. The court secretary used the opportunity to ask him a few questions, so they conversed comfortably and quietly, as if in the privacy of his chambers behind the courtroom.

As long as Judge O'Brien was still in the courtroom, conversation among everyone else was slow to return to the pre-hearing level. People spoke in hushed tones, as the bailiffs rose from their chairs to return Stela to jail.

She held up her shackled hands, patting the air as they approached counsel table. "Could I talk to my lawyer for two seconds, please?"

Monica's stomach lurched, as she turned to face Stela. "Yes?"

Stela removed a paper from her trial binder. "Here's the list of clothes I'd like you to buy. There's a gentleman in the back of the courtroom. Don't look now."

Monica was about to turn but caught herself. "All right."

"He has black hair, glasses, and is wearing a gray parka. He'll meet with you outside and give you cash for the clothes."

Monica was speechless. She folded the list and stuffed it in her blazer pocket. "Got it. Anything else?"

"Yes." Stela tore off two more sheets of paper, both covered top to bottom in her cursive writing. "Here's the statement you can give to the media today."

"Come again?"

Stela angled her head and indicated toward the back of the courtroom. "To the TV reporter."

"You want me to give an interview?" Monica asked.

"No, silly. I want you to read this statement and only this statement. You are to indicate that you're reading my statement, not your own. Don't go off script, and for sure, don't give an interview after you read my statement. Remember, the only thing that makes you newsworthy is me, so don't try to leverage this trial into advertising for yourself."

Monica was insulted by the rebuke. "Let me be clear, Ms. Reiter, I'm not advertising for more criminal clients. I don't practice criminal law, and I don't want to start. I'm here because the court appointed me to be here. I have a thriving legal practice that doesn't include representing killers. This assignment is crushing my productivity at work and providing me no benefit, monetary or otherwise. "

"Your disdain for my case is obvious. You ignored my request to get the DA's file two days ago."

Monica shrugged indifferently. "I planned to ask in person today."

"Fine." Stela picked up the papers with her shackled hands and thrust them at Monica. "Read my statement to yourself, so we know you can read my writing."

Monica lowered her eyes to the old-fashioned cursive handwriting that was probably the product of some Romanian nun standing over her with a ruler. After Monica read the statement, which she couldn't believe she was about to read on TV, she asked, "You're sure you want me to read this? I see two problems. First, the judge won't like it because it will make it harder to find jurors who aren't prejudiced by TV coverage. Second, the prosecution will have a preview of your testimony, so she'll be better prepared."

"I can see you're thinking strategically. That's good. Go read the statement." Stela tipped up her chin toward Tiffany Rose, who seemed to sense they were talking about her.

"Okay," Monica said. "Just making sure. Tiffany will want to talk to me anyway, so now I'll have something for her."

"Thank you." Stela turned and closed her binder.

"Time's up. Let's go," the large male bailiff said.

Stela stood and picked up her binder, her chained wrists clanking loudly. "One second," she said to the bailiff. She leaned around Monica and said in a loud voice to Dominique. "Excuse me, District Attorney Bisset?"

Dominique turned. "Yes?"

"Attorney Spade will give you my email address. I expect you to share your entire file with me by the end of today."

Dominique's cool, calm exterior never wavered. "I'll see what I can do."

If Stela thought she was going to get a rise out of Dominique, she was wrong.

Dominique looked at Monica, then added, "We'll email what we have to Attorney Spade. She can forward it to you."

The bailiff reached for Stela's arm.

"I want it sent to my email address," Stela said, as she reluctantly turned with the bailiff.

"Not going to happen," Dominique said to Stela's back. "I can't communicate directly with you. I'll send it to Ms. Spade."

Stela slumped as she shuffled, then said in her sweet voice for anyone who was listening. "Very well. Have a nice day." The bailiffs closed the metal door behind her.

Monica turned and glanced around the room, her eyes roaming the pews. She saw the fellow with the black hair, glasses, and gray parka. She nodded and made eye contact, but didn't make a move toward him. She grabbed her attaché case and proceeded toward Tiffany, who was now looking at Monica, waiting in anticipation like a toy poodle expecting a treat.

"Hey, Tiffany. Do you have a minute?"

"For you? Anytime," Tiffany said.

"Stela Reiter gave me a handwritten statement that she wants me to read for you on TV."

"Fabulous." Tiffany beamed. "Let's do it right here with the courtroom in the background."

Monica stepped aside, so people could walk around her. Tiffany cozied up to Monica, her large microphone in hand. She shoved it under Monica's chin and exchanged some words with her cameraman. "You're on."

Tiffany's posture straightened, and she announced in her on-screen, bright tone, "The preliminary hearing for the Boyfriend Killer, Stela Reiter, just finished, and Ms. Reiter's special counsel, Attorney Monica Spade, has a statement to read on behalf of the Boyfriend Killer." Tiffany looked at Monica. "Go ahead."

"Before I read the statement, I'd just like to clarify that I'm not Ms. Reiter's lawyer. I was appointed by the court to act as standby counsel, which means I'm available to Ms. Reiter, who is representing herself, to answer questions about the judicial process."

"Yet, you're sitting next to her counsel table, are you not?" Tiffany asked.

"Yes," Monica said. "That's part of my role."

"Do you chat with her often?"

"I'm not at liberty to discuss our interactions."

"Very well," Tiffany said with a pout. "Please read the Boyfriend Killer's statement."

Monica raised the piece of paper a little higher, so she could read it while facing the camera. "My name is Stela Reiter, and I'm from Romania. While studying chemistry in America, I started dating a young man named Andy Nelson. Everything was fine at first, but then he became increasingly violent during sex, telling me that he wanted to engage in BDSM activities. He wrote out his fantasies about nonconsensual, violent sex, including cutting up his sexual partner for his own pleasure. He made me read his journal and asked me if I wanted to participate. I told him I wasn't interested. He didn't bring it up again for a long time, so I thought he had dropped the idea. Then, one day he drove me out to the country, and we parked in a farmer's field. After we went for a walk, he suggested we kiss in the back seat of his car. He blindfolded me, and, when he got on top of me, he began taking off my clothes and cutting me. He put his hand on my neck, under my chin, and choked me while he cut me. Fortunately, I was able to break free and grab his knife. I had to stab him to save my own life. I didn't mean to kill him, but I was terrified that he was going to kill me. I could see it in his eyes. I hope you understand. I will defend myself in court, having heard many wonderful things about the fairness of the American judicial system."

Monica looked up at Tiffany. "That's it."

"She gave us an appetizer this statement on the record today, wouldn't you agree?" Tiffany said.

"I'm not going to comment," Monica said. "That's all I have for now. Thank you."

Tiffany did her wrap up, and the camera turned off. As soon as she lowered the microphone, she turned to Monica. "Thanks for giving me the scoop. If anything else comes up, will you call me?"

"I'll see you here, I'm sure."

"Something might come up outside of court. You never know. You have my cell number, right?"

"No. I'll just call the station…" Monica let the sentence fade in hopes of curbing Tiffany's enthusiasm.

"I might not be there. Let me get you a card." Tiffany quickly moved to her pastel-colored designer purse on the pew and retrieved a business card for Monica. "My cell phone is listed on it."

"Thanks." Monica stuffed it in her blazer pocket. "I have to run."

Tiffany touched Monica's arm. "Talk to you later, I hope."

"Yeah." Monica turned and rushed through the doors into the hallway. She spied the man in the gray parka standing at the opposite end of the hallway from the main entrance.

He watched her walk to him.

"Are you Stela's friend?" she asked.

He nodded but didn't shake her hand or introduce himself. "Yes. Did Stela give you the list of clothes?"

"Yes," Monica said, looking past his glasses into steely gray eyes that matched his parka. "She said you were going to give me some money?"

He removed a white envelope from the inside pocket of his parka and handed it to her. She quickly dropped it into her attaché.

"There's two thousand dollars in there," he said in an accent. "That should be enough to cover everything, no?"

"Yes." Monica noticed that he, like Stela, added "no" to the end of his questions. "Is there anything else?"

"Not right now."

"Will you be here throughout the trial?"

"Probably not."

"How do you know Stela?"

"Too many questions, Ms. Spade. Remember, you and I don't enjoy the attorney-client privilege." His voice held an edge, his stare hostility.

"That's correct. Nice meeting you."

He turned and left through the back door of the courthouse without saying goodbye.

Monica had a strong premonition that he wasn't in America to study at the university either. The university stint was just cover.

She retraced her steps to the front door of the courthouse, ignoring curious glances from people milling about. Lost in thought, she tromped through the snow toward her white truck.

16

As Monica drove by Half Moon Lake on her return to the office, she saw at least 20 more ice fishing shacks than last week's record number of 100. The village was multiplying during the tourney, drawing anglers from near and far for the grand prize of a new pickup truck. She wondered if all the augered holes damaged the integrity of the ice, as she envisioned the entire village submerging, the shacks slowly sinking to the bottom of the lake. *How many holes and shacks are too many?*

When she entered the sun-filled, peaceful reception area of her law firm, a space that Kathy and Janet had decorated, Monica immediately felt at home, casting aside the emotional body armor she had worn in the courtroom.

Kathy looked up from her monitor. "Hey Boss, how did the prelim for the Boyfriend Bobber go?"

Monica rolled her eyes. "It was a circus, and I learned that Stela is quite comfortable playing the role of ringmaster."

"Oh really?"

"No joke. She obviously has court experience, despite her cover story of a chemistry student at the university. She even had a trial binder prepared with arguments and case citations. If this woman wasn't a lawyer back in Romania, or wherever the fuck, then I'm not a lesbian."

Kathy raised her eyebrows. "Well, isn't that quite the development?" One side of her mouth angled up. "Her being a lawyer, that is. Not you being a lesbian."

"More importantly," Monica said, not accepting the invite for that bird walk, "I met with a mysterious associate of Stela's after the hearing. He gave me $2,000 cash for her trial wardrobe." Monica fished the envelope out of her attaché and Stela's list of clothes from her blazer pocket. "Here."

"Let's take a look." Kathy picked up the list and glanced through it. "I think Kohl's would be the best place to buy all of these pieces. The ensemble is pretty much an office wardrobe, with the exception of a pink cardigan and some pastel-colored blouses. She specifically requests chiffon blouses with pussy bows. Can you believe she wrote 'pussy bows?'"

Monica squinted. "Are you putting me on?"

Kathy showed the list to Monica. "Didn't you read it?"

"No. I just assumed it would be ordinary stuff. I don't even know what a pussy bow is."

"It's short for 'pussycat bow.' You've seen them a hundred times. Just two pieces of thin fabric coming off the neckline that you can tie into a loose bow." Kathy demonstrated with her thick hands.

"Good to know. I've never owned a shirt with a bow on it."

Kathy waved over Monica's front. "A pussy bow would look ridiculous on you. You're the quintessential tailored look."

Monica circled back. "Can you buy those clothes for Stela?"

"Sure," Kathy said. "When?"

"Things are moving really fast. In the next few days, if you have time."

"I'll make the time," she said. "I sort of like the idea of working on this case."

"I appreciate it. Maybe I'll have a few more assignments." As Monica took a few steps in the direction of her office, her stomach growled.

Kathy laughed. "I heard that. There's food in the kitchen."

"That was a loud growl, wasn't it?" Monica disappeared down the hall and into her office. She booted up her computer and caught up on emails. She was at least 40 emails deep when she received one from Dominique Bisset attaching a large file.

Dominique wrote, "Dear Attorney Spade, Attached is the file of documents intended for Defendant Stela Reiter. Please forward it to her."

Monica didn't waste any time forwarding the email to Stela at her jail account, lest she be accused of withholding critical information. Next, she opened the file herself and began reading. Dominique was right. There were hundreds of documents in the file. Monica realized she had to organize them, or it would turn into a paper blizzard.

She spent the next few hours categorizing the documents and creating electronic folders, so she could access them on her laptop in court. She noticed Dominique had a laptop on her counsel table so could easily navigate to documents, some of which were bound to become trial exhibits. Monica also jotted down notes about facts in the police reports, the lab findings, and the forensic pathology on Andy Nelson, which did not mention a severed penis, but did include a stab to his scrotum.

She paused over a cache of several photos of the scene that were as gruesome as anything Monica had ever seen. Blood stains were smudged helter-skelter throughout the back seat of the car—the backs of the front seats, the console, the floor, the ceiling, and the doors. A large pool of blood on the seat had soaked through and turned a deep shade of macabre maroon.

Several photos of the ground outside of the white, four-door sedan were filled with tiny evidence stickers indicating small blobs of blood amongst clumps of dirt and leaves on the snowy terrain. Even taking into consideration the possibility of ground saturation, the amount outside the car was miniscule compared to that within.

She carefully studied two photos. One of the murder weapon—a Trident kitchen paring knife. The other, Andy's cell phone—the screen smashed. Both had dried blood smeared all over them, and the State Forensic Lab Report indicated that the blood matched Andy's DNA. The police found the two items in a ditch about halfway between the car and the farmer's house where Stela had run for help. She admitted to carrying them with her and "dropping" them along the way. She didn't admit to smashing the phone, however.

That doesn't look good for her, Monica thought. *If she were innocent, why would she smash the phone and dump the phone and knife in the ditch? Wouldn't she have left them at the scene?*

The police also had visited Andy's work—*Voila!*—which had been making small appliances like waffle irons, deep fryers, rice cookers, egg cookers, and pressure cookers for over 100 years in Apple Grove. A staple of the local economy, *Voila!* employed about 1,000 Apple Grove residents.

Monica learned from the reports, however, that Andy didn't work in the kitchen appliance section. He worked in the weapons division. Weapons division of a small appliance manufacturer? She was stunned. Apparently, a segment of the company supplied nuclear warheads and guidance systems to the U.S. military. *Voila!* was a defense contractor. Monica had no idea, and she had lived in Apple Grove for three years now. She'd heard of companies diversifying, but from waffle makers to weapons systems sounded like a big leap.

She googled *Voila!* and was shocked to see how much information was available to the public about its weapons division. *Voila!* originally made ammunition for the military during World War II. Having banked a fortune from that, it must have invested in R&D because the sophistication of its offerings grew with technology. As she studied the public financial brochure, she learned that the weapons division drove the bottom line, and the small appliances were just a side show.

Connecting the dots in subsecond time, Monica inhaled deeply to slow her pulse, as she realized the gravity of Andy's relationship with Stela, and what could have been Stela's real motives. She stared mindlessly at the computer while her mind catalogued the possibilities.

She recalled the pre-murder photos she had seen of Andy, and while a nice-looking Wisconsin lad, he wasn't exactly Brad Pitt. In fact, Stela ranked an easy seven with makeup—if she lost her glasses—and Andy was, at best, a four with money.

Monica deduced there was no way Stela would have dated Andy if he weren't rich, a rock star, or, as was the case, worked on top secret weapons that she wanted. The only question was: "Who hired Stela to seduce Andy Nelson?"

Clearly, the police were thinking the same thing, because their most recent reports were full of interviews with Andy's co-workers and bosses, asking if any products or materials had gone missing, if they had any internal concerns about Andy, if he had been behaving differently at work, and the like. His co-workers reported that he seemed happier than he had been in a long time, and they attributed his happiness to his relationship with Stela, whom they had met at their company Oktoberfest party.

They described Andy as responsible, considerate, and trustworthy. He had been working for *Voila!* for six years, his first job since he had graduated from the University of Wisconsin with an engineering degree. Everyone liked him.

Monica stopped reading, rested her elbows on her desk and dropped her head into her hands. *You have to be kidding me! Just get a search warrant for his bank accounts or search his house for a stash of money.* She massaged her scalp through her long, black hair, wondering how she could sit next to Stela, knowing that Stela killed Andy, but also suspecting that Stela had used Andy to pirate top-secret information about nuclear weapons and guidance systems. She didn't know whether she was petrified or outraged, or both, but she was overdue for nourishment, so she shoved away from her desk and went in search of food and water.

When she entered the kitchen, the first smell to greet her was a veggie tray on the conference table. The onion and dill dip in the center had developed a filmy residue on top, and the carrot and celery sticks looked dry. After studying the gory photos, the ripe smell, reminiscent of body odor, made her stomach gurgle.

She went to the fridge and removed a can of Ginger Ale, seeking to calm the growing disaster known as her digestive system. She took a long swig, allowing the cold carbonation to act as an elixir. She leaned against the counter and stared at the face of the battery-operated clock on the wall. As she watched the second hand sweep efficiently around the face, she could hear the barely-audible ticktocks.

She nursed her soda and contemplated the grisly crime scene—including the photo of Andy hanging out of the car with his neck skin filleted open—when a burp bubbled up and out of her. She watched the red second hand. Blood red. Andy's face replaced the face of the clock, his right temple gored. The red second hand swept around his face. Ticktock, ticktock...

Suddenly, an unmistakable snake of bile lurched up her esophagus. She set down her soda and ran to the bathroom off the kitchen, barely arriving in time to vomit into the toilet. She hadn't even closed the door, so she retched in full view of the kitchen and within earshot of her coworkers. Her eyes threatened to bug out of her head, as her stomach rebelled against the onslaught of gory images. Her throat screamed in agony from the insult, which left her coughing and gagging.

Finally, she was able to flush the toilet and grab some toilet paper to wipe her face, as the sweat beaded on her forehead. She tossed the fistful of used toilet paper into the toilet and flushed again. With effort, she straightened, only to see Janet hovering outside the bathroom door.

Monica would have been mortified but for the look of compassion and empathy on Janet's middle-aged face. "Need help?"

"No, thanks," Monica said into her hands. "I'm sorry I didn't have time to close the door. I feel like an idiot. Just give me a minute to wash up, and I'll be out."

"I'll be here," Janet said.

Monica used Clorox wipes to clean off the toilet then ran soap and water over her hands, arms and face. She opened the cupboard to her personal stash of hygiene and used her toothbrush and toothpaste.

Satisfied that she was presentable, she exited to Janet's patient face and Jim crunching a celery stick. The sight and smell of the dip just about made her return to the bathroom, but she swallowed hard and proceeded to the cupboard for a glass, which she filled with ice water. She sipped at the cool liquid, willing herself to calm down.

"Got the flu bug?" Jim asked, piercing the yellow veneer over the dip with a carrot.

"Is there anything we can do?" Janet added.

Monica felt her cheeks redden. "No. I'm sorry I didn't have time to close the door. The nausea snuck up on me. I guess I was grossed out—traumatized, actually—from looking at the police photos of Andy Nelson's murder."

"I should have warned you." Jim said, crunching. "Murder scenes can do a number on you."

"Thanks," Monica rasped. She sipped more water. "That, and sitting next to, then talking to, Stela Reiter in court today. All of this is disgusting and disturbing and devastating and depressing..." She ran out of words.

"And, dangerous," Janet added.

"Yes!" Monica said, pointing her finger at Janet.

"All the 'd' words," Jim added with a twinkle in his eye.

At least he made Monica smile.

"Want to tell me about it?" he asked.

She took the next 20 minutes to download what had transpired and what she had figured out on her own from the police file.

He whistled through a mouthful of carrots, spraying some on his beard. "I don't doubt it for a minute. People have underestimated what goes on at *Voila!* manufacturing. That company has become a cornerstone of weapons technology for the Defense

Department, and hardly anyone in Apple Grove even knows about it."

"I remember my mother working there in the 1970s," Janet said. "She was making ammo for guns and grenades."

"Really?" Monica asked. "I had no idea that division even existed."

"I'm not surprised," Jim said. "Mostly just us old-timers know about the history of *Voila!*. So, you think Stela Reiter was either spying on Andy Nelson or buying info from him?"

"Time will tell," Monica said. "Tiffany Rose has cast Stela as 'the Boyfriend Killer,' but I'm willing to bet Andy confronted Stela about her real motives."

"It sounds like the police suspect the same thing." Jim paused for a minute. "Can you still fulfill your duty as standby counsel given your reaction today?"

Monica drained her glass of water and inhaled deeply. "I wouldn't miss this for the world."

Jim smiled. "That's my girl."

Janet applauded. "I'll order some Pepto Bismol for you."

17

Since Monica couldn't stomach the thought of eating anything at work the remainder of that afternoon, she was ravenous when she walked into her dark house after five. At least, most of it was dark. Her bedroom light was on, which wasn't routine, but she assumed she had forgotten to turn it off in her rush to get to court that morning.

She decided to take a quick shower to wash away the events of the day, more specifically, the images of the murder scene.

While under the hot spray, Monica reflected on Stela's case and concluded that deciphering Stela's motive had made her vomit rather than merely looking at the photos. Fear thrummed through her. Not the theoretical fear that something somewhere might happen to someone, but real, tangible fear. Her instincts told her she had entered a world and touched people who could harm her if she crossed them.

While she was rinsing the shampoo from her hair, she thought she heard her kitchen door close, so she expected Shelby to bound into the bathroom any second. While Monica waited, she quickly lathered her entire body, then rinsed away the suds, a cold shiver snaking up her spine despite the hot spray.

She was slightly disappointed that Shelby didn't duck into the bathroom, but Monica lingered under the spray for a few more moments, breathing in the steam, encouraging it to permeate her lungs since it was so brutally dry outside. Humidity was at an all-time low in the dead of winter, and her body craved the moisture. She longed for a tropical beach somewhere, frolicking in the surf with a bikini-clad Shelby. Ah, the romantic thought of it.

She reluctantly ended the hot shower and toweled off, then opened the bathroom door to a dark hallway. "Shelby, is that you?"

Silence filled the space.

"Shelby?"

Dead silence.

Monica wrapped the towel around herself and tentatively tip-toed to the kitchen. She felt anxious, as if she had consumed too much coffee. Something had shifted inside of her, and she didn't like it.

Fortunately, a bag full of groceries sat on the dining table, then Monica caught sight of Shelby closing her car door and bringing in another bag.

Monica quickly scooted over to the door and opened it. "Hey."

Once inside, Shelby let her eyes travel up and down Monica's towel-clad body. "Hello, beautiful. Exciting to come home to a wet, naked woman."

Monica blushed. "I just took a quick shower. I thought I heard you come in, but I wasn't sure. How long have you been here?"

"Just got here right now. Brrrr. It's cold out tonight. Ten below zero, according to the thermometer on my car." Shelby placed another bag of groceries on the table, dropped her backpack, then turned and kicked off her boots. Rubbing her hands together briskly, Shelby advanced on Monica.

"So, you didn't get here like, ten minutes ago?" Monica asked, covering Shelby's hands with her own to warm them. Shelby's strong fingers were icicles.

"More like two minutes ago. Why?" Shelby asked.

"I thought I heard the kitchen door while I was in the shower. Must have been my imagination," Monica buried her face in Shelby's soft, chestnut curls. "Mm. Missed you today."

"I missed you too," Shelby said, easing back, so she could find Monica's mouth.

As Monica fell into Shelby's warm kiss, she cast aside all stress from the day and floated through the universe, suddenly warm and cozy.

After kissing each other into oblivion, Shelby said against Monica's lips, "How about some steamy sex on the dining room table?"

"As enticing as that sounds, I'm not really into exhibition for my neighbors."

"I bet they'd love it, but if you insist, we'll take our sex life to the bedroom." Shelby pressed seductive kisses on Monica's eyelids, then moved to her cheekbones, then dropped down to her chin, and finally trailed her tongue along Monica's neck.

A fuse crackled from Monica's jugular to her core, exploding in lust. She longed to feel Shelby's skin next to her own, see the passion in Shelby's eyes, and feel her body shudder in climax.

"To my bedroom." Monica turned and led the way, but didn't make it more than a few steps before Shelby nicked Monica's towel, throwing her into nudity. Monica resisted the urge to turn around and demand her towel, instead picking up the pace and fleeing toward her room.

Shelby gave chase, managing to slap Monica's ass once before she dove under the comforter on her magnificent bed. "You'll pay for that!"

"I can't wait!" Shelby quickly shed her clothes and joined Monica under the covers, scooting over, so they were skin-on-skin. She leaned down, her long tendrils creating a curtain around their faces, her hot breath over Monica's mouth. "I love you."

Before Monica could reply, Shelby's mouth claimed hers. Punch drunk with desire, Monica liked the newly assertive Shelby. Talking dirty. Chasing her. Taking command. Monica felt adored. Desired. Wanted. She skated her hands over Shelby's perky ass then rested them below the crescent moons where her fingers could tickle Shelby's inner thighs.

Shelby cooed with delight, not breaking their kiss, as she pushed up to rest on her right elbow, giving Monica full access to her fit body.

Monica's fingers worked in a slow tease from Shelby's inner thighs to her bottom, until she brought one hand around to Shelby's front and slid her fingers through the thin patch of hair to Shelby's oh-so-wet folds, circling and playing.

Shelby squirmed, her hips moving against Monica's busy fingers. On a groan, she left Monica's mouth and tracked punishing kisses down Monica's neck until she landed on one breast, circling Monica's nipple, then moved to the other.

Monica curled into Shelby, so her fingers could explore deeper while Shelby ravished her breasts. She coiled with desire—Shelby pulling whimpers from her —then slid two fingers into Shelby's tight wet heat.

Shelby thrust her hips into Monica's strong hand, writhing faster now, as Monica's thumb found her clit, circling, teasing, and gliding over it, building a rhythm. Shelby arched her back with wanton desire, her mouth leaving Monica's breasts. Her gaze dropped to Monica's, pure hunger lighting up her eyes. Need. Possession. Pleading.

The ferocity of Shelby's stare while Monica played with her clit and sunk her fingers into her center drove Monica wild. Her instinct to please, then claim, Shelby overcame her. She wanted all of Shelby, her body, her soul, her heart. She pulled out and slapped Shelby's ass, eliciting a yelp.

Shocked, Shelby rasped, "Do it again!"

Monica spanked Shelby's cheek on the only fleshy spot, the sweet sting signaling sexual promise.

"Flip around," Monica said, "I want to bury my face in you."

Shelby's eyes dove a shade darker, her lips pulling up in a devious smile. Limber as a cat, she rubbed her nipples across Monica, as she slowly moved her legs to plant her knees on either side of Monica's head, licking a trail from breasts to her pussy.

"You're so beautiful," Monica said into Shelby's pussy before she attacked it, arching her own hips into Shelby's probing tongue.

The air in the room sizzled with moans and smacks until both women tensed simultaneously then exploded in release, their bodies heaving and shaking against each other. Sex-scented sweat fused their skin, as they wrapped their arms around each other, rolling from side to side, surfing the waves of passion until their bodies went limp with satisfaction.

***

An hour later, Monica jolted awake to a snoring Shelby, her face resting on Monica's chest. Monica wished she could have stayed in that position all night, but her tummy screamed in protest that it needed food—NOW! She kissed the top of Shelby's head and gently eased her from her shoulder onto the pillow.

Shelby moaned, her eyes fluttering open. "Hey, beautiful." Her voice was groggy from satisfying sex and a nap.

"I'm sorry to wake you," Monica said, "but I'm starving. I didn't get lunch today." Punctuating her statement, Monica's stomach growled loudly.

Shelby giggled. "You better feed that machine for round two tonight."

"I'd love that. Feel free to stay in bed. I'm going to make something for dinner." Monica slipped out of bed and searched her room for comfy clothes.

"I brought the makings for burgers and grilled asparagus," Shelby said.

Monica moaned. "You're not going to make me grill in this weather, are you? With the current windchill, it would be torture to step outside on the deck, even for a minute."

Shelby sighed. "I suppose not. I can fry the burgers in an iron skillet if you want." She threw back the covers and picked up her bra from the floor. "Do you have anything warm for me to wear?'

Monica dug in her dresser drawer and tossed a tank, a sweatshirt and yoga pants over her shoulder at Shelby.

Later, as they prepared their meal, Monica opened a couple of Snow Drift Vanilla Porters and poured the dark liquid into beer glasses. Not only was the ale's name appropriate for the weather, but its creamy dark consistency was practically a meal in itself. She turned on the local news to Keith Hoyt on WQOD in mid-report. When he mentioned the murder trial of the Boyfriend Killer, Monica turned up the volume, as the coverage switched to Tiffany's recorded interview of Monica inside the courtroom.

Shelby stopped forming hamburger patties, washed her hands, and went to her backpack. She retrieved a new pair of glasses, a thread of lavender running through the aqua-colored bows, and watched in fascination.

When Monica finished reading Stela's statement on TV, Shelby said, "You've got to be kidding me! You read her statement on TV?"

"Well, I'm deathly afraid of her, so I agreed to."

"That had to be a creepy day. How do you do it?"

Monica took a long drink of her dark beer. "I have a legal role to play, so I just focus on my responsibility to the court." She ate some chips and watched the news coverage switch back to Keith at the anchor desk.

Keith continued, "The police reported that they searched the victim, Andy Nelson's, house again today, discovering two lead-lined carrying cases in his garage. Apparently, these cases are used to transport radioactive materials like enriched uranium and plutonium, which are used for making nuclear devices. Given Nelson's employment in the Defense Division at *Viola!*, the police immediately suspended their search. They returned a few hours later in Hazmat suits with a Geiger counter. They reported that the Geiger registered significant amounts of radiation in Nelson's garage and trace amounts in his house."

"What the actual fuck?" Monica breathed, the hairs on her arms standing on end. "This is what I was afraid of—that Stela was stealing information from Andy. But nuclear materials? That takes it to a whole new level." Monica turned to Shelby. "Stela Reiter didn't come here to study chemistry. She probably already has a chemistry degree." Monica cocked her head back and looked at Shelby. "Wait a minute. Did you get glasses?"

Shelby blushed, ripping them off her face. "Yes, and I don't like them one bit, but I'm going blind, so I had to. The optometrist told me I have to wear them to drive now." She sputtered in disgust and quickly turned her back to Monica.

Monica grabbed Shelby's wrist before she could walk away. "I think you look adorable in glasses. Put them on again."

"Don't be ridiculous." Shelby hunched over in embarrassment.

"Please," Monica pleaded in a gentle voice. "I want to see you in them."

Shelby reluctantly moved them into place, and Monica stared lovingly at her. "The little lavender thread running through the bows matches the streak in your hair." Monica fingered the lavender corkscrew hair to the tip, then released it, so it snapped back into place. "I think you're sexy as hell in glasses. Please never be shy about wearing them around me."

"Oh, stop it." Shelby rolled her eyes.

"I'm serious. They add another dimension to 'sexy Shelby' that wasn't there before. Kind of mysterious and intellectual. Total turn-on."

"Now I know you're lying," Shelby said.

"I am not. Come here." Monica coaxed Shelby by the chin until they were lip-to-lip. "You're beautiful." She kissed Shelby to prove it, taking her time to suck on her lower lip.

Shelby smiled. "I guess I'm a little self-conscious."

"You won't be after you wear them to bed. You. Naked. With only those glasses on? My sexy, naughty, teacher-fantasy come true."

"Now I know you're putting me on." Shelby returned to the kitchen to finish the hamburger patties. "Sexy teacher fantasy. Seriously," she muttered as she formed the burgers.

Monica joined her at the counter, resting her hand on Shelby's perky ass. She pressed her thumb into Shelby's glute and did a little circle, massaging there.

"Mm," Shelby whispered.

"Back to talking about Stela Reiter," Monica said. "I'll bet you a dollar that she works for some underworld figures in Eastern Europe, and is buying and smuggling radioactive materials."

"Where did you say she's from? Romania?" Shelby asked. "I'm not even sure I can picture that on a map."

"Close to Russia and the countries that splintered off from the U.S.S.R. when it fractured in the early 1990s."

Shelby washed her hands and sipped her beer. "I remember studying that in high school. Wasn't there a coup attempt against Gorbachev? The one who tore down the Berlin wall?"

"If memory serves," Monica said, "then that Yeltsin guy came in and made a bunch of democratic reforms. That's when Ukraine and other countries became independent. I think Romania is close to Ukraine."

Shelby plopped the hamburger patties down in a hot iron skillet. "So, I'm not sure we can link a young Romanian woman to the black market for nuclear materials just because she's from that region."

"What other motive would she have to kill Andy, who by all accounts seemed like an ordinary, nice guy?"

"She said he was trying to rape her," Shelby said.

"Possible, but I sense that there's something deeper at play here, and now that they discovered lead-lined carrying cases for radioactive materials at his house, I think he could have been stealing materials from work and selling them to her."

Shelby whistled. "That sounds a little farfetched to me, Mon. Even if she bought plutonium from Andy, how the heck would she get it back to

159

Romania? And, what does Romania have to do with anything? I haven't seen them in the news lately."

"I have no idea how she'd transport it back to Romania. Maybe she wouldn't have to. Maybe she was just the point-person to buy it, then it was her job to transfer it to someone who would smuggle it out of America. I mean, I have no idea how much is needed for a bomb or how to smuggle it."

"But, Romania?"

"Well, it's close to Ukraine, and isn't Ukraine currently at war with Russia? Doesn't Putin want to take back Ukraine?"

"I have no idea," Shelby said, drinking her beer. "Again, it all sounds a little too complicated for a simple murder in Apple Grove."

Monica moved around the kitchen island. "Not when you consider that *Voila!* is a defense contractor. I googled them today and learned that they have three separate companies that make various weapons of destruction. Andy Nelson worked there, so he was a target for an international arms dealer like Stela to seduce him into the world of corporate espionage—"

Shelby's laugh interrupted Monica. "Espionage? That's sounds like a novel, not our Apple Grove. I'm sure *Voila!* keeps its uranium and plutonium under lock and key. I seriously doubt there are barrels of it sitting in a warehouse somewhere for Andy to dip into and bring home to Stela-the-Boyfriend-Killer."

"I wonder exactly how much is needed for a bomb," Monica said, not listening to Shelby's doubts. "I'll google it after dinner." She dedicated herself to cutting buns and adding fixings for their cheeseburgers.

"I don't know about you," Shelby said, "but I'm not in the mood for asparagus. Can we just have burgers and chips?"

Monica kissed the back of Shelby's neck while she flipped the burgers. "A girl after my own heart."

After dinner, they cuddled on the sofa and prepared to catch up on their new favorite series, *The Morning Show,* with Jennifer Aniston, Reese Witherspoon, and Steve Carell. As riveting as the show was, Monica couldn't shake her quest for knowledge about Stela's motive. With on eye on the drama, she googled facts about plutonium and uranium.

Monica learned there was, indeed, a robust black market for both elements, and lead-lined carrying cases were the preferred method of transfer. She considered the implications of Andy's job, and what he could steal from *Voila!* while going unnoticed. Shelby was right, they probably kept their plutonium and uranium under tight security. Monica would just have to watch the facts play out, as the police continued their investigation. As much as she wanted to interview Andy's boss at *Voila!*, that was a job for Detective Matt.

Shelby nudged Monica when the episode ended. "Are we going to the early CrossFit class tomorrow?"

Monica sent out feelers to her sore muscles. "Um. Would you mind terribly if I went to hot yoga instead? My entire body aches, and I feel like I just need to stretch out."

"Yoga?" Shelby asked in an *Are-you-crazy?* voice.

"What's wrong with hot yoga?"

"At The Yoga Studio?" Shelby asked suspiciously.

"Uh-huh. Why?"

"I won't step foot in there," Shelby grumbled.

Monica quickly realized she needed to tread carefully around this apparent land mine. "Which makes sense because you don't like yoga."

Shelby absent-mindedly fingered the cartilage piercing in her ear. "A few years back, I spent quite a bit of time there...um..." Shelby shifted uneasily on the sofa, pulling her knees up to her chin. "Remember when you asked me about the diamond stud in my ear, and I sort of blew up at you?"

Monica's heart lurched. "Like it was yesterday."

Shelby lay her hand on Monica's leg. "I'm sorry, I just couldn't bear to explain at the time that I had a girlfriend who's a yoga instructor there. She still is. I don't want to get into it, but I'm never setting foot in that place again." She shimmied her shoulders with a chill. "Baaaad memories."

In addition to major jealousy instantly coursing through Monica, a thousand questions came to mind. "Girlfriend? When?"

Shelby's face tightened into a moue, which would have been unattractive on a woman less beautiful, but on Shelby, her pouting lips simply accentuated her prominent cheekbones. "I love you, Mon, and I don't want to hurt you. It was a year ago, so can we just leave it at that?"

Monica didn't want to leave anything at that. In fact, leaving it alone was the last thing she wanted. She wanted to know what had gone on, and if she had competition out there, like a yogi who could steal Shelby back. "Um. I'd sort of like to know more... When you're comfortable talking about her, that is."

Shelby was now perched on the edge of the sofa like she was prepared to spring up and run out of Monica's house any second. "I'll let you know. Right now, it's too painful, okay?"

Painful? That isn't a good sign. "Sure. When you're ready." She put her hand on Shelby's shoulder and leaned over to kiss her temple.

"I'm sorry I'm not ready to talk about it yet."

An awkward silence fell, Monica's shallow breaths the only sound. Under her black lashes, Monica studied Shelby. Not detecting any hostility, she wrapped her arms around her and rested her chin on the top of her head.

Shelby moved her hand to Monica's breast, caressing lightly then skating her thumb across the nipple. "In the mood for round two?"

Monica couldn't speak for a second then whispered, "Are you trying to distract me with sex?"

"Absolutely not. I'm trying to win you over with sex."

"In that case, let's go." Monica allowed herself to be conquered, but she knew in her heart that sex wasn't the answer. She had to find out what had gone on…for her own peace of mind.

18

When the alarm sounded at o'dark thirty the next morning, Monica quickly dressed in her tights and a yoga top. In an effort to soften her departure from Shelby's side, Monica muttered something about doing CrossFit only so many days in a row before she needed a break. Shelby rolled over with a sleepy moan.

Despite Shelby's dire experience with her ex-lover at The Yoga Studio, or perhaps because of it, Monica was determined to resume classes there, so she could learn who had ravished, then hurt, her beautiful Shelby. Her search for answers to life's riddles frequently got the better of her, but she couldn't tolerate the idea of Shelby's ex-lover remaining an unsolved mystery. She needed to get to the bottom of Shelby's broken heart—one way or the other. She would sleuth surreptitiously, keeping a low profile. She didn't have a name to go on, but she was confident she could figure out the woman's identity through simple observation and deduction.

The thought of Shelby falling for a yoga instructor struck at the core of Monica's body image issues. All of the yogis had slim bodies and came across cooler and more hip than Monica, wearing their long beaded necklaces and rustling bracelets. She told herself she was a beautiful, smart woman with her own constellation of attributes, but that never seemed to erase her insecurity in the milieu of athletic, beautiful women. Monica's self-esteem reservoir was drained every time she entered the space.

That morning, Monica's yoga instructor had been a woman in her early twenties and so straight that Monica had quickly concluded she couldn't have been Shelby's ex-lover. In any event, Monica got the feeling that Shelby had been the naïve one in the relationship, perhaps falling prematurely, or maybe for the first time, so Monica was on the lookout for a woman slightly older and more sophisticated than Shelby.

***

Now at the office and facing a deluge of work, Monica dragged herself from such unproductive emotional meanderings. She returned to her email inbox, which brimmed with requests from hospital clients for Monica to review everything from their campus-wide no-smoking policy—with a question about exceptions for people who were on hospice and wanted one last cigarette before they died—to a new set of bylaws for the stadium complex, since McKnight Construction had withdrawn from the deal, leaving only the university and the hospital to carry forward the dream of a revered hockey stadium with an attached medical office building.

When there was a knock on her door, she looked up to see Nathan Taylor, trial attorney extraordinaire, standing before her in a new suit, perfectly tailored to his slim build. He looked happier and healthier than she'd seen him since they had started as associates back in the day at SWD. Unbeknownst to her at that time, Nathan had also been in the closet. Once he came out, however, they became close friends, and she came out soon after.

"Good morning," he said. "Is now a good time?"

"Now is perfect." She scooted her chair to the side of her computer screen for an unobstructed view of him.

"I should bring you up to speed on the Darcy Lemon litigation," he said.

"I'm all ears."

"The court set a briefing schedule for my motion to dismiss. Wally's opposing brief is due in five days."

"Nice," Monica said. "That will let her know that we mean business, forcing her to do some work if she's going to sue us. What about the veterinarian exam of Marcus? Did that happen yet?"

Nathan chuckled conspiratorially. "Darcy brought him to our expert vet, who checked him out head-to-toe then tested him with tasks and whatnot. The vet's conclusion is that Marcus is intelligent, happy and well-adjusted. Darcy, on the other hand, not so much, but the monkey is fine."

"Oh really? What did Darcy do during the interview?"

"He said she talked nonstop, getting herself worked up over Marcus' stay at the hospital, becoming practically hysterical. Then she started pumping him for information about animal rights, going off on a tangent about the ospreys who nest on top of the outdoor stadium lights at Carson Park baseball stadium."

"What do humans have to do with the osprey nests?" Monica asked in exasperation. "The ospreys chose to make their nests close to Half Moon Lake for fishing, and they have an awesome view of the baseball field. What more could you want? Fresh fish and America's favorite pastime."

"She thinks the stadium lights shouldn't be turned on for night games because they heat up the nests and could cook the eggs or osprey chicks."

Monica covered her face with her hands and moaned. "Is that true? How hot do those lights get?"

"Hot enough for an osprey omelet."

"What about the chicks? Do they die from the heat?"

"Not that I know of. You'd think the local media would be all over the story if any chicks died," he said.

"I mean, I'm all for animal rights," she said, "but based on my personal experience with Darcy, she's a nutroll."

"No kidding. When the vet visit was finished, he told me that Marcus clung to him, not wanting to go back to Darcy. He thinks Marcus knows she's crazy too. The vet will mention that in his report."

"Good gravy," Monica said. "I can't believe this is an actual lawsuit. Will you do a short email to Al Bowman summarizing the status of the case? He really expected you to get it dismissed right away, so it will come as a bit of a blow that he's going to have to set aside a budget for litigation."

"I understand. There's still plenty of opportunity to get it dismissed. I just want to employ a few tactical maneuvers, so we're sitting in a position of strength. I want to put some pressure on Wally-the screeching-crane, to the extent she'll listen to reason."

"Good luck. I think she's just as crazy as Darcy. Maybe Darcy actually hired Wally because she looks like a bird—a crane in a peasant skirt."

Nathan smiled then asked, "So, what's the latest in the Boyfriend Killer case?"

"Did you see the news last night?"

"Yeah. They found traces of radioactive materials at Nelson's house, huh?"

She nodded. "Frankly, I'm a little concerned about being associated with Stela in any way, shape, or form. In addition to being a sociopath who murdered a man, she also might be an underworld arms dealer."

"Did she tell you that?"

"She doesn't tell me squat, but I think it's obvious."

"What are you going to do now?"

"Continue to serve in my role, but try as hard as I can to keep my distance from her. I need to remain just another person in the judicial process. Neither good nor bad. Unmemorable when she leaves our little town."

"You're assuming she'll be acquitted?"

"You never know, do you? She comes across as a trial attorney in a former life." Monica held up her fingers, and ticked off one-by-one as she spoke. "She asked me to hire an expert physician to testify. She cites caselaw to the court. She's writing out cross-examinations. She has a trial binder. She thinks strategically. She argues motions like a pro."

"In that case, whatever you do, don't piss her off."

"Thanks for your sage advice."

"The more you're on TV with her, though, the better advertising it is for our firm," he said with enthusiasm. "Kathy told me a few people called this morning to see if you could represent them."

"I'm afraid to ask who," she said, surprised that Kathy hadn't told her.

"Upstanding members of our community who've been charged with drug possession and DUIs."

"Just who I want as clients."

"Well, If they can pay the bills, then I'm all for it. I told her to send them to me, because I didn't think you'd want to be bothered. For criminal work, I charge a minimum $20,000 retainer, and $180 per hour. One guy hung up as soon as I quoted my rates.

The other guy, a professional in town, hired me on the spot. I hope you're okay with that."

"Gosh yes. Are you going to expand your practice in that direction?"

"Maybe. I hate to turn away work. If you're going to be the rainmaker, then I'm going to catch every drop in my bucket."

"A lawyer bucket," she said with a Texan twang. "You and Jim are the true litigators. I don't know what the hell I'm doing in court."

"Fortunately, you don't have to do much for your standby counsel role. I'd love to drop by the trial to see Stela Reiter in action."

"Please do. She's a piece of work." Monica stood to leave. "Thanks for taking on new clients to pay the light bill."

"My pleasure."

On her way back to her office, Monica stopped in the kitchen and made herself a chai tea. When she returned to her desk, she saw a new email from stela1034@jail.wis.gov, and the bottom fell out of her stomach. The message said, "The FBI wants to interview me at one o'clock. I need you. Please come to the jail."

"Fuck. I'm not your lawyer!" Monica hissed at the computer screen. She pushed away from her desk and trudged over to Jim Daniel's office.

He looked free, so she marched in and plopped down in a guest chair.

"Yes?" he asked in amusement.

She told him about the email.

"Are you going to run over to the jail for the meeting?" he asked.

"Why?" Monica asked. "I'm not her lawyer, and the FBI interview doesn't have anything to do with the murder case."

"How do you know?" Jim asked. "You have to go."

"You're not backing me up here," she said.

"Do you want Stela pissed off at you?"

"No, but—"

"For that reason alone, you should go. You don't have to say a word. In fact, tell her you can't say a word. Just observe, listen and memorize. I wouldn't even take notes if I were you."

Monica fidgeted with a stray thread on her pinstripe trousers. "Fine. But this sucks."

"Sometimes assignments get sucky."

She flipped him off as she left, inviting a hearty laugh from behind his thick beard.

19

Monica arrived at the gray citadel ten minutes before one. No one was in the reception area, so she figured she had beat the FBI to the party.

"Cold enough for ya?" Bob, the guard with the calm manner asked.

"Horrible out there," Monica said. "Hot yoga is the only thing that warms me up."

He peeked in her attaché case and waved her through the metal detector. "That sounds nice. It's always cold on our wedding anniversary."

"Happy anniversary," she said. "How many years?"

"Thirty-six," he said warmly.

"That's commitment," she said.

"She's a saint," he said.

The thick metal door opened, and Cliff appeared. "Ms. Spade. The Romanian is waiting for you. She's glowing today."

"From handling radioactive materials," Bob said, laughing.

"Hi, Cliff." Monica glanced between the two of them. "Saw the news last night, huh?"

"Makes more sense now," Cliff said. "I never believed she was just dating him. She seems more—"

"Diabolical," Bob supplied.

"Yeah. That and well-traveled," Cliff said.

"The FBI agents aren't here yet, are they?" Monica asked.

"No, but I heard they were coming to talk about the nukes at Nelson's house," Bob said.

"Let's not jump to conclusions," Monica said, trying to appear neutral. "I'll go chat with her while we wait."

She followed Cliff, the door slam still startling her.

"I also heard she's excellent in court," Cliff said over his shoulder, as they proceeded down the gray hallway.

"You have good intel," Monica said.

He led Monica to the windowless conference room. Stela was seated in her usual spot on the other side of the metal table, slouching. She acknowledged Monica with a casual nod.

Cliff smiled politely at Monica and closed the door behind him.

"Hello." Monica thought Stela looked a little tired this afternoon. Her eyes had lost some of the alertness Monica had seen in court, and her hair was pulled back in an oily bun.

"Do you know what this is about?" Stela asked before Monica could take her seat.

"No clue," Monica said honestly. She didn't want to share her own conjecture about radioactive materials trading hands, because she was mindful that Stela most likely hadn't seen the local news from her jail cell. It wasn't Monica's job to educate her, so she elected not to.

"When they get here, sit on my side of the table, and don't say a word," Stela said. "Don't ask any questions. Just sit here. Don't take notes either."

There were show horses and work horses, and Monica sensed that Stela had decided Monica was going to be a show horse for this meeting.

"I'm down with that," Monica said equably.

"Fair enough." Stela sat calmly, openly assessing Monica's appearance. After a time, she said, "Nice suit."

"Thanks. How are they treating you in here?"

"Better than most jails."

Monica registered loud and clear that Stela experience with imprisonment. "Do you need anything? Writing supplies for your trial or anything?"

Stela's expression remained resolute. "No. They supply me with everything I need."

"Good to know." Since Stela didn't seem very talkative, Monica sat calmly, trying not to make eye contact with those flat, dark eyes.

There was a knock on the door then the click of the lock. Cliff entered, followed by two skinny men in dark suits. While they thanked Cliff, Monica rose and scooted around the table next to Stela.

Peter McCoy and Steven Scott introduced themselves as FBI agents, sliding their business cards across the table, as they sat. Monica studied their cards and reciprocated with her own.

"Do you know why we're here?" Peter, the older one, asked Stela.

"To make this nightmare go away?" Stela asked in a serious tone.

Peter stared at her for a second, then shook his head. "The police detected high levels of radiation in Andy Nelson's house and garage. They found two lead-lined carrying cases in the garage. They now suspect that he was selling enriched uranium and plutonium to you." His tone dove to a condescending pitch. "Very sloppy, my dear..."

Stela's lips compressed into a thin line, as her eyes volleyed back and forth between the two men.

After some silence, Peter asked, "What did you do with the nuclear materials?"

"Stop it," she said in a lifeless whisper.

"Where did you stash them?" Peter asked.

"I don't know what you're talking about. I was just his girlfriend." She didn't flinch.

Steven, the younger one, said, "You have a record on INTERPOL of criminal activity in Moldova, Ukraine and Poland."

Stela stared hard at him.

Monica made a mental note.

"As in smuggling uranium, plutonium and cesium," Steven added. "Easy for the local police to discover."

"You can't believe everything you read on INTERPOL," Stela said, no hint of surprise in her voice.

She didn't deny it, Monica thought.

"We need your cooperation if you want to beat this charge," Peter said.

Stela regarded Peter with mild amusement. There was something between them. A familiarity.

"The DA is one mouse click away from discovering and introducing your INTERPOL record at trial. The jury will convict you like that." Peter clicked his fingers.

Stela sat motionless, not a rattle from the chains around her wrists or ankles.

"Your bosses will be so very disappointed," Peter said sarcastically.

Still nothing from Stela.

"Where is Yuri Zaleski?" Steven asked.

Stela's eyebrow quirked, but she remained silent.

Peter ran his bony fingers across his clean-shaven chin. "If you work with us, we can help you make this mess go away." He glanced at Monica, then said to Stela in a low voice. "We need to know where the nukes are."

Stela's lips remained pressed shut, not even a moan issuing forth, but her jaw flexed, as she stared them down.

"Once this information comes out in your trial, there's no way the jury will believe Andy was trying to sexually assault you," Peter said. "Your only chance for freedom is to cooperate with us."

Stela stared at Peter, processing. Her hands rested on her lap and were hidden from view of the agents, but Monica noticed Stela's thumbs urgently smoothing over her knuckles in a nervous gesture.

"Is Yuri Zaleski really worth life in prison?" Steven asked, his youthful voice incredulous.

Stela rolled her shoulders back then said in a Romanian accent, "The false accusations you're making aren't admissible at my trial. I'll keep them out of evidence."

Peter shrugged with skepticism then took a new tack. "See if you can keep this out. The Wisconsin State Crime lab found three sets of DNA at the murder scene."

Stela openly blanched.

Peter had her attention. "Andy Nelson's, which is no surprise. DNA that matches your blood, putting you there. And, a third blood sample that doesn't match either yours or Mr. Nelson's. Since DNA doesn't lie, we know there was a third person there. The police are looking for Zaleski."

Stela's thumbs rubbed furiously over her knuckles.

"We can keep you safe," Peter said.

She snorted. "Your track record sucks."

"There are new people in charge," Peter said.

"You?" she asked in disbelief.

He visibly bristled at the insult and rocked back in his chair. "Why don't you think about it for a few days. We'll be back in touch. If you cooperate, you might get out of here. If you don't..." He swept his hand around the room, "...you might as well hang some curtains, because you'll be here for a while. Your choice."

Pleased with themselves, the thin, clean-shaven men in dark suits shoved their chairs back and stood.

Peter turned to Monica. "Thank you, Ms. Spade."

Shocked, but defaulting to politeness, Monica said. "Nice to meet you." She shook their hands, then returned to the opposite side of the table after they departed. She raised her eyebrows at Stela, waiting for an explanation.

"Here's what I need you to do," Stela said, her voice calm and low. "Contact Dr. George Popovich. Tell him he needs to come and testify at my trial."

"About what?"

"Never mind that. Just explain what the FBI agents said about three sets of DNA, and he'll know what he has to say."

"What type of doctor is he?"

"He's an oncologist and hematologist," Stela said.

Monica tilted her head, thoroughly confused. "Okay. That sounds way off-topic, but I'm sure you have a plan, judging by the way you handled those guys. Do you have any contact information for Dr. Popovich?"

"Yes." Stela rattled off a memorized phone number.

"Just a sec." Monica grabbed her legal pad from her attaché and wrote his name and phone number on it. "Do I use the Eugène Ionesco currency with him too?"

"I see you're a quick learner. Yes."

After making a note, Monica looked up. Instinct told her not to reveal to Stela that she had read a few of Ionesco's cracked plays.

"That will be all for today, Ms. Spade." Stela stood.

"One more thing," Monica said.

Stela looked down at her expectantly.

"Is the guy who gave me money for your wardrobe Yuri Zaleski?"

Stela squinted. "The less you know, the better. Trust me."

Monica suddenly felt stupid and careless for asking. She held up her hand. "Of course. You're right. It won't happen again."

"Guard!" Stela yelled, sending Monica into the air like a startled cat.

The edge of Stela's lip briefly quirked up.

So, she gets off on scaring me, Monica thought, resenting her for it.

Cliff swung the door open and allowed Stela to pass first. He made to close the door with Monica still in the conference room, but she wedged her boot against it, preventing him. He smiled mischievously and pushed it back for her. "Go to the end of the hallway and knock. Bob will let you out."

Monica was a little surprised that Cliff allowed her to walk alone to the exit while he went in the opposite direction with Stela. She was proud that he was treating her like a big girl who knew the ins and outs—especially the outs—of jail.

She knocked, and Bob unlocked the door and met her on the other side. Relief flooded her, as she relaxed her jaw and rolled her shoulders, trying to shake loose a new knot between them.

"That didn't take long," Bob said. "The FBI agents left already."

"They're efficient." She buttoned up her Italian wool coat and pulled on her knit hat.

"Keep your eyes open," he said.

"Will do, but in this cold, I wouldn't be surprised if my eyelashes froze shut on the first blink." She smiled appreciatively and left.

On her way back to the office, she found herself wishing her old truck had heated seats and a stronger fan. On the other hand, the sentimentality of her grandfather's truck outweighed the lack of creature comfort. She forced herself to focus on Stela's case rather than how cold she was. The FBI wanted to make a deal with Stela. *Why don't they just take custody of her?*

After the short drive, Monica again was filled with gratitude when she entered her law firm to find Kathy at the reception desk, actually on the phone. Kathy made slashing motions in the air with her nail file, punctuated by a few stabs, as Monica passed her.

Monica shed her coat and picked up a half full cup of cold tea from her desk. That wouldn't do. She needed hot tea to take the chill off of all that running around outside.

In the kitchen, she was immediately enveloped by the aroma of something sweet and glorious baking in the oven. While making her tea, she stole glances at the dish, which appeared to be a cake or brownies.

She microwaved some whole milk then frothed it with a handheld device that Kathy had given her for Christmas. She used the restroom while her tea was steeping and returned to find Sandie and Cheryl on break. Cheryl, the blonde of the group, with dimples and a ready smile, removed the pan from the oven.

"That smells delicious," Monica said.

"Trust me, it is," Cheryl said.

Monica studied the dark, molten chocolate with swirls of white and caramel. "Brownies?"

"S'mores," Cheryl said. "One of my favorites."

"I'm sure they're to die for," Monica said.

"Better than sex," Sandie said, as she poured herself a cup of coffee.

Monica tilted her head but didn't reply.

"She's not going to agree with you," Cheryl said to Sandie while pointing at Monica. "She and Shelby are still in the sizzle stage."

Monica's chest tightened, as she wondered why they were having this conversation. After a pause, curiosity got the best of her. "What comes after the sizzle stage?"

"Fizzle," Sandie said with glee.

"Good night, Irene," Monica said at the same time Cheryl said, "Don't listen to her."

"If it isn't fizzle, then what is it?" Monica asked, turning to Cheryl.

"If you love each other, you settle into a long-term romance known as chisel," Cheryl said.

"What happens during the chisel stage?"

"That's when you mold your partner—in my case, Mike—into what you want him to be," Cheryl said.

Sandie made a gagging gesture.

"I'm supposed to chisel Shelby into what I want her to be? That sounds like a lot of work, and I'm not sure what I would change about her."

"Remember," Cheryl said, "It isn't changing the person. It's just fine-tuning. I've never tried it on a woman, but Mike is easy. It's a delicate balance between food and sex."

Monica's ears turned pink. "I'll keep that in mind." She cleared her throat and asked, "If you don't love each other after the sizzle stage, then what happens?"

"Kaput," Sandie said, pointing her thumbs down. "We call that drizzle."

"Oh dear," Monica said. "I hope Shelby and I hit chisel instead of drizzle or fizzle."

"I'm sure you will, dear," Sandie said, "but the sex still won't be better than Cheryl's s'mores bars."

"Ha!" Cheryl exclaimed. "Speak for yourself."

"Well, you're married to Mike!" Sandie said.

"But you have Tim!" Cheryl said in a high-pitched screech. "We all know he's the hottest!"

Sandie shook her head, as a slow smile spread across her face. She had been fishing for that all along and now claimed her victory.

Monica still found it hard to believe that a dessert could be better than sex. Sex with Shelby *was* dessert. "Well, I have to go make some phone calls. Enjoy your dessert bars."

"Do you want me to bring you a bar when they cool off?" Cheryl asked.

"Absolutely," Monica said, as she left the kitchen. Sex or not, she wasn't passing up those bars.

20

Monica returned to her desk and marveled at Cheryl and Sandie's descriptions of the stages of a relationship. They were right about one thing—she and Shelby were in full-on sizzle right now—savoring every second of heated contact. *Could we ever fizzle? How would that happen to us?*

Batting away those thoughts as the worst kind of self-doubt, she forced herself to focus on work, retrieving the note pad from her attaché case.

Previously motivated by not making an enemy of the judge, she was now motivated by not making an enemy of someone more powerful—Stela. She picked up her desk phone and dialed the phone number for Dr. George Popovich.

"This is George," a man with an accent answered.

"Hello, Dr. Popovich. This is Attorney Monica Spade. I'm standby counsel for Ms. Stela Reiter. She's on trial in Wisconsin for murdering Andy Nelson." Monica paused to let him digest her opening salvo.

"Who's on trial?" he asked with a thick, Eastern European accent.

"Stela Reiter. You can google her after we hang up. She told me to mention Eugène Ionesco, and that she needs you to testify as an oncologist in her defense. I have no idea what the connection is."

Silence renewed itself while he processed, and she could have sworn he muttered, "Ahh, my Mila," under his breath.

Monica scribbled, "Stela=Mila?" on her notepad.

"You said she's on trial for murder?" he asked.

"Yes."

"Who are you?" he asked.

"Attorney Monica Spade." She told him the story as she knew it, which took about 10 minutes. She could hear him typing on a keyboard as she spoke, obviously taking notes, or perhaps googling Stela, or both.

"At what point did she tell you she need me?" he asked, eliding the "ed" for the past tense of need.

"When the FBI told her they found three sets of DNA at the murder scene. They accused her of having an accomplice, and they mentioned a gentleman by the name of Yuri Zaleski."

She heard him clap loudly then discharge a litany of harsh words in a foreign tongue. She assumed he was speaking Russian or Ukrainian, because it wasn't as smooth as the Romanian that Stela occasionally mumbled.

"From where you sit, is there any other proof that Zaleski was at the murder scene?" George asked.

"Not that I've seen, but we haven't received a full copy of the prosecutor's file yet. Actually, come to think of it, I think they're still investigating the case."

"Send me everything you've got so far," he said.

"I'll need to get permission from Stela to do that."

"Of course." He sighed heavily and muttered some more words she didn't understand. His language sounded abrupt, giving it a choppy cadence in contrast to Stela's smooth slur of consonants.

"I'll email her today and get back to you," Monica said in a pleasant voice. "What's your email address?"

He supplied it.

"That's all I have. Do you have any questions for me?" she asked.

"What's your email address and phone number?"

"I'll email both to you when we hang up," she said.

"Okay," he said in an uncertain tone, then added with more confidence, "Okay."

"Goodbye," she said.

He didn't bother saying goodbye, so she hung up and immediately emailed Stela, asking what, if anything, she was allowed to email to Dr. Popovich.

Not expecting to hear back right away, Monica opened the file that Dominique had emailed her earlier, beginning with the State Crime Lab forensics report. Monica read that there were, indeed, three sets of DNA found at the scene.

She also pulled up a police report and discovered that Detectives Matt Breuer and Brock Curfman had visited Racy's Coffee Lounge on Water Street to talk to employees about Stela, who they discovered spent a great deal of time there. One of the employees was none other than Yuri Zaleski. The report was over a week old, well before the nuclear materials story had broken on the news.

The report indicated that Yuri admitted to knowing Stela, claiming that he met her at Racy's. He told Matt and Brock that they chatted frequently there but nowhere outside of the lounge. He remembered seeing her there with Andy Nelson, snuggling on the sofa and drinking coffee while they ate a variety of pastries and sandwiches, depending on the time of day. He said Andy always paid for himself and Stela. Yuri didn't notice anything out of the ordinary about either one of them.

Of course you didn't, Monica thought, *you were in cahoots with her. By bringing Andy to Racy's, Stela enlisted your help to double-team him.*

The detectives asked him where he was on the day of the murder, and he claimed he had worked an eight-hour shift at Racy's.

That's an alibi that's easy to confirm, Monica thought.

The report indicated that they checked the coffee lounge manager's records, which reflected that Yuri had been clocked in from 9 a.m. to 5 p.m. on January 4th, the day of the murder.

Maybe he snuck out of work and someone else clocked him out, Monica thought.

Monica continued to read that Matt and Brock asked Yuri to write a statement of his alibi, which was a short paragraph describing his arrival at work, clocking in, working the entire day, and clocking out. He expressly stated that he couldn't remember the names of any patrons who could confirm his presence. He relayed that his manager was in and out of the lounge that day, so the police could talk to him. Yuri's narrative was attached to the police report, and Monica noticed that his cursive was similar to Stela's.

The report indicated that Matt and Brock asked Yuri to voluntarily submit to a cheek swab for DNA testing, but he had refused.

Duh, Monica thought. *He's guilty.*

The report didn't include what Monica really wanted to see, which was a photo of Yuri to confirm he was the gentleman who had given her the money for Stela's wardrobe. Monica would have to wait in suspense for that because googling his name turned up nothing.

Monica called Kathy at reception.

"What can I do for you, my dear?" Kathy asked.

"I'm wondering if you're in the mood to do a little detective work outside the office?"

"Always," Kathy said.

"Can you visit Racy's Coffee Lounge on Water Street and ask the manager for a photo of former employee, Yuri Zaleski?"

"Sure."

"Also, ask him how an employee clocks in and out, and whether Yuri could've left early and asked someone else to clock him out."

"I'm on it."

"Thanks."

Monica returned to the DA's file. There were also police reports of conversations with Julia Brown, the SANE nurse, Dr. Jim Tollefson, the Emergency Department physician who treated Stela and wrote in his note that her cuts were self-inflicted, and Dr. Bart Karey, the psychiatrist who attended to Stela on the Behavioral Health Unit.

Stela's medical records were all attached as well, so Monica dove into those. Since she was familiar with physician-speak, she read between the lines that the providers were sort of suspicious of Stela's story. They indicated that her detached demeanor and reticence weren't consistent with sexual assault victims, and, at the time she was seen in the ED, the providers didn't know that Stela had killed her alleged attacker. They were operating under the assumption that she was an innocent victim.

Stela had been admitted directly to Behavioral health from the ED that Saturday night, and the next day, Detectives Matt and Brock had visited her, but she didn't tell them anything.

Late Sunday evening, Dr. Karey's notes took on a more defensive posture after he rounded on her. He mentioned that she had entertained a male visitor earlier that day, but that she still claimed amnesia from PTSD, the veracity of which he openly questioned in his note, describing it as "factitious." Monica mistakenly thought he meant "fictitious," so she googled "factitious" and was shocked to learn that it was a technical term that meant "contrived."

Instead of taking Stela's presentation at face value, Dr. Karey had diagnosed her with dissociative and personality disorders, concluding that she had engaged in self-cutting and most likely was withholding information. His diagnosis was huge for the prosecution.

Monica envisioned the physicians and SANE nurse testifying, and based on their notes, she concluded their testimony wouldn't be favorable to Stela. Monica assumed that was the reason Stela requested Monica to contact Dr. Karpenko—to rebut the testimony of her treating physicians. She was impressed with Stela's ability to forecast what the physicians would testify to and build a defense accordingly. Of course, Stela had been a participant in her own care, so she was proving herself capable of creating cover for her failure to tell her providers what had transpired between Andy and her.

By the time Monica finished reading the prosecution's file, it was the end of the day, and she had surprised herself by almost filling a legal pad with notes. She rubbed her hands over her face and sighed. From where she sat, things didn't look good for Stela. If Monica were in Stela's shoes, she'd take the FBI agents' offer in a heartbeat.

She also was curious whether Stela's INTERPOL record would be admissible by the prosecution. Monica suspected that evidence of prior crimes wouldn't be admissible to prove the guilt of Stela for the current crime, so she googled some caselaw and read a few on-point cases. After confirming that legal precedent, Monica again rubbed her eyes and pushed away from her desk.

She called Detective Matt on his cell.

"Hello?"

"Hi. I tried to access INTERPOL, but it requires law enforcement credentials."

"Yup."

"Maybe you should do that and share your results with me."

He thought about that for a minute. "Deal. Thanks for the tip."

"My pleasure."

They rang off.

She wandered over to Jim Daniels' office and saw that he was on the phone, so she detoured for a glass of water, and, by the time she returned, he had ended his call.

"Yes?" he asked, waving her in.

She explained what she had read in the prosecution file and told him about the FBI interview of Stela. "Doesn't the FBI have jurisdiction over this case?" she asked.

"You're asking whether stealing radioactive materials trumps a state charge for homicide?"

"I guess so," she said.

"I don't think so." He rubbed his beard.

"The FBI agents made it sound that way," she said. "They kept using phrases like, if Stela cooperated, they could get her out of here and set her up with a new identity. Otherwise, her sexual assault defense looked flimsy in the face of evidence of a radioactive materials deal gone bad."

"They always start with the carrot," he said, "then wield the stick."

"I sensed a certain familiarity between Stela and the agents."

He considered that for a moment. "Small world that deals in nukes. Maybe they've heard of her. I expect they would have visited the *Voila!*

manufacturing plant by now to see if Andy's bosses had noticed any material gone missing.*"*

"The police already did," she said. "Whatever *Voila!'s* safety procedures are for handling and storing radioactive materials, they were completely breached by Andy."

"Even if he had legitimate access to radioactive materials, he left the building with them and stored them at his house," Jim said. "That's pretty crazy. You'd think *Voila!* personnel would be working with the FBI and local police to help them identify and clean up any residuals at Andy's house."

"Maybe they are," she said, "but there hasn't been anything on the news, and I didn't see anything in the DA's file that Dominique emailed to me.

"Speaking of Dominique, I'd better get home." He looked at his watch. "It's my turn to make dinner, and she doesn't like it if I'm late."

Monica smiled. "I know the feeling." She returned to her office and gathered her belongings then turned off the lights. She and Jim met at the reception area and locked up, as they were the last to leave.

When Monica pulled into her driveway, Shelby's Jeep was already there, tucked away in the one-stall garage. Monica felt a smidgeon of irritation but immediately suppressed it, as Shelby had been the first person home and it was only logical that she should pull into the garage. Monica closed the garage door and swallowed the disappointment that she would be emerging to a cold truck in the morning that would need its windows scraped.

She entered her cozy little house.

"Hey, love," Shelby said over her shoulder from the stovetop. Spicy aromas wafted and warmed Monica, as she removed her coat then sat on the bench to remove her boots. Maybe dinner was a prime trade-off for the garage spot.

"Hope you're in the mood for stir-fry," Shelby said, keeping her attention focused on the wok before her. "We haven't eaten very many veggies this week, and I really miss them. I could eat veggies for every meal."

Ugh, Monica thought to herself but said aloud, "Sounds terrific. Is there any meat in the stir-fry?"

"Shrimp!" Shelby said enthusiastically.

Monica pictured a bag of frozen shrimp that Shelby had thawed and rinsed. On an unforgiving winter night with subzero temperatures and darkness by four o'clock, Monica desired something heartier— like bison or beef. Since Shelby was cooking, however, and Monica worshipped the ground she walked on, Monica wouldn't complain. If Shelby loved vegetables, then Monica would pretend to as well.

21

"This is really tasty," Monica said later, as they ate at the dining nook. "I love the flavors."

"It's my proprietary blend of hoisin sauce, fresh ginger, fermented black bean sauce and some other spices," Shelby said, her expression radiant over her forkful of broccoli, her face flushed from working over the hot wok.

Monica was hoping for a large bowl of white rice with her stir fry, but no such carbs were in sight. *Is she putting me on a diet?*

"How was work today?" Shelby asked.

"A grind," Monica said, pretending to enjoy a bite of broccoli.

"Busy with the Boyfriend Killer?"

"Very." Monica stabbed a sliced carrot and shrimp. *How many shrimp can I eat without looking like a glutton?*

"Tell me about it."

"I don't want to share too much with you because I was told that the less I know, the better, so I have to believe the same holds true for you."

"I'm not afraid of the Boyfriend Killer," Shelby said with a cheek full of food. "A jury will convict her in two seconds, and off to prison she'll go." She chewed triumphantly, the veggies inexplicably energizing her.

"I wouldn't be so sure of that," Monica said, eating another shrimp. "There are forces at play that are even more powerful than the local District Attorney."

Shelby's chestnut eyebrows knitted into an adorable frown. "Are you in danger?"

"I hope not."

"A mysterious Monica is a sexy Monica," Shelby said playfully.

Monica half-smiled, as she dutifully chewed. She was speechless when Shelby looked at her like that—lust blazing a hole through her heart.

Later, while doing dishes, Monica turned on the WQOD evening news to Keith Hoyt reporting that specialized personnel from *Voila!* were assisting the police in the search and decontamination of Andy Nelson's garage and home. They sampled his septic system and found more uranium and plutonium, so they called Earl, the owner of Honey Wagon Septic, whose slogan was, "We're number one in the number two business. We haul only American-made products."

When interviewed by Keith, Earl laughed in response to the police's suggestion that Earl pump out Andy's radioactive septic tank. "Was the dumb [bleep] eating plutonium?"

Keith said, "The police think either Andy Nelson, or someone else, flushed the radioactive materials to hide the evidence."

Earl scratched at the greasy hair under his hat. "Wouldn't be the first time someone flushed evidence of a crime. The police better not ask me to put on a diving suit to look for glowing [bleep] in his septic tank."

"Will you pump it out and carry it away?" Keith asked.

"I'm not contaminating my used virgin meals on wheels," Early said. "I've already got a spot in heaven for the [bleep] I carry, but I don't want to get there too soon, you know?"

Keith chuckled in spite of himself. "I understand. Do you know someone who could haul it?"

"I sent the police to Milwaukee," Earl said.

Back at the news desk, Keith confirmed that a Milwaukee hazardous waste septic truck would pump out and transfer the contents to a specialized processing center where they would separate the shit from Shinola, so to speak, in an attempt to isolate the radioactive materials.

Still reading the news, Keith stressed that the County Health Department was conducting tests of neighboring wells, but they didn't anticipate any leakage issues because Andy Nelson's septic system was relatively new.

What a load of crap! Monica thought. *The nuclear experts make a big deal out of using lead-lined containers for radioactive materials, but the Health Department is saying that radioactive materials in Andy's septic system won't contaminate the surrounding environment? That doesn't make any sense. Surely, Andy's tank isn't lined with lead.* She turned off the TV.

Monica glanced at Shelby, who was a few feet away in the laundry room off the kitchen. "What do you want to do tonight?"

"Well, it's a school night, and it's super cold out, so staying home sounds nice," Shelby said.

"Uh-huh," Monica said. "I have a lot of energy, though, so I don't want to sit around reading Eugène Ionesco plays."

"What?" Shelby peeked her head around the corner. "I thought you didn't like them."

"I don't, but there's something—" Monica started to say but remembered she couldn't because some things were too dangerous for Shelby to know. "Never mind. Want to go to a movie?"

Shelby turned on the washing machine and returned to the living room. "Again, school night and the temperature is in the deep freeze." She directed her attention to her cell phone and tapped the screen. "It's 12 below zero right now, and will get even colder by the time the movie ends. Do you know how cold that will feel when we exit a theater?"

Do you know how cold that will feel tomorrow morning when I go out to start my truck? Monica thought but didn't say. "You're right. Maybe we should watch something here, so I can distract my mind from work."

"Too bad we finished the last episode of *The Morning Show*. I wonder if they're making another season," Shelby asked.

"I hope so," Monica said in a lame voice.

They joined each other on the sofa and scooted together, as Monica brought up options on her smart TV. After a few minutes of clicking on titles, reading the descriptions, and even watching trailers, Monica found herself thinking about Stela's upcoming trial, and the FBI agents who had accused her of being involved in an international smuggling ring. *Could they deliver on their promises to erase the realities of being held accountable for murder if Stela confessed and ratted out her bosses, and potentially their bosses?*

She was jolted from her thoughts by the front door bell, which sent her springing from the sofa and mindlessly flinging the TV remote up to the ceiling, where it cracked open and fell in pieces behind her.

"What the hell, Mon?" Shelby asked, quickly covering her head. "It's just the doorbell, for God's sake. What's wrong with you?"

Shelby rose, but Monica patted the air in front of her, forcing her back down. "It might not be safe. I'll get it."

"Not safe? You need to simmer down. It's probably your neighbors inviting you to a Super Bowl party." Shelby rose and placed her hands on Monica's love handles, pushing her toward the front door. "I'm right behind you." She giggled as they stumbled to the door, Monica trying to push away Shelby's groping hands.

Monica peeked out the window at the top of the thick door. Peter McCoy and Steven Scott stood on her front stoop in their black stocking caps, black coats and black leather gloves.

"Fuck. I knew it," Monica whispered.

"Knew what? Who is it?" Shelby asked.

"A couple of FBI agents I met today."

"I didn't do it!" Shelby exclaimed then laughed at her own joke.

"This isn't a laughing matter," Monica whispered in reproach. "Be serious." She turned the bolt lock and opened the door. "Hello, Peter. Steven."

"Hi, Ms. Spade. Do you have a few minutes to talk?" Peter asked.

"Of course," Monica said in her professional voice. "Please, come in."

The men entered, ushering in a cloud of chilly air behind them.

"It's a cold one tonight," Monica said.

Their faces pale and stern, the men quickly observed their surroundings, their eyes coming to rest on Shelby.

Monica cleared her throat. "This is my girlfriend, Shelby St. Claire. Shelby, these are FBI Agents Peter McCoy and Steven Scott."

With eternal brightness and charm, Shelby said, "Nice to meet you. Would you like me to take your coats while you chat with Monica?"

No one shook hands, but the men quickly removed their outerwear, handing them to Shelby, who draped them over a nearby chair. "Would anyone like a cup of herbal tea? I was just about to make one for myself."

"If it wouldn't be too much trouble," Steven said, rubbing his hands together.

"That's very kind of you," Peter said. "Please."

"Thanks Shelby," Monica said then turned to the men. "Let's sit over here." She motioned to her corner area where a loveseat was positioned in front of the gas fireplace. As they made their way over, she flipped on the lamps and picked up the remote for the fireplace, turning the flame to high.

She claimed her favorite recliner with a view of her snow-covered yard, then turned her attention to the gaunt men on the loveseat across from her.

Peter glanced at the bank of windows. "Do you have someplace more private?"

"If you were tailed, or my house is being watched, we might as well chat in the open. If it makes you feel better, you can cover your mouth with your hand like a baseball catcher talking to the pitcher on the mound."

Neither Peter nor Steven smiled at her suggestion.

"What can I do for you?" Monica asked, placing her hands in her lap.

"We're working with the Apple Grove Police on their investigation of Andy Nelson, Stela Reiter and Yuri Zaleski."

"I recall you asking Stela if she had seen Yuri Zaleski. Did you read Detective Matt Breuer's report about interviewing Yuri at Racy's Coffee Lounge?"

Peter and Steven exchanged a look. "Yes, well, Detectives Breuer and Curfman spoke to him before we got involved," Peter said.

Monica waited.

Peter clasped his hands. "There are, perhaps, details surrounding Ms. Reiter and Mr. Zaleski that we cannot tell you."

Monica held up her hand. "I assumed as much, and I'd like to keep it that way. I'm just acting as standby counsel for Stela because she fired her public defenders."

"We'd like you to work with us to right the ship."

"What ship would you be referring to?" Monica asked, "because Stela appears to be on the Titanic from my perspective." Monica heard the clank of mugs being placed on the kitchen counter, grateful that Shelby was busy not hearing this conversation. To keep it that way, she hopped out of her chair and closed the door between the former porch and main house. "It's probably best if my girlfriend doesn't hear any of this."

"Good thinking," Peter said. "Over the years, I've made a point of separating my work from my personal life. We don't want to jeopardize our loved ones in our line of work, do we?"

Monica returned to her chair. "Just to be clear, Mr. McCoy, my line of work isn't your line of work, and I want to keep it that way. The fact that my involvement in this trial might expose Shelby to your world makes me nervous."

"Please, call me Peter."

"Our worlds aren't as different as you might think," Steven said.

She ignored him.

"We're not asking for much," Peter said. "We just want you to contact us if Stela tells you something about smuggling nuclear materials, especially with Yuri Zaleski. We weren't joking when we said they're involved with a ring of international professionals. Their associates have been arrested in the past for transporting small amounts of plutonium-239 in lead-lined cases."

Monica nodded thoughtfully. "How much is a small amount?"

"Only 12 ounces or so, but you can make a dirty bomb with as little as two pounds, so 12 ounces is a lot in the world of enriched plutonium."

"How much does an ounce of plutonium cost?" Monica asked.

"Depending on location and quality, about $5,000 per gram," Peter said.

"That equates to roughly $140,000 per ounce," Steven said.

Monica whisper-whistled. "About the cost of my house, give or take a few thousand."

"That's right," Peter said. "So, you can see why it would be lucrative for a young man like Andy Nelson to sell some on the side."

"Have you or the police checked his bank account or found any money at his house?" she asked.

"The police found a hidey hole in his kitchen—a false back to a cupboard—containing $20,000, but that's all so far," Peter said.

The door creaked, and they all looked up to Shelby carrying in three mugs of hot tea that smelled of peppermint, ginger and a hint of lemon. The aroma was eclipsed by her beauty, however, as she handed each person a mug. She angled her face away from Peter and Steven and winked at Monica before leaving. They all mumbled thank you, and Shelby gently closed the door behind her as she left.

Monica would forever associate all sweet smells with Shelby, as she sipped her tea, the steam caressing her face, her heart bursting with pride that Shelby was her girlfriend.

"This is very good tea," Peter said then took another sip. "Where was I? Oh yes, only $20,000 in cash has been recovered, but our team is currently chasing down Mr. Nelson's bank accounts and transfers. Could be a needle in a hay stack at this point if Stela electronically wired money to an offshore account for Mr. Nelson under an alias."

"That sounds plausible," Monica said, blowing at the tea. "However, it doesn't concern me. I'm just part of the due process Stela is supposed to receive while she stands trial for homicide in our little corner of the world. You need to understand that she enjoys attorney-client privilege with me, so I won't be sharing any information I learn with you."

Steven's young features hardened. "You don't want to be charged with obstruction of justice, Ms. Spade."

Monica smiled at him with steadied patience. "Asserting the attorney-client privilege doesn't come within spitting distance of obstruction, Mr. Scott."

Peter took back the conversation. "We aren't asking you to violate any ethical rules. We're just giving you the broader picture, so you understand what to look for and what her motive might have been for killing Andy. There's more at stake here than murder. Our country's national security is in jeopardy if people like Stela Reiter and Yuri Zaleski can freely enter the U.S. and buy black market plutonium and uranium, then smuggle it out. We need to stop the entire operation, not just her."

"I agree," Monica said. "Why don't you just arrest her for that, take her into custody, haul her off to some interrogation cell at Langley or wherever, and do whatever it is you do to extract information from people like her?"

Peter sighed. "If it were only so easy. Unfortunately, we have this thing called the Constitution, and DA Bisset told us that Ms. Reiter has demanded a trial, so we have to honor that under the law. Basically, Ms. Reiter's homicide trial takes precedence over our investigation, if she wants to roll the dice on a trial, that is. We tried to throw her a lifeline today when we met with her, but she didn't bite. If she insists on trying her murder case, then we have to sit on our hands and patiently wait."

Monica noticed his mixed metaphor but let it pass without remarking that one does not bite a lifeline. "Hm...interesting." She sipped her tea.

"The DA wasn't in a mood to negotiate," Steven added. "When we pressed, she became hysterical, threatening to go over heads." He shook his head at Dominique's supposed hysteria.

Monica wouldn't entertain disparagement of Dominique under any circumstance, much less from this arrogant youngster. She was reminded of the sexist white men at her old law firm, and the memory struck a raw nerve. Somewhat scarred by their attitudes, she confronted Steven's innuendo. "If DA Bisset's legal position is correct, then she was emphatic, not 'hysterical.' I suspect you'd never say that about a male DA."

"What?" he asked, caught off guard by Monica's remonstration.

"I get the sense that you're used to dealing with men, so, even if a woman gives you the same message as a man, she's 'hysterical,'" Monica said with air quotes.

"Well, uh, I don't think—" he sputtered, his face pinching with embarrassment.

She narrowed her eyes. "You need to show us the same respect in our roles as you automatically would give a man."

Peter quickly flicked his hand as a signal for Steven not to speak. "Thank you for educating Steven, Ms. Spade."

Steven bristled at Peter, opened his mouth to say something, then wisely shut it.

Monica smiled, warming to Peter but not necessarily believing what he said. Any of it.

"Now, if we could just return to the topic at hand," Peter said.

Monica picked up where they left off. "If Stela is acquitted, are you going to take her into custody?"

"Probably," Peter said.

Monica processed Stela's situation. "She has a chance at freedom if she stands trial, but probably no chance if she goes with you."

"That isn't entirely true," Peter said. "If her intel is good, we might be able to work a deal with her. We're more interested in Zaleski than Stela, but she's protecting him."

"I see." Monica allowed a pause for tea before saying, "Based on the way she was furiously rubbing her thumbs today, I don't think she believes you. Either she doesn't trust you, or she knows the power and reach of her comrades. I'm guessing they're ruthless and could find her anywhere in the world, even if you give her a new identity with a job somewhere far, far away."

Steven shrugged, and Peter's face remained frozen, which was a sign to Monica that she was close to correct in her assessment.

"I'd suggest that you continue to investigate the old-fashioned way and not attempt shortcuts by trying to get me to breach my ethical duty to the court," Monica said. "Remember, snitches get stitches."

Neither Peter nor Steven cracked a smile at Monica's attempt at levity.

"Yes, well. Let's see how the process plays out during her trial, shall we?" Peter drained his cup in one giant swig. "Thank you Ms. Spade, and please extend our gratitude to Ms. St. Claire for the tea." He stood, his clone following suit.

In that moment, Monica had little hope that her speech had landed between Steven's ears. On the positive side, however, she noticed he had drunk all of his tea too, so she was sure that Shelby had made a good impression.

She followed the men to the chair with their outerwear piled on it. No one spoke while they shrugged on their coats and hats to face the brutal elements.

As they prepared to leave, Monica asked, "Am I in danger?"

"No more so than you were before we visited," Peter said. "Romanians, Ukrainians, Russians, whoever is helping Stela, aren't known for playing nice."

"That doesn't sound reassuring," she said.

"It wasn't intended to," he said.

Her chest tightened as an image of her delicate Shelby being harmed appeared in her mind. "I'll take that into consideration. Good night, gentlemen."

"Thank you for your hospitality," Peter said.

They shook hands and departed.

22

The next morning, Monica woke well before the alarm on her cell phone was scheduled to ring. She tiptoed to the bathroom and checked the temp on her phone—26 degrees below zero. The cold floor and cool air lurking in the corners of her house confirmed the deep freeze. As much as she wanted to return to bed to snuggle with Shelby, she knew her mind wouldn't settle while she was swimming in this cesspool of a murder trial. She decided to rise and shine for the day, sparing Shelby more tossing and turning.

The only upside of waking so early was that she had plenty of time to drink coffee, eat some yogurt, and prestart her truck for the early bird yoga class. She did a gut check as to whether she wanted to brave the cold to continue her personal, and potentially damaging, search for the identity of Shelby's ex-girlfriend. The inexplicable answer was yes. Information was power, and Monica decided she needed as much power as possible if she wanted to understand the nuances of Shelby.

Wrapped in her microfiber robe and a down jacket, she opened the kitchen door to the dark, hostile air, her nostrils flash-freezing on inhalation. She treaded carefully in her Birkis down the slippery steps to her truck and opened the squeaky door. Perched on the frozen seat, she jimmied the key into the ignition and turned. A sputtering sound signaled that the battery still had enough spark to breathe life into the old gal. Monica revved the engine, cranked the heater to high, and went back inside.

Ten minutes later, she was dressed in her camo Athleta leggings and a yoga tank, her water bottle in hand. She pulled on her thickest, heaviest boots and bundled up in the down parka that fell to her knees.

The neighborhood was dead silent when she emerged the second time, the streets deserted during her pre-dawn drive to The Yoga Studio.

The contrast between the outdoor polar air and the indoor studio air was more than 100 degrees when she shed her outerwear and lay her mat on the heated floor. She was one of only four women who had suffered the intolerable conditions for the promise of enlightenment. They quickly and quietly congratulated each other on their courage and commitment, then, one by one, assumed relaxing positions to begin their collective yoga practice. Monica chose the heart-opener.

Just as Monica's body was thawing out, and her mind relaxing enough to forget her conversation with Peter and Steven the night prior, the glass door pushed open and a sexy, curvy, captivating woman in her mid-thirties entered. Her long, blonde hair looked freshly styled, framing bright blue eyes and lashes as long as an opera singer's. A new dimension of energy parted the air before her, as she smiled at the small class and rolled out her mat. She carried with her the authority of a leader and the presence of an entertainer, clearly feeding off the delight of being the center of attention.

Monica knew without asking that this woman had to have been Shelby's lover, her poise and sophistication something to which Shelby would have been attracted.

"Good morning, everyone. My name is Coco. I have the privilege of being your instructor today," she said, her voice smooth yet animated. Her bright blue eyes swiveled to Monica. "For those of you who don't know me, I'm the owner of the studio."

Monica nodded, and Coco smiled warmly. She started the class, taking them through standard warmup positions then transitioning into a flow from one position to another, Monica's muscles waking to the challenge.

What type of name is "Coco?" Monica wondered, as she moved through warrior-two, extended side angle, and all of its machinations.

Adopting a mask of pleasant focus, Monica followed Coco's cues like a devoted student, surreptitiously studying Coco's figure whenever she could sneak a peek. A petite woman, Coco was smooth and supple. Monica immediately pictured Shelby touching Coco, and jealousy in its most primal form exploded in her chest, as she went from down dog to tree pose. Monica found the emotion difficult to process, as a newfound feeling of possessing Shelby overcame her.

Being an attentive yoga instructor, Coco seemed to intuit Monica's discomfort, their eyes meeting periodically in the mirror. Monica attempted to divert her gaze, but probably revealed too much in her emotional state. She felt immature, wanting to be the bigger woman and smile, or at least appear neutral, but jealousy was overtaking her usually rational brain.

By the end of class, sweat dripping from her brow, Monica could have strangled the dazzling woman who obviously had fucked her girlfriend. Contrary to the purpose of yoga, Coco had succeeded in provoking, rather than releasing, Monica's anger.

While everyone sprayed and wiped down their mats, Coco sauntered over to Monica, who was on her knees, wiping her mat vigorously.

"Hey, thanks for coming this morning," Coco said. "I didn't catch your name."

Monica glanced up through the strands of hair falling over her perspiring forehead. "I'm Monica. Great class. Just what I needed. Thanks."

"I hope you come again," Coco said. "You have nice form." With that, she turned and opened the door, allowing the cooler air from the common area to enter their room, feeding the women fresh oxygen.

A few minutes later, standing by the front desk—her coat and boots at her feet—Monica found herself alone with Coco.

"Do I know you from somewhere?" Coco asked in a smooth, flowing voice. "You look so familiar to me."

"I don't think so," Monica mumbled, as she pulled on one boot, then began loosening the laces on the other for her sweaty, bare foot.

"Do you work in town?" Coco angled her head in curiosity.

"I'm a lawyer." Monica grunted while struggling into the second boot. "Monica Spade of Spade, Daniels & Taylor."

Coco's eyes glinted with recognition. She clicked her fingers, as she watched Monica shrug on her long, insulated coat and zip it up. "That's it! I saw you on the news at the Boyfriend Killer trial. You read her statement."

At least she didn't accuse me of being Stela's lawyer. "That's right," Monica mumbled. "Very astute of you." Monica pulled on her chopper mitts and rested her hand on the door. "I should get going."

Coco turned up the wattage on her smile, her voice going into full flirtation mode. "I'll keep a lookout for you—on TV and here. I hope to see you again."

Monica would have to be insensate not to pick up on Coco's overture. No wonder Shelby had fallen. The charisma. The body. The beauty. And a sexy, sophisticated accent. *Italian?*

"Thanks again. Bye," Monica said, her tone uninviting. She pushed through the door into the morning air and was relieved to discover that the bitter edge had come off with the rising sun. She checked her phone and saw that the temp had risen six degrees while she had been inside—to a whopping 20 degrees below zero. Her increased body temp carried her through the shock of a cold seat for several blocks, however, when the heater finally kicked in and produced something warmer than freezing.

When she rolled into her driveway, she saw fresh tire tracks on the snowpack and assumed Shelby had awakened and left for CrossFit from Monica's insulated garage—where Monica's pickup had not spent the night. *I have to stop thinking like that. She's my lover and guest, and I want her to be comfortable here.*

Shelby would shower at the CrossFit Box and go straight to work, so Monica wouldn't see her until that evening. Monica was secretly relieved because she wasn't sure she could look at Shelby the same way after meeting her former lover—a woman who was so out of Monica's league that her own self-doubt practically engulfed her. If Coco ever wanted Shelby back, Monica wondered how on earth Shelby would resist such beauty, athleticism, charm...

Monica was convinced that Shelby would drop Monica like a bad habit if Coco clicked her fingers. She sighed, chastising herself with internal dialogue. *Why do I let my curiosity get the best of me? What do I have to show for it, except jealous insecurity? Do I understand*

Shelby any better? Women in general? Mystery Shelby. Mystery Coco. Mystery Stela. I'm surrounded by mysterious women.

Monica turned off her truck and got out, only to be met by a man standing at the bottom of her stoop. Her heart skipped a beat on a jagged intake of breath. She hadn't seen him when she pulled in, and now wondered where he had come from. Had he been inside her house? She swallowed a scream and glanced over his face, barely visible under his hat and the down hood of his gray parka. His unshaven face had frost forming on black stubble, but she recognized the black glasses, hostile eyes and gray parka.

He advanced on her. "You remember me, Ms. Spade. I'm Stela's friend. The one who gave you money for her clothes."

Monica reflexively stepped back against her truck, a backstop that prevented her from escaping. She couldn't be sure whether she peed herself or her tights were sweaty from yoga, but the cool air snaked around her damp legs. "Of course. Why are you here?"

"That isn't a very polite greeting," he said.

Being accused of not being courteous to a menacing intruder confused her.

"No worries, Ms. Spade," he said, reading her mind. "This isn't a social call."

"What are you doing here?" she croaked.

"I need you to deliver something to Stela at the jail for me. Obviously, I can't visit her with the CIA watching. I saw Peter and Steven visit you last night."

On a first name basis? "They're CIA? They told me they were FBI."

He scoffed. "Peter is old-school CIA. Steven is a newbie. Peter and I were working on a project together, but our interests diverged when Stela got arrested."

"I didn't tell them anything," Monica said defensively. "I'm holding everything Stela tells me in confidence."

"I know you didn't." He shrugged. "I bugged your house."

She gasped. "You were in my house?"

"Of course," he said. "Don't bother looking for the microphones. You'll never find them."

Her blood ran cold. All of her conversations with Shelby—listened to by this shady, very scary, character. She mentally retraced everything she had said about Stela and the trial, silently congratulating herself for not telling Shelby much.

"Was that when I was...in...the shower the other day?" she sputtered

He nodded.

Her legs trembled now. "What do you want?"

"Keep lawyering for Stela. Keep Peter and Steven away from her. And..." He reached into his pocket and removed a small, plastic vial that he held out to her. "Give this to Stela."

She moved to accept it from him with her mitted hand, but their fingertips collided, and the vial fell to the ground. He reached down and grabbed it. The plastic was tan-colored like a prescription bottle, but the size of the vial was much smaller in diameter. She heard the rattle of what sounded like a single pill inside, as he carefully placed the vial in her outstretched chopper mitt.

His voice was colder than the air temp, as he said, "I'm trusting you to give this to Stela. Don't open it. Don't test it. Don't show it to anyone. Just give it to her."

"What is it?" Monica asked instinctively.

"Her health is none of your business. Just give it to her."

"Um…will there be more?" She shook the bottle and looked at it, confirming there was one pill inside.

"Never mind that!" he barked, scaring her. "You just need to follow instruction, and do what I tell you." His accent thickened, as he chopped off his words.

Monica didn't appreciate heavy-handedness by thugs or the feds, so instinct prompted her to push back. "Listen, Yuri, or whatever your name is, I'm not your drug mule, and I have half a mind to report that you've bugged my fucking house. You've completely invaded my privacy and are threatening me. I didn't sign up for this shit, and I'm not part of your international arms dealing ring, so don't try to suck me into—"

Suddenly, his large gloved hand was around her neck, and, with remarkable strength, he squeezed until she couldn't breathe. "You want to play hardball with me, you cunt? I teach you how we do business in my country, no?"

She wheezed for precious air, stars floating around her vision.

"You give this vial to Stela, or I'll take your sweet little Shelby for a drive in the country that she'll never forget. You understand?"

Monica tried to nod in acknowledgement, but her chin hit his gloved hand. Her eyes bugged out of her head, so she squeaked, "Yes."

He removed his hand, and she gulped for air, doubling over and placing her hands on her knees. The vial once again had fallen to the ground. She bent over and picked it up, as he loomed over her.

When she straightened, he stuck his face dangerously close to hers, his eyes predatory, and his breath like a dragon's. "I'm glad you see things my way."

"No worries," she rasped. "I'll give this to Stela. Will you be at the courthouse?"

"No," he said, and without further ado, turned, and disappeared around the back of her house, his large boots crunching on the packed snow.

Monica stared at the empty space that Yuri and his powerful grip had occupied only seconds earlier. She had the strange sensation of wondering if that entire exchange had really happened.

It all seemed so surreal, yet here she stood, her throbbing neck a testament to the grim truth. Visions of Shelby being attacked by him flashed through her mind, and she felt guilty beyond belief to have exposed her girlfriend to this mess. She had to warn Shelby to watch her back, but she didn't know how to do that without spilling the entire story, thereby endangering Shelby even more. She wanted no part of this deadly world.

23

Chilled to the bone and shaking uncontrollably, Monica entered her unlocked house. Once inside, she turned the bolt lock in the door, then stared at it, realizing with a chill that it was ineffective against Yuri. She kicked off her boots, and shed her coat, which was damp with sweat-induced trauma. She was relieved to discover she hadn't peed herself, though.

Mindful of the deep invasion of her privacy, she moved through her house in horrified silence, refusing to give Yuri any information through his clandestine microphones. Her mind raced with the possibilities of how she could out-maneuver the real-life checkmate in which she found herself, yet simultaneously fulfill her legal duties to the court, an entity to which she had taken an oath.

If she resigned as counsel, then surely Yuri would return, or worse, harm Shelby. Monica had to figure out a way to serve in her role while not setting herself up for blackmail. She was at an important crossroads.

She considered turning to Peter and Steven, since they seemed more powerful than the police, but they weren't even clever enough to find Yuri, and Steven seemed overly confident, emboldened by his badge. *Should I believe Yuri that Peter and Steven are CIA? Working with him?*

In a supreme state of paranoia and hopped up on adrenaline, she quickly showered and dressed for work. She needed a strategy that extricated her from Yuri's grip, but didn't piss off Dominique Bisset, Judge O'Brien, or Matt Breuer. Jim and Nathan could help her manage those relationships, since Jim was an extension of Dominique and Nathan of Matt. About the only thing she had going for her was the home-field advantage.

Later, when she entered her law office, she felt comforted by Kathy's smile and warm greeting. "I made a pot of oatmeal. It's on the stove in the kitchen."

Monica's usual enthusiasm for food was eclipsed by her sore trachea and the urgency with which she needed Jim's advice. "Thanks," she muttered. "Is Jim here yet?"

"He is," Kathy said, pointing with her thumb. "In the kitchen drinking coffee and eating oatmeal."

Monica dumped her coat and gear in her office and proceeded to the kitchen, where she turned up the volume on the morning news program, followed by turning on the faucet to a strong stream of water. Both acts invited a bewildered look from Jim. "What the—"

Monica shushed him with a finger to her lips.

He frowned and removed his half-glasses, setting them on a document he had been reading. "What's up, buttercup?"

She squinted in irritation and moved a chair close to him. She sat and relayed to him in a whisper-voice befitting of a church service what had transpired at her house that morning.

When she finished, he rubbed his beard, knocking off some oatmeal. "Guessing by the volume on the TV and running water, you think our offices might be bugged as well?"

She nodded.

"This Yuri character is probably bluffing," he said.

She glared at him.

He sighed. "I know a guy who specializes in electronics and bugs. He can sweep our offices, your house, and Shelby's house." He paused and stared at the coffee maker steaming. "He should probably sweep the DA's Office and Dominique's home as well."

The gravity of the situation hit home for both of them.

"Who knows?" she said, "Some of the bugs might be from the CIA, or FBI, or whoever Peter and Steven work for."

He frowned. "They wouldn't have probable cause to eavesdrop—"

"When did that ever stop them?" she sneered.

Sensing an overreaction nearby, he said, "Let's not jump to conclusions. We can address the immediate threat—that being Yuri—if he's the one who throttled you this morning."

"It would be nice to know if he really is Yuri Zaleski. Who's to say there aren't a couple of guys helping Stela?"

"I'm guessing this is a two-person team, and if you can believe anything he says, he's probably skipping town, and the country for that matter, because the FBI has probable cause to take him into custody and question him about buying radioactive materials."

"Peter and Steven also said they found three sets of DNA at the murder scene, so he probably was an accomplice to Andy's death."

"All of that tells me he's going to lay low or leave," Jim said. "In fact, there's probably a warrant out for his arrest."

"No matter where he is," she said, "he could still listen to our conversations through his bugs."

"I'll call my guy. Don't worry about it." He switched gears. "What about the pill in the vial? What do you suppose it is?"

"I asked him, but he wouldn't tell me," she said. "I wonder if it's some type of cancer-treatment drug. Stela told me to hire an oncologist to testify at her trial, so I'm guessing she has cancer."

"Cancer?" he exclaimed. "If that were the case, Stela could tell the jail nurse about her medical problem, and they'd bring her to Community Memorial Hospital for treatment."

"She probably doesn't realize that," Monica said. "She told me this is the nicest jail she's stayed in."

"Do you plan to deliver the pill to her soon, so you don't end up on her shit list?"

"Of course." Monica flicked a wisp of hair from her face, unaware of how agitated the gesture made her appear.

"In the meantime, you should warn Shelby—"

Jim was interrupted by a special news bulletin on TV. Tiffany Rose, as beautiful as a fresh flower, stood next to a highway in a white, snowy landscape. In the background, a blackish, brownish muck rolled over the brilliant, white snow, across the highway, and down the ditch, where a septic truck, festooned with hazardous waste triangles, lay on its side.

Tiffany was dressed in a white hazmat suit that was made for someone much larger. Both Jim and Monica looked up to Tiffany's voice, yelling against a strong wind that pummeled the microphone in her hand.

"I'm standing on County Highway F, and, in the distance behind me, you can see a septic truck that was hired by the Apple Grove Police to pump out Andy Nelson's septic tank, where they believe radioactive materials of enriched plutonium and uranium were located."

"I hope she's upwind," Jim said.

The camera briefly left Tiffany and focused on men in yellow hazmat suits, wearing specialized hoods with clear plastic facemasks, standing at the perimeter of the amoeba-shaped pool of waste, its dark contours a vivid contrast against the white snow.

The shiny, silver truck lay askew on its side halfway down a hill, the leakage of its contents having left a fifty-foot trail of muck.

"The driver was taken to a local hospital but is reported to be in fair condition," Tiffany said. "He told the police that he hit a patch of ice while going around a corner and slid off the road so quickly that he didn't have time to react."

"Holy shit!" Jim exclaimed.

"Glowing shit," Monica said.

Tiffany continued, "Since the spill is being treated as highly toxic with radioactive materials, the police have closed County Highway F in both directions. The road will remain closed until this mess is cleaned up. Here with me is Police Detective Matt Breuer."

The camera panned out to include Matt, Nathan's boyfriend, who was much taller and wider than Tiffany, actually filling out his one-size-fits-all hazmat suit.

"Detective Breuer, is there any danger to local residents?"

"No," Matt said in his deep, authoritative voice. "Fortunately, there aren't any homes along this stretch of road, so we aren't ordering any evacuations."

"When do you expect this mess to be cleaned up?" she asked.

"A replacement truck and specialized cleanup team are on the way," he said. "I'm hopeful that the area will be safe sometime tomorrow. They also have to excavate some soil along with the snow for remediation of the spill."

"Can you confirm that the spill is from Andy Nelson's septic system?" she asked.

"I can, and it is," he said.

"How does this relate to his murder?"

"We're not sure the radioactive waste in his septic system directly relates to his murder, but it does implicate him in stealing the material from *Voila!,* his employer."

"Has *Voila!* confirmed that it's missing nuclear material?"

"Yes."

"How much?"

"We haven't completed our investigation."

"Is the woman who is on trial for murdering him, Stela Reiter, involved in stealing radioactive materials from *Voila!?*"

"We haven't completed our investigation."

"Was she buying nukes from Andy Nelson?" Tiffany asked against the wind. "Is that why she murdered him? To silence him?"

"Again, Tiffany, I can't comment because we haven't completed our investigation."

"Will your investigation be completed in time for her trial?" she asked.

"I can't comment one way or the other."

"Thank you for your time, Detective Breuer."

The camera dropped Matt from the picture and focused on only Tiffany once more. "Again, if you joined us late, County Highway F is closed between the intersections of Priory and Giese Roads due to a radioactive spill from a septic truck that pumped out Andy Nelson's septic system, the man who was murdered by Stela Reiter, the Boyfriend Killer. I'm Tiffany Rose for WQOD news."

The screen indicated "Special Report" for a few seconds then went to a commercial.

Nathan chose that moment to enter the kitchen. "Good morning. Kathy said there's oatmeal in here." He stopped and looked at the loud TV, noted the running water in the sink, then looked down at Jim and Monica in confusion. "Why is the TV so loud? Why is the faucet on?"

Monica summoned him closer with the curl of her index finger. "We think the office has been bugged by Stela Reiter's accomplice, Yuri Zaleski. While he was choking me this morning, he told me that he bugged my house."

"What the fuck?" Nathan exclaimed then sat down and leaned in close.

In hushed tones, Monica and Jim relayed everything to him.

With his customary flare for the dramatic, he said a little too loudly for Monica's taste, "Those motherfuckers! Wait until Matt hears about this."

"You're not telling Matt," Monica said.

"Bullshit!" Nathan said urgently. "I don't know why you didn't call the police right away."

"Um, probably because I'm afraid Yuri will kill Shelby if I do."

"Right," he sighed. "Nonetheless, Matt stayed at your house during the last murder trial, so there's no reason he can't stay with you again. It sounds like you're up against some Ukrainian thugs."

"They're ruthless. A few days ago, Yuri was in my home while I was in the shower."

"What?" Jim and Nathan asked in unison.

"I got home from work and my bedroom light was on. I thought I must have left it on, but while I was in the shower, I heard the kitchen door. I thought it was Shelby, but when I got out, she had just arrived, so the sounds I heard while I was in the shower couldn't have been her. This morning, I asked Yuri, and he confirmed it."

Nathan slapped the table. "I've heard enough. Matt is staying with you."

Monica squirmed uncomfortably in her chair, scrunching her face in protest.

"I think you need to set aside your privacy with Shelby for the sake of your safety," Nathan said.

"It isn't our privacy I'm worried about," she groaned. "I'm worried about the optics of having the detective investigating Stela's case live with me while I'm her standby counsel. It's too cozy. It would look to her and Yuri, and the FBI for that matter, that we're in cahoots."

"That's going a little far—" Nathan began, but Jim cut him off.

"I agree with Monica," Jim said. "She needs to maintain an air of independence from law enforcement."

Monica nodded. "How about we just get rid of the bugs for now, and we worry about someone staying with us later? I have a bunch of stuff I need to do, not the least of which is to warn Shelby to be careful today."

"Good plan," Jim said, patting her shoulder. "I'll call my electronics guy. I need the keys to yours and Shelby's houses for him."

"They're in my office," she said. "I'll bring them to you."

They broke their conference. Once seated at her desk, Monica googled "cancer treatment pills," and at least eight oral chemotherapy drugs populated on her screen, all with unique names like Femara and Zytiga. She dug the vial out of her coat pocket and looked at the pill through the plastic. She couldn't see any writing on the oblong-shaped pill, so she shook it to flip it over. No writing on the opposite side either. Well, so much for that query.

Next, she emailed Stela at her jail account, telling her that she planned to stop by after work to deliver something. Monica didn't expect to hear back from her, but she thought it was wise to keep Stela in the loop. Having completed her task under the threat of Yuri's gloved hand, she turned to warning the love of her life.

She texted, *Hey, some things happened this morning on my case that mean you and I have to watch ourselves. Please have someone accompany you to your car after school and plan to stay with me tonight. I gave your house key to my partner, Jim, because he's going to have a guy sweep your house for hidden microphones. I know it sounds crazy, but it's a new reality. I can explain more in person later. Just watch your back today, okay? Sorry for this text, but I didn't want to call and interrupt your class. Call me if you want to talk. xxxooo*

Monica knew it was a shitty way to communicate a possible life-threatening situation, but she wanted to warn Shelby as soon as possible, and Shelby had told her she couldn't take phone calls during class, but she did periodically check her phone throughout the day.

Monica returned to her email inbox and discovered that Dominique had emailed her another file of police reports, documents, and photos. Monica quickly glanced through them, but didn't see anything exculpatory. She hastily forwarded the information to Stela.

For the remainder of the morning, Monica committed herself to analyzing the entire file that Dominique had sent. She pulled out her legal pad and flipped to the middle where she had left off. From the information provided in the police reports, Monica began to create a chronology of Stela and Andy's movements on the day of the murder. She also wrote down key facts about the crime scene, including that the murder weapon, a Trident paring knife, apparently matched a set in Andy's kitchen.

Usually, Monica would surmise that *he who owns the knife probably brought it to the party*. Given that Stela was Andy's lover and over at his house, however, she suspected Stela plucked it from his wooden block of knives in premeditation and brought it with her in the car that day. *Did Stela intend to kill him or just threaten him? Did he flush the pellets down the toilet to piss her off or was he panicking?*

24

As the January sun descended over the snowy horizon well before five, Monica stopped working on Stela's police file, marked her time down for reimbursement from the state, and turned off her computer. She was packing her things when Jim Daniels darkened her doorway.

"Hey, Jim. I was just headed to the jail to deliver Stela's pill."

"Good," he said, leaning against the jamb. "I'm not sure that's a kosher move, so you might want to keep it on the down-low."

"Right."

"I wanted to tell you what my electronics guy found."

She froze. "What?"

"You had bugs all over in your house," he said. "Your friend, Yuri, wasn't bluffing."

Her legs gave out, forcing her to sit back in her chair. "What are we going to do?"

"My guy removed them."

"How do we know he got all of them?"

"Trust me," Jim grunted. "If he found them in the first place, then he removed all of them."

She stared at him, paranoia gripping her. "What if there are smaller, more sophisticated ones that he couldn't detect?"

Jim shook his head. "It doesn't work like that. Your house is clean now."

"When Yuri figures that out, he might come back!"

"I have a plan for that too," he said.

She covered her face with her hands. "Did he find any at Dominique's office or home?"

"Yes."

"And?" She looked at him through her fingers.

"He found a few microphones at each place."

"I'm scared, Jim."

"No need to be," he said.

"Easy for you to say."

"I know." He scratched his beard. "I'd sleep better if a guy I know stayed at your house."

"Police?"

"No. He owns the shooting range. Ex-military. He does special assignments for me sometimes."

"God, I just don't know," she said in a bit of a whine. "Shelby and I like our privacy, and we're sort of early in our relationship."

"I get it," he said. "Why don't I ask Todd to arrive at your place about nine, after you and Shelby have enjoyed your evening together?"

She moved her hand to her neck, the pressure of Yuri's death grip still fresh in her memory. "As much as I don't like having to take this step, I have to admit that personal security sounds nice."

He clapped. "Excellent. Share a bottle of wine with Shelby, enjoy dinner, do whatever you do in the evenings, and Todd will ring your doorbell around nine."

"What does he look like?"

"Scary as hell, which is why I like to use him for assignments like this. Big red beard. Six feet, five inches tall. He makes other men shrink with just a glare."

"I like him already. I hope he fits in the extra bed. It's only a double."

"His feet will probably hang over, but I'm sure he's used to that."

"I look forward to meeting him. What does he charge?"

"Don't worry about it," he said. "We're going to add it to your bill to the state with an explanation when this trial is over."

"That's why we're partners. You think of everything." For the first time that day, she smiled. Her day had started out shitty, so she hoped against hope that it didn't end that way.

"All right," he said. "Go deliver the mystery medicine to Stela."

"Can't wait."

Monica arrived at the jail with renewed energy. Jim had been right about bugs and security. Having Todd stay over soothed her.

Bob waved her through security—which was good since she had a pill in her coat pocket that Jim told her wasn't allowed—and Cliff escorted her to the conference room.

"The Romanian Boyfriend Killer awaits you," he whispered before unlocking the door.

Monica was becoming so seasoned to the drill that she simply shook her head and rolled her eyes at him, drawing a smirk.

"I'll be right outside," he said.

"Thanks."

Monica entered to a sullen Stela. "Hey. I have something for you."

Rather than speak, Stela raised her chin, as if summoning a valet at a motel. Under the veneer of deadly killer was a second layer of arrogance.

Mindful of the security camera in the upper corner of the room, Monica sat across from Stela and unbuttoned the top button of her coat. "Rest your hands on the table in front of you."

Stela did as instructed in a casual, natural gesture.

Monica pulled out her legal pad and flipped back the pages to an arbitrary page with writing on it. She turned the pad and showed the arbitrary page of her notes to Stela. While Stela looked at it, Monica retrieved the vial from the inner pocket of her coat along with a black pen. She moved her hand, the vial hidden in her palm, pretending to point with the pen at a sentence. Simultaneously, Stela moved her palm next to Monica's, and Monica rolled the vial into it.

"I see you've been reading the police file," Stela said, pointing to the page for real.

"I made my way through it," Monica said. "I roughed up a few cross-examination outlines for the police detectives if you're interested."

Stela smiled, as she leaned back and casually moved her hands to her lap, where Monica assumed she did something with the vial.

"I might be. We'll see. Did you read Andy's journal entries? Pretty scary, no?"

Monica wasn't prepared to discuss Andy's sexual fantasies. "I read a few lines, but I couldn't really get into them. I'm not much for philosophy, especially about nonconsensual sex and cannibalism."

"I'm deciding which excerpts to use. I'll show them to you when I see you next."

"I look forward to it," Monica said, the instinct of deceit guiding her. She slid her legal pad back to her own side of the table and flipped the pages over to their resting place. "Anything else?"

"No," Stela said. "Thank you for bringing this. You have no idea what it means to me."

Monica nodded curtly. "Happy to be of service." She opened her mouth to add something about Yuri's stranglehold but decided against it.

"Is there something else?" Stela asked, her flat, assessing eyes scanning Monica's face.

"Um…Yeah." Monica cleared her suddenly-dry throat. "Your friend, Yuri, or whatever his name is, choked the shit out of me this morning."

A slow, satisfied smile spread across Stela's lips. "He can be very passionate about me."

Just the reaction Monica expected. "He doesn't need to choke me. Remember, I'm actually here to help."

Two sharp barks of laughter erupted form Stela. "Let's not pretend, Ms. Spade. You live here and work with these people." She raised a hand to the end of the shackle chain and motioned toward the outside.

"I took an oath to uphold the law, Ms. Reiter. Rest assured that I'll honor the legal and ethical duties that that my profession demands of me. There's no need to resort to violence."

There was a loud silence while Monica fought back the impulse to issue a few threats of her own.

Finally, Stela said, "He's gone now, so you don't have to worry."

Monica squinted, wondering how Stela knew Yuri was gone if she supposedly didn't have any contact with him. "Okay."

In a blatant change of topic, Stela asked, "Are you ready for my trial to start in two days?"

"What?" Monica wondered if she'd heard her correctly. "Two days?"

"Didn't you get the email from DA Bisset?" Stela asked.

"Email? When? I've been at my office all day."

"It came about 10 minutes before you arrived. The trial starts day after tomorrow. We have a lot of work to do. I'm sure I'll be up all night preparing."

"That's what you wanted, right?"

"Absolutely." Stela examined the nail on her left index finger then bit it. "The sooner, the better."

"I'll prepare some themes and notes. Want to meet tomorrow to go over your defense?"

"I prepare on my own. You can show me your notes in court on the first day."

"Will you be testifying?"

"Yes."

"Do you want to do a dry run of that?"

Stela smiled as if Monica's suggestions were childish. "Later."

"As you wish," Monica said. "Will there be anything else?"

"I'll need my clothes. Have you purchased them yet?"

"Um…Someone in my office is doing that. I'm sure she has. I'll have her deliver them directly to you tomorrow."

"Very well."

"Is there anything else you'd like to discuss?"

"No." Stela suddenly lapsed into thought, staring past Monica.

Monica was so accustomed to Stela yelling, "Guard," that she was surprised when she didn't. "Are we finished?"

"Yes," Stela said softly, then her head snapped up from her train of thought, and she yelled, "Guard!"

Even though Monica was expecting the shrill command, she still jumped. Judging by Stela's pouty smile, she was tickled.

Life's small pleasures.

Cliff opened the door and gestured for Monica to leave, waiting for Stela to walk in the opposite direction, the direction Monica didn't want to see or visit—ever.

As shocked as Monica was about the rapidity with which the court had scheduled the trial, especially since Detective Matt had told Tiffany in his interview that their investigation was still pending, part of Monica was relieved to get this assignment-from-hell over with. She didn't want any more contact with the killers, and would consider herself lucky to make it through the entire ordeal unscathed.

She practically ran out to her white truck and headed for home. When she turned into her quaint neighborhood, she waved at a few people walking their dogs. She entered her driveway and pushed the remote on her visor to open her garage door, expecting to see Shelby's Jeep ensconced there. The garage was empty, so Monica pulled in.

As soon as she was inside the house, before she could even kick off her boots, she texted Shelby. *Hey, r you coming over tonight? There r some things I need to explain.*

After changing into a thick pair of sweats and a hoodie over a tank, she checked her phone. Still no reply from Shelby.

Following routine, she went to the kitchen and poured herself a can of sparkling water over ice, while considering side dishes to go with chicken for dinner. As she assessed the veggies in the fridge, she thought it was uncharacteristic of Shelby not to reply to her text. Her heart lurched, so she called Shelby, who picked up right before Monica was going to click off.

"Yes?" Shelby asked curtly.

"Hey, gorgeous. You aren't replying to my texts. Is something wrong?" Monica asked, her stomach a ball of nerves.

"Are you spying on me?" Shelby asked.

"What?"

"You heard me. Are you digging into my past?"

"What do you mean?"

"I heard you're making friends over at the Yoga Studio." Shelby's tone was as cold as a hoar frost.

Monica had no idea what to say, since she was, in fact, guilty of satisfying her curiosity about Shelby's ex-lover—fucking Coco. In reality, her pre-dawn yoga session seemed so trivial now in light of the rest of her day.

"Well?" Shelby asked.

Monica took a calming breath and kept her tone even. "You know I go to hot yoga to stretch out. I'm a friendly person, but I wouldn't say I'm 'making friends' over there." She adopted a light note of curiosity. "Why do you ask?"

"Because word has it that you're flirting with my ex," Shelby said through gritted teeth.

Bingo. Mystery solved.

Monica attempted a nonchalant chuckle. "Shelby, you know I don't flirt with anyone but you, and even then, I'm not practiced in the art. I have no idea who your ex is, so this entire conversation is moot."

"Don't try fancy lawyer talk on me!" Shelby exclaimed, her voice rising in pitch and volume.

"Sorry. I was just trying to tell you that I didn't flirt with anyone at yoga."

There was a prolonged silence on the other end of the line.

25

After enduring few beats, Monica asked, "Can we discuss this in person, so I can tell you how much you mean to me, and I can reassure you that I'm not spying on anyone at yoga?" Even though she was, but not in the way Shelby thought. Well, probably exactly in the way Shelby thought.

"Not tonight," came the terse reply.

Monica felt a prickle of anger rise to the surface. "You know, if you'd just come clean and tell me who I'm supposed to avoid, it might make my life easier. I've been nothing but loving and loyal, but you kicked me out of your house when I asked you about your diamond stud, and now you're accusing me of something that completely and totally baffles me." Because her motives were altruistic; truly they were.

"Fine. I'll think about it."

Her voice still testy, Monica, said, "You do that. In the meantime, I'm going to live my life like a normal person, not trying to avoid these invisible land mines that you scattered all over town."

"Fuck you!" Shelby said unexpectedly, but Monica had the feeling Shelby had been itching to say it all along.

"See? That's what I'm talking about! Why the anger?"

"Because you're stirring up something that hurts!" Shelby yelled. "A lot!"

Monica's heart sank with the news that Shelby wasn't over Coco, the energetic sex magnet. *I'll never be able to compete with Coco.*

Shelby breathed hard on the other end, then, in a small voice, said, "Maybe we should take a breather."

Monica's heart constricted. "What does that mean?"

"I think I'll stay at my place tonight. We can catch up later this week."

Monica's careful security plan with Todd flashed through her mind. She'd sooner die than see any harm come to Shelby. Monica had brought Shelby into this mess, and she wouldn't leave her unprotected, regardless of Shelby's ambivalence about their relationship.

"Ah, listen," Monica said in a serious tone, "I wasn't joking earlier today when I texted that you need to be careful. A guy associated with Stela Reiter showed up at my house this morning and choked me."

"Choked you?" Shelby screamed. "Oh my God! How are you?"

"I'm fine now. I'm not telling you this because I want your sympathy. I'm telling you because he also threatened to harm you if I didn't do what he asked, so I arranged for security at my house tonight." She paused and sighed. "If you don't want to come over, I can send the security guy to your house. His name is Todd, and he'll be there at nine o'clock."

"But, what about you?" Shelby sputtered, "Is another guy coming to your house?"

"No," Monica said resolutely. "I did what he asked, so I shouldn't be in danger tonight. He knows who you are though, so…"

Shelby didn't speak, but Monica could hear her rummaging around, her breathing growing heavier with movement. "Fuck that. I'm coming over. Even though I'm angry, I won't steal your security guard. If there's only one guy, then we need to huddle together."

Relief flooded Monica.

"If I come over, do you promise not to ask me any questions about my ex?"

"Do you promise not to get angry at me for going to yoga?"

"Yes."

"Deal. I'll start dinner," Monica said.

"Be there in twenty minutes."

They rang off.

Monica reopened the fridge and removed a plastic container of chicken breasts marinating in teriyaki sauce. She grabbed some broccoli and washed and sliced it. Despite that mofo Yuri making her newly afraid of the dark, she planned to brave the deep freeze on her deck to grill the chicken. She'd be damned if she'd be forced into her house like a jail cell. Her cabin fever was already at an all-time high this January, so she wasn't about to compound it with a fear-based lock-in.

She opened a box of brown rice and quickly prepared it on the stovetop, then went outside to start the grill.

When she stepped onto the crunchy snow on her deck, she listened for anyone and anything, but it was cold and silent, not even a hoot from an owl or a yip from a coyote. She followed the narrow path to her grill and lifted the lid. The knobs were harder to turn in the extreme cold, but once she pressed the ignition switch, the flame came to life. She returned to the kitchen to stir the rice. The grill would need several minutes in this cold to warm up to a decent cooking temp.

She removed a pineapple from the fridge—a special shipment having arrived at the local market to ward off scurvy—and peeled and sliced half of it into thick discs. She planned to grill those and chop the other half for a light salsa.

As she thought about Stela, Yuri, and how they had used Andy, she diced tomato, sweet onion, and mango into a bowl, then ran outside with the platter of chicken breasts and placed them on the hot grill. She set the timer on her Apple Watch and returned to the kitchen.

Deep in thought about Stela and Yuri, Monica diced the avocado and added it to the salsa. She heard Shelby's Jeep in the drive, and a few seconds later, Shelby opened the kitchen door.

Monica stopped mid-air to read Shelby's expression—sweet princess or Tasmanian devil—

While Shelby's face was tight with tension, there was a flicker behind her soft, brown eyes that heated every fiber of Monica.

"Hey," Shelby said in a conciliatory tone.

"Hi, beautiful." Monica set down the knife and opened her arms.

"I'm so sorry," Shelby whispered, as she rushed to Monica. "I don't know what came over me. You were in class this morning with a friend of mine, Allison, and she said my ex was staring at you, then she flirted with you afterword."

Going in for the kill right away, Monica thought, but took satisfaction in learning that her suspicions about Coco-the-dazzling-blonde were correct. "I didn't notice any of that, hun, and I don't know who your ex is, so I'm in the dark here. Clearly, Allison, who I don't remember meeting, didn't tell you that I was oblivious to this entire subtext. I was there for yoga and only yoga." Which wasn't true, but sometimes romantic harmony demanded white lies.

Shelby pushed back enough to lock eyes with Monica. "I know that now. Here. In your arms, and seeing the honesty in your eyes, I believe you." Her smiled faltered, and her eyes suddenly misted over.

"Coco seduced me into an intense relationship then cheated on me, and all the while she insisted she was loyal. So, I went crazy with jealousy, and it turned out I was right. That was like, in the last year...so...once burned, twice shy, you know?"

"You mean, once burned, twice as suspicious?" Monica smiled, then adopted a more serious expression. "I'm not her. I won't cheat on you. I'm in love with you." Monica thumbed away a tear under Shelby's eye.

"Thank you." Shelby attempted to blink away the moisture, but a few more fell.

"I'm so sorry. That won't happen with me. You know that, right?"

Shelby anchored a wisp of Monica's hair around her ear then placed her thumb along Monica's jaw. "I've been trying to protect my heart and not give it to you because Coco broke it, and I barely had time to recover before I met you at CrossFit."

Broke it? Oh no, what if I'm her rebound? Monica thought, sure that the expression on her face portrayed her thoughts.

Shelby's gaze pinged between Monica's eyes, as she continued, "But the more time I spend with you, and look into your emerald eyes, so honest and sincere, I fall deeper in love with you. I just need time to assimilate coming off a big relationship and falling in love with you, okay?"

Monica kissed Shelby's forehead. "That sounds like a lot to process, especially since Coco-the-cunt still lives in town."

Shelby smiled then leaned into Monica and said into her neck, "Rivelli."

"Coco Rivelli? She has to be a sexy Italian, doesn't she?" Monica blurted before she could stop herself.

"Sicilian," Shelby murmured.

Great. She's probably a good cook too. And sensual lover. And, and…a hundred others things that I'm not.

Shelby continued torturing Monica by confiding, "We had talked about getting married, and she gave me the diamond stud as an engagement present. That's why I flipped out about it when you initially asked."

"Oh," Monica said against Shelby's forehead. *And you kept it?*

"Then she—"

The timer went off on Monica's Apple Watch, startling them.

Shelby pulled back. "What's that for?"

As much as she didn't want to throw a blanket on the big reveal, Monica broke contact and headed toward the sliding door. "I'm sorry. I need to put the chicken on the grill. Be back in a sec."

Shelby looked equal parts surprised and relieved, as Monica walked out the door. The cold air punched Monica in the gut but made her focus on something other than Shelby's fantastic former fiancée. She quickly added the chicken, and when she returned, she sensed a shift in the intimate confession. Shelby was standing at the stove, her back to Monica.

Monica strolled up behind her and wrapped her arms around her, lowering her face to Shelby's ear. "Thank you for confiding in me. If it makes you feel any better, I'll look up who the instructor is before I go to yoga, so I don't take any classes from Coco."

Monica felt Shelby's spine go rigid. "You'd do that for me?"

"Yes."

"Good." Shelby softened into Monica's body, even arching her butt against Monica's pussy. "The thought of her teaching you makes me sick to my stomach."

"Me too," Monica said, her curiosity about Shelby's past now mostly satisfied. "I can do less yoga and come to CrossFit more if you want."

Shelby lay her head against Monica's cheek. "I'd like that. I miss you at class."

"The next few weeks might be tough because the murder trial starts, but I'll try to come regularly after that. Not every day. But a couple of times a week, okay?"

"I hope I can make you come more than a couple of times a week," Shelby said in a seductive voice, quickly turning in Monica's arms and pressing her mouth to Monica's.

They were tongue-deep in a passionate kiss when Monica's Apple Watch timer went off again.

Shelby jumped. "We need to do something about that timer."

Monica planted another kiss on Shelby. "Let me finish grilling the chicken then take you to bed. We have a few hours before Todd gets here."

Shelby's eyes danced. "Fuck before dinner? How radical. I love switching up the routine."

Monica laughed and disappeared outside. When she returned, Shelby was quickly slicing the remainder of the avocado into the bowl. "Do you have any cilantro?"

"In the bottom drawer of the fridge." Monica tipped up her chin in the direction of the fridge while she set her watch to flip the chicken and pineapple slices.

While Shelby quickly chopped and added cilantro to the salsa, Monica turned off the rice and added a can of black beans to it. That could sit while they enjoyed their appetizer in bed.

Shelby placed plastic wrap over the salsa and set it in the fridge. "Are we ready?"

"Let me just grab the chicken and pineapple. She ran out to the grill and quickly put the chicken on a platter with the pineapple slices, coving them with aluminum foil."

As soon as she returned to the kitchen, Monica kissed Shelby silly until she broke briefly to lead her down the hall to her bedroom.

Once in the bedroom, Shelby looked fiercely into Monica's eyes before throwing herself at her in a frenzy of kisses and tangled limbs. She was nothing if she wasn't passionate. Monica staggered off balance before they toppled onto the bed, clothes flying off with speed and wild abandon.

If Monica had wanted slow and sultry, she was out of luck. Shelby's knee was already between Monica's legs, as Shelby stayed on top of Monica, kissing her neck, then moving lower. She ripped off Monica's bra, sucking Monica's nipple with a loud smack. Monica arched in delicious shock.

Shelby gingerly nipped Monica's nipple, sending her one sensation short of yelping, but a ripcord between her nipple and her hotspot pulled, as Shelby finally smothered Monica's breast in a sloppy, wet kiss. She positively devoured every inch of Monica's body, as she roamed downward, over her tummy and through her trimmed patch of hair to her center, where she glommed on so tightly that Monica squealed.

Shelby giggled in a low, guttural tone, as she mercilessly wolfed Monica until her hips rose off the bed in a crescendo of fireworks, leaving her breathless and ecstatic. She hadn't expected to come so fast, barely getting into the heat of lovemaking. As Monica floated down from the high, Shelby scooted up and kissed Monica's mouth with a sensuous, tangy kiss.

"I love you," Monica said when they broke apart. "That was awesome. One for the record books."

"I love you too," Shelby whispered, her own body writhing over Monica like a cat in heat.

Monica smiled at Shelby's wanton horniness. "How do you want it?"

"Any way you want to give it to me."

"Let me get my riding crop."

"What?"

Monica laughed.

***

Later, after they had napped and dressed, they sat at Monica's dining nook, the flickering candles casting a warm glow over Shelby's sated eyes.

"Why does food always taste so much better after sex?" Monica asked.

"And beer," Shelby said, sipping her light beer between bites.

They momentarily got lost in each other's smiles before returning to eating. Monica was ravenous from her busy day and bed sport, recalling that she hadn't eaten any of Kathy's treats at the office.

"What time does your security guy get here?" Shelby asked.

"Nine."

"Have you met him?"

"No."

"How will we know it's him?"

"Red beard. Big man."

"Tell me about your traumatic choking this morning."

"Ah, that's a hard pass."

Deep concern furrowed Shelby's eyebrows. "I'm worried about you. You won't tell me anything but you're clearly in danger. We're in danger."

"The less you know—"

Shelby spoke over Monica, "The better. I know. Fuck that. Who was he? I need to know what to look out for too, you know."

Shelby did have a point. Monica said, "Black hair. Black glasses. Gray parka. Medium build and height. I think his name is Yuri Zaleski. He's gone now, though."

"Thank you for telling me that much. What did he want you to do?"

"Deliver a pill to Stela Reiter at the jail."

Shelby blanched in surprise. "That hardly seems worth choking someone."

"He was showing me who's boss."

"Fuck, Mon."

"That's why the red-bearded Todd is staying with us."

"Do the police know?"

"Ah…"

Shelby put her hands on her hips and tilted her head.

"The people who need to know have been informed."

"Oh, for God's sake."

Later, as they were doing dishes, the evening news with Keith and Tiffany came on. Tiffany was once again at the radioactive septic spill site.

"As you can see," Tiffany said, making a wide, sweeping gesture with her arm, "there are protesters here." The camera panned wide to include a small group of people, at the front of which was the infamous Darcy Lemon. She was holding a sign that said, "Boycott *Voila!* for nuclear negligence!"

"Cool," Monica said. "There's Darcy. Maybe she'll focus on this cause now instead of her bogus lawsuit against the hospital where, I might add, her monkey enjoyed a few days of vacation from her."

Shelby laughed. "I can just picture a monkey frolicking down the hospital hallways, peeling a banana."

"That pretty much sums it up," Monica said.

Shelby pointed at the TV. "There are at least 15 protestors behind her, freezing their butts off in front of a toxic shit storm."

"Where does she find the time to organize these?" Monica asked rhetorically. "Doesn't she work for a living?"

"She's obviously very committed, but you know what?" Shelby said with sudden clarity, "We need people like her to remind us that things aren't always what the big corporations say they are."

Here we go… I like big corporations. They pay the bills. Monica decided an abrupt change of topic was needed before she and Shelby fell into political disagreement. "You know what we should do?"

"What?" Shelby scooted closer and ran her fingers over Monica's neck, making it difficult for Monica to remember what she had planned to say.

"After this trial, we should get the hell out of this frozen tundra and go on a vacation someplace warm."

"That sounds nice. You know I can't leave until school spring break, right?"

Right. Forgot about that. "When is that, exactly?"

"The third week of March."

"That's not very far away," Monica said. "Where would you like to go?"

"You mean, 'where can I afford?'"

"How about where *we* can afford if we pool our resources?"

Shelby glowed with excitement. "Someplace exotic and romantic!"

"With deep blue waters and a white, sandy beach."

"Not Costa Rica," Shelby said with a scowl.

Monica eyed her suspiciously. "Got it. I assume you went there with Coco-the-cheating-cunt, so we don't need to belabor it."

Shelby nodded then narrowed her eyes. "You don't need to be jealous, you know."

"I'll make a note."

After googling vacation spots and dreaming together, they made some tentative plans. The doorbell rang, startling them, and this time, Shelby overreacted, throwing a pillow across the room.

Monica laughed and rose. "Relax. I'm sure it's Todd." She walked to the front door, and through the porch windows, she saw something akin to Hagrid with the reddest beard she'd ever seen.

26

Two days later

A cross-section of 60 Apple Grove residents sat in the gallery of Judge O'Brien's courtroom. Selected from the registered voter rosters, these 60 unlucky people comprised the jury pool for the Boyfriend Killer trial.

Through the process of *voir dire*, the large number would be winnowed to 14 people who would sit through the trial, and, of those, 12 would remain to deliberate and come to a verdict. Two people served as extras in the event illness or some other family emergency required a juror to leave. If all 14 were still present at the end of the trial, there would be a random selection of two names from an old fashioned tumbler. Those two jurors would be thanked for their service and dismissed by the judge.

Presently, a low level of chatter spread over the jury pool until the side door to the court opened, and Stela appeared, escorted by two sheriff's deputies who were assigned for the duration of the trial. They would briefly tag out for breaks, but otherwise would provide a constant sentinel.

Through a brown curtain of somewhat greasy bangs, Stela glanced at the massive pool of people, as she walked timidly to the counsel table where Monica awaited her. Stela's bearing was all a carefully orchestrated act for the potential jurors and TV cameras. She stood next to Monica and placed her three-ring binder in front of her on the counsel table. Monica was impressed that Stela had created a trial binder at all, much less one so complete, the tabs indicating her outlines for examining various witnesses, her opening statement, and her closing argument.

Next to the trial binder, Stela lay a Redrope stuffed full of papers that included exhibits, photographs and medical articles.

Judge O'Brien was announced by the court secretary, as he bustled in, commanding everyone to sit, as he, too, quickly lowered himself to his leather chair.

Ever-conscious of the TV audience and people directly behind her, Stela carefully tucked her gray skirt with both hands in a lady-like gesture, as she sat in her chair and rolled up to the table. She smoothed down her pink cardigan and looked expectantly at Judge O'Brien.

He welcomed the room full of potential jurors then had the court secretary randomly select 14 people to come forward and be seated in the jury box for questioning. He would first ask the jurors questions to determine their suitability to serve with an open mind, objectivity, and most importantly, no overt bias, then, the DA and the defendant would have a crack at them.

Judge O'Brien used about an hour to question each individual juror, dismissing a few because their relatives either worked at the police station or courthouse or they, themselves, had been through the criminal justice system and had opinions oh-so-strong that they professed lack of objectivity. By 10:30 a.m., everyone who remained looked like their eyeballs were floating, so the judge ordered a fifteen-minute restroom break.

Stela left with her female deputy escort to use the restroom too. She returned quickly, well before the jury. Monica observed Stela draw a matrix of 14 squares on a paper then number the boxes. Either Stela had read a book on jury selection, or she had done it before, because the matrix was the first step in keeping track of who was who, so that each party could exercise three peremptory strikes to rid the jury of someone who appeared biased against them for one reason or another.

After the break, everyone resumed their seats, and the judge invited Dominique to ask her list of questions. He'd heard Dominique's inquiries many times during criminal trials, so he relaxed and looked at his computer screen.

Dominique adjusted the left lapel of her suit and leaned into the microphone on her counsel table. "Thank you, Your Honor. I, too, would like to remind the jury that this is a homicide case, so we will be discussing the details of the stabbing and showing photos of the scene to the jury. Are there any of you who, for one reason or another, would have trouble looking at that evidence and deliberating over it?"

One man in the back row raised his hand, juror number eight. Stela marked his box.

"Yes, sir," Dominique said. "You raised your hand?"

"Yeah. I don't think I could handle that."

"What do you do for work?"

"I take tickets at Carmike Cinemas," he said, "and I play video games in my free time."

"What kind of video games?" she asked.

"Just video games," he mumbled then looked down at his lap.

"Is there some specific reason you couldn't listen to or look at the evidence in this case?"

"My childhood," he said, still looking at his lap.

"I see. Thank you," Dominique said, then looked expectantly at Judge O'Brien.

"You may be excused, Mr. Olson," Judge O'Brien said.

The gamer rose and clumsily scurried out of the jury box.

The court secretary called another name and a new person walked from the gallery to the jury box, taking the gamer's warm seat. Stela erased Olson's name from her juror matrix and replaced it with the new person.

A real pro, Monica thought, *using a pencil rather than a pen. She's obviously done this before.*

Dominique continued with her questions. "I'd like to point out that the defendant is originally from Romania and holds a Romanian passport. Do you all feel that you can be objective regarding the defendant's national origin, as you consider the facts of this case?"

A plump, sturdy-looking woman in her mid-seventies raised her hand from the back row.

"Yes?" Dominique asked, then glanced down at her matrix. "Mrs. Popa?"

"Is it okay that I'm first-generation Romanian?" Mrs. Popa asked, her red-colored hair shimmering under the fluorescent lights.

"Can you be objective and apply the law to the facts of the case, as the judge instructs you?" Dominique asked.

"I think so. I'm proud to be Romanian. The defendant," Mrs. Popa pointed at Stela, "sort of reminds me of my granddaughter, who's in college now."

Stela smiled sweetly at the grandmotherly compliment.

"Thank you." Dominique wrote a note to herself on her matrix and proceeded with her questions. As the process continued, two more jurors were replaced with new ones, so Dominique had to circle back and repeat some of her questions for them. Time slowed to a glacial pace, and just when Monica was losing concentration in the tedium, Dominique announced she was done.

Judge O'Brien turned to Stela. "Does the defendant have any questions for *voir dire?*"

Stela attempted to charm the jury with her demeanor and smile. "I apologize for asking this, but it's all part of the process," Stela gestured toward the judge and prosecutor's table. "Is there anything about me—the way I look, talk, dress or behave—that you don't like? Anything at all that might interfere with your ability to remain objective during this trial?"

A gentleman in blue trousers and a sweater raised his hand.

Stela looked down at her matrix of names. "Yes, Mr. Everhart?"

His face twitched, and his eyes darted around the room before they came to rest on Stela. "No offense, but I don't care for you at all. The way you look, talk, anything. I didn't know the victim, but I just find a hard time believing anything you say, so….ah…no matter what you do here…" He thrust his arm out in an angry gesture, "I think you're guilty as hell, and I'd put you in jail and throw away the key." He jutted out his chin at her in defiance.

"Very well," Stela said in a saccharine voice. She turned to Judge O'Brien, expecting him to excuse the juror, but he didn't. She waited an interminable minute, but he just looked at her.

"Do you have any other questions for the jury?" Judge O'Brien asked her.

"Yes. I'll be brief." Stela regrouped at Judge O'Brien's refusal to excuse the juror for cause, made a notation on her matrix, and directed her attention toward the jury as a whole. "Would any of you have a problem hearing evidence that I acted in self-defense when my boyfriend was trying to fulfill some BDSM fantasy about having sex with a woman who was screaming and bleeding?"

No one raised a hand.

"Would those facts affect you so deeply that you couldn't be objective and follow the judge's instructions?"

No one raised a hand.

"Nothing further, Your Honor," Stela said.

"Okay," Judge O'Brien said. "At this time, I would ask the prosecution and defendant to use their peremptory strikes on paper to strike any remaining jurors currently seated.

Surprised that the judge made her use a strike, Stela wrote down Mr. Everhart's name and handed the piece of paper to Dominique, who wrote down Mrs. Popa.

As soon as Stela saw Dominique's strike of Mrs. Popa, she looked at Judge O'Brien, and asked, "May we approach the bench, Your Honor?"

Monica couldn't tell who was more surprised—Judge O'Brien or Dominique.

"Please do," Judge O'Brien said, giving the impression it was normal practice for a *pro se* defendant to make such a request.

Dominique led, followed by Stela and Monica. The female bailiff positioned herself between the judge and Stela.

Judge O'Brien covered the microphone with his hand and leaned down, directing his comment at Stela. "I hope you understand that having a conference outside the hearing of the jury at the bench is a practice to be used sparingly."

"Of course, Your Honor," Stela said impatiently in the manner of someone who already knew that and was anxious to move on. "When you hear my concern, I think you and the District Attorney will be relieved that I didn't say it out loud."

"What is it?" he asked.

Stela handed the peremptory strike sheet to the judge. "The District Attorney struck Mrs. Alina Popa, juror number 11, the Romanian immigrant."

Judge O'Brien peered over his glasses at Dominique. She shrugged. He returned his attention to Stela. "And?"

"I object because the only basis upon which the District Attorney exercised her strike was Mrs. Popa's national origin. That's unlawful discrimination."

Judge O'Brien squinted his eyes and looked at Dominique. "Any response?"

"That's absurd," Dominique said, her nostrils flaring. "I based my strike on the fact that Mrs. Popa looked adoringly at the defendant and said she reminded her of her granddaughter. National origin was incidental."

The judge nodded. "That's true." He swiveled his eyes back to Stela.

Stela's eyes remained flat and her voice devoid of passion, all sweetness gone. "Because she's Romanian, and I'm Romanian. That was the reason Mrs. Popa verbalized. National origin. Then, the District Attorney asked Mrs. Popa if she could be objective, and Mrs. Popa said yes. She said yes. That should be the end of it. If the District Attorney is now striking Mrs. Popa, then the only reason can be that of national origin, and that's discriminatory."

Monica watched Judge O'Brien process Stela's argument—obviously a new one for him. There was no doubt in Monica's mind that he was calculating whether he could be overruled by the Court of Appeals for granting Dominique's strike of Mrs. Popa in the face of a discrimination claim by Stela.

Stela had clearly set Dominique back on her heels, and it showed in her rigid body posture and shallow breathing.

After weighing the legal arguments, most likely forming a decision that he thought would be bulletproof on appeal, Judge O'Brien said, "I'm going to deny the prosecution's strike of Mrs. Popa because it was motivated by a shared national origin with the defendant. Mrs. Popa indicated she could be objective, so she can stay on the jury. I'll keep the strike sheet here for the record. If that's all, counsel and the defendant can return to your tables."

Dominique turned, her face frozen in shock, and walked back to her table like a robot.

Stela practically skipped back to her table in her gray skirt and pink cardigan, looking like a school girl who had just won the spelling bee. Once seated, she leaned over and whispered to Monica, "I think Dominique was just adjudicated a racist."

Monica nodded in disbelief. If this was a harbinger of what was to come, Monica was in store for a show. She didn't dare glance in Dominique's direction.

27

After they replaced the angry Mr. Everhart, the final, complete jury was seated. Judge O'Brien dismissed the larger pool of people who waited restlessly in the gallery. Disguising their smiles, so their friends and neighbors who remained in the jury box wouldn't see their relief, the dismissed folks quickly grabbed their outerwear and fled from the civil duty of deliberating a gruesome murder trial.

Lucky bastards, Monica thought, as she watched them go.

"At this time," Judge O'Brien said, addressing the jury, "you are the 14 jurors who will remain for the duration of this two-week trial. We usually start court at 8:30 a.m. every morning and go until about 4:30 p.m. each afternoon. I usually have a break at 10:15 in the morning and another one at about 3:00 in the afternoon. Whether the jury goes out for lunch or orders in, our lunch break is about one hour. Does anyone have any special dietary requests or problems with this schedule?"

A young female juror raised her hand and Isla, the elderly jury bailiff, dashed over to her. They had a hushed conversation, then Isla went to the Judge's bench and conveyed the message in whispered tones.

The judge nodded his understanding, and Isla returned to her seat. Judge O'Brien thought about his choice of words for a second, then said, "We're going to revise the schedule somewhat. We'll break for lunch around 12:45 each day for an hour. After we resume court, we'll take a break a few hours later. For the first couple of days, our afternoon will be flexible until we fall into a routine. Does this sound acceptable to everyone?"

Even though he used the word "everyone," he specifically focused on the juror who had relayed her request to Isla. She smiled and angled her head, patting her heart. The women on the jury warmed to Judge O'Brien for his accommodation, and Isla looked proud of herself, winking at the young female.

"What was that all about?" Stela asked Monica.

"Looks like that juror has a special need. I'll find out at break."

"Do that. It might affect my case."

Exercising great restraint, Monica didn't say, *Not everything is about you,* because the reality was that this entire trial was about Stela. *She probably has the IQ of a genius*, Monica thought. *And she's paranoid, but that's probably the result of her line of work. Who wouldn't be? Am I paranoid if a guy shows up at my house and strangles me?*

Judge O'Brien cleared his gravelly throat and resumed speaking. "Okay, since it's about lunchtime now, we're going to break. I understand your box lunches are here. When you return, I'll read some instructions to you, then each party will give their opening statements. At this time, the jury is excused. All rise."

Everyone in the gallery rose and watched the jury unenthusiastically shuffle out, with the exception of the Romanian grandmother, who had a spring in her step and a smile on her face.

After the jury left and everyone resumed their seats, Judge O'Brien asked, "Is there anything the parties would like to take up before we break?"

Out of habit, he looked at Dominique first, and she shook her head no.

Almost reluctantly, he swiveled his gaze to Stela, who had her hand raised slightly and her index finger pointed toward the ceiling, indicating she wanted to be heard.

"Yes, Ms. Reiter?" he asked.

"I do have a pre-trial motion, Your Honor."

"Please, go on." He flicked his hand, the sleeve of his black robe flaring.

Stela scooted up to the microphone, her shoulders hunched, her elbows resting on the table. "I move the court for an order prohibiting the prosecution from using the word 'murder' during this trial." Her tone was so polite that she could have been ordering a burger and fries.

Dominique wasn't amused. Every strand of her platinum, shoulder-length hair swung in concert, as she turned to look at Stela in disbelief.

"Do you have a basis for this motion?" Judge O'Brien asked.

"Yes," Stela said. "It isn't that uncommon of a motion because "murder" is different than homicide, and I'm charged with first degree intentional homicide. Not all homicides are a crime, but murder is, in fact, the unlawful taking of someone's life with malice aforethought." She paused and watched the judge absorb her tsunami of semantics.

"I'm not sure I follow," he said, "can you elaborate?"

"Even though Andy Nelson died by homicide, it was justifiable in this case because he was assaulting me with the intent to kill me. At least, I thought he was going to kill me. So, I engaged in justifiable homicide, not murder. There is no 'justifiable murder' under the law. While it may seem like I'm parsing words, like it or not, words are the currency of advocacy, and I'm striving for accuracy here."

She continued, "The prosecution is going to pummel the jury with the term over and over—murder, murder, murder—to the point where, subconsciously, the jury will equate my act of self-defense with murder, which can never be justifiable under the law. In this case, the prejudice to me by the prosecution using the term 'murder' far outweighs its probative value, of which there is none, of course, because advocacy isn't evidence."

Stela briefly glanced over at Dominique, who stared straight ahead, possibly in shock, but Monica couldn't tell, because her expression was once gain inscrutable.

Stela lowered her voice and continued, "There is absolutely no harm in prohibiting the prosecution from using the word 'murder,' because they still get to describe their case in legal terms of 'first degree intentional homicide.' On the other hand, there's a distinct, definable, and irreparable harm to me from which I won't be able to recover while explaining, and proving, self-defense that required my use of deadly force in a justifiable homicide." She stopped briefly, gathering her thoughts for a summation.

Her face pink with passion, Stela said, "I believe this very issue went to the Supreme Court of the United States, and the Supreme Court upheld the lower court's ruling in favor of the defendant on this issue, barring the prosecution from using the word 'murder' in a homicide trial. That case is on all fours with mine, because that defendant was engaged in a struggle with the victim and used deadly force in self-defense as well."

"What's the citation for the Supreme Court case?" Judge O'Brien asked.

Stela glanced down at her trial notebook, and there was a single case written in blue ink under the heading "Pre-Trial Motion." She read it aloud. "State versus Martinez, 184 S. Ct. 324 (1984)."

"Okay, I'll read the case over lunch and rule on your motion when we resume in 30 minutes. That will give us plenty of time before I bring the jury back in. If either side has any more matters to bring up before opening statements, please do so when we return. Court is hereby adjourned for 30 minutes." He slammed his gavel and rose.

After he left, Stela turned to Monica. "Read this case and tell me if I'm missing anything. Let me know what you think Dominique's comeback will be, okay?"

"Right. I'll do that while I eat my peanut butter and jelly sandwich. See you in thirty." She watched as the deputies escorted Stela to the side-door. Monica was surprised that Stela had left her three-ring binder on the table.

"Stela," Monica said.

"Yes?"

"Do you want your binder?"

"No need," Stela said. "I have my opening memorized, and I assume no one will touch my work product." To punctuate that statement, she peered around Monica and locked eyes with Dominique, whose expression was a study in apathy.

After Stela disappeared with the deputies, Dominique floated over to Monica. "So, what gives? Are you feeding her all of that caselaw, or did she go to Harvard Law School before she became a 'murderer?'" Dominique said in conscious imitation of Stela.

Monica raised her eyebrows. "I've haven't given her any caselaw—mostly because I've never been involved in a case like this—and she hasn't discussed her arguments with me. Although, she did ask me to read the Supreme Court case over lunch. Are you familiar with it? Is it still good law?"

"Yes, it's still the law, but under very narrow circumstances that don't apply here. I'd tell you what I'm going to argue, but I don't want to put you in an ethical bind."

"I understand. No need." She let that topic die before saying, "Do you know what the issue was with respect to the young, female juror, and why she requested the judge to change the daily schedule?"

"Yes," Dominique said, "She needs to pump breast milk every day at 1:30 and 4:30. That's what Isla relayed to the judge."

"Oh," Monica said. "Good for her, and I'm glad Judge O'Brien accommodated that."

"Me too," Dominique said, turning back to her table. "Off to lunch."

"I think I'll sit here and eat my sandwich," Monica said, googling the case that Stela had cited.

As she was a few pages into the case, Tiffany approached her. "Hey, Mon."

Monica's eyes traveled to Tiffany's short dress, the fabric of which was more befitting of a summer barbecue than a winter trial. Monica wondered how Tiffany's bare legs survived the cold from her car to the courthouse doors. "Hi."

Tiffany rested a hand on counsel table next to Monica's laptop, and tilted her hips in a sexy pose. "What do you think of the Boyfriend Killer's request to prohibit the prosecution from using the word 'murder?'"

"No comment, Tiff. You know I'm not going to give you quotes during trial, right?"

Tiffany slumped with a pout. "Fine. Talk after court, though?"

"I'll think about it," Monica said.

Tiffany squinted hard at Monica then sashayed to the back of the courtroom.

Amused, Monica watched her until her eyes caught like a fish hook on two gaunt gentlemen in black suits sitting in the gallery. Agents McCoy and Scott. She tipped her chin, and they nodded in return, reminding her that they wanted something from her.

She returned to reading the case at hand, quickly eating her sandwich. As her eyes traveled over the words, she thought about the evening she had enjoyed with Shelby, exploring vacation possibilities in either Belize or Hawaii. They hadn't made a final decision, so Shelby planned to follow up on resorts and airfares today between classes.

After glancing through the case, Monica used the restroom and returned to see Dominique and her paralegal, Lori, at their counsel table. The judge bustled in and ordered the bailiff to bring in Stela, who entered a few seconds later with her deputy detail. She looked surprisingly rested and calm, not like someone who was about to put her life on the line while advocating her own case.

Judge O'Brien turned to Dominique. "Let's go on the record. Does the prosecution wish to be heard on the defendant's motion about the use of the word 'murder?'"

"Yes," Dominique said. "The case cited by the defendant is outdated and not on all fours with this case, as represented by the defendant. The Supreme Court has ruled in later cases that *State versus Martinez* was a unique case, and should be construed narrowly. As a result, it's rarely cited as precedent. Recently, in another Supreme Court opinion, Chief Justice Roberts opined that state law should be followed, and matters of terminology should be decided by the trial judge in his or her discretion. Under the law of

Wisconsin, it's perfectly appropriate for the prosecution to use the word 'murder' during a homicide case, even though the statute uses the word 'homicide.' Here, we've charged the defendant with first degree intentional homicide, which is the same as murder. Both require 'malice aforethought,' which doesn't mean days of planning, it just means premeditation in the sense that the defendant planned, or designed, the murder before the act of killing occurred. We will show the steps the defendant took on that day to kill Andy Nelson to satisfy the state's burden. She murdered him, and the State should be allowed to use that term when describing her conduct. That's the law of Wisconsin." Dominique rested.

"Any response from the defendant?" Judge O'Brien asked.

"I think the prosecution just made my argument, Your Honor," Stela said. "The statute uses the term 'homicide' not 'murder.' We all know, and the court can take judicial notice of the fact, that the word 'murder' is used in everyday language to mean an illegal killing. That's not what happened here, so I should not be prejudiced by the prosecution repeatedly using that word." Stela leaned away from the microphone and rested her hands in her lap, her thumbs rubbing over her knuckles like a dog licking a wound.

"Very well," Judge O'Brien said. "I read the case myself over lunch. Having heard both parties' arguments on the matter, I hereby rule that the prosecution is prohibited from using the word 'murder' during this trial. The prosecution should hew to the statutory language of homicide. Is there anything else before we bring the jury back in?"

Dominique seethed. Stela had scored a huge point, boxing in Dominique. What a pain in the ass, Monica thought, which is, no doubt, what Stela had plotted all along—to be a pain in Dominique's ass and throw her off her game.

"I do have something else," Stela said.

"What would that be?" Judge O'Brien asked impatiently.

Stela removed a stack of photos from her Redrope file. All were numbered with white stickers. "The prosecution provided 30 photos to me a few days ago that she intends to use during opening statement and in her case in chief."

"Yes?" Judge O'Brien asked.

"I move that some of the photos not be displayed on the overhead screens."

Judge O'Brien indicated genuine interest in this motion. "What photos are you referring to, Ms. Reiter?"

"There are several taken of me at the hospital, Your Honor, if I can direct you to the prosecution's exhibits 11 through 18. Of those, I'm nude in a few that capture the cut marks to my groin area and upper thigh. I move that those not be displayed on the overhead screens, but published privately to the jury."

"Any objection?" Judge O'Brien asked of Dominique.

"Yes," Dominique said. "These photos demonstrate self-cutting by the defendant, which is a cornerstone of the prosecution's case—that she killed Mr. Nelson then stayed at the scene and cut herself to make it look like self-defense. The photos will help establish her deliberate self-cutting. In addition, the SANE nurse and ED physician are expected to use them during their testimony."

"Is there any reason they can't be circulated only to the jury during the nurse and physician testimony?" Judge O'Brien asked.

"Yes," Dominique said, "it will make it more difficult for me to question the witnesses on the specific style of cutting. I'd like them to point with the laser on the big screen while they testify."

Stela started to speak, but the judge held up his hand to stop her. "I think their testimony will go smoothly by privately publishing the photos to the jury. I hereby rule that the nude photos will not be shown on the overhead screens."

Stela checked off an item on her list.

"Any other photos?" Judge O'Brien asked Stela, in a business-like tone that he routinely used with lawyers, dropping his earlier weary tone.

"Yes," Stela said. "The photos of the autopsy numbered 22 through 28 have problems, Your Honor."

"Just a second, let me get there," Judge O'Brien said, turning to them. "Those are photos of some of the stab wounds. What's the problem?"

"These photos—lacerations to the neck, stab wounds to the head and abdomen—are not only unduly gruesome and unnecessary to the State's case, but inflammatory and prejudicial to my case."

"How so?" Judge O'Brien appeared genuinely curious.

"Well, for instance, despite the clean cut to Andy's neck," Stela said, using his name without a hitch in her voice, "this photo at the medical examiner's office looks like I took a chunk out of his neck. The reality is that his skin was finely cut with one swipe." Stela demonstrated with a single-handed slice through the air.

Monica instinctively flinched.

Unaware of how incriminating the gesture looked, Stela continued, "but the neck skin flaps later fell open—possibly during transport of the body— making the precise slice look like I chopped at him." She tsked. "It looks amateurish and sloppy, but more importantly, if some of the jurors are visual learners, they might think, 'Oh my gosh, she really butchered him.' Whereas, in reality, they were quite precise and small, and executed very quickly. Almost painlessly."

Stela's revealing account sucked all the oxygen from the courtroom, drawing a sob from Andy Nelson's mother, Sharon. Stela had just admitted she was a professional killer with a knife, tantamount to a surgeon, who usually took pride in the precision of her deadly slashes. But here, the neck incisions later fell open, resembling a sloppy hack job that was unbefitting of a professional.

No stranger to interacting with violent criminals, even Judge O'Brien looked rattled by the description. "Ahem. Would the prosecution care to address displaying the neck wound photos on the overhead screens?"

"Yes," Dominique said, standing. Monica could tell she was bristling, her own professional pride on the line, especially since she had lost the 'murder' motion. "The photos need to be published to the jury and on the big screen while the pathologist testifies. When the defendant slashed Andy Nelson's neck, that's what the wound looked like when he reached the medical examiner's office. No one tampered with the wound. It's an accurate depiction of a knife wound to the neck. It also establishes the force used, and apparently the lack of professionalism involved, based on the defendant's remarks,"

"Objection!" Stela exclaimed, jolting Judge O'Brien.

"The jury isn't present, Ms. Reiter, so you don't need to object." He regarded her. "What are you objecting to?"

Monica realized in that moment that Judge O'Brien's perspective of Stela had changed—he was treating her with more respect. She could almost hear him thinking that this was a once-in-a-lifetime experience from the bench, as he regarded Stela with genuine fascination.

Stela said, "The prosecution's use of the phrase, 'professionalism.' It's just this type of careless language and overt prejudice that I fear DA Bisset will use in front of the jury. I will be forced to move for a mistrial if the DA attempts to paint me as an assassin or experienced killer when the jury is present. We all know that past crimes aren't admissible to show intent in the present case."

A chill spread through Monica's body. If there had been any doubt about Stela's violent past, she had laid that to rest today as quickly as she had killed Andy.

Judge O'Brien nodded thoughtfully. "Understood. I don't think that will be necessary, but thank you for the reminder." He turned to Dominique. "Please continue, District Attorney Bisset."

Dominique shook her head at the insanity. "Anyway, as I was saying, the defendant can cross-examine the pathologist about the skin flaps on the neck regarding what happens to a wound during transfer. All of these wound photos," Dominique gestured to the stack on her counsel table, "demonstrate the amount of force the defendant used—like stabbing the victim in the temporal skull and deeply into his organs. The photos are evidence of intentional homicide versus defensive cuts made during the act of protecting oneself. Even the number of wounds—13 to be precise—seems to go beyond the pale of self-defense." Dominique paused and looked squarely at Stela. "Certainly beyond the pale of a professional."

Stela's eye twitched and her hand flinched.

Monica scooted her chair back a few feet.

Dominique resumed. "I don't ask jurors lightly to look at bloody, gruesome photos, but when a homicide involves sharp-force injuries from a kitchen knife, the jurors need to see the wounds to understand the material facts of the case. Like, the amount of blood that would be lost from each wound and what the defendant claims Mr. Nelson was doing while the defendant stabbed him in the head. If we aren't allowed to publish these photos to the jury and on the screens, then why are we here?"

Judge O'Brien rubbed his eyes then shoved his square glasses back on his head. "Having heard both sides, I agree with the prosecution and will rule that all of the autopsy photos will be shown to the jury in their entirety as material evidence in this case, as well as projected on the big screen. While gruesome, this is a homicide trial, so bloody, gruesome photos are to be expected. Is there anything else before we bring the jury back in?"

Stela sighed. "Not at this time, Your Honor."

Even though she didn't get everything she wanted, she certainly knows how to shape a case for trial, Monica thought.

"Okay," Judge O'Brien said. "Here's another reminder for both parties before the jury comes in. Let's keep opening statements to the facts. This isn't an opportunity for argument. Having said that, however, I don't want a bunch of objections from either party during opening statements. Let's be respectful. If you must object, then approach the bench. Understood?"

Both Dominique and Stela nodded.

"Bailiff, please bring in the jury."

28

The jurors resumed their seats in the box, looking well-fed and alert for opening statements. If there was an award for enthusiastic juror expressions, Mrs. Popa would have won. She positively glowed warmth as she stole glances at Stela.

Judge O'Brien called the court to order, read instructions to the jury about opening statements, including telling them they weren't allowed to take notes because openings weren't evidence, then invited Dominique to address the jury.

Dominique, wearing a black A-line skirt and a wine-colored herringbone jacket, moved to the podium in front of the jury box. She placed her yellow legal pad, plump with handwritten notes, in front of her and flipped back the first few pages. She took a deep breath and adjusted the left lapel of her blazer, which had an American flag pin on it.

"Ladies and gentlemen of the jury. This is a homicide case. Stela Reiter, the woman sitting before you today at counsel table," Dominique stopped and politely, but fearlessly, pointed at Stela, "is charged with the intentional homicide of killing Andy Nelson."

While Dominique lowered her arm, she still stood at an angle, addressing both the jury and Stela. She wasn't intimidated by the cold-blooded criminal who was on trial.

"Ms. Reiter isn't the meek and well-mannered woman you see here today, dressed in her pink cardigan. She's a killer. She seduced Andy Nelson into a relationship for the sole purpose of buying nuclear materials from him, materials that he stole from *Voila!*

Industries where he worked as an engineer in the defense division. Andy and Stela had a sexual affair, and all the while, she manipulated him into stealing and selling enriched plutonium and uranium to her."

While not using the word "'murder," Dominique had liberally substituted "killer." Monica wondered if Stela resented Dominique's clever sidestep. In anticipation of Dominique's next attack, Monica felt Stela's body tense. A lethal amount of energy poured off her. Monica felt like a coiled snake was seated next to her, so she divided her attention between listening to Dominique and watching out for a swift, venomous strike.

"When their nuclear materials deal went bad— perhaps over money or the fact that Andy's bosses were starting to question him about inventory—Stela took him for a drive in the country and killed him. She planned it, even taking a paring knife from the block of Trident knives in Andy's kitchen. She killed him in cold blood, stabbing him over and over, in 13 places to be exact, including the scrotum. She might have planned a clean kill with precision, but it didn't turn out that way. It was a bloody mess. Their vicious struggle—her slashing his neck open—resulted in multiple blood smears and stains in the back seat of Andy's car. Andy was in a fight for his life. A fight he lost. By her own admission, we know that Ms. Reiter slashed and stabbed him repeatedly, forcefully, and brutally until he died."

"The DNA in the blood spots at the scene is incriminating in this case. There are three sets of DNA. Andy's is all over the interior of the car. Stela's is in a small smear on the rear car door and a few droplets on the ground. And a third set of DNA is in some droplets smudged on the trunk. Since DNA doesn't lie, the pathologist will testify that Stela had an accomplice with her."

"We will prove that Andy's DNA was found in two other places. First, in the self-cutting marks on Stela's groin, which makes sense because she cut herself *after* she used the knife to kill him. Second, his DNA was in the blood under Stela's fingernails, which also makes sense because he hemorrhaged a lot of blood, as she stabbed him repeatedly, so her fingers and hands were drenched in it, as was her outer layer of clothing."

As Dominique published photos on the overhead screen of Stela's clothes—an insulated flannel with mud and blood all over the front, the jurors faces went ashen. A T-shirt that had a clean, straight cut down the center. The T-shirt had no mud or blood on it. And a clean tank top with a single cut down the front. The cuts were so clean, they looked as if scissors had been used to create them.

"A very cold and calculating Stela told the police the second time they interviewed her that Andy was trying to sexually assault her in the back seat. She said that's why her clothes had a singular cut on the front of them, and she had cut marks to her right groin, outer right thigh, and palm of her left hand. She was lying. The reality is that she—or her accomplice— made all the cuts to her clothes and to herself *after* she killed Andy. The cut clothes and her self-inflicted lacerations were her cover story."

"How do we know this? For starters, Andy's DNA wasn't found on her vaginal area by the Sexual Assault Nurse Examiner at the hospital. Ms. Reiter submitted to a full SANE exam, telling Emergency Department physician and nurses that she was sexually assaulted. She never told them that she killed the alleged assailant, but she did tell them that she was assaulted. She consented to a full exam, which included swabs of her bottom and vaginal cavity. There was nothing found. Nothing. No DNA from Andy Nelson on her. No evidence of a sexual assault."

"You will hear testimony from Dr. Tollefson, the ED physician, Julia Brown, the SANE nurse, and Dr. Karey, the psychiatrist. They all treated Ms. Reiter at Community Memorial Hospital. They will tell you that, by the nature of Ms. Reiter's cut marks, they were self-inflicted. At the time Ms. Reiter was in the ED, the physician and nurse were concerned she had been sexually assaulted then cut herself as a result of the emotional trauma. They had no idea that she had killed Andy Nelson, so they consulted the psychiatrist. They will tell you that the cut marks—made in parallel lines, all at a shallow depth, in a very controlled fashion—were consistent with self-cutting. Not the type of random, deep cuts one would suffer in a knife fight when defending oneself."

Dominique walked to her laptop at counsel table and clicked until photos appeared on the overhead screen for the jury.

"Let me show you a photo of the cut marks on Ms. Reiter. Here are three parallel lines on the inside of her left palm, her nondominant hand. She's right-handed, so she used the blade to carve these superficial marks into the palm of her left hand. During her second interview, she told Detectives Matt Breuer and Brock Curfman that she suffered these cuts while trying to wrest the knife away from Andy Nelson. Dr. Tollefson will testify, however, that the cuts on her palm are too shallow and patterned to have come from grabbing a knife blade during a fight. Moreover, people usually grab with their dominant hand when fighting, and these cuts are on her nondominant palm."

Dominique clicked on a photo of Stela's inner thigh. "Similarly, these cut marks on Ms. Reiter's inner right thigh in the groin area are evenly spaced, parallel lines that scratch the top layer of the skin to create some oozing and scarring, but they aren't the deep, jagged gashes that would be consistent with a significant, unpredictable force used in a knife fight."

Dominique next displayed a photo of Stela's outer thigh. "Similar to the groin and palm cuts, these self-inflicted cuts on Ms. Reiter's outer thigh barely break the skin. They're about three inches long, placed next to each other in parallel lines, and are consistent with an upward cutting motion, as she held the knife in her right hand and pulled upward."

Dominique stepped away from the podium and demonstrated with her right hand pulling up against her right thigh. "Arm's length. Not too deep. Just breaking the surface of the skin. The experts who regularly see wounds like this in their medical practice will tell you these, too, are consistent with self-cutting."

"This next sequence of photos will be graphic," Dominique warned as she displayed photos of Andy's body on the pathologist's table at the medical examiner's office. There was a collective intake of breath by everyone in the courtroom, as Andy's naked, white body lay on a metal table before them. Monica felt badly for his family having to endure the photos of his disfigured body in repose.

"These photos were taken by the forensic pathologist, Dr. Bud Linden, who will testify that the force used to create these stab wounds to Andy Nelson's skull, neck, abdomen, lungs, back, scrotum, was a powerful force, both purposeful and intentional. These are not the type of wounds one would see in self-defense, but rather in a full-on attack filled with rage. Note the depth of the wound to Andy's right temple. His *right* temple. If Ms. Reiter were underneath him on the seat of the car being sexually assaulted, how could she reach around with her right hand and stab him in the right temple?"

"The State will prove that Andy Nelson's wounds indicate Ms. Reiter most likely surprised him with her initial attack, stabbing him in the back first, then she used great force to stab him repeatedly until she killed him."

While the photo of Andy's gored body was still on the overhead screen, a female juror in the front row sneezed and coughed simultaneously. Dominique grabbed a tissue box from a shelf on the podium and approached the jury box. She extended her arm, offering a tissue to the juror, but the juror grabbed the entire box, held it to her face, then sprayed explosive vomit, splattering the jury rail and Dominique's skirt. Acting fast, Dominique grabbed the trash can from under her counsel table and quickly heaved it up and over the jury rail for the juror to use.

Dominique turned around to the judge and muttered something Monica couldn't hear.

"Okay, everyone," Judge O'Brien said. "We're going to take a short break. Court is in recess for 15 minutes."

Everyone stood while the jury left through the back door, Isla helping the sick juror. Stela left with her deputies, and Monica, like everyone else in the courtroom, wanted to bolt from the sight and smell of fresh puke. On her way down the aisle, Monica avoided eye contact with Peter and Steven on one side, and Tiffany on the other, as she made a beeline for the courthouse steps.

She burst into the mid-afternoon sun, the wind coming at her and stealing her breath. Every bit of stale, courtroom air rushed from her lungs, replaced by stinging polar air. She couldn't blame the puking juror, as Monica had done the same thing the first time she had looked at the photos.

A moment later, she was joined by Peter McCoy and Steven Scott, who also breathed deeply.

"I don't see Ms. Reiter winning this trial," Peter said into the wind.

Monica felt cornered. "Agent McCoy, I'm not going to dissect every phase of this trial with you during breaks. I have things I need to do and think about that don't include your obscure agenda."

"Read between the tea leaves, Ms. Spade," Peter said in a low voice.

From that mixed metaphor, Monica didn't know if she was supposed to deduce what he really wanted or predict the outcome of the trial. "Speak clearly, Agent McCoy."

He looked at her peripherally while keeping his nose to the wind. "We want you to call us if Yuri Zaleski shows up at your house."

Monica's eyes suddenly filled with tears, so she stared straight ahead, remaining silent.

"We heard he paid you a visit."

"Where did you hear that?"

Peter didn't answer her. "You need to call us if he shows up again."

"You know, that's kind of hard to do while I'm being choked. If you two would've been doing your jobs in the first place, then I wouldn't have been throttled by that monster."

"We can't be everywhere all the time, Ms. Spade."

"From where I stand, it looks like you can't be anywhere any of the time. Get your priorities straight, will you?"

Peter's ears turned pink with offense. "We believe we have; but what can we offer you?"

"If you want my help, put some security on Shelby."

Peter glanced at Steven then said, "We could alternate tailing her to and from school."

"Well, thank you," Monica said, surprised at his agreement. "I'll tell her."

He jerked his thumb toward the courtroom. "You saw firsthand how Stela and Yuri operate. They're used to doing business in Ukraine, not being held accountable in America. They're vicious animals who will stop at nothing to get what they want, and right now, they want Stela out of here."

"From my perspective, Stela is a ruthless killer, but an educated one," Monica said. "You heard her pre-trial motions. She obviously practiced law somewhere." Monica was beginning to wonder if Peter was good at his job.

"I assumed you coached her," Peter said.

She grunted. "You can't coach that. It's all her. No wonder she fired her two public defenders."

"What did Yuri tell you?"

Delivering the pill to Stela flashed through Monica's mind, but she thought better of telling him about it. "He gave me money to buy clothes for Stela and told me I needed to help her get acquitted."

"Uh-huh," Peter said, encouraging more.

"He also said he's known you for years—that you're CIA, not FBI—and working on a project with him." She watched him from her peripheral vision.

"Classic misinformation," Peter said, turning toward the door. "Should we go back in?"

From whom? she wondered.

They returned to the courtroom, where the cast of court personnel was reassembling. Andy's family members looked sad and stricken, especially his parents, Harold and Sharon.

Dominique was back at the podium, her laptop close by, so she could publish more ghoulish pics on the overhead screens. She was wearing slacks now instead of the barf-splattered skirt.

The bailiffs brought in Stela and Judge O'Brien entered shortly thereafter.

Once the jury was reseated, Dominique picked up where she left off. "I apologize for the gory photographs, everyone. Homicide is a nasty, distasteful crime, but it's my job to prove that Stela Reiter drove Andy Nelson into the country where she mercilessly killed him."

"You will hear from a local resident who drove by the entrance to the farmer's field at roughly 3 p.m. and saw both Ms. Reiter and Andy Nelson in his car. Ms. Reiter was driving. She later told Detectives Breuer and Curfman that Andy drove her out there, but that was a lie. She drove; not Andy."

Dominique glanced over at Stela, "Then, and this is especially diabolical—"

"Object, Your Honor," Stela said loudly.

"Sustained," Judge O'Brien said.

Dominique continued, "Again, the defendant's actions demonstrate those of a cold and calculating killer—"

"Object, Your Honor," Stela said loudly again.

"Sustained," Judge O'Brien said, giving Dominique a look.

Dominique ignored Stela. "Ms. Reiter ran from the scene that she carefully staged after she killed Andy. She took his phone, so he couldn't call for help.

She actually smashed it to prevent him from using it, then took it. She also took the murder weapon—a Trident paring knife—and she ran toward a farmer's house about a mile away."

"Object, Your Honor. 'Murder' weapon," Stela said.

"Sustained."

"Habit," Dominique muttered to him, as she walked to a table next to the court secretary and carefully lifted a box containing the bloody paring knife. The blood was dark and crusted, mixed with mud. She walked along the jury rail, holding the box open for them to see the knife. "This is the knife Ms. Reiter used to kill Andy Nelson. That's uncontested. She admits she killed him with this knife. She simply disputes bringing it along."

Dominique returned the knife to the table and came back to the jury with Andy Nelson's bloody, dirty, smashed cell phone. She held it out for the jury to see, as she walked along the jury rail. "This is Andy's smashed cell phone. The police found it in a ditch next to the knife, halfway between the crime scene and the farmer's house where Stela ran. Stela didn't use it to call for help. No. Instead, she smashed it and tossed it with the knife, thinking no one would find them. She deprived Andy of a lifeline for help."

"Objection," Stela said.

"Overruled," Judge O'Brien said.

"Andy was alone in the back seat of his car, bleeding uncontrollably. Dying alone. Dying a painful death. Dying at the hands of the defendant Stela Reiter. And she made sure he couldn't call for help by stealing his phone."

Dominique let those statements settle in the air, as she returned the cell phone to the evidence table.

Both Harold and Sharon Nelson cried openly, his face red with fury and hers mostly covered with a tissue.

"Then," Dominique said on her way back to the podium, "Ms. Reiter ran to the farmer's house and asked him to call an ambulance. He called the police instead. When the police arrived, she told them she woke up in a field after having been sexually assaulted, but she couldn't remember by whom. They brought her to the hospital where she said the same thing, not providing any details."

"The police visited her first thing Sunday morning, but she insisted she couldn't remember anything aside from being assaulted, pointing to her lacerations."

Dominique glanced disapprovingly at Stela.

"Sensing something was amiss, Detectives Breuer and Curfman returned to the farmer's house on Sunday afternoon. They searched the area and found Andy's car with his body hanging out the back door."

"On Monday morning, they returned to the Behavioral Health Unit and questioned Ms. Reiter about Andy. All of a sudden, she had a recollection, but it was limited. She admitted to killing Andy, but claimed she did it in self-defense. She claimed her self-cutting lacerations were actually battle scars from fighting off Andy, as he tried to sexually assault her. She didn't explain anything else, though. Instead, she apparently saved the details for you during this trial."

Dominique turned another page. "As you will see and hear during this trial, the DNA evidence and testimony from a number of witnesses will undermine the defendant's contention that she killed Andy Nelson in self-defense."

Dominique turned to Stela again, locking eyes with her. "The evidence will show that Stela Reiter is guilty of first degree intentional homicide. At the end of this case, I will address you again during closing arguments. At that time, I'll ask you to follow the judge's instructions and return a guilty verdict." She turned back to the jury. "Thank you for your attention."

There was a heightened sense of relief in the courtroom now that everyone got a preview of the cold-blooded facts that were about to play out over the next several days. Based on Dominique's delivery, Monica thought she had a lock on a guilty verdict.

Dominique, conscious of the fact that she had savagely nailed her opening, sauntered back to her counsel table.

"The court will take a short recess before we hear the defendant's opening statement," Judge O'Brien said. Everyone stood while the jury shuffled out.

After the jury left, Judge O'Brien turned to Stela. "Are you ready to deliver your opening?"

"Yes."

"Did Ms. Spade explain to you that this is a preview of the evidence only? There is to be no argument."

"I'm well aware, Your Honor. Perhaps your admonition would have been better suited to the prosecution."

Dominique fired a scornful look at Stela, then said, "That's nonsense, Your Honor. I would request the court to remind the defendant that this forum is a judicial one, not an arena for her to lob insults at me."

"Very well," Judge O'Brien said. "Ms. Reiter, please keep your editorial opinions to yourself."

Stela patted the air in a conciliatory gesture, indicating she had heard him loud and clear.

"Return in 10 minutes," Judge O'Brien said, and got up and left.

29

Monica naturally assumed that Stela would leave for a tinkle break before she delivered her opening statement, so she was surprised when Stela remained seated and waved off the deputy escort.

Ignoring Monica, Stela turned to the tab marked "Opening" in her trial binder and focused on the typewritten pages, adding a few notations in the margins from notes she had taken during Dominique's opening. Monica noticed that Stela's was a complete narrative, not just an outline.

Since Monica wasn't needed for this exercise, she rose to stretch her legs, and if she was being honest, to get away from the killer who was masquerading as a meek librarian with the skillset of a trained lawyer.

As Monica walked down the hallway, she wondered how Dominique managed to present murder scenes in such a business-like tone, reviewing whose blood was whose per the DNA, as if negotiating terms of a contract. Maybe she had become desensitized... Monica entered the women's restroom to find Dominique smoothing her already smooth hair while staring at her better half in the mirror.

Monica quickly glanced around the space, registering they were alone. "Nice opening."

"Thanks. I felt like I wasn't at the top of my game."

"I thought it was very effective. I like how you addressed Stela head-on."

"I do that in all of my openings and closings. I have to demonstrate to the jury that it's our job to confront the accused and hold her accountable. We can't be intimidated."

"Good strategy."

Dominique smiled and left.

When Monica returned to the courtroom, Stela sat erect in her chair, staring at the wall above the witness box. For the first time, Monica noticed a TV camera attached to the rail of the witness box that was pointed directly at Stela and her. She found it disconcerting, hoping she hadn't pulled any faces that were captured and broadcast.

When Monica rolled her chair up to the table, Stela glanced over and said, "I have another motion for the judge when we start."

"What's that?"

"You'll see."

Monica closed her eyes at the gamesmanship.

The door behind the judge's bench squeaked, and Judge O'Brien entered and sat in his highbacked leather chair. He looked at Dominique and Stela. "Are we ready to bring the jury in?"

"In a minute, Your Honor," Stela said. "I have a motion."

His face tightened, as he squinted at her. Dominique sat back in her chair, giving the impression she was prepared for some good entertainment.

"Go on," Judge O'Brien said to Stela.

"I move the court to order the TV station in the back, namely Tiffany Rose and her cameraman, to stop filming me when the jury leaves. The camera next to the witness box is on and trained on me during break, which is an invasion of my privacy. I need to be able to have attorney-client discussions with my counsel, and they're filming that, maybe even going in for a closeup and reading my lips for the newscast. There's no reason they need to film me when court isn't in session."

Judge O'Brien's eyes traveled to the back of the courtroom, then volleyed back to the camera on the witness box, as if he, too, were seeing it for the first time. He nodded at Dominique, inviting her to remark.

"The State has no position on the matter, Your Honor," Dominique said.

"Very well," Judge O'Brien said, "I hereby order that the TV cameras not film during breaks. You can film only when the jury is present. Moreover, no closeups of the lawyers and parties talking to each other. Understood?"

Tiffany nodded from the back.

"Let's bring in the jury," Judge O'Brien said.

After the jurors were seated—Mrs. Popa, the Romanian grandmother looking especially eager— Stela took the podium. She wasn't as confident as Dominique, perhaps trying to provide a contrast between Dominique's commanding style and Stela's supposed demure persona. Even so, everyone knew that Stela could take Dominique in a knife fight.

Stela placed her notes on the podium and turned back to the Judge, "May it please the court." She turned and politely gazed at Dominique, "Counsel." She skipped Monica and faced the jury.

"Ladies and gentlemen of the jury. Thank you for your civil service as jurors in this most important trial about my life. I'm from Romania, which has a different judicial system, so I'm honored to be given the opportunity to represent myself in this homicide trial where my defense is that I was fending off a twisted sexual assault by my then-boyfriend, Andy Nelson."

From Monica's vantage point, the jurors looked equal parts scared and intrigued, but in a wide-eyed fashion full of disbelief, as one might gawk at a car accident.

Stela smiled and let her arms fall to her sides. "Let me start with some background and context about my relationship with Andy. I've been in America for five months. I started fall semester of last year at Apple Grove University, studying chemistry. Early in the semester, I met Andy at Racy's Coffee Lounge on Water Street. He approached me, not the other way around. He bought me a coffee and we got to talking. I had no idea he worked at *Voila!*, which he ultimately shared, but he described it as a small appliance manufacturer of waffle irons and the like. I had no idea *Voila!* designed and sold armaments to the military."

She glanced over at Monica, then let her eyes drift toward the back of the courtroom where Tiffany's TV camera was pointed directly at her. Stela's expression was so angelic that Monica thought a halo might appear any second.

"Andy and I started dating, and it's true that we became lovers. That's true, but in the most honest, genuine sense, not in the ruthless transactional sense that the DA would have you believe. We hung out at Racy's and his house on the outskirts of town. He was teaching me about American culture, helping me navigate the university system, and we were enjoying ourselves as couples do."

"Unfortunately, I came to learn that Andy also had a dark sexual side. I don't want to use the word 'depraved,' but it was something so close to depraved that I don't know how else to describe it. He kept a journal of his philosophies about life, including sex. Fantasies, really. His journal was a small notebook on the bedside table that he would scribble his thoughts in. Often, his thoughts were sexual, and he was slowly, but surely, introducing me to his secret desires for rough sex. I have some excerpts of his writings that the police recovered from his home. I'll put them up on the big screen now."

She snapped her fingers once and pointed to Dominique, apparently using her as a projector bitch during opening. At least Stela couldn't complain about the fairness of Dominique's approach in the courtroom.

Several excerpts of handwritten notes appeared on the screen.

Stela explained, "These are excerpts from Andy's sex journal. He wrote them over the last couple of months, but I put together a few of them yesterday to give you a flavor of his mindset, and the reason I was legitimately afraid when we were in the back seat of his car."

"Let me read them." Stela turned to face the big screen over the witness box, as the jurors' heads turned like they were watching a tennis match.

"'Your body is a work of art that creates an adventure for my mind. I want to give you every part of me while I take every part of you. Dreams and anguish bring us together as we give and take in equal measure. Consent, in its most abstract form, is a total gift of the body, releasing itself from the soul in existential rapture, for the lover to enjoy on his own terms. Consent means nothing when desires of the flesh blossom…Isolating the concept of cannibalism, one can say it's morally reprehensible to kill another to eat her flesh, but I've always been suspicious of collective truths. I want to eat you while you still live and breathe—to taste your blood, lick your wounds, taste your torn skin…The beauty of release through pain. We have not the time to take our time…Our ties that bind aren't enough anymore…We can predict our fate only after it has happened.'"

The jurors were glued to the screen, almost afraid to look away and risk making eye contact with anyone. In that moment, Stela had them.

Monica's jaw hit the floor. She quickly typed some notes on her own laptop then refocused on the screen overhead, watching and listening in rapt curiosity.

Stela cleverly left the words on the screen and remained silent for a few seconds. When she turned to refocus on her notes, Dominique clicked the excerpts off the screen.

Stela whipped around and looked at her, using her sweet voice, "I would request the prosecutor to leave the quotes on the screen while I expound upon them."

Dominique quickly illuminated the big screen with the quotes once again.

Monica studied the traditional cursive writing of the excerpts, neat and straight. She pictured Andy Nelson writing in bed or at an awkward angle, Stela looking over his shoulder. It didn't fit.

Stela resumed, working up to her fervent Romanian accent, "Early in our relationship, Andy introduced me to some playful, light sexual play. He covered my eyes with a scarf while doing things to me. Enjoyable things. I was uncomfortable at first, but I obeyed because it made him happy. Soon, he escalated to tying my wrists to his bed, and then my feet. Being completely tied up is unnerving, but I obeyed, because it pleased him. One night after dinner, he showed me a new toy he had bought—a whip. I drew a line in the sand at that. 'No way,' I said. He whined and pouted until I relented. It was painful, and I didn't like it. The welts made it difficult for me to sit in class in my jeans, and they took forever to subside."

"Excuse me, I need a drink of water." Stela turned to walk toward the counsel table where a glass of water was, but she collapsed halfway and fell to the floor, as limp as a ragdoll.

Oh, nice move, Monica thought. She glanced at Dominique, who raised her hand to her mouth and bit her knuckles. Monica was close enough to see the edges of Dominique's lips curl up in amusement.

Judge O'Brien peered over his bench. "Ms. Reiter? Are you okay?"

She lay still, her eyes closed. Some jurors looked alarmed while other's openly smirked, clearly thinking —*fake faint, fake faint, fake faint.*

Her eyes closed, Stela didn't move.

The pill that Yuri had given to Monica for Stela flashed through Monica's mind. *Maybe she really is sick.* Reluctantly, Monica rose from counsel table and walked around to kneel beside Stela. "Stela? Are you okay? Can you hear me?"

No movement. Eyes closed. Monica could see Stela's chest rise and fall, but she seemed legitimately unconscious. Monica turned to the judge and shook her head.

Judge O'Brien pinched the bridge of his nose and addressed the jury. "Okay, we're going to take an unexpected break. The jury is excused for 15 minutes. All rise."

Everyone except Monica and Stela rose to watch the jury leave. Once they were gone, Judge O'Brien asked, "Do we need paramedics?"

"I don't know," Monica said, assessing Stela. She picked up her limp wrist and felt for a pulse. It was present. Her medical skills now exhausted, Monica looked at the female deputy hovering over them.

Deputies take basic life support classes, don't they? The deputy didn't move.

Just as Monica was considering suggesting the paramedic route, Stela's eyes fluttered open, but they looked vacant and glassy. Not glassy with tears, but glassy opaque.

"What happened?" Stela asked.

"You fainted?" Monica suggested.

Stela rubbed her forehead, her eyes darting from Monica to her surroundings. She muttered something in Romanian that sounded like expletives to Monica, then said, "Did the jury... Did I faint in front of the jury?"

Monica nodded. "Yes. How are you? Do you need something?"

Stela said just above a whisper, "I have a serious medical problem—anxiety-induced seizures. I probably just had one. This cut short my career in Romania. Stage fright in front of juries." She sat up.

Oh what the courtroom lost when you decided to become a killer, Monica thought. "Did you take the medication Yuri gave you?"

Stela dismissed Monica's question with a grimace.

"Do you need to go to the hospital?" Monica asked.

Stela shook her head and smoothed out her skirt. "No."

"Can you continue your opening?"

"No," Stela said. "I can sit in the chair, but I don't have the energy to speak. Probably, I will just faint again, no?"

"In that case, I'm sure the judge will break for the day," Monica said. "You can resume giving your opening tomorrow."

Stela grasped Monica's forearm, scaring her. "You."

"What?" Monica asked, not comprehending.

"You give the rest of my opening."

"Ah...no thanks," Monica said. "That's waaaay outside the scope of standby counsel."

"What's going on down there?" Judge O'Brien asked from the bench.

Monica looked up, having forgotten that he was waiting for a condition report. "It appears that Ms. Reiter is suffering from a medical condition, and most likely just had an anxiety-induced seizure. She's strong enough to sit through court for the rest of today, but she just requested me to give the remainder of her opening statement."

Judge O'Brien's expression went from concerned to relieved. "That's a splendid idea. Let's keep this trial on schedule."

"I told her 'no,'" Monica said, making Dominique crack the slightest bit of a smile, careful to keep her face angled away from the TV camera at the witness box.

"What's the issue?" Judge O'Brien asked.

Monica, still kneeling on the floor next to Stela, said, "I have no idea what she was going to say."

Stela said from the floor, loud enough for the judge to hear, "It's all typed out. All you have to do is read it."

"Very well then," Judge O'Brien said, "Ms. Spade is going to read the rest of Ms. Reiter's opening. Just tell the jury what you're doing. You'll be fine."

"But—" Monica said.

"It's settled," Judge O'Brien said, "Let's bring the jury back in."

Monica's stomach burned, and she broke out in a sweat, as she reluctantly helped Stela to her feet. Hunched and almost doubled over, Stela shuffled back to her seat at counsel table, took her chair, and sat as straight as she could while propping herself with her elbows on the table.

Dominique and Judge O'Brien watched, Dominique's hand now covering her smile. When Monica and Dominique's eyes briefly met, Dominique winked. Monica didn't know if Dominique was teasing or sending encouragement. Either way, she felt like the butt of a huge joke. She'd never given an opening to a jury. She'd never tried a case. Yet here she was in a homicide case involving arms dealers, about to give an opening statement.

Baptism by fire, she thought. *Fuck me.*

30

Stela leaned over to Monica and whispered, "The typed pages are on the podium. Just read them word-for-word." She paused a second, then said in a louder whisper, "Try to put some passion into the words, no? This is my life we're trying to save."

If Stela had intended her words as some sort of pep talk, they couldn't have landed further from the mark. She was imploring Monica to "save her life" after intentionally taking Andy's life? Hardly.

Monica's heart began racing, and her palms broke out in a sweat. Like it or not, she was now a character in Stela's tragic play. Monica wanted to run rather than address the jury on Stela's behalf.

"Are we ready to bring the jury back in?" Judge O'Brien asked, staring directly at Monica.

"Yes," Monica croaked, her nod serving as reluctant assent.

Stela leaned forward and poured Monica a glass of water. "Clear your throat and bring this to the podium with you."

"Thanks," Monica said.

"Deep breaths, and remember—passion," Stela said in a steely whisper while fist-pumping her own heart.

Judge O'Brien observed their quiet exchange then said, "I'll make a few remarks when the jury comes in, so they know what's going on."

Everyone stood, including Stela, as the jury reassembled in their assigned seats. One by one, they all looked at Stela to see if she was still there.

"Welcome back," Judge O'Brien said. "As you saw, the defendant fainted during her opening statement.

We're going to resume proceedings, and Standby Counsel, Monica Spade, is going to read the remainder of the defendant's opening statement. Ms. Spade isn't counsel for Ms. Reiter. Ms. Spade was appointed by the court to explain judicial process to Ms. Reiter throughout the trial. Nevertheless, upon Ms. Reiter's request, Ms. Spade graciously agreed to step in and read the remainder of Ms. Reiter's opening statement."

The judge looked at Monica. "Ms. Spade, are you ready to proceed?"

"Yes, Your Honor." Monica rose, rubbed her sweaty palms on her blazer, and took the podium, where she set her glass of water on the first shelf. Not a complete stranger to public speaking—actually enjoying giving presentations to hospital personnel about much more benign topics—Monica took a deep breath and said in her low, calm, speaking voice, "Good afternoon. I'll do my best to read Ms. Reiter's remarks. Please forgive me if I stumble over a few words here and there, having never seen this statement before today."

Monica lowered her eyes, only to discover that the type was in incredibly small font. Rather than strain with her head lowered—talking straight into the podium—she picked up the papers and held them in her hands, so she could project her voice to the jury. Her trembling hands shook the papers.

"Let's see, where did we leave off?" Monica asked rhetorically while scanning the document. "Oh here." She cleared her throat and read.

"So, Andy told me it was a Wisconsin tradition to have sexual relations in the outdoors—while in the car, of course—but in the 'great outdoors,' as he called it. He suggested we go for a car ride to find the perfect spot, so he drove us to the snow-covered road in the woods next to the farmer's field." Monica felt her ears prickle with the heat of embarrassment, as she motored on.

"I really felt like we were in the middle of nowhere, and Andy was acting strangely. Uptight. Nervous. Like he was preparing to try something. Upon his suggestion, we moved to the back seat. I was fine with the adventure, don't get me wrong, but shortly after we started kissing, him on top of me, I became suspicious because he seemed preoccupied, like he was up to something."

"He removed my spectacles, which always makes me a little nervous unless I'm going to sleep because I can't see without them. Then, out of nowhere, he produced a bandana and placed it over my eyes without asking. He had blindfolded me before, and it hadn't been too bad, so I didn't protest, thinking it might be okay if I just relaxed. Obviously, it meant a lot to him, so I acquiesced to his wishes."

"Not much time passed before I freaked out because he was treating me really rough. I asked him to stop, but he just mumbled that I was beautiful, and he wanted all of me. He pinned my arms above my head. The seat wasn't long enough, so our legs were bent, and our feet were crushed against the car door."

"He leaned up, put his knee between my legs, and I felt something sharp cut my jeans. I lowered my head, but I couldn't see under the bandana. I panicked, yelling, 'That hurts! Are you cutting me?'"

"He told me he was, but that I should fight through the pain and lie still. He kept telling me to 'be still.' I saw white lights and felt unbearable pain, but he put his forearm over my chest to hold me down, as he cut through my jeans, making the perfect lines on my inner thigh. I lay frozen in fear. Frozen! I'd read the fantasies he'd written, and all I could picture was him chopping me up for his own twisted pleasure."

"I screamed at him to stop, that I was in pain, so he finally set the knife aside and removed my jeans. He said he was turned on by the blood, so he wanted to cut some more. He started cutting on my outer thigh, and I screamed again. He wouldn't stop. After a few more cuts, I ripped off the bandana, so I could see what he was doing. When I saw the evil glint in his eyes, I became more scared. I yelled at him to get off me, that I didn't want to be there, and that it was over between us."

"He held the knife under my chin and told me that I needed to help him act out his fantasies. Then, he made a tiny cut on his palm, much tinier than the cuts he had made on me, and put his palm on my outer thigh, chanting about 'mixing our blood, mixing our blood…'"

"I thought to myself that this was where I was going to die—in the back seat of a car in the dead of winter next to a farmer's field in America. Just like that. Never to be seen or heard from again because my American boyfriend wanted to act out his sadistic fantasies on me. My poor parents, back in Romania. Never to hear from their only daughter again. I couldn't let that happen, so I decided to act fast to save myself."

Monica stopped and took a drink of water, swallowing hard with everyone staring at her. She briefly locked eyes with Dr. Lisa Gilmore, a physician on the jury, who wore an empathetic expression for Monica's plight. Familiar with her from working with Community Memorial Hospital, Monica knew her to be intelligent and kind. Monica found her place on the page and continued, "I knew I had to fight or die, so the instinct to survive surged through me. Fear turned to rage, and I blew up. I reached down to grab the knife with my left hand because Andy was right-handed, and he was holding the knife above me with his right hand. I managed to get the knife from him but not before the blade sliced my palm."

Monica glanced over at Stela, half expecting her to hold up her palm, but she didn't. She stared at Monica with those cold, assessing eyes.

Fearing another visit by Yuri for a good choking, Monica injected a little more passion in her voice as she read the next passage. "I tried to scoot around him to get out of the car, but he put his hand over my throat. I dropped the knife on the floor of the car, but felt around for it until I got it again. Since it was in my left hand, I jabbed it as hard as I could into his right temple. That's why he has a stab wound there. That was my first stab. I mistakenly thought that's all I would need to do to stop him, but it infuriated him. He flailed around, trying to get the knife from me, so I just started stabbing wherever I could. Maybe that's when I stabbed him in the back. I don't know. The fight is a blur. It went on forever. Him hitting me. Grabbing me. Choking me. Me stabbing anywhere to stop him. The blood was spurting everywhere, but he wouldn't stop. He wouldn't stop."

Monica saw a bracketed note for a photo exhibit to be displayed. She turned to Dominique. "Could you please put exhibit number 23 on the overhead screen?"

They all watched as Dominique complied, and a photo of the back seat appeared with a huge, dark stain of blood on the cushion. Below it, on the floor mat, lay a clump of long, brown hair.

"Here's a photo of the scene that the prosecution didn't show you. That's my hair," Monica said emphatically. "That's a clump of my hair he pulled out while I was struggling to get away. He kept clawing at me. Grabbing at me. Pulling my hair. So, I stabbed again and again, not even knowing where I was connecting, but I was terrified he was going to kill me if I didn't stab him."

Dominique took down the photo.

Monica continued in a softer voice. "I managed to get out of the car, but he came after me like he was superhuman. I just wanted him to stop, but the more I stabbed, the more enraged he became. He was like a wild bull, grunting and snorting. I was afraid and confused, but I managed to get out of the car. He tackled me in the snow, so I stabbed him again. Maybe that's when I stabbed him in the scrotum. I don't know. It wasn't on purpose. It was just instinct."

Monica paused while she set down the page of notes she had just read.

"He fell down to the ground, finally stopping his assault, so I got back in the car and sat there, overwhelmed. Stunned. Exhausted. In shock. Traumatized. I don't know how long I sat there. I might have fallen asleep or blacked out. I don't know, but I awoke to the cold. I was shivering and terrified. I wasn't wearing any shoes, socks or pants. My clothes were cut in the front, so I was exposed. I found my spectacles and put them on, then surveyed the scene. It was a nightmare. A bloody nightmare. I found my pants and put them on, then I saw Andy's cell phone on the seat. I wanted to dial 911, but my hands were shaking and slippery with blood, so I couldn't enter his passcode, which he had given to me. I didn't see my shoes or socks, so I decided to run for help before it got dark. I don't know why I grabbed the knife too, but I did. Maybe because I was scared. I had the phone and knife in my hands. Maybe it was my instinct for survival, to bring the weapon with me. I don't know. I wasn't thinking clearly, and I was scared. Really scared."

Monica continued in a solemn tone, the grisly scene of Andy's murder hitting her in the chest. "I ran down the path of tire tracks in the snow, falling and sliding because my feet were numb and didn't work right. I turned on the road and ran toward the lights at the farmer's house. I fell several times, and one of those times, I dropped the knife and phone. I didn't try to hide them from Andy or anyone else. I just dropped them. Maybe that's when the phone got smashed."

"I ran. I fell. I ran. I saw the farmer's house and ran up the steps. I was out of breath. I banged on the door. I was so scared and cold. When he came to the door, I asked him to call an ambulance. I don't know what happened after that. I just remember crumpling to the floor and closing my eyes. He might have asked me some questions, but I don't remember what they were, or what my answers were."

"The next thing I remember is that I was at the hospital. It's true that when I was there I told them I was sexually assaulted. I didn't know how else to describe it. I was in shock. They asked me a ton of questions, but I couldn't talk. I couldn't think. I was suffering from brain shock. Emotional shock. Physical shock. I just wanted help. Someone to hold me. Help me. They insisted on taking photos of me and examining me. It was uncomfortable and embarrassing, but I complied. I remember being so cold. The lights were so bright, and my mind was so dark. Everything felt like it was going black."

"The next thing I knew, I was on the Behavioral Health Unit meeting with the psychiatrist. He, too, asked me a bunch of questions that I didn't feel ready to answer. Couldn't answer."

Monica turned to the last sheet of paper.

"In my defense for this trial, I will testify. You will hear directly from me when it's my turn to present my case. That will be in a few days. I would ask you to keep an open mind until then."

"You will also hear from two expert witnesses on my behalf. An expert psychiatrist to testify about the symptoms of PTSD, which is what I had after the assault. His name is Dr. Delaney Karpenko. He's a practicing psychiatrist in Cleveland, Ohio, but is coming here in person to talk about my PTSD, and why it wasn't so strange or suspicious, as the prosecution would have you believe, that I couldn't talk the first few days after the assault. Dr. Karpenko will tell you why it was normal for me not to remember what happened when the physicians, and later, the police, asked me what happened."

Monica looked at Dr. Lisa Gilmore, the only physician on the jury. She wondered what Dr. Gilmore thought of Stela's version, and of Monica reading it.

"Finally, you'll hear from Dr. George Popovich. He's an oncologist and hematologist, a physician who specializes in treating cancer and the blood. He'll explain why there were three sets of DNA found at the scene of Andy's death. There wasn't a third person there—an accomplice, as the prosecution asserted. It was just Andy and me. It might appear to the police that there were three sets of DNA, but Dr. Popovich will explain that I have two sets of DNA."

Monica squinted, wondering if she was reading this passage correctly. "Yes. That's right. My body has two sets of DNA, because several years ago, I had a bone marrow transplant for cancer treatment. Now, my body has my original DNA and the donor's DNA inside of me. My blood is a mixture of the two. I know it sounds confusing, but Dr. Popovich will explain it all to you."

Monica found that difficult to believe. Was that even possible? She glanced over at Dominique, whose facial expression was as calm as a granite statue, but her sharp eyes were bright with surprise. Monica returned to reading the final remarks.

"After you've heard my side of the story and the expert physicians testify, I will ask you to return a verdict of not guilty. Thank you."

Monica scooped up the papers and returned to her seat next to Stela.

31

"Thank you for delivering Ms. Reiter's opening statement," Judge O'Brien said. He turned and addressed the jury. "Since it's almost 4:30 p.m., I'm going to dismiss you for today. I remind all of you not to read any local news, look at social media, watch the news on the TV, or talk to anyone about the trial tonight. You are not to gather facts or evidence on your own. Court will resume tomorrow morning at 8:30 sharp. Thank you."

Everyone in the courtroom rose, as the jury left.

Once the jurors were out of earshot, Judge O'Brien looked at Dominique. "Who is the prosecution's first witness tomorrow?"

"Detective Matt Breuer," Dominique said.

"Okay. Will the parties be ready to start at 8:30? Ms. Reiter, how are you feeling?" Judge O'Brien asked.

Stela held up her hand, signaling she was fine. "I'll be ready at 8:30 tomorrow, Your Honor."

"Very well then," he said. "Court is adjourned for today." He abruptly rose and left through his door behind the façade.

Monica got the impression that he had had enough courtroom drama for one day, and frankly, so had she. He had been elected to preside over this bullshit. She, on the other hand, had tried to avoid it, yet here she was—stuck between a man in a robe and an assassin in a pink cardigan.

"You did a nice job with the opening," Stela said, interrupting Monica's dark mood.

"Thanks," she said, then forced herself to ask, "How are you feeling?"

"Better. I think I was overwhelmed by the enormity of the situation, had nerves, and a seizure followed."

Yeah right. One woman's seizure is another's acting class. "I'll see you tomorrow morning."

The deputies hovered over their table until Stela said, "I'm coming already."

While Monica stowed her laptop in her bag, Dominique sauntered over. "Stela played that well—fainting so you could read the opening. Your delivery was much more effective than hers ever could have been."

"Thanks, but I'm not too happy about having to do it," Monica muttered.

"You underestimate your abilities."

Monica thought Dominique was mocking her, but when she looked at Dominique's eyes, she didn't see anything but earnestness there. "Maybe I just know my limitations. Court isn't my jam. You, on the other hand, charmed the jury today."

"Except for the Romanian lady," Dominique said.

"Yeah, she seems smitten with Stela," Monica said. "Go figure." Monica shrugged on her black wool coat and slung her laptop strap over her shoulder.

"Ready to go?" Dominique asked.

"Yep. Unlike you, I don't have to work all night on trial prep," Monica said in a teasing voice.

Dominique threw a fake scowl at Monica, as they walked together toward the back of the courtroom.

Tiffany smiled at Dominique as she passed but stopped Monica.

"Nice delivery, Monica," Tiffany said, her voice more business-like than usual.

"Thanks." Monica paused next to her. "Your coverage of the toxic septic spill has been... enlightening for lack of a better word."

Tiffany's expression brightened at the compliment. "That's what I want to be known for—my investigative journalism of a massive shit show. The smell was horrendous." She scrunched her nose in a tease.

Monica smiled. "No doubt. Now you know how I feel. It's not like I want to be known as 'the Boyfriend Killer's lawyer.'"

"Guess we sometimes don't get the choice assignments, huh? Do you have any comments for the record today?"

"Most definitely not," Monica said.

"Do you think Stela's fainting was real or manufactured?"

"I have no comment," Monica said.

"I'll pin you down one of these days," Tiffany said flirtatiously.

"Maybe. Maybe not," Monica said playfully. "Have a good night."

"See you tomorrow."

When Monica entered the hallway, she saw Peter and Steven lurking near the coat racks. She stifled a groan, having no desire to interact with them. Fortunately, she had the sudden urge to pee, so she angled toward the women's restroom before they could intercept her.

She didn't think she had consumed that much water during court, but the pressure to go was suddenly strong. There was no way she'd make it home. She removed her coat and went into a stall. When she sat down and tried to pee, barely a drop came out. *That's strange,* she thought, *maybe this trial is more stressful on my system than I thought.*

She washed her hands and put on her coat again, then made her way out to the parking lot with the court personnel who were going home. The sun was already setting on the snowy horizon, pink clouds streaming like cotton candy across the sky.

Her truck door protested with a loud creak, as she got in and sat on the iceberg of a seat. While she turned the key and started the engine, her bladder screamed that she had to pee again. *Maybe it's because I'm cold. I can make it home.*

She drove faster than she usually did for fear of peeing her pants, the fifteen-minute drive taking forever. When she arrived home, she didn't even care that Shelby had taken the spot in the garage. Monica was happy to park next to the kitchen door, race up the steps, kick off her boots, and run into the bathroom without removing her coat or greeting a surprised Shelby.

When Monica sat down, her bladder spasmed like she was going to pee like a race horse, but, again, only a few drops came out. Then, a burning sensation shot up her urethra and fired up her bladder to spasm again.

She didn't know whether to be shocked or scared. Never had she experienced such a jolt of pain, similar to menstrual cramps but *on fire*.

She rose, washed her hands and removed her coat. The pressure to pee still lingered.

When she wandered out to the kitchen, Shelby looked up from slicing an onion. "Hey. You don't look so good."

"Thanks," Monica said. "I feel sort of weird."

"I'm sorry. Maybe some wine would help. Want a glass?"

"No thanks," Monica said, the thought of wine making her ill. She disappeared into the bedroom and changed into jeans and a sweatshirt. Ignoring Shelby, she sat down at the kitchen table and opened her laptop.

"Are you working?" Shelby asked while sautéing onions.

"Ah, no. I just want to research something real quick, then I can help with dinner."

Monica googled, "I feel like I have to pee, but nothing comes out." The first few hits included pecker problems, so she refined her search to focus on only females. The most noteworthy answer was, "If a person has a constant urge to pee but little comes out when they go, they may have an infection."

An infection? She scanned the page for information and her eyes rested on a sidebar that described the symptoms of a urinary tract infection: Discomfort when urinating, foul smelling urine, or blood in urine.

The discomfort was definitely present, but she hadn't noticed a smell, and she definitely hadn't looked in the bowl for blood. *Why do they always ask me questions too late? I was supposed to smell and inspect my pee?*

Her bladder interrupted her google search with another spasm, making her head pop up with the intensity of it. She shoved away from the table and returned to the bathroom. While sitting on the toilet, Monica's bladder shot off a stream of fireworks. Sparks roared through her urethra, but only a few drops came out.

She left the bathroom and went straight to Shelby at the stove.

"Hey, I think I might have a bladder infection."

Shelby turned from the pan, her eyes wide and concerned. "What?"

"Yeah. I googled the symptoms, and I think I have them." As if on cue, Monica winced, as a bladder spasm hit her.

Shelby rested a caring hand on Monica's shoulder. "Feels like you really have to go, then stings like holy hell when you pee, but hardly anything comes out?"

"Exactly." Monica was immediately relieved that Shelby understood.

"Uh-huh. Been there. We're going to Urgent Care right now. Come on." Shelby turned off the stove and put her hand on Monica's elbow.

"Are you sure? When I googled it, they recommended drinking cranberry juice."

Shelby laughed sarcastically. "You need antibiotics, girl. Trust me."

Monica suddenly doubled over in pain, her bladder sending flaming pinballs in Brownian motion through her abdomen. She turned to walk back to the bathroom and actually found it difficult. As she sat on the toilet, Shelby standing in the doorway staring, Monica spasmed in pain. Shelby was right. She needed medical intervention.

"I'm just so shocked at how sudden this came on!" Monica moaned.

"Finish up, sweetie. We should go. They give you a pain med for your bladder that really helps."

Shelby gingerly guided Monica to her truck, tucked her in the passenger seat, and drove straight to Urgent Care. She dropped Monica at the revolving doors. "Check in, and tell them your symptoms."

Monica checked in, and, as soon as she explained her symptoms, the nurse sent her to the lab on the lower level. "This will speed up the process. The doctor will have your lab results when he sees you."

"Good call," Monica said and disappeared down to the lab. She texted Shelby where she was. By the time Monica found herself in a bathroom peeing in a cup, she actually had to pee. Her bladder applauded her for peeing but immediately went into another spasm, causing her to sit back down on the toilet, wondering if more would come out. When nothing happened, she finished and labored back up the stairs.

Walking like she had a corn cob up her ass, she joined Shelby in the lobby and waited until she was called back to see the doctor. "Want to come with me?"

"I'd be happy to," Shelby said.

Monica leaned on Shelby, as they followed the nurse down the hallway to the exam room. The nurse was sympathetic to Monica's plight, so very quickly took her vitals. Shortly after she left, a male doctor in a plaid shirt and brown corduroys entered the room.

"I'm Dr. Attenborough." He shook her hand, and Monica introduced herself and Shelby.

"What brings you in today?"

"My bladder is on fire. I feel like I have to pee, but when I go, nothing comes out and then my bladder spasms."

There was a knock on the door, and the nurse stuck her head in. "The lab results came back. They're in the system." She nodded at the computer on the desk in front of the doctor, so he focused his attention on the screen and clicked a few times.

"You have a bladder infection, Ms. Spade," he said. "Ever had one before?"

"No. I'm so shocked at how suddenly it came on."

He turned to face her, his cheeks ruddy and eyes compassionate. "I've never had one, but I've practiced medicine long enough to know that when a woman tells me she has a bladder infection, she has a bladder infection."

"I can vouch for the fact that the symptoms are as bright as a neon sign," Monica said.

"I'm going to prescribe you an antibiotic and a medicine called Pyridium. It acts like an anesthetic on your bladder, so the spasms should subside. Take it right away, and you should notice some relief in an hour or so."

"Oh God, thank you," Monica said. "I wouldn't be able to sleep with this going on." She motioned to her belly.

"That's what I hear," he said. "The pharmacist will go over the antibiotic doses with you. Any questions?" He looked at Monica then Shelby.

Neither had any.

"If you don't feel better by tomorrow evening, then you'll want to come back in. Also, if you get a fever, then come in right away, okay?"

"Okay," Monica said. "I'll have to buy a thermometer."

He typed on the keyboard then clicked to close out of her medical record. "All done. I'll let you go, so you can get some relief. Nice to meet you both."

"You too. Thank you so much."

They picked up the prescriptions and a bottle of water. As soon as Monica was in the car, she swallowed two Pyridium tablets and guzzled the water. As Shelby drove them home, Monica could feel every bump in the road reverberating through her spasmodic bladder.

"We'll be there soon," Shelby said, patting Monica's leg.

"It just hurts so bad. My bladder feels like a bass drum that the car is pounding with every bump."

"Breathe through the spasms. The Pyridium really helps once it kicks in. Trust me."

"When will that be—exactly?" Monica asked through gritted teeth.

"Soon."

When they arrived home, Shelby helped Monica to the door.

As soon as they entered the house, Monica rushed to the kitchen, poured herself a glass of cranberry juice and washed down an antibiotic pill. She rested her hands on the cool counter, absorbing another spasm. "Yowzah, this hurts."

"Maybe a warm shower would help," Shelby said, turning on some lights. "When this happened to me, I felt better just sitting in the shower for a while and letting the water massage me."

"That does sound nice." Monica came to Shelby and lay her hand in hers.

Shelby led her to the bathroom and carefully pulled her sweatshirt and tank over her head, which was difficult due to Monica's hunched over shoulders and belly pain. Shelby turned on the shower and helped Monica in. "Do you want me to join you and soap your back?"

Monica grimaced. "As nice as that sounds, I can barely stand up straight with these spasms. The thought of someone touching me kind of scares me a little. Sorry."

"No worries," Shelby said. "Just holler if you want me to help you get dressed."

Left alone, Monica embraced the spray, letting it soothe her face and chest. She turned around, allowing the water to gently warm her back. Then, she lay her arm on a ledge and rested her forehead on it, inviting the spray to massage her neck and shoulders. She remained in the shower as long as she could stand, the soothing nature of the ritual distracting her from the bottle rockets in her bladder.

After toweling off, she decided she was too weak to put on clothes, so she wrapped herself in her microfiber robe and joined Shelby on the sofa.

"Hey, feel better?" Shelby asked, opening her arm for Monica to curl up next to her.

"A little." Monica barely got comfortable when spasms overtook her again. She moaned as she stretched out, which was a mistake. Pulling her bladder taut seemed to exacerbate the problem. Beyond embarrassment at that point, she flopped down to her knees on the floor and rested her head on the seat, moaning like a child.

She felt Shelby's hand on her head, gently stroking her hair. "There, there. It's going to get better. I promise. You've been through the worst part. Hang in there until the painkiller works."

Monica moaned. *It's been a half-hour.*

She flipped and flopped against the sofa for another 30 minutes until she couldn't take it any longer. "I'm going to try lying down in bed. Maybe I'll fall asleep, and when I get up, this bladder torture will be over."

Shelby gave Monica the most compassionate look, no hint of amusement on her face. "I'll come with you. Do you mind if I look at my iPad while you try to sleep?"

"Not at all. I'd love it if you were with me."

"Is big, red Todd coming over again tonight?"

Monica tried to focus through her discomfort. "Not unless we call him. We left it that he would be on standby. Do you want him here?"

"No. I feel fine."

"I wish I could say that," Monica said on her way to the bathroom.

While Shelby turned off lights and locked the doors, Monica hauled herself into the fetal position in bed. She felt a sudden lessening of the wildfire in her belly, grateful for the medication that must have kicked in.

A few minutes later, Shelby crawled in next to Monica and rubbed her shoulder. "How are we doing?"

"A smidgeon better," Monica said, cuddling next to Shelby's warm body.

"Good to hear. Take some deep breaths and focus on falling asleep."

"Will I feel better in the morning?"

There was a long pause, then Shelby said, "It's different for everyone, but I'm optimistic. For now, just focus on lying still and ignoring the spasms. Sleep will help."

"Okay." Monica fought the urge to toss and turn, or get out of bed to sit on the toilet, despite the fact that her body was signaling in every way for her to go to the bathroom. "Am I going to pee the bed if I don't get up?"

Shelby chuckled. "No. As long as you just tried, I think you're fine for a few hours, don't you?"

"I usually am, but this is so fucking weird. I'm afraid that, if I ignore the spasms, I'll pee myself."

"I don't think that will happen," Shelby said, "but if it does, I won't think less of you. We'll just change the sheets and go back to sleep. Okay?"

"Okay," Monica mumbled, and her last thought before she slipped into sleep was that she was going to pee the bed, but her last sensation was Shelby's warm, comforting hand on her shoulder.

32

Monica woke with a start at five the next morning, her bladder signaling it was stretched to the max and needed to be emptied. The burning sensation had subsided, so she hoped this was the real deal and not a repeat of last night's false alarms. She turned to look at Shelby sleeping next to her, her button nose pointed in the air, her curls cascading down the white pillow. Monica's heart squeezed. If she could awaken to Shelby beside her for the rest of her life, she'd be a happy woman.

She slipped out of bed, went to the bathroom and actually peed, but she still felt horrible, like a truck had run over her. Her entire body was sore, not just her bladder. She moped out to the kitchen and took an antibiotic pill—best to stay on schedule with those —washing it down with some water and half of a banana. She crawled back into bed with her iPhone, trying not to jostle the covers. It was still dark out, and she suspected Nathan was still asleep, but she had to contact him sooner rather than later.

Attempting not to wake Shelby, Monica texted Nathan. *Hey, I came down with a nasty infection. Can u sub for me in court this morning? If I can sleep for a few more hours, I'm sure I can be there by noon.*

She didn't expect to hear back from him for an hour, so she cuddled up to Shelby's warm back, gently slid her arm over her ribs, and drifted back to sleep.

She awoke an hour later to her phone ringing. She grabbed it off the nightstand and saw it was Nathan.

"Hey," she said.

"An infection?" he asked playfully. "Does someone have courtitis?"

"Very funny. My bladder. I saw the doctor last night and got some antibiotics and painkillers, but I'm laid up this morning. If you can sub for me, I promise to get there by noon."

"Ah…I don't know about that," he said.

She could hear the trepidation in his voice? "Why not"

"Matt is supposed to testify first thing. I can't be in the position of cross-examining my boyfriend."

"No worries. You aren't there to cross-examine him. You're there to explain stuff to Stela. Big difference," she said reassuringly.

"He won't see it that way," Nathan said. "Maybe Jim can do it."

"Jim's in a real conflict," Monica moaned. "The DA is his lover."

"Why is his conflict more real than mine?"

"It just is. You know Dominique would be furious with him if he showed up at counsel table across from her. He wouldn't be able to stop himself from kibitzing with Stela, whispering all sorts of questions for her to ask Matt." Monica had to pause to catch her breath, surprised at her lack of energy.

"I'd rather have Dominique mad at Jim than Matt mad at me," Nathan said.

"Well, Jim didn't add my name to the criminal defense counsel list, and I'm sure Matt will understand. Just text him in advance."

"I won't have to do that," Nathan said. "He's in the shower at my house."

"See? Problem solved. Tell him I'm really sorry that I'm sick and put you in this bind. I'll make you both a homemade dinner in return. If you just stick to your standby counsel role, you'll be fine." She already felt tired, needing to wrap up this conversation, so she could fall back asleep.

Releasing an exaggerated man sigh, Nathan sounded like he was in more pain than she was. "Fine, but you owe me."

"You signed me up for this," she fired back.

"I'll see you at noon," he said and hung up. She was so exhausted from that short exchange that her eyes were already closed. She immediately fell back into a profound sleep, surfacing only for a fleeting second when Shelby planted a kiss on her forehead as she left for school.

***

A few hours later, Monica was jolted awake by her cell phone ringing. She grabbed it from the nightstand and automatically answered in a groggy voice.

"Hello?"

"I'm looking for Monica Spade," an unidentified, yet familiar, female voice said.

Through the cobwebs of sleep, she garbled, "This is Monica."

"This is Cassidy Ness at Triple A," the young woman said in her perennially-bored voice. "You asked me to call you if Darcy Lemon booked another banner."

Monica's mind chugged, sputtering to life. "Of course, Cassidy. Thanks for calling." She rubbed her eyes, as she pictured Darcy Lemon and the airplane banner. "Is Darcy running the same banner or a new one?"

"A new one. It says, 'Boycott *Voila!* for nukes!'"

"*Voila!?*" Monica asked.

"That's what it says," Cassidy said through gum smacks.

"Not the hospital?"

"Nope."

"Awesome. She isn't attacking the hospital. Go ahead and sell her the spot. Only call me if she books another banner mentioning the hospital, okay?"

"I live to serve," Cassidy said sarcastically and hung up.

Monica looked at her phone, puzzled that Cassidy was so pissy.

She yawned and stretched, sending out feelers to her bladder and urethra, looking for signs of pain. Nothing. Her mind and body felt refreshed from sleep and the initial doses of antibiotics, but she was starved. Food was a must before she went to court.

She stumbled out to the kitchen and made coffee, eggs and toast, topped off by another antibiotic pill. While eating, she googled Eugène Ionesco again and looked up several of his famous quotations from plays and other writings. Something niggled at the back of her mind from Stela's opening statement, just within reach if Monica could sort out the word salad that Stela had thrown at the jurors as Andy's sex journal excerpts.

She removed her laptop from her bag and navigated to Stela's exhibit of Andy's sexual fantasies. Monica compared the excerpts to a long list of Ionesco quotes. She chuckled cynically under her breath. Next, she pulled up her file from the DA's Office and located the written statement that Yuri had supplied to Matt and Brock. She compared the handwriting and quotations, confirming her suspicions.

Energized, she felt ready to head to court like a bird dog set loose in the woods.

33

Even from a distance, Monica could see the agitation in Nathan's body language, as she made her way toward him in the hallway filled with spectators, reporters, and Andy Nelson's family and friends.

Anxious to leave, Nathan was buttoned up in his camel overcoat with a matching Burberry plaid scarf coiled around his neck. He raked his hand through his longish brown hair. "About time you got here."

She put her hand on his arm. "Thank you for pinch-hitting for me. I was really sick. How did it go?"

He closed his eyes for a second and said before re-opening them. "Not well. Matt is furious with me."

"For sitting next to Stela?"

"Not exactly just sitting there."

"Did you feed her some questions?"

"Unfortunately, yes. I just couldn't stop myself. It's my job to test the prosecution's case—to put them to the standard of *beyond a reasonable doubt*, you know?"

"What questions did you feed her?" she asked, fighting back a smile.

He moaned in agony. "I just pointed out that Matt's report didn't mention Stela's clump of hair on the floor of the back seat nor did they have direct proof that Stela brought the Trident paring knife from Andy's kitchen. It's not like they got that on video or anything."

"Astute observations."

"Matt saw me whisper to Stela before she grilled him."

"And?" she asked. "There has to be more since that doesn't sound so bad."

He shifted his weight on his expensive brown brogues, his gaze falling to the floor. "I sort of, kind of, pointed out that, when Matt and Brock found Andy's body in the field Sunday afternoon, Stela immediately became a suspect since she had been picked up at the farmer's house and told the police that she had been assaulted. Thus, when Matt and Brock visited her on the Behavioral Health Unit Monday morning to interview her, they should have Mirandized her because they suspected she killed Andy."

"I never thought of that," Monica said. "Did Dominique rehabilitate Matt on redirect?"

"She actually asked to be heard outside the presence of the jurors, so Judge O'Brien dismissed them. Dominique made the usual arguments about Stela not being in custody, thus Matt and Brock weren't required to Mirandize her."

"How did Judge O'Brien rule?"

"He found that they didn't need to Mirandize her at the hospital, so the statements she made while being interviewed on the Behavioral Health Unit are admissible testimony from Matt."

"So, what's the big deal?"

"You know cops. Dominique understands, but I'm sure Matt feels like I frosted his balls."

Monica wondered whether he meant cold or a sugar coating. She shook off the image, grateful that she wasn't attracted to men. "Gosh. I feel horrible for putting you in that position."

"No worries. I deserved it by signing your name to the volunteer list, and I could've remained quiet, but I didn't. Matt and I will survive this."

"Frosty balls or not." Monica smirked then looked around to make sure no eavesdroppers were nearby. "Let me help you get back into Matt's good graces. I had the chance to sleep on something, and the facts crystallized in my mind. I have a tip for Matt to follow up on."

Nathan cocked his head. "Tip?"

"Yes, but don't tell him it came from me."

"I'm all ears."

She told him what she had pieced together.

"Brilliant," he said. "I'll relay it right away."

"Thank you," she said in a softer voice. "I'll make you two dinner when this is all over."

He winked. "I had fun."

After he departed, she entered the courtroom and took her chair at counsel table.

Dominique came bustling in with her paralegal on her heels. "Hey Monica, feeling better?"

"Much."

Dominique came closer, so they wouldn't be overheard. She was wearing a navy blazer with a lapel pin in the shape of Wisconsin with the state crest emblazoned in gold on it. Monica thought it was a nice alternative to the American flag pin. "Nathan said you had an infection. Not the flu, I hope."

"No. Bladder infection. I've never had one, and boy, did I learn they're painful."

A look of familiarity crossed Dominique's face. "Oh yes. Thank goodness for antibiotics, and that special bladder pain reliever they give you."

"Righto." Monica smiled, then switched gears. "I heard Nathan created a dust storm this morning."

"Storm?" Dominique waved off the characterization. "More of a dust *up* if you ask me. The clump of hair isn't exculpatory, and I don't need to prove who brought the knife."

"Nathan said Matt got angry."

"Cops always get angry when they're cross-examined. He'll cool down. I told him it was no big deal."

Monica was again struck by how unflappable Dominique was in her arena, thinking on her feet and arguing every day, composed even in front of the TV cameras.

"Good to know," Monica said.

Judge O'Brien entered the courtroom 10 minutes before court was scheduled to begin. Dominique consulted her watch and returned to her counsel table.

"Ms. Spade, good to see you again. Decide to sleep in this morning?" Judge O'Brien asked.

Monica felt her face flush. "Hardly, Your Honor. I was quite ill. I brought my physician discharge summary from Urgent Care if you'd like to see it." She started digging in her bag for it.

He chuckled. "No need. I believe you. Are we ready to proceed this afternoon?"

"Yes," Dominique said.

Judge O'Brien's gaze roamed from the empty chair next to Monica to the metal door at the side of the courtroom. "Where's the defendant?"

"We still have ten minutes before our scheduled start," Dominique said.

Something must have been in the air because the side door opened, and the deputies escorted Stela to her spot next to Monica. She wore a black blazer and gray skirt, and carried her trial notebook under her arm. If not for the hovering deputy escort, she looked like a lawyer.

"Hello, Ms. Reiter," Monica said.

"You again?" Stela asked. "I was just getting used to your colleague, Mr. Taylor. He's very... What shall I say? Smooth?"

"That's why I called him to sub for me this morning. He's an experienced trial attorney."

"I could tell. Quick on his feet, and he gave me some insightful ammo to use on cross."

"Maybe you shouldn't have fired your public defenders," Monica said, feeling as though her own time wouldn't have been wasted if Stela had accepted a full-blown defense attorney.

"Nonsense," Stela said in a flat tone. "After interviewing them, I could tell they weren't as good as Mr. Taylor. He, on the other hand, would have been acceptable."

Monica nodded but thought better of saying more.

"Any chance I could have Mr. Taylor for the remainder of the trial, and you could return to your sleepy little office practice doing…" Stela fluttered her hand in the air, "whatever it is that you do?"

Monica plastered a smile on her face, and said, "I'm afraid you're stuck with me, Ms. Reiter. Court orders. Plus, Mr. Taylor has a busy litigation practice right now."

"Nothing is more important than this trial." Stela shimmied up to the microphone. "I'll ask the court."

Unfuckingbelievable! Monica clenched her jaw, and waited for Stela to spring her new demand on the judge.

Judge O'Brien repeated his earlier question. "Is there anything we need to take up before we bring in the jury?"

"Yes, Your Honor," Stela said.

"What is it?"

"I'd like to move the court for a substitution of standby counsel. I want Mr. Taylor back."

Monica heard a modest snicker from Dominique, but when Monica glanced over, Dominique had already reset her face to Inscrutable2.0.

Judge O'Brien's eyebrows shot up, and he looked at Dominique. "Does the State have a position on the defendant's motion?"

Dominique immediately recognized that he was looking for her to make a compelling argument, so his ruling would have some substance.

"The State opposes the motion, Your Honor. The defendant already fired two public defenders, then insisted on representing herself *pro se*. Given the nature of the charges, the Court properly appointed standby counsel to explain matters of judicial process to the defendant during the trial."

Dominique breathed, adjusted her lapel, and continued. "Ms. Spade has done an exemplary job of fulfilling the role of standby counsel, but was out ill this morning with an infection for which she saw a physician last night. Mr. Taylor, a seasoned trial attorney, substituted for Ms. Spade and slightly exceeded the parameters of standby counsel by feeding the defendant questions for the cross-examination of Detective Matthew Breuer, then making a motion regarding a Miranda warning. Those two actions go above and beyond the scope of standby counsel. Ms. Reiter agreed to them, even praising Mr. Taylor's efforts, but the record should reflect that she is still a *pro se* defendant."

Dominique turned to her paralegal, Lori, and whispered something. "One second, Your Honor."

They waited while Lori thumbed through some files in a Banker's Box then handed Dominique a manila-colored file. Dominique opened it, glanced over some material and looked up.

"There is legal precedent in Wisconsin that a *pro se* defendant is not entitled to defense counsel halfway through her trial because she suddenly realizes she might benefit from it. The cite is *State v. Monroe*, 134 Wis. 2d 67 (1997)."

Judge O'Brien wrote down the case number.

Dominique continued, "That precedent is for *actual* counsel, not standby counsel. Here, the defendant wants to have her cake and eat it too. She wants the legal right to run her own defense but also wants a super-lawyer standby counsel who periodically represents her like defense counsel would. That's an improper use of standby counsel that isn't supported in the law. There's a Seventh Circuit case with relevant language, and here I quote, 'In delineating the duties of standby counsel, the court may take into consideration avoidance of abuse of counsel by an opportunistic or vacillating defendant.' The citation is *State v. List*, 880 F. 2d 1047 (7th Cir. 1989), Your Honor."

Dominique looked up from her folder. "As such, the defendant isn't entitled to new standby counsel in the middle of a trial. The defendant hasn't cited any reason, factual or legal, for her request, other than she preferred Mr. Taylor's style, which again, was akin to a public defender, two of whom the defendant fired. For these reasons, the State opposes the defendant's motion."

The creases in Judge O'Brien's forehead smoothed, as his eyebrows lowered to a resting pose. He turned to Stela. "Does the defendant have anything more to say?"

Stela leaned into the microphone. "In the interest of fairness, Your Honor, I didn't realize how helpful standby counsel could be. I'm not requesting full-blown defense counsel, but I would like someone with more experience. No offense to Ms. Spade, but she isn't a trial attorney."

Judge O'Brien looked at Dominique again.

"Again, Your Honor, Ms. Spade's role isn't to try the case. It's simply meant to explain judicial process and the court's rulings. Ms. Spade is perfectly competent to do that, and has been doing a commendable job thus far."

Judge O'Brien nodded, signaling he was ready to rule. "The court has considered the law and arguments from both parties regarding the defendant's motion for a substitution of standby counsel."

He ignored them for a second and turned to his computer screen, frowning as he looked for something. After a few seconds, his eyes brightened, and he said, "Here it is. My letter to Standby Counsel Spade. At the beginning of this case, pursuant to the defendant's wishes, as stated on the record when she fired her second public defender, I sent this letter to Attorney Spade outlining her duties, and copied the defendant, so she would have a clear understanding. In my letter, I said, in part, that standby counsel 'should not speak on behalf of the defendant, and refrain from giving the impression to the jury that she represents the defendant.'"

He turned from the flat screen and looked at the parties.

"The defendant hasn't cited any factual reason, other than a personal preference for Mr. Taylor, or any legal precedent for her request. Having observed Ms. Spade in her role, it is the Court's observation that she is performing as well or better than any standby counsel who has ever served previously in that role. Moreover, the law cited by the prosecution is familiar law and provides precedent for my ruling. I hereby deny the defendant's motion."

Stela slumped in her chair and savagely opened her trial binder, slamming the cover on the table. The deputy closest to their table rose from his chair and walked over to sit directly behind her. Even though Stela pretended not to notice, she shifted in her chair and lay her hands on the table in full view.

Monica glanced back at the deputy then put some distance between Stela and herself.

Judge O'Brien surveyed them. "Is the State ready to call its next witness?"

"Yes, Your Honor," Dominique said.

"Who will that be?"

"Julia Brown, the SANE nurse from Community Memorial Hospital."

"Very well," Judge O'Brien said. He turned to the plump, elderly Isla, who was sitting in the jury bailiff chair next to the empty jury box. "Please bring in the jury."

34

As the jurors filled their empty seats, each, in turn, glanced at Stela's table to register that Monica had replaced the dapper Nathan.

Judge O'Brien broke the silence. "Welcome back. I hope lunch was satisfactory. The prosecution will now continue with its case. District Attorney Bisset, please call your next witness."

"The State calls Nurse Julia Brown."

A woman with shoulder-length, chocolate-colored hair entered the back of the courtroom, a tentativeness in her mannerisms and step. Dominique beckoned her forward, then motioned her over to the court secretary for administration of the oath.

The nurse carried with her a small white box, which she clutched like a baby. Once she was settled in the witness chair, Dominique began with the preliminary background questions.

"Please state your name for the record."

"Julia Brown."

"What is your profession?"

"I'm a nurse."

"Where do you work?"

"Community Memorial Hospital."

"What kind of nursing do you practice?"

"I'm a sexual assault nurse examiner."

"Did you go to school for that?"

"Yes. I have a four-year college degree, followed by forensic nursing training."

"Turning now to the issue before us, do you remember the evening of Saturday, January 4, 2020 in the Emergency Department?"

"Yes. I was at work that night."

"Did you take care of the defendant, Stela Reiter?"

"Yes. I conducted a sexual assault nursing exam of her and gathered evidence."

"Can you identify Stela Reiter in the courtroom today?"

Nurse Brown pointed to Stela. "Yes. That's her, directly in front of me."

"Let the record reflect that the witness pointed at the defendant," Dominique said. "Did you make a note of your exam of Ms. Reiter that night?"

"Yes."

"Approach the witness, Your Honor?" Dominique asked.

"Of course," he said.

Dominique delivered a document to Nurse Brown.

"I've given you what's been marked as Exhibit 48. Is that a nursing note of your exam with Stela Reiter on January 4th?"

Nurse Brown looked at it. "Yes."

"What time did you arrive at Stela Reiter's exam room?"

"7:22 p.m."

"Who was in the room?"

"When I entered, Ms. Reiter was lying on the bed, and an ED technician was sitting next to her."

"Was law enforcement present?"

"Yes. He was standing outside the room."

"Please briefly explain what a SANE exam is for the jury."

Nurse Brown turned to the jurors, and said in a tutorial voice, "We're trained to examine a patient who presents with a history of a possible sexual assault. We help facilitate evidence collection for law enforcement and the patient. We conduct a head-to-

toe exam, talk to the patient, and collect pieces of evidence."

"What is your role?"

"I'm there to collect evidence and preserve it for law enforcement if the patient wants to report the event. I'm not the patient's nurse for care purposes."

"Are you trained to follow a protocol?"

"Yes. We're trained by the International Association of Nurses. We assess the patient for medical needs and collaborate with the treating nurse and physician. Then, we collect evidence and maintain chain of custody to protect it."

"Let's talk about your initial evaluation of Ms. Reiter. Is there a form you follow?"

"Yes. First, we do an interview, hopefully helping the patient recall what happened to him or her. Our first concern is whether the patient is hurt or has any trauma."

"Looking at page one of your assessment, did you ask Ms. Reiter what happened?"

"Yes."

"What did she tell you?" Dominique asked.

"She said she couldn't remember. That she'd lost her memory."

"Did you ask her if she lost consciousness?"

"Yes."

"What did she say?"

"She might have blacked out. She muttered something about seizures, but then denied having any condition that would lead to seizure activity." She raised her shoulders in question.

"Did you ask her about the physical surroundings of the alleged sexual assault?"

"Yes. She said, 'I was with my boyfriend. That's the last thing I remember.' I asked if she remembered any details. That's when she said, 'I don't know. I think I was raped. It hurts.'

"Did you ask Ms. Reiter whether there was any injury to her assailant?"

"I did. I wrote 'unknown' on my intake form because she said she couldn't remember."

"Did you ask about sexual contact?"

"Yes."

"How did she respond?"

"She couldn't remember the details, so I wrote 'unknown' on my report. She initially said she was raped, but she couldn't elaborate."

"Did you ask if his penis touched her? If so, how did she respond?"

"Yes. She couldn't remember, so I wrote 'unknown' on my report."

"Did you ask if his fingers touched her?"

"Yes. She couldn't remember, so I wrote 'unknown' on my report."

"Did you ask if his mouth touched her?

"Yes. Again, she couldn't remember, so I wrote 'unknown' on my report."

"Did you ask if anything touched her genitals?"

"Yes. She couldn't remember, so I wrote 'unknown' on my report."

"Do you usually do any follow-up to confirm what a person is telling you?"

"Um. Not really. Based on what the patient tells me, I check the boxes for 'yes, no, or unknown.'"

"Do you conduct a physical exam as well?"

"Yes, but it's a SANE exam, not an exam for treatment purposes. So, I check the body for injury or evidence of contact with an assailant."

"Did you observe any injuries on Ms. Reiter?"

"Yes."

"What were those?"

"Self-cutting lacerations."

"Where were those?"

"Her left palm, her right groin, and the outer aspect of her right thigh."

"Why did you describe them as 'self-cutting lacerations' in your report?"

"Because they looked consistent with every self-cutting laceration I've encountered on patients during my career."

"First, what's a laceration?"

"It's a cut to the skin, usually made with a sharp object."

"Can there be various depths to a laceration?"

"Yes. Ms. Reiter's lacerations were shallow. What we call 'superficial.' Just the top layer of the skin was cut very carefully and in a controlled manner."

"Are there certain characteristics you look for to define self-cutting?"

"Yes."

"Please explain what those are."

"Self-cutting is usually superficial because of the pain involved, and the patient isn't anesthetized like in surgery. It doesn't take much of a cut to the skin to create pain. The cuts are usually very controlled rather than the slashing stabs and gashes we see with an actual knife fight. Self-cutting is usually in a pattern, or a diagram, or words. It's usually in a spot on the body where the person can see what he or she is doing while they're cutting. The cuts are usually within easy reach while using a knife, or other instrument, to do the self-harm."

"Thank you, Nurse Brown," Dominique said. "Did you ask Stela Reiter how the cuts on her left palm, right groin and outer right thigh got there?"

"Yes."

"What did she tell you?"

"She couldn't remember."

"Okay. Did her cuts require any treatment like stitches or bandaging?"

"No. Just some antibacterial ointment."

"Thank you. Let's move to your actual physical exam of Ms. Reiter. I noticed you brought a white box with you today. What is it?"

"This is a Wisconsin State Crime Lab Medical Evidence Kit."

"What is it used for?"

"These are the kits we use to take evidence."

"Were you trained in how to use the items in the kit?"

"Yes."

"Please open the kit and explain what's inside for the jury."

Nurse Brown did as requested, holding up various items, so the jury could see them. "This piece of paper is a listing of the order in which we collect evidence, and where we collect it from. There's an evidence drying kit with labels for swabs. Here's a cervical swab. Here's an oral swab," she said, holding them up for the jury to see. "After we take a swab sample, we put the swab in the drier then put it in the correlating envelope."

"What else is in your kit?"

"There's a toxicology gathering vial, swab and form."

"Do you take bodily fluid samples?"

"Yes."

"What kind?"

"Blood, saliva and urine."

"Why?"

"To detect drugs or alcohol in the patient, as well as get their DNA to compare it to the DNA of the assailant."

"During your examination, did you take a blood sample from Ms. Reiter?"

"Yes."

"Did you include it in the kit?"

"Yes."

"Did you take a saliva sample?"

"Yes."

"Did you include it in the kit?"

"Yes."

"Why?"

"Because Ms. Reiter didn't remember what happened, so maybe clues would be in the evidence collection. We always recommend blood, urine and saliva if the patient doesn't recall the events of the assault."

"Did you ask Ms. Reiter to consent to all of this?"

"Yes."

"Did she?"

"Yes."

"What about the oral swab? How do you collect that?" Dominique asked.

"The oral collection is by both swab and flossing. We asked her to floss her teeth, then we put that in the envelope that's labeled 'floss.' After that, I swabbed her mouth then put the swab in a rack to dry. I also got Ms. Reiter's DNA with a cheek swab."

"Did you include those in the kit?"

"Yes."

"Did you collect a hair sample?"

"Yes."

"Urine sample?"

"Yes."

"You also got fingernail evidence?"

"Yes."

"How did you do that?"

"We have a smaller and pointier swab for that. We have the patient hold her hand over a paper to see if something falls out. If anything falls, we collect it. Then, we use a swab under the fingernails to collect DNA."

"Did you do that here?"

"Yes."

"Did you collect clothing?"

"Yes. By the time I arrived, the ED staff had already bagged her clothes in brown paper bags."

"What else did you collect from Ms. Reiter?"

"We collected dirt from her hands."

"What else?"

"We collected dried blood secretions from her right thigh."

"Can you explain that for the jury?"

"We used a light source and a moistened swab to collect secretions from her right thigh where the self-cutting marks were."

"Did you swab the top of her pelvis?"

"Yes, we swab that area when there isn't any pubic hair, and she didn't have any pubic hair."

"Did you do external genital swabs?"

"Yes."

"Where are those collected from?"

"The outside of the vagina and labia, and crevices between the pubic bone and thigh."

"Did you do a vaginal swab?

"Yes."

"How?"

"We use a speculum and light to look for any injury or trauma, then we take four different swabs inside the vagina."

"Did you observe any physical injuries or trauma?"

"No."

"Did you also do an anal swab?"

"Yes."

"How?"

"We just did an external anal swab here, because she said her anus wasn't violated."

"Okay, switching to another part of her body, did you observe any injuries to her neck?"

"Yes. The right side of her neck, right below her jaw, was reddened a little. The skin wasn't broken."

"Did you photograph it?"

"Yes."

"Prior to testifying today, did you review an electronic copy of the photos?"

"Yes."

"Are these exhibits, numbers 11 through 18, true and accurate copies?"

"Yes."

"Your Honor, I move to publish the photographs to the jury," Dominique said.

Stela raised her hand and interjected, "Since these photos are intensely private, I request that they be published only to the jury and not on the overhead screens."

"Granted," Judge O'Brien said. "The Court requests the District Attorney to do so."

Dominique gave the first photo to Isla, who rose from her chair and handed it to the juror nearest her.

"What is this photo of?" Dominique asked Nurse Brown.

"This is a photo of the patient's perineal area."

"What is the next photo?"

"It's a different angle of the same shot of perineal area, groin and right thigh."

Dominique gave that photo to Isla to circulate to the jurors. "Are there any injuries?"

"There are superficial lacerations of self-cutting."

"What is the next photo?"

"Those are the patient's hands. Abrasions and dirt are present."

"Ms. Reiter hadn't showered, right?"

"Correct."

"This is how she presented to you, right?"

"Correct."

"What's the next photo?"

"It's her hand laceration with a ruler overlaying it to gauge the length of the lacerations."

"During your examination, Ms. Reiter told you that Andy had made these lacerations to her palm, correct?"

"Yes. She couldn't remember much, but she mumbled a couple of times, 'He cut me. He cut me.'"

"Did you ask her how?"

"Yes."

"What did she tell you?"

"She said she couldn't remember."

"Okay. How long were you with Ms. Reiter?"

"I arrived at 7:22 p.m. and left around 11p.m."

"Thank you. I have nothing further for this witness," Dominique said, as she returned to her chair, leaving the photos in the jurors' hands to circulate.

Judge O'Brien looked at Stela. "Does the defendant have any questions?"

"A few." Stela remained in her chair and leveled her gaze at Nurse Brown. "Before you examined me at the hospital, I was in the custody of law enforcement, right?"

"That was my understanding—that you were brought in by law enforcement."

"The law enforcement personnel were all males, correct?"

"Object, Your Honor. Relevance," Dominique said.

"Overruled," Judge O'Brien said.

"I don't know," Nurse Brown said.

"The guard outside my room was male, correct?"

"Yes."

"Okay," Stela said. "During your exam of me, you asked if I had taken any drugs or alcohol, right?"

"Yes."

"I reported that I hadn't, correct?"

"Correct."

"I was sober, no?"

"Some illicit drugs don't show up on tox screens, but you appeared sober."

"I was cooperative and consented to everything, right?"

"Yes."

"I didn't object to anything?"

"You didn't object."

"In your experience, do victims of sexual assault exhibit signs of PTSD?"

"Yes."

"Is one of the signs of PTSD lack of memory?"

"Sometimes."

"Not all sexual assault victims you've treated have a perfect recollection of what happened, do they?"

"No."

"Likewise, not every sexual assault victim you've treated is talkative either, correct?"

"That's correct."

"It isn't uncommon for a victim to recall more details later, like the next day, and the next, and so forth, correct?"

"I suppose, but I don't usually see victims later, so I couldn't tell you for sure."

"Fair enough," Stela said. "Let's put up on the screens the photo of the right side of my neck that was reddened due to the strangling." Stela nodded at Dominique to do so, which Dominique quickly did from her laptop.

"This is a photo you took of me that night, right Ms. Brown?"

"Yes."

"The red mark was just below my jaw, yes?"

"Correct."

"You've treated sexual assault victims who have reported that they've been strangled or choked, haven't you?"

"Yes."

"In my case, that's a pretty obvious red mark, isn't it?"

"Yes."

"Even if the patient can't tell you what happened, this mark is important evidence, isn't it?"

"Yes."

"This red mark is consistent with strangulation, isn't it?"

"It could be."

Stela paused a moment, glanced through her notes, and continued, "I signed releases of all of my health care information for law enforcement, didn't I?"

"Yes."

"That means that I allowed law enforcement to get the results of your exam, correct?"

"Yes."

"I also consented to photographs of my entire body for law enforcement, didn't I?"

"Yes."

"Nothing further, Your Honor," Stela said.

"Any redirect by the prosecution?" Judge O'Brien asked.

"Just a few questions, Your Honor," Dominique said.

"Nurse Brown, did you examine Ms. Reiter's eyes?"

"Yes."

"Specifically, did you look for evidence of strangulation?"

"Yes."

"Describe for the jury signs of strangulation in the eyes."

"Petechiae—specifically, bright red patches in the whites of the eyes—are sometimes present with a strangulation because of the stress on the blood vessels of a sudden decrease in oxygen."

"Were there any petechiae present in Ms. Reiter's eyes?"

"No."

"Let's turn to Ms. Reiter's neck. Did you look at both sides of her neck?"

"Yes."

"Were there marks on both sides?"

"No. Just the one side."

"In the case of strangulation with the hands, you usually see redness around the entire neck, don't you?"

"Yes."

"Whether it's a two-handed strangulation or one-handed, there are usually symmetrical red marks, aren't there?"

"Yes," Nurse Brown said.

"Nothing further, Your Honor," Dominique said.

"Any re-cross by the defendant?" Judge O'Brien asked.

"Yes," Stela said. "Strangulation doesn't always leave petechiae, does it Ms. Reiter?"

"In the ones I've seen, it does."

"You haven't treated every strangulation case, have you?"

"Of course not."

"In addition, petechiae is merely reported in the literature as one sign of strangulation, isn't it?"

"An important sign."

"Let's discuss the literature and your training. When you train to become a SANE nurse, you get the accumulated knowledge of a lot of patients from your text books, literature and instructors, don't you?"

"Yes."

"A large body of patients for purposes of data collection and teaching, correct?"

"That's correct."

"So, when they teach you that petechiae can be a sign, in addition to other signs of strangulation, that's from a wider body of knowledge than what you see in your own practice, isn't it?"

"I suppose."

"You have no reason to disagree with what you've been taught, do you?"

"No."

"I have nothing further," Stela said.

Monica thought back to her own strangulation by Yuri. His hand had been gloved, but she could still feel the pressure he had exerted on her neck, depriving her of precious oxygen. She had noticed her skin was mildly red later, but she hadn't experienced petechiae.

"Very well," Judge O'Brien said, visibly pleased that the examination of Nurse Brown by Dominique and Stela had gone smoothly, without any drama that would necessitate his intervention. "Nurse Brown, you may be excused from the witness box." He turned to Dominique. "Is the prosecution prepared to call its next witness?"

"Yes," Dominique said.

"Who is that?"

"Dr. Tollefson, the Emergency Department physician who treated Ms. Reiter."

The remainder of the day was filled with Dominique questioning Dr. Tollefson then Dr. Karey, the psychiatrist. Both testified that it was strange that she wouldn't talk about the incident, or couldn't remember the incident, despite her assertion of PTSD. Both physicians were familiar with PTSD and treating patients with PTSD. Both insisted that Stela didn't act like someone with PTSD. Rather, she acted like she was hiding something. Dominique emphasized with both of them that PTSD certainly didn't cause a person to lie, and they agreed.

35

A few days later

Monica was setting up her laptop on counsel table when she heard the star *matadora* enter the arena. Without looking, Monica knew it was Dominique by the greetings from Andy Nelson's family and the decreased chatter from onlookers in the gallery.

Monica was startled when Dominique leaned over her shoulder and whispered so quietly that she strained to hear what Dominique was saying.

"Thanks for telling Nathan to relay to Matt that he go to *Voila!* to get a writing sample from Andy's employment file. Andy didn't create a lot of handwritten material at work, since they mostly do their reports on the computer, but we got a few samples. In addition, Andy's mother has a letter she received from Andy last year at this time. She was thinking the same thing as you when Stela put those bogus journal entries on the overhead during her opening statement. You won't be surprised by Mrs. Nelson's testimony."

"Is that right?" Monica said noncommittally, glancing nervously toward the metal side door, afraid that Stela would emerge any second and bust them strategizing. "Glad I'm not the only one who noticed."

Dominique patted Monica on the shoulder and returned to her own counsel table to set up her laptop and confer with Lori about files she would need for the day. She was wearing a tailored navy jacket and matching skirt with a crisp, white blouse, the American flag pin displayed on her lapel.

Monica turned around and allowed her eyes to sweep the courtroom, which was slowly filling with people. In the back row, she spotted Agents McCoy and Scott, looking as suspicious as two raccoons in an overcoat. Shelby had confirmed they had tailed her to and from school, as one of them usually rested against the outside of the car—in plain view—until she got in her Jeep and drove off.

They hadn't been present in court for the last couple of days, so had missed the nurse and physician testimony as well as the pathologist's description of every single stab wound and gash to Andy's body.

Monica's gaze drifted to Tiffany, who was standing next to her cameraman, her shoulders rounded and chin down while she typed on her cell phone.

Directly behind the prosecution table, the family and friends of Andy milled about, talking in hushed tones, as people do at solemn occasions. Andy's trial was like an extended funeral service, which had been held before Monica had become involved in the tragedy. People remained sad, tearful, and respectful of his memory while they endured photos of his gored body. Monica also sensed increasing anxiety over the justice the family no doubt hoped the jury would deliver.

The court secretary and reporter scurried in like church mice and sat at their stations, portending Judge O'Brien's arrival like a well-rehearsed play, everyone with a specific role to play, beginning with scene one of the day. Now sensitized to the definitive sound of the opening and closing of the large metal door behind the backdrop to the judge's bench, everyone in the courtroom quieted as Judge O'Brien came in and situated himself in his massive chair.

"Please be seated," he said to the courtroom in general. "Is there anything we need to take up before we bring the jury in this morning?"

"Ah. Your Honor, the defendant isn't here yet," Monica said.

He looked at the empty chair next to her. "Right you are, Ms. Spade. Is there something delaying her that I should be aware of?"

"Not to my knowledge," Monica said.

"Carry on, then." Judge O'Brien turned his attention to the computer on his desk.

The low level of chatter among the family and spectators returned slowly.

Monica felt a tap on her shoulder and looked up to see Kathy, her receptionist.

"Hope you don't mind if I attend for a few hours?"

"Not at all. Glad you're here."

"I have some info for you." Kathy removed a copy of a passport photo from her bag. "This is a copy of Yuri Zaleski's passport photo. The manager at Racy's Coffee Lounge had it for tax purposes."

Monica studied it. "Yep. That's the guy who choked me."

"I also asked the manager if employees clocked out for each other, and he confirmed it happened occasionally. He didn't dispute that someone could've clocked out for Yuri on January 4th when Andy was killed. Yuri could've given a coworker his work I.D., then the coworker would wait until the end of shift to slide it through the machine."

"That's what I suspected," Monica said. "Thanks, Kathy. You're a gem."

"I'll just sit a few rows back and watch the show."

"Enjoy," Monica said.

A few minutes later, the side door opened, and Stela moped in with her deputy escort. She looked disheveled. Her hair was greasy, and she had made no attempt to tame her bedhead, a loose ponytail resting at her nape. Further evidence of a lack of shower hit Monica's nostrils when Stela sat down next to her.

"Good morning," Monica said, wondering why Stela hadn't showered. The jail had showers.

"Hi," Stela grunted. "Did you know about this?" She shoved a revised witness list across the table to Monica, the stamp indicating it had been filed by Dominique at the close of business yesterday. Monica read it and saw the addition of Sharon Nelson, Andy's mother, and a man whose name she didn't recognize, Harry Hebl. His job title was listed as, "Manager, Weapons Division, *Voila!*"

"No," Monica said. "I didn't see that. I suppose Mrs. Nelson will testify about the family's heartbreak over Andy's passing, and I have no idea why the prosecution would call someone from Andy's employer. Do you?"

Stela shook her head, indicating no, but her disbelieving eyes methodically assessed Monica's expression.

Monica held Stela's stare, hoping Stela wasn't as good at detecting deception as she was with a knife.

"Are there any matters we need to take up before we bring in the jury?" Judge O'Brien asked, interrupting their uncomfortable exchange.

"Yes." Stela held up the revised witness list. "I just received the prosecution's new witness list. There are two people on it who weren't listed before, and no information was provided about the nature of their testimony. This is trial by ambush, denying me due process. We all know I'm supposed to get advance notice in time to prepare."

Judge O'Brien's eyebrows knitted together in interrogation of Dominique. "District Attorney Bisset, can you please explain?"

"The State is wrapping up its case this morning by calling Sharon Nelson, the mother of the victim, and Harry Hebl, the victim's boss at *Voila!*"

"What are the general areas of their testimony?" Judge O'Brien asked.

"They will both testify about the victim's handwriting."

Judge O'Brien nodded, not yet connecting the dots, then volleyed his gaze back to Stela. "Is that satisfactory, Ms. Reiter?"

Stela had already connected the dots, as evidenced by her quivering lower lip and trembling hands that she tried to soothe by rubbing her thumbs over her knuckles.

"No, Your Honor," Stela said. "Getting notice right now isn't satisfactory. I haven't had time to prepare a cross-examination of either of these witnesses. Moreover, I question the relevance of them testifying about Andy's handwriting."

Nice touch, Monica thought, *pretending like you don't have a clue even though you probably directed Yuri to write those journal entries.*

Judge O'Brien looked at Dominique, who dropped the hammer.

"The relevance is that the defendant introduced Mr. Nelson's handwritten sexual fantasies as evidence of her state of mind when they were in the back seat of his car. They allegedly support her claim of self-defense. She even requested that law enforcement go back to Mr. Nelson's house to search for and seize the spiral notebook. Mrs. Nelson and Mr. Hebl will testify about Andy's handwriting, which differs from that in the spiral notebook, thereby calling into question whether Andy wrote any of it."

"Ah, I see," Judge O'Brien said. "Quite relevant then, aren't they?"

"Yes." Even though Dominique had swiftly stuck a dagger into Stela's case, her expression remained impassive and all-business. Her tone was neither passionate nor cynical, always playing to the cold facts and applicable law.

"Who is your first witness, DA Bisset?"

"Mrs. Sharon Nelson."

"Okay. Let's have Mrs. Nelson testify, then we'll take an extended morning break during which the defendant can work on her cross-examination with the assistance of Ms. Spade, if the defendant so desires."

Monica's stomach lurched. She couldn't imagine helping Stela craft a cross-examination of two witnesses she had suggested that Matt find to affirm Andy's handwriting.

As soon as Stela had displayed the journal excerpts in her opening statement, the serpentine of memory had reminded Monica of several Eugène Ionesco quotes she had read in the strange plays after meeting with Stela at the jail.

While eating breakfast after her bladder infection, Monica had studied Stela's exhibit of Andy's journal excerpts, and highlighted the following phrases: "Your body is a work of art that creates an adventure for my mind," and "Dreams and anguish bring us together," and "I've always been suspicious of collective truths," and "We have not the time to take our time," and "We can predict our fate only after it has happened."

Interspersed among Andy's alleged ruminations about consent and cannibalism, the Ionesco quotes had jumped out at Monica. She had confirmed that they were, in fact, lifted from Ionesco writings.

So, in a nutshell, Stela had killed Andy and now was attempting to make a mockery of the trial by manufacturing false evidence. And, imbedded in that evidence, Monica couldn't help but wonder whether there was a message for someone else located far, far away. Specifically, the phrase, "We have not the time to take our time," seemed like a call to action, but to whom? For what? And, when?

She returned her attention to the pecker pruner.

"How about allowing me a day to prepare my cross-examination, Your Honor?" Stela asked.

Since Stela's question was delivered in a challenging tone, Judge O'Brien's eyebrows instantly pulled back like a dog ready to bite. "That won't be necessary, I'm sure. The witnesses' testimony should be straightforward about a topic with which you're familiar. It isn't as if they're providing expert testimony regarding lab results or something. I think one hour should be adequate. If something changes between now and then, we can revisit the plan before the break."

Monica watched Stela scribble on her notepad, *They aren't experts. They can't give opinions on handwriting.*

"If there isn't anything else, let's bring the jury in," Judge O'Brien said.

The jury door opened, and the pale jurors moped in wearing turtlenecks, sweatshirts and sweaters, some sporting the Packers football logo. Monica thought their appearances matched the overall mood of the courtroom—dreadful—everyone held hostage to Stela's psychopathic mind.

"Good morning," Judge O'Brien said to the jury, attempting enthusiasm, but he came off as a seventh grade substitute teacher—pathetically unconvincing.

"We have two witnesses scheduled this morning." He turned to Dominique. "The prosecution may call its next witness."

Dominique leaned into her microphone. "The prosecution calls Mrs. Sharon Nelson."

A woman rose from the gallery immediately behind Dominique's table. Her pained face was framed by gray hair and black glasses. A woman in her mid-sixties, she was dressed in modest clothing over her sturdy build. After being sworn in, she tentatively entered the witness box and sat uncomfortably in the chair facing Dominique. Under the fluorescent glare, Monica could see the deep lines of grief etched into Mrs. Nelson's face. Sadness clung to her. Not only had she lost her son, but under wretched circumstances that had to be confusing and horrible to bear. Monica's heart went out to her.

"Please state your full name for the record," Dominique said.

"Sharon Nelson."

"How did you know the victim, Andy Nelson?"

"He was my son."

"I'm going to ask you some questions about Andy's handwriting, if you don't mind."

Mrs. Nelson swallowed hard, looking as if torture were imminent.

Dominique asked, "When was Andy born?"

"He was born on September 13, 1990, at Community Memorial Hospital."

"Did you and your husband, Harold, raise Andy in your household?"

"Until the day he left for college," Mrs. Nelson said, her voice raspy and weepy. "And, again during the summers while in college."

"Okay. Did you watch his handwriting evolve through the years? From elementary school to college?"

"Oh yes. I'm familiar with Andy's handwriting."

"Did he ever write any letters to you?"

A wistful smile appeared then quickly pulled down the corners of her lips. "Yes. We exchanged cards and letters while he was in college because we both liked the tradition of it. Sure, we texted and spoke on the phone too, but there's something special about receiving a note in the mail, you know? Looking at the person's handwriting makes you feel like you're connecting in a way that texting doesn't convey."

"Did you and Andy continue that tradition even after he graduated from college?"

"Yes. Even though we both lived in Apple Grove, we would send each other a postcard, or actual card or letter, when we were on vacation."

"When was the last time you received a letter from Andy?"

"Last year at this time. My husband, Harold, and I were in Florida during January. We're both retired, so we like to spend some time there during the winter. Anyway, Andy sent me a few letters while we were there."

"Approach the witness, Your Honor?" Dominique asked.

"Yes," Judge O'Brien said.

Dominique rose and swung by Stela and Monica's table, handing Stela a copy of a document, then walked to Mrs. Nelson at the witness box. "I'm showing you what's been marked as Exhibit 110, Mrs. Nelson."

Dominique returned to her counsel table and fiddled with the mouse on her laptop until a handwritten letter was projected on the overhead screen. It began with "Dear Mom," making Monica's heart squeeze.

"Is this one of the letters you received from Andy last year at this time?" Dominique asked, while pointing to the date in the upper right corner—January 11, 2019.

"Yes," Mrs. Nelson said.

"I apologize for asking you to do this, but could you just read the first paragraph of that letter, please?"

Mrs. Nelson nodded, indicating she had expected this, then read, "'Dear Mom, Hope you and dad are enjoying sunny Florida. We're in the deep freeze up here. It was 18 below when I left the house for work this morning. Not much new here. Went ice fishing with Sam and Steve last weekend. We caught some crappies on Lake Wissota...'" At this point, Mrs. Nelson's throat constricted, and she burst into tears.

"I'm so sorry." Dominique delivered a box of Kleenex to her, and Mrs. Nelson liberally dabbed at the waterfalls under her eyes.

Dominique gave her a moment to collect herself. "May I ask you a few more questions?"

"Yes. I'm sorry I broke down."

Dominique held up her hand. "No need to apologize. We understand. Would it be fair to say that you recognize Andy's handwriting?"

"Absolutely," Mrs. Nelson said. "He was my son and frequently wrote to me."

"Before we discuss another writing, let me ask you whether you met Ms. Stela Reiter before this trial."

Mrs. Nelson's face pinched into a scowl, as she scanned Stela. "No."

"It appears she and Andy had been seeing each other for a few months. Did he usually introduce his girlfriends to you?"

"We had met a few in the past. I don't know why he didn't bring Ms. Reiter to the house for dinner or something."

Dominique nodded, then turned her attention to her laptop. With a few keystrokes, she swapped out Andy's letter for the excerpted journal entry that Stela had put on the overhead during her opening statement.

"Is the excerpt I'm showing you now on the overhead as exhibit 29, and represented by the defendant to be Andy's writing in his journal, in Andy's handwriting?"

"No," Mrs. Nelson said at the same time as Stela said, "Object, Your Honor."

The jurors were as startled as Mrs. Nelson at Stela's objection.

Careful not to ruin this line of questioning, Judge O'Brien said, "Approach the bench."

Monica followed Stela to the bench where they met up with Dominique. Judge O'Brien covered the microphone and leaned over the desk. "What's the basis of your objection, Ms. Reiter?"

"That Mrs. Nelson isn't an expert on handwriting, so she shouldn't be allowed to give an opinion that Andy's journal doesn't look like his handwriting. She can testify as to receiving letters from him as a fact witness, but she isn't a handwriting expert, so she shouldn't be allowed to give an opinion on his journal entries."

Dominique countered, "I'm not offering her testimony as an expert, but, as a fact witness who received numerous writings from Andy and who recognized his handwriting as well as any other human could. I think she's entitled to say that the journal entries don't look like his handwriting to her. Ms. Reiter can point out on cross-examination that Mrs. Nelson isn't an expert at analyzing handwriting."

"I disagree," Stela said. "Allowing Mrs. Nelson to testify that the entries don't look like Andy's handwriting to *her* is, in fact, opinion testimony by a lay witness who doesn't have any specialized knowledge, training, or skill to assist the jury in analyzing the handwriting."

Dominique's tone became more insistent. "I laid an adequate foundation that Mrs. Nelson does, in fact, have specialized experience and knowledge of Andy's handwriting because she's seen it since he was born. Again, the defendant can point out on cross-examination that Mrs. Nelson isn't a handwriting expert."

Stela started to speak, but Judge O'Brien shushed her. "I'm going to allow Mrs. Nelson to say whether she thinks the entries are in Andy's handwriting based upon her experience with his handwriting, but I'm limiting it to that. She isn't an expert, so I'm giving you a very narrow window here, Attorney Bisset."

"Understood," Dominique said.

When they returned to counsel tables and sat, Dominique again asked Mrs. Nelson, "Based upon your experience in receiving numerous writings from your son, is the handwriting I'm showing you now, on exhibit 29, and represented by the defendant to be Andy's writing, actually Andy's handwriting?"

"Same objection, Your Honor," Stela slipped in before Mrs. Nelson could answer.

"Overruled," Judge O'Brien quickly added.

"No," Mrs. Nelson said with emphasis and a clear voice.

"Why not?" Dominique asked.

"It just doesn't look like his writing," Mrs. Nelson said.

"Thank you," Dominique said. "Nothing further for this witness."

Judge O'Brien looked at Stela. "Did the defendant wish to take a break before the cross-examination?"

Contrary to her earlier protests, Stela said in her sweetest of sweet voices, "No, Your Honor. I'm fine. I just have a few questions."

Surprised, Judge O'Brien said, "Please, go ahead."

"Mrs. Nelson, I'm sorry to ask you a few questions, but I must. You don't have any training, background, education or experience in the analysis of handwriting, do you?"

"No."

"In other words, you're not a handwriting expert, are you?"

"No. I'm the mother of the son you killed."

The jury gasped, and the courtroom became deathly quiet.

Shouldn't have asked her that, Monica thought.

Through the uncomfortable silence, Stela finally said, "Thank you. Nothing further."

"Does the prosecution have any more questions?" Judge O'Brien asked.

"No, Your Honor," Dominique said, wisely letting Mrs. Nelson's last statement punctuate her testimony.

"The witness may step down," Judge O'Brien said to Mrs. Nelson.

After Mrs. Nelson returned to her seat in the gallery, Judge O'Brien invited Dominique to call her next witness, who was Harry Hebl, Andy's boss at *Voila!*.

A thick man who was vertically challenged walked from the back of the room to be sworn in. He wore polyester navy trousers and a short-sleeved button down shirt with his phone in the left breast pocket.

"Please state your full name."

"Harry Hebl."

"Where do you work?"

"At *Voila!*"

"What's your position there?"

"Manager, Weapons Division."

"How long have you worked there?"

"Thirty-two years."

"How did you know Andy Nelson?"

"I hired him."

"Was he a good employee?"

"Yes, until very recently."

"What do you mean by that?"

"We discovered we were missing some inventory of classified materials, so the VP of Human Resources and I met with everyone in my division, including Andy."

"How did that meeting go?"

"Not very well," Harry said, folding his arms over his belly.

"Please explain."

"After we told Andy we were missing enriched plutonium and uranium, he became red in the face and very defensive. He asked if we were accusing him of stealing."

"What did you say?"

"That we were meeting with everyone, so we weren't accusing him of anything."

"How did he take that."

"He calmed down, but he wasn't his regular self. I planned to follow up with him in a few days, but I never got the chance." Harry lowered his head.

"I see," Dominique said. "I need to ask you about his handwriting as well. Do you think you can answer some more questions?"

"Sure," Harry said in a sad voice.

Dominique continued, and Harry's testimony was similar to Mrs. Nelson's from the limited writing samples he had of Andy's work at *Voila!*

Stela attempted to nail him on cross for not being a handwriting expert, but the jury wasn't behind her in either spirit or legal distinction. Monica actually felt embarrassed for Stela's continued persistence. Not embarrassed enough to erase the satisfaction of having the fictitious journal entries exposed for what they were, however. Monica pictured Yuri creating them then planting them at Andy's house. At least that very possibility had come out in the wash. As the finder of fact, the jury would decide the fate of the salacious entries, whether fabricated or authentic.

36

After Dominique wrapped the prosecution's case in mid-afternoon, Judge O'Brien excused the jury, sending them home so they could shovel out their driveways from the snowmageddon that had been pummeling Apple Grove since early morning, threatening to shut down the town.

Once the jury was gone, Judge O'Brien asked the parties, "Is there anything we need to take up before the defendant presents her case tomorrow?"

"No," Dominique said.

"No," Stela said.

"Who is your first witness tomorrow, Ms. Reiter?"

"I am," Stela said, surprising Monica.

"Will Ms. Spade be asking you questions while you testify?" Judge O'Brien asked.

"Yes."

"The Court assumes you and Ms. Spade have prepared?"

"We haven't, but we will," Stela said, again surprising Monica.

"Ms. Spade, are you on board with the plan?" Judge O'Brien asked.

"Yes, Your Honor. Ms. Reiter and I can meet after court today."

"Very good. How long do you think your testimony will go, Ms. Reiter?"

"I'll talk for about an hour, then I'm sure District Attorney Bisset will have a vicious and lengthy cross-examination of me."

Before Dominique could speak, Judge O'Brien pointed at Stela. "I know passions can run high during a trial, Ms. Reiter, but we need to stay civil.

This is a court of law, and it's the District Attorney's job to prosecute the charges, which necessarily involves cross-examining you if you decide to testify. I would remind you to stay civil during your testimony tomorrow. Of course, you have the right not to testify if you wish."

Stela squinted at him through her thick glasses, as she transformed from her sweet face for the jury to her resting killer face that scared the shit out of Monica. "Of course, Your Honor. Civility won't be a problem."

"Good. Do you plan to call any other witnesses?" he asked.

"Yes. Dr. George Popovich, the oncologist/hematologist who will testify about my DNA profile, and Dr. Delaney Karpenko, the esteemed psychiatrist from Cleveland, Ohio, who will testify about my PTSD."

"Arrangements have been made for these physicians to testify in person?" Judge O'Brien asked.

"Yes, Your Honor," Stela said, making Monica's head spin. *When and how had Stela arranged that? Is she sending emails to them from jail? Did Yuri communicate with them?*

"Very well," Judge O'Brien said. "Is there anything else?"

"No," Stela said.

Dominique shook her head indicating no.

"Court will stand in recess until tomorrow morning at 8:30 a.m., weather permitting. We might need to push back the start time if we get significant accumulation of snow tonight. The court secretary will contact you if that's the case." Judge O'Brien slammed his gavel, pushed back from his bench, and left in a rush.

Monica turned to Stela. "So, ready to work on your testimony?"

"Yes. Meet me at the jail conference room."

"Will do."

Stela departed with her deputies, and Dominique approached Monica. "Have you met these physicians?"

"Of course not," Monica said.

"According to Stela's opening, Dr. Popovich is going to say that she has two sets of DNA, right?" Dominique asked.

"I guess so," Monica said. "Stela doesn't tell me shit. I didn't even know she had arranged for them to testify. She must be emailing them directly from her jail computer."

"Well, her DNA voodoo doesn't make sense anyway," Dominique said.

"Perhaps it's best if you don't tell me the reason," Monica said.

"You're right. Good luck prepping her." Dominique's smirk was unmistakable.

"Thanks for your support," Monica said sarcastically. "I think I need a cup of coffee before our prep session."

"Or something stronger," Dominique quipped as she walked away.

***

By the time Monica and Stela finished their prep session, the sky was dark, and thick sheets of snow blanketed the parking lot. The clouds hurled pellets of ice against Monica's face, as she walked through the drifts to her lonely pickup truck. At least six inches had accumulated since she had been cloistered away in the depressing citadel housing the courthouse and stinky jail.

She unlocked her ice-mobile, got in, and started the engine. As she waited for it to warm up, she got out and cleared the snow from the windshield with a long scraper. Her coat and boots now covered in snow, she slid behind the wheel and drove toward home, visions of a warm dinner with Shelby playing through her mind.

Her phone rang. "Hello?"

"Not a wise move, Ms. Spade, tipping off the DA that the journal entries weren't in Andy's handwriting," a male voice said.

Monica's blood ran cold. "Who is this?"

"Your old friend, Yuri. Remember my glove around your throat?" He paused, his heavy breathing the only sound coming through the line.

"You can't blame me for every flaw in Stela's case. His mother noticed the handwriting wasn't even close to Andy's. A stupid idea," Monica said with more bravado than she intended.

"But I can blame you for tipping off the police, can't I?" His tone was so confident that Monica wondered how the hell he had figured out that she had told Nathan to suggest to Matt that he get Andy's writing samples.

In the interest of self-preservation, she said, "I'm sorry, Yuri. You lost me. I'm in the dark as much as you are. Why are you calling me?"

"To make a deal."

She sighed. "Listen, I'm exhausted, cold, and hungry, and I just want to get home. I'm all out of deals for the day."

"You arrogant cunt!" he snarled. "Stop sabotaging Mila's case and start helping her!"

"Mila? Who's Mila?" Monica asked over the thumping of the windshield wipers.

"I meant Stela." His voice turned angry and loud. "You know who I mean!"

Her neck instantly prickled. "Okay. No need to get riled up. That's what I thought I was doing… helping Stela. I just spent the last few hours at the jail with her, going over her testimony for tomorrow. What more do you expect from me?"

"Not to work with the police and DA," he snarled. "We both know you gave the handwriting tip to the DA, but that's all going to change now. As long as you're in control of something that's special to me, I'm taking control of something that's special to you."

Monica's heart stopped, her mind racing to a nightmare she could only sense was about to unfold. "What?"

"That's right," he said. "You heard me. I have your precious Shelby here with me, and she's going to stay with me until the trial is over. If Stela goes free, your Shelby goes free. If Stela is found guilty, then I'm going to find your Shelby guilty. And, in my world, we enjoy capital punishment."

Monica's throat constricted, as she pulled over to the side of the snowy road, unable to process his threats and drive at the same time. Her hands were shaking so violently that she was barely able to move the gear shift into park.

"I don't believe you," she croaked.

"Maybe hearing your lover's voice will convince you," he said.

Monica heard some rustling in the background then a female whimpering in pain.

"Monica?" Shelby asked in a terrified whisper.

"Oh God," Monica said. "Shelby? Are you okay?"

"He's got me," Shelby squeaked, then Monica heard commotion followed by a door slamming.

Yuri came back on the line. "She's back in her safe little spot, where she'll remain until my Stela is set free."

"Anything," Monica sputtered. "I'll do anything you want."

"Now, we get somewhere," he said in a thick accent. "I need you to convince the DA that Andy wrote that journal. Make sure she doesn't argue against it in her closing remarks to the jury."

"Got it," Monica breathed. "I'll try."

"You need to do better than try."

"Yes," Monica whispered, then in a louder voice repeated, "Yes!"

He paused a second. "Now, for the big ask."

Her mind reeling with abject horror, Monica would agree to fly to the moon if he asked. "What?"

"I need your help getting Stela out of the courtroom before Agents McCoy and Scott grab her."

"They're going to grab her?"

"Isn't that what they told you since you're friends with them now?"

"No! They aren't my friends. I don't like them any more than you do!"

"Then it shouldn't be difficult for you to get rid of them, so Stela can sneak out to me when she gets the not-guilty verdict."

"How on earth am I supposed to do that?"

"You're the lawyer. Be creative."

Her mind was completely blank—utterly incapable of visualizing a plan—as she watched the wipers fight a losing battle against the thick snow. "I'm sure I'll think of something. How do I get in touch with you?"

"Don't worry. I call you," he said and hung up.

"Hello?" She looked at her phone to confirm he had cut the line. Her heart thundered, and her ears rang at full volume. *He has Shelby! Fuck!* She pictured Shelby's sweet face and angelic body, and prayed that Yuri wouldn't harm her...or worse. Panic engulfed her.

She needed help. Advice. Muscle. Brains. Guns. A plan. To whom could she turn? She took a deep breath, eased the truck back into traffic, and drove straight to the office. There was only one person she wanted to see, and he usually stayed late. Minutes later, she tapped on Jim Daniels' door and walked in before he could speak.

His eyes moved from his screen to her face. "You look like hell. Something wrong?"

She let loose a torrent of words, peppered by sobs and tears. She told him everything, admitting that she had tipped off Matt to check Andy's writing.

"Oh right," Jim said. "Dominique told me about Matt's miraculous epiphany to get Andy's notes and writings from work and his mother. Once she compared Andy's real handwriting to the fabricated journal writings, there was no doubt in her mind that someone else had written them. Are you telling me that you figured it out because quotes from a French-Romanian playwright were dropped into the entries?"

"Yes. They jumped out at me after I recently read some Ionesco plays. I mean, why did Stela use Eugène Ionesco as a codeword, then blatantly use the quotes in the journal? Did she want me to figure out that Andy wasn't the author?"

He stared at the dark bank of windows for a second. "Maybe only Yuri wrote the fabricated journal entries after Andy died, and Stela didn't know Yuri was going to drop Ionesco quotes into them—"

"That makes sense," Monica said. "They both might regularly use the Ionesco name, but maybe Stela didn't even recognize the quotes in the excerpts."

"Depends on how into his plays they actually are, or if Yuri took it to an absurd level," Jim said. "But why? Why would he use quotes in them?"

"More coded language for someone outside the courtroom to see?" Monica said.

"I think you're onto something," Jim said. "Sending messages back home."

"We need to focus on Shelby," Monica sobbed. "I think Yuri will kill her if I don't deliver Stela free and clear of the FBI."

Jim jumped up from his chair and came around the desk to sit next to Monica. He patted her leg. "We're not going to let that happen. Trust me. That fucker doesn't know who he's dealing with. We'll get Shelby back tonight. Listen to me carefully. I need you to keep your wits about you and follow my plan. Do you think you can do that?"

Stunned by Jim's warp speed, she swallowed hard and focused on his intense eyes. "I'll try."

"Good. Put your coat and gloves back on, and go out the basement door. Cut into the woods and meet me at Prairie Drive where I'll pick you up. If you're being watched—by Ukrainians or FBI agents—I want them to think you're staying at the office late. I'll leave through the front door and lock up."

"Okay." She wiped her eyes. "Where are we going?"

"You'll see. Just leave your office light on to make it look like you're still here."

"Right. I'll see you in a few minutes."

"Good girl." He patted her knee and stood.

Minutes later, Monica was lying in the back seat of his car, trying not to roll off, as he rounded corners too fast and braked suddenly at intersections.

"Where are we going?" she asked, her hand on the back of his seat to brace herself.

"To Nathan's house."

"Nathan? How can he help?"

"Matt is over there."

"Oh."

Jim must have texted Nathan in advance of their arrival because the garage door was open, so Jim quickly pulled into a vacant stall. Before he could cut the engine, the garage door went down.

"You can get out now," he said to Monica from the front seat.

They were greeted by Nathan and Matt. Nathan hugged her first, as she started crying again, unable to talk. Jim relayed the details to Matt.

Matt looked at Monica and took her hands in his. "I need you to collect yourself, so you can answer some questions for me. Can you do that?"

Her chest jerked with a hiccup, the tears running like faucets. "Yes."

"Okay. Does Shelby's phone show up on your iPhone as a Device or People in your Find-My-iPhone app?"

Monica's mind went blank. She'd never looked. She removed her phone from her coat pocket and unlocked it. "Here."

Matt took it and navigated to the app. "Excellent," he mumbled, as he swiped up with his thumb to discover that Shelby's name was, indeed, listed as one of the people in Monica's app. He clicked it open, and a map of Apple Grove suddenly displayed with a blinking phone icon in the name of Shelby in the center.

He showed the screen to Monica. "Is this your street?"

"Yes," she said.

"Is that the precise location of your house, where the phone icon is blinking?"

She focused on the screen, which was no small task through tears. "Yes."

He frowned. "Okay. I doubt she's at your house, but I'll have a uniform swing by and check. I suspect only her phone was left at your house, so that won't be any help in finding her, but we always check the victim's phone first."

"Victim?" Monica gasped. "Please don't call her a victim… I can't take hearing that word applied to her."

"I understand," he said. "I'm sorry."

She felt Nathan's arm around her shoulders, as they watched Matt navigate to "recent calls" on Monica's phone. He swore under his breath.

"What?" she asked.

"Yuri used a burner phone with an untraceable number to call you. I need to add an app to your phone. Are you okay with that?"

"Sure, what is it?"

"It will give us Yuri's GPS coordinates if he calls you again."

Her eyes lit up. "Seriously? There's an app for that?"

"If you keep him on the phone for at least one minute, the app can locate his GPS. It doesn't always work, but we can give it a try. The hardest part is staying on the phone for one minute. It's longer than you realize."

"I'll do whatever you need," she said.

"Answer if he calls again. Play dumb and ask as many questions as you can if he gives you instructions. Just keep him talking."

"Where will you be?" she asked.

"I'll pick up Brock, and we'll hit up our usual go-to people in town who might have heard or seen something."

"You mean, like informants?" she asked.

"Yeah. Good old-fashioned detective work. It can be painstaking, but if you go to the right bars and talk to the right people, you'd be surprised what you can learn."

Matt strapped on his shoulder holster, added a large handgun, then shrugged on a heavy coat. He pulled a slate-colored knit cap over his thick, black hair. "I'll be in touch. Hang in there." He hugged Monica, nodded at Nathan and Jim, and left.

37

"Now, what do we do?" Monica asked into the stillness of Matt's departure.

"We let him do his job," Nathan said, going to the kitchen sink and filling a pitcher with water, which he poured into his coffee maker.

Lingering by the door, Jim said, "If you two are comfortable without me, I'd like to go home to Dominique."

"Of course," Monica said. "Thank you for helping."

"Anytime. Trust Matt. He'll find Shelby."

Monica's throat was so constricted, she couldn't even reply.

Soon after Jim left, she and Nathan sat at his kitchen counter, drinking coffee. "Where would that motherfucker take her?"

"Didn't you say Stela was renting an apartment in town?" Nathan asked. "Maybe there."

"Too obvious," Monica said. "First place the police would look, don't you think?"

"Matt and Brock are probably there now."

Monica clicked her fingers. "That does give me an idea, though. Maybe Yuri is communicating with Stela about where he is."

"How? He can't visit her at jail, and she doesn't have a cell phone."

"Yeah, but she has a computer, and she's been emailing her physician witnesses through her government account to arrange for their testimony."

"The police monitor that email account," Nathan said. "She and Yuri wouldn't dare—"

"I didn't realize that. I thought they just eavesdropped on all phone conversations through the glass."

"Nope," he said. "They monitor the email of a jail account too. Inmates sign a release allowing them to in exchange for the privilege of getting an account."

She thought about that a minute while she drank some coffee. "What if Stela created a new account on Gmail or Yahoo?"

He nodded. "Should we hold a gun to her head and make her email Yuri?"

"Ha!" Monica barked. "Wouldn't I love to do that! She never would, you know. She's probably been trained to withstand torture as harsh as waterboarding. No, I think we need to hack into her account and figure it out ourselves. Maybe we could text Matt and ask him to arrange for an officer to meet us at the jail."

"It's worth a try," Nathan said.

***

Thirty minutes later, Monica and Nathan were at police headquarters meeting with Janki Perinchery, one of the detectives who specialized in computer forensics.

"Thanks for working with us tonight, Detective Perinchery," Monica said.

"Please call me Janki. I work the night shift anyway. How can I help?"

"One of the inmates, Stela Reiter, has been using her government account to email quite a bit, and now my girlfriend has been taken hostage by Ms. Reiter's associate, Yuri Zaleski. We want to see if they've been emailing back and forth."

Janki squinted her eyes in skepticism. "I've been keeping up with the trial. Stela seems smarter than the average bear, so I doubt she and Zaleski would be so reckless as to email about his location, but we can check if you like."

"If it wouldn't be too much trouble," Monica said. "My girlfriend's life depends on it."

Janki's eyes quickly traveled over Monica in appreciation, then she turned and led them to a room filled with computer work stations. No one else was present. She sat down at a station, and Monica and Nathan rolled over chairs on each side of her. Janki entered the governmental network and navigated to Stela's account. She pulled up the email inbox.

"Go slowly," Monica said, scanning the names and information. "I recognize the names of her physician witnesses for the trial, but maybe she's passing messages through them to Yuri. You never know."

The three of them read each incoming and outgoing message carefully, including the deleted items, studying them for any clue as to Yuri's current whereabouts. After a while, Monica rubbed her eyes in defeat and desperation. "I don't see anything helpful."

"Neither do I," Janki said.

"Stela easily could have created another email account, though," Monica said. "Is there a way to check her browsing history on your system to see if she set up a Gmail, Yahoo, or other account?"

"Sure," Janki said. "Give me a minute."

They watched as Janki rapidly clicked and typed through a series of screens with commands that were foreign to Monica. Long minutes ticked by, each marked by Monica's escalating fear. She suddenly realized that her knee was nervously bopping up and down, and she was clenching her jaw so tightly that her teeth hurt. She channeled yoga class, breathing in slowly and deeply, and controlling her exhale. After several calming breaths, her eyes brightened at the sight of an email account on the screen.

"Found one," Janki said. "Looks like she set up a Gmail account. Let's open it."

Yuri wasn't identified by name, but there was only one other person with whom Stela was communicating, and he was identified as "Ionesco."

"It's either Yuri or another associate," Monica said.

"Alias?" Janki asked.

"It's a code name she's been using. Eugène Ionesco is a French-Romanian playwright, long since dead. I have no idea of the significance."

"How did you figure it out?" Janki asked.

"Stela gave me Ionesco's name to use as a code when I initially contacted her physician experts to testify. They snapped to attention as soon as I dropped it. Then, she and Yuri used Ionesco quotes in the journal entries they fabricated as Andy's. I mean, seriously, they aren't very adept at covert communication."

"Or, you're just smart," Janki said, casting a sidelong glance over Monica. "Or, maybe their quotes were intended for someone else. Someone who couldn't be at the trial but might see them on TV."

"Great minds think alike," Monica said. "We can figure that out later. Right now, let's just read these emails."

The three of them studied the emails from the last several days while Stela had been in jail. Some were revealing of Stela's disappointment over getting caught, but completely devoid of emotion over killing Andy. As the trial grew near and began, the tone changed to frustration, nervousness, then anger over how the trial was going.

"You can see she's beginning to panic about her performance in these recent emails," Nathan said, pointing.

"Look at this one from yesterday," Monica said. "Yuri writes, 'Don't worry. I have an idea to put some pressure on Spade.'"

They read Stela's reply of "Anything would help."

"Look at today's exchange," Nathan said.

Janki scrolled to Yuri's message. "I now have something precious of Spade's."

Stela had replied to him after court that very day, asking, "Where are you?"

Yuri responded, "Dive motel outside of town."

Monica clapped her hands. "That's it! That's where he's taken Shelby. To a dive motel outside of Apple Grove!"

"If the town he's referring to is, in fact, Apple Grove," Janki said.

"It has to be," Monica said. "He just took Shelby today, and he's hanging around until the end of the trial." She pointed at the computer screen. "Google motels within 50 miles of Apple Grove."

"Let's start within 20 miles," Janki said.

"I'll text Matt and let him know what we're doing," Nathan said.

Janki pulled up half a dozen motels, and hotels, on the outskirts of Apple Grove, most along a divided highway running north.

"Yuri described it as a 'dive motel,' so I think we can exclude those three that are nice hotels," Monica said, pointing for Janki.

"That leaves three for Matt and Brock to check out." Monica turned to Nathan. "Here, give them these three names—Do Dodge Inn, Antler's Motel and the Roadway Inn."

Monica stood, reinvigorated by the information. "Thanks for your help, Janki."

"My pleasure. Do you want to give me your cell number, and I'll text if you if I discover anything else?"

"Good idea." Monica and Janki exchanged contact information while Nathan texted Matt.

"They're going to the Do Dodge Inn first because it's closest to where they are right now," he said.

"Great. Let's meet them there," Monica said.

"No way." Nathan jangled his car keys in his coat pocket. "We aren't the police, so we're not tagging along."

"We'll see about that," Monica said.

"I would discourage going to the scene," Janki said. "There might be gunfire."

"That's precisely why we're going," Monica said. "My girlfriend is the one being held hostage, and I want to be there when she's rescued." She turned on her heel and marched out to Nathan's fancy SUV.

Nathan caught up to her, not bothering to talk, as they braced the angry wind. Once inside the car, he turned to her. "Seriously, Mon. I love you as a friend, so I need to stop you from getting involved in police business."

"We're wasting time here," she said. "If you won't drive us to the Do Dodge Inn, then drive me back to the law firm, and I'll get my pickup truck and go myself."

He drove out of the parking lot. "You're serious, aren't you?"

"Dead."

"We probably will be if we drive over there." He sighed. "Fine, but we're not getting out of the car."

She didn't commit to that.

On their way, his dash screen lit up with a text from Matt. Nathan pressed a button on the steering wheel, and they heard the computer voice transcribe, "Nothing at Do Dodge Inn, going to Antler's."

Monica quickly plugged in the address for Antler's Motel and rattled it off to Nathan, who drove like an old lady.

When they arrived at the rundown motel, about 20 minutes west of Apple Grove, Nathan spotted Matt's car in an adjacent driveway belonging to a storefront whose faded business sign said, "Phuk & Assoc., Marketing Your Name is Our Specialty." He grunted in amusement.

"Insane," Monica said, briefly glancing at it then more broadly at the sketchy surroundings.

"Look," Nathan said, pointing out her window. "Matt and Brock just went into the motel office."

38

Matt and Brock snuck into the office through a streaked sliding glass door that the owner quickly closed behind them. He drew the drapes and turned to them. "I'm Jack. Come right this way."

They showed him their badges then followed him around the reception counter to his small office. "As we said on the phone, we're looking for a male in a gray parka who might have brought a female into his room."

"I'm glad you called in advance." Jack cued up some surveillance video, which was black and white, and at a 12-foot height, but still good enough for them to identify Yuri checking in at the office counter.

"That's our man," Matt said. "Do you have any video of the woman with him?"

"It isn't very good," Jack said. "He pulled his car right up to the room door." He cued up another clip, and they watched Yuri remove someone from the back seat. From her body size and shape, they could she was a woman, but they couldn't identify her as Shelby because of her bulky coat and the hat on her head. She also leaned heavily into Yuri, as he walked her into the room.

"That's enough for me," Matt said. "Tell us about the room."

"It's just around the corner," Jack indicated with a nod. "You can walk under the car port, and it will be on the right-hand side. Your guy is in room nine, and the one to the right of it, room ten, is empty. The room to the left, number eight, has someone in it."

"Gotcha," Matt said. "Draw me a quick floorplan."

Jack did as requested while Matt and Brock studied the box with a bed to the right and a bathroom at the back.

"Too bad there's a picture window in the front. Is there a window in the back where the bathroom is?"

"Yes," Jack said. "It's a small horizontal window above the shower. Not big enough for a person to fit through."

"Okay," Matt said. "Do you have a spare key?"

Jack reached under the counter and pulled out an old-fashioned, diamond-shaped, plastic key ring with a tarnished key "Here."

"You'll lead us to the room?" Matt said.

"Absolutely not." Jack walked to his office window and pointed. "It's to the right of the stairwell. Over there, but there's no chance in hell I'm going over there."

"Fair enough." Matt scratched his head through his knit cap.

"Thank you," Brock said to the motel owner. "We're going in. If you hear gunfire, hit the floor."

"Wouldn't be the first time. If you shoot everything up, the city better reimburse me."

"I'm sure the city administrator will be in contact," Matt said.

The detectives unholstered their handguns and slid back the actions, loading the chambers. Matt led, the key in his left hand and his gun in his right, and Brock followed with a flashlight in one hand and his gun in the other.

They quickly made their way under the carport, then hugged the exterior wall on the opposite side of the parking lot, as they ran in a crouched position. They passed room ten uneventfully, then saw they would have to pass in front of the picture window of Yuri's room, the bottom of which was at knee height.

From inside Nathan's car, Monica said, "I think I saw a flashlight beam go around the other side of the office."

"Me too," Nathan said. "Sit tight. This will be over in a few minutes."

She put her hand on the door handle and cracked the door.

He quickly grabbed her arm and held her where she was. "Close your door. You're not going anywhere. The only thing you could do is screw up their rescue, putting Shelby's life in danger."

She reluctantly closed her door. "But I can't see anything."

"Be patient."

They sat in darkness.

Matt and Brock stopped at the edge of Yuri's room. The orange street lamp in the parking area would no doubt illuminate their silhouettes if they walked past the window. There was no way to get to the room from the opposite side without being seen, however, because the motel was built in a U-shape around the parking area.

Matt stopped and turned to Brock. He made an army-crawling motion with his fingers and pointed at himself. Brock nodded.

Matt army-crawled on his belly under Yuri's window to the door. Once on the other side, Matt sprang to his feet, then held the key to the doorknob. He tipped up his chin at Brock, who turned on his flashlight, carefully angling it away from the window. Matt turned the key and opened the door, shouldering through the flimsy chain that was hooked to a latch, throwing the door wide into the wall on the left.

Brock sprinted past the window and was by Matt's side, his flashlight sweeping across the room to the bed on the right. The beam landed on Yuri, propped against pillow, a shocked look on his newly awakened face.

Even in his sleep state, however, Yuri had a trigger finger, greeting Matt and Brock with the deafening sound of gun shots.

Matt hit the floor, but not before he logged Yuri's position on the bed. He hadn't seen Shelby on the bed, and his suspicion of her location was confirmed when he heard a scream from behind the bathroom door.

Without raising his body, Matt rested his hand on the foot of the bed and shot at the headboard. He heard a groan, but he wasn't sure if it was Yuri or Brock. They were plunged into darkness again.

Matt looked across the carpeting toward Brock, and saw that the flashlight had rolled out of his hand and under the bed. Brock lay with his face down, so Matt nudged his shoulder with his boot. Nothing. He nudged harder, rocking Brock's shoulder. Nothing. Fear shot through Matt's veins, but he couldn't stop to tend to Brock without knowing whether Yuri still posed a threat.

That fucker can't still be alive, he thought, as he removed his own flashlight from the side pocket of his pants and shined over his right shoulder, into the mirror above the desk. He saw Yuri's bloodied face, his head slumped against a pillow and blood stains behind him. His open eyes had the faraway stare of the dead, and his mouth hung slack, his tongue lolling out.

Matt sprang to his feet, his gun at the ready and his flashlight pointed squarely at Yuri, who was dead as dead can be. Matt moved to the side of the bed and removed the gun lying by Yuri's limp hand.

"Shelby!" Matt yelled at the bathroom door. "It's Matt. Are you in there?"

"Yes!" came a terrified scream.

Matt shone his flashlight on the bathroom door, and saw that Yuri had screwed a hinge into the jam and locked it with a padlock. Matt would have to frisk Yuri for the key. "Give me a minute. I have to find the key."

"Okay," she squealed.

Before searching for the key, Matt turned to Brock and fell to his knees beside him. He rolled him over and saw that he had taken a bullet to his chest and arm. Matt knew Brock was wearing a bulletproof vest, but the shot to his arm didn't look good. Blood had already soaked through his shirt and into his jacket. He, too, had a limp body and slack jaw, but his eyes were closed. Matt felt for a pulse in Brock's neck. Present and strong.

Time slowed, becoming an obstacle, as Matt turned on the overhead light in the room then clumsily removed his belt, cinching a tourniquet around Brock's arm. "You're gonna make it, buddy." Matt called 911.

He finished the call then reluctantly left Brock on the floor to turn his attention to rescuing Shelby. He moved to the side of the bed where Yuri was lying askew. "You cocksucker. Which pocket did you put the key in?" Yuri didn't answer, so Matt jammed his hand into Yuri's pocket, locating a small key.

His hands trembling now, Matt went to the padlock on the bathroom door and inserted the key. As soon as he opened the door, a disheveled and frightened Shelby stared at him. She was wearing a

South High sweatshirt and jeans, and her hands were zip-tied together at the wrists.

"Oh Matt! I'm so glad to see you." She lurched forward to hug him, stopping suddenly to stare at his bloodied jacket. "Oh my God! Are you hurt?"

He looked down. "No. Brock's blood."

"Is he alive?" she asked through a gulp, her eyes scanning the room.

"Yeah. Yuri, on the other hand—" Matt glanced over his shoulder at Yuri's bloodied face. "Ah. You shouldn't come out here just yet—"

"Bullshit. I'm getting the fuck out of here." She elbowed him aside and strode through the room, stepping over Brock's legs, to the outdoor sidewalk, where motel residents were cracking their doors and peering through curtains. Leaning her bound hands against the exterior wall, Shelby pulled in several deep breaths of subzero air, grateful to be set free from her prison.

Matt didn't have time to check her for injuries, as he heard Brock moan in pain. He knelt beside him.

"What the fuck?" Brock muttered, looking around then down at himself.

"You've been shot in the chest and arm," Matt said. "Lay still. The ambulance is coming."

Brock raised his good arm and felt of his chest, his finger locating the distinct bullet hole in the bulletproof vest. "This thing good..." He breathed in shallow bursts. "Chest hurts like hell."

"I'm sure it does," Matt said. "The bullet probably cracked a few ribs. Your arm didn't fare so well, though, so don't move, okay? I made a tourniquet, but it isn't very strong."

"Shelby?" Brock whispered. "Okay?"

"She's good." Matt pointed over his shoulder with his thumb. "Standing outside."

"Yuri?" Brock asked.

"Dead," Matt said in a flat tone.

"Good." Brock lay his head back.

Matt stayed by Brock's side but yelled to Shelby, "Are you okay out there? There's an ambulance on the way."

"I'm a little scraped up," she said, "but I'm fine. I'd come back in, but I can't take it."

Matt hopped up, removed his coat, and met her at the door. "Put this on. More police will arrive in a few minutes."

She held up her wrists. "I can't."

"Let me get those." He removed a pocket knife from his jeans pocket and slit the plastic, then helped her shrug on his coat.

"Thank you." She rubbed her bloodied wrists where the plastic had cut into her skin.

Matt hugged her briefly then returned to Brock. He didn't know whether two or ten minutes passed, but multiple police cars and an ambulance eventually arrived, lighting up the parking lot like a fireworks finale.

The EMTs quickly loaded Brock on a gurney and hoisted him into the back of the ambulance, giving Matt the opportunity to talk to Shelby.

"What happened to your head?" he asked, pointing to a cut on the right side of her forehead.

"He must have hit me with his gun or something when I got out of my car at Monica's. That was after work. The next thing I knew, I was in that fucking motel bathroom."

"I'm so sorry," he said. "We need to get you to the hospital. I think you need stitches."

"I'm exhausted," she said. "Maybe I can lay down."

"My car is over here." His arm around her waist, he helped her walk from the grisly motel to the Phuk & Associates parking lot.

As they drew near Matt's car, the interior lights of another car came on, and Nathan and Monica burst from it.

"Shelby!" Monica said, running toward her, slipping on the icy drive.

They collided in a heap, falling into a snowbank.

Monica held Shelby's face in her hands. "Oh my God! Are you okay?"

"Yes." Shelby sobbed into Monica's neck, shivering uncontrollably.

"She needs to go to the hospital," Matt said, towering over them. "She has a cut on her forehead and her wrists look like hamburger. Come on." He helped Shelby to her feet while Monica got ahold of herself.

"You can ride along if you want," Matt said to Monica.

Monica turned to Nathan, a panic-stricken look on her face.

He read her mind. "Yes. I'll cover court tomorrow morning. Go. Go with Shelby to the hospital."

"Thank you!" Monica exclaimed. "I love you."

"You're welcome." Nathan turned to Matt. "See you later."

Matt smiled and held the passenger door for Shelby while Monica got in the back.

As Matt was pulling out of the parking lot, Shelby yelled, "Stop!"

He slammed on the brakes.

She opened her door and leaned out, spraying the snow with vomit.

He put the car in park and fished around in the console for a package of antibacterial wipes and tissues. "It's okay, Shelby. Happens to us all the time," which was a lie, but he wanted to comfort her.

She coughed and sputtered while holding her hair back. When she finished, she closed the door and covered her face. "God. So sorry."

He removed a wipe from the package and handed it to her. "It's a natural reaction to what you've experienced. We've all been there."

He and Monica helped her clean up, then they sped off toward the hospital.

On the way, Monica asked, "And, Yuri?"

"I shot him," Matt said.

"Is he—"

"Dead."

She patted his shoulder from the back seat. "I know that has to be hard on you, but he deserved it."

He didn't reply.

"I just thought of something," Monica said.

"What?"

"Are you going to get samples of Yuri's hair, saliva and blood to see if any match evidence from Andy's murder scene?"

"They're doing that right now," he said.

"I bet that Yuri's blood matches the third sample taken from the crime scene."

"I won't take that bet," Matt said.

39

Monica sat on the edge of Shelby's hospital bed, holding her hand. There was a jagged laceration in Shelby's forehead, high above her left eyebrow, along the hairline. Her chestnut hair was wet and matted down next to the wound, the adjacent skin stained with betadine.

"What's taking the doctor so long?" Shelby asked.

"I guess they're really busy." Monica turned her concerned gaze on Shelby. "Did Yuri hurt you?"

Shelby nodded, fighting back tears. "Yes...with his pistol, I think." Her lower lip trembling, she formed the words and moved her mouth before she could articulate them. "I remember...pulling into your driveway and getting out of my Jeep, then everything went black...until I woke up on the floor of the motel bathroom, my wrists bound in those fucking zip ties." Shelby's face contorted in pain.

Monica glanced up at Nurse Diane, who came in to check Shelby's IV line. "The doctor is on her way."

Monica felt exhausted, her heart broken for Shelby. "That had to be horrible, but you're here now. Safe with us."

Shelby openly cried, muttering, "Okay...I'm okay."

Monica took Shelby's hands in her own and cradled them, gently rubbing her thumbs in circles on Shelby's palms. "I won't leave you."

Shelby visibly relaxed, her rigid body melting into Monica. "I think the worst was when he made me talk to you on the phone." Tears flowed steadily over

Shelby's long lashes. "He jerked me around by the hair, and sort of punched me in the direction of the bathroom."

Monica held Shelby. "Where did he punch you?"

"The ribs," Shelby said, shivering from the memory. "My arms."

Monica delicately placed her hand on Shelby's back and patted while they cried together.

"I'm so sorry," Monica said after a few minutes. "If it weren't for my job, this wouldn't have happened to you."

Shelby hiccupped. "Who could've predicted... stupid court assignment...not...your fault."

"But—" Monica looked into Shelby's troubled eyes.

"Not your fault."

They heard footsteps, then the curtain was pulled aside by a female physician in scrubs and a white doctor coat. "Hello, Ms. St. Claire. I'm Dr. Ajir."

"I'm Shelby, and this is my girlfriend, Monica Spade."

"Nice to meet you both," Dr. Ajir said, moving to Shelby's side of the bed and looking at, but not touching, Shelby's forehead. "Can you tell me what happened, Shelby?"

Monica pushed herself up, so Shelby and Dr. Ajir could converse, but she still remained on the edge of the bed.

"Yes," Shelby said, swallowing and sitting up a little straighter. "I think he hit me with his pistol... then held me hostage..."

Dr. Ajir sat on a nearby stool and rolled over to Shelby. "I'm so sorry that happened to you. Do you hurt anywhere else besides this cut on your head?"

"My ribs...my arms. My wrists," Shelby said.

"Mind if I take a look?" Dr. Ajir asked.

"Please do," Shelby said.

Dr. Ajir scooted close and cautiously placed her hands on Shelby's abdomen over the gown. "I'm going to press down in a few places, okay?"

Shelby nodded, scrunching her lips in anticipation.

Dr. Ajir palpated each rib, one-by-one.

"That one!" Shelby exclaimed through a hiss.

Dr. Ajir immediately released her fingers and muttered a number to Nurse Diane, who entered it in the electronic medical record.

"I'm going to touch your tummy now."

Monica could tell by Shelby's clenched jaw that she was anticipating more pain.

"Does it hurt anywhere in this area?" Dr. Ajir quickly pressed in a few spots.

"No," Shelby said.

As Dr. Ajir released the pressure on Shelby's tummy, she smiled reassuringly. "I think you have a few bruised ribs, but I don't think they're broken. Mind if we take an X-ray to confirm?"

"Go ahead," Shelby said.

"Did he hit you anywhere else besides your head, right rib cage, and right arm?"

"No."

"Can you show me your wrists?"

Shelby held them out. The plastic had cut away the skin circumferentially.

Dr. Ajir took Shelby's hands in her own, as she inspected Shelby's wrists. "How did this happen?"

"He zip-tied my wrists in the front of my body."

"I'm so sorry," Dr. Ajir said. "We'll put some antibacterial cream on them and bandage them for you, okay?"

"Thank you."

Dr. Ajir nodded at Nurse Diane to make a note in the record.

"While we wait for the X-ray machine, I can stitch up the laceration along your hairline. Do I have your consent to do that, Shelby?" Dr. Ajir asked while gently palpating its jagged contours.

"Please do. Will I have a scar?"

Dr. Ajir focused on the wound, saying under her breath, "Not too deep. Diane did a good job washing it out." Then she said in a louder voice to Shelby, "The laceration is on the edge of your hairline, so I'll hide the bulk of the stitches there. I think you'll be able to cover up the tiny scar with your hair."

"That's a relief," Shelby said in a shaky voice. "How many stitches do you think?"

Dr. Ajir turned to a tray of equipment and picked up a syringe. "A dozen or so. I'm going to numb up the area with some lidocaine, okay?"

"Uh-huh," Shelby said, her hand searching out Monica's.

While the lidocaine was taking hold, Dr. Ajir prepared a suture and gently asked in a serious tone, her voice carrying a slight Middle Eastern accent, "Did he do anything else to you, Shelby?"

Shelby tilted her head, not catching the nature of Dr. Ajir's question.

Monica squeezed Shelby's hand.

"Did he sexually assault you?" Dr. Ajir asked.

Shelby shook her head vigorously. "No. Thank God, no." She squeezed Monica's hand in return. "Aside from roughing me up a little, he left me alone."

Dr. Ajir nodded. "I understand from Detective Matt Breuer that you were present for the shootout and saw what there was to see?"

Shelby pressed her eyes shut, trying to block out the memory of Yuri's bloody face. "Yes.

Psychologically, I think that was the worst part of the experience."

"That sounds like a very gruesome and troubling scene," Dr. Ajir said. "Would you like a referral to a counselor?"

Her eyes still closed, Shelby whispered, "Maybe."

"I think it sounds like a good idea." Monica again squeezed Shelby's hand. "I'll come with you if you want."

Shelby nodded, and Dr. Ajir moved the suture to Shelby's forehead, hovering over it. "I'm going to ask you to hold still now. Do you think you can do that?"

"Yes." Shelby kept her eyes closed and lips pursed.

Dr. Ajir proved to be efficient and dexterous, trailing the stitches expertly into Shelby's hairline. Afterward, she handwrote the name of a therapist on the back of her own business card and gave it to Shelby. "I hope you go see Wendy. She's one of the best therapists I know. Very calm and caring. It will help you work through this experience and decrease the chances of developing PTSD."

"That sounds like a good plan," Monica chimed in.

"I'll go," Shelby said, glancing at Monica.

"You have my business card," Dr. Ajir said. "I don't give a card to everyone, but you've been through quite a lot. Call me if you need anything."

After Shelby was discharged, they drove to Monica's house. "Do you want to stay here?"

The dimples above Shelby's eyebrows grew deeper with angst. "I just don't know...I feel... discombobulated..."

"Let's take our time."

They got out, and Monica helped Shelby find her phone on the floor of the Jeep, along with a bag of groceries and her backpack.

"I totally forgot that I'd stopped for groceries," Shelby said, swaying against the side of the Jeep.

Monica went to her, and looped her arm around Shelby's waist. "Let's go inside."

Shelby crumpled into herself, using Monica for support. "I'm so scared...don't want to be alone... and cold..."

Monica's heart liquified, a war raging inside of her. She wanted to kill Stela with her bare hands.

"I need you," Shelby said in a tremulous voice. "Will you help me?"

"Of course. I'm here."

After they shed their outerwear, Monica asked, "Do you want to take a shower? Maybe that would help you feel better."

Shelby nodded like a child, her usual wide smile gone. Monica led her to the sun-filled bathroom, helped her to undress, and turned on the shower. "I bet I have a shower cap to protect your sutures." She began rummaging through the vanity drawers. "I could've sworn I brought one back from a hotel stay."

"I'll be careful," Shelby said, getting in the shower and sliding the door shut.

Monica quickly texted Nathan. *Hey, Shelby is in really rough shape. Shock from trauma. I can't leave her alone. No court for me today.*

Nathan replied instantaneously. *Totally understand. Stay with her... I've got this.*

Not one to indulge in emojis, Monica nevertheless texted several hearts to Nathan. She opened the shower door a crack. "How are you doing?"

Shelby tried to smile through tears while haphazardly running her trembling hands over her arms, giving the impression she was cold. "I don't know."

"Want me to come in?" Monica said, now coming into the full realization of how broken Shelby was.

"Yes," Shelby said. "I'm afraid to face the spray."

"Give me a sec to get out of this suit." Monica quickly removed her clothes, suddenly realizing that she'd been wearing the same suit for 24 hours. To say she needed a shower, too, was an understatement.

She scooted in behind Shelby, so she could embrace her. They stayed under the spray for long, tender minutes, holding on for dear life. Monica knew she would do anything—anything—for Shelby, to help her recover from this disaster.

40

Nathan bypassed everyone in the courthouse hallway, not making eye contact. When he entered the courtroom, Tiffany Rose stood before him in the aisle, her pencil-thin skirt barely covering her thighs, her sheer blouse barely hiding her skin.

"Good morning, Mr. Taylor." Her doe-like eyes scanned Nathan's cashmere coat. "Subbing for Ms. Spade again?"

"Yes."

"Does her absence have anything to do with the shooting at the Antler's Motel last night?"

Nathan cocked an eyebrow.

"Police scanner."

"Ah," he said noncommittally, then left her wondering, as he proceeded to his counsel table. As he was making himself comfortable, Dominique entered and dropped her laptop and files on her table. She scooted over to him and leaned down. "Monica texted Jim last night that they rescued Shelby. How is she?"

"She was scraped up and really shaken, so Matt and Monica took her to the hospital."

"How devastating," Dominique said. "I assume you're taking over as standby counsel?"

"Just for today," he said.

"Good to have you back." She patted his shoulder and returned to her own table.

Stela entered through the side door with her deputy escorts, positively radiating energy in her white schoolmarm blouse and pink cardigan. She looked freshly showered and well-rested, ready to take on the world.

"Good morning, Mr. Taylor," Stela said brightly. "Is Ms. Spade sick again?"

"Something like that." From her demeanor, he concluded she didn't know about the shootout or Yuri's death. Stela probably assumed that Monica was out because she was distraught over Shelby's disappearance.

"I rehearsed my testimony with Ms. Spade, but I'm sure you can ask me the list of questions. You're much more experienced than she is." Stela scanned his face intently.

"Slide them over." Nathan glanced through them. "Easy enough."

"Put some life into it, will you?" She flashed her eyes, smiling victoriously.

Disgusted with her deadly games, Nathan rose and paced the aisle, thinking about Shelby and Monica.

Stela ignored him, rubbing her hands together and warming up for her performance.

Judge O'Brien entered the courtroom and focused on Nathan. "Substituting again, Mr. Taylor?"

"Yes, Your Honor."

"For good reason, I hope?"

"Yes. Ms. Spade had to go to the hospital to visit a friend."

That update drew a curious glance from Stela.

"I see." Judge O'Brien looked at Stela and raised his eyebrows.

She shrugged, still assuming she and Yuri were in control.

"Very well," he said. "Let's bring in the jury."

Once the jury was seated, Judge O'Brien said, "Now, it's time for the defense to put on her case. Ms. Reiter, who is your first witness?"

"I am," Stela said brightly, as if she were delivering a gift for all. "Attorney Nathan Taylor will be asking me questions."

"Please proceed." Judge O'Brien gestured for Stela to be sworn in.

She rose and scurried over to the court secretary then took the witness chair.

With a dark scowl, Nathan asked, "Please tell us your name and a little about yourself."

"My name is Stela Reiter, and I'm from Romania. I went to high school and college for chemical engineering, and I wanted to take some chemistry classes in the United States. Apple Grove University has an excellent program with graduate-level classes, so I signed up for classes in your lovely city."

"How long have you been in America?"

"Since last August," Stela said. "I arrived shortly before the fall semester was scheduled to begin. I had rented an apartment online, sight unseen, and it turned out well."

"Jumping ahead to the question that's on everyone's mind: 'Did you kill Andy Nelson?'"

"Yes," Stela said from behind her schoolmarm getup.

Nathan wanted to say *no further questions* and fold his arms over his chest, but he owed a duty to the court, so he asked, "Why?"

Like a faucet eager to be turned on, Stela gushed, "Because he was on top of me, cutting me, about to rape me, and going on and on about fulfilling his twisted fantasies. He had the knife in his right hand, and his left hand held my throat, pinning me to the seat. I was terrified. Terrified that he was going to kill me. That I would die in America in the back seat of his car. In the frozen field. So, I acted on instinct, doing the only thing I could. I wrestled the knife from him, cutting myself in the process," she held up her left palm for the jury, "and jabbed it in his right temple first because that's the angle I had. Remember, my glasses were off, so I stabbed wildly, not knowing what I was doing, just trying to stop him."

Stela manufactured a cough that turned into a cry, wiping nonexistent tears from her eyes. Nathan allowed Stela's performance to play for a few seconds, until some jurors turned to look at him for the next question.

"All right," Nathan said in a business-like tone. "Let's take it from the top. How did you and Andy meet?"

Stela threw her hair back and walked the jury through the beginning of their relationship at Racy's Coffee Lounge. Their initial dating seemed ordinary, even normal, until she started talking about their sex life. "He introduced me to blindfolds during sex, which I went along with because they seemed important to him. Being in control seemed important to him."

"Did his requests escalate?" Nathan asked, careful to hold the piece of paper before his face to demonstrate that he was reading, lest anyone think he was helping her.

"Yes. Week-by-week, he shared his likes and dislikes, ultimately reading his journal to me in bed. At this time, I request District Attorney Bisset to display exhibit 29, the essay excerpts," Stela said, looking at Dominique, who tapped on her laptop, so the journal entries appeared for everyone to see.

Stela waited a second, then read the excerpts out loud again—as she had in her opening statement—

seemingly oblivious to the fact that Sharon Nelson's testimony discredited them.

"As I told you in my opening statement, he also used a whip on me, creating huge, painful welts. I was sore for two weeks. That's when I put my foot down and told him I wouldn't consent to whipping."

"And?" Nathan asked in an apathetic monotone.

"A month later, he gave me his latest fantasy to read, the one about tasting my torn skin. I asked him what he meant by that, and his eyes went dark. He got a crazy look in his eye. You know it when you see it, no?" She pointed at her own eyes, talking to the jurors as if they were sitting in a coffee shop, except their stricken faces regarded her warily. "He said he meant exactly what it said, and asked if he could tie me up and play around on me with a knife."

Her expression froze in a conscious imitation of horror, as she paused for an eternity.

Nathan couldn't take her theatrics any longer, he rolled his hand in the air, motioning for her to speed it along. "And what did you say?"

"Of course, I told him 'no.' No!" Stela repeated with mock virtue. "I mean, who in her right mind would agree to such things? I would never allow him to cut on me for his sexual pleasure. That would be insane! The fact that he said this was a fantasy of his, a hidden desire, made me sick, and scared me a lot. So, I closed his journal," She demonstrated with her hands, "and set it back on his bedside table. I told him that I never wanted to read them again, and I didn't want him to read them to me either."

"Let's talk about the day of the homicide. You were at Andy's house?"

"Yes. I prefer to think of it as the day of the *assault and* homicide," Stela said. "It was a Saturday, and we slept in. After brunch, he became excited and animated, telling me we needed to go on an adventure. I pictured the movies or something, but he said he wanted to take me on a drive in the countryside, maybe find a roadside restaurant for dinner. Just a spontaneous tour."

"What happened next?" Nathan asked with genuine disinterest.

"We were on a country road, and he suddenly turned onto a snowy path along a corn field that had withered to stubble. It was bumpy and slippery, the car fishtailing and losing traction, but he said it looked like a good spot to enjoy ourselves."

"And then?" Nathan asked in lawyerbot tone.

"We got out and walked around a little. He might have relieved himself on a cornstalk, then we got in the back seat. He was playful at first, but soon, as I told you in my opening statement, he removed my glasses and blindfolded me. I obeyed at first, but when he put his knee between my legs, I felt something sharp cutting my jeans. I lowered my head, but I couldn't see under the bandana he had put over my eyes."

Nathan stared at Stela in disbelief.

Stela ignored him, gathering steam. "I panicked, saying something like, 'Bloody hell! Are you cutting me?'"

"He admitted he was, but that I should fight through the pain and lie still. He kept telling me to 'be still...be still.' I'll never forget how he spat those words at me while I saw white lights of unbearable pain behind my eyelids. He had to put his forearm over my chest to hold me down, as he cut through my jeans, making the perfect lines on my inner thigh. I lay frozen with fear, not moving an inch for fear he'd lose control and make a deep stab into my flesh. From his twisted journal, all I could picture was him cutting me to pieces."

Stela worked herself into a frenzy, her face frantic and voice pleading, maintaining absolute fidelity to her story.

"I screamed at him that I was in pain! For him to stop. He finally set the knife aside and removed my jeans. He said he was turned on by the blood, so he wanted to cut some more. He started cutting on my outer thigh, and I screamed again. After a few more cuts, I ripped off the bandana, so I could see what he was doing. When I saw his eyes—dark and evil—I yelled at him to get off of me."

Her hands gestured wildly in front of her, as she re-enacted bits and pieces. "But he didn't move. Instead, he held the knife under my chin and told me that I needed to help him act out his fantasies. Next, he made a tiny cut on his palm, much tinier than the cuts he had made on me, and put his palm on my outer thigh, chanting about 'mixing our blood, mixing our blood…'"

To embellish the chant, she made squirrelly motions with her hands, wiggling her fingers wildly, imitating a witch over a cauldron of brew.

"So, that's when I grabbed the knife and stabbed him again and again. He fought, pulling out a thick clump of hair. Again, the pain." She touched the side of her head, showing the jury a depilated spot. "That was when I realized we were in a fight to the death. It was either him or me. At some point, he opened the door, and we both tumbled out of the car. He attacked me in the snow, and I stabbed him again. I thought he was done. He was down on the ground, wounded, so I got back in the car for a minute, but he got up and came at me again, so I had to stab him over and over…over and over…until he died."

She skewered the air several times then covered her face with her hands, her entire body shaking. When she again looked up, her face was reset to a permafrost expression.

"Then what did you do?"

"I grabbed his cell phone and tried to dial 911, but my fingers were too wet and cold. I didn't know what I was doing. Perhaps I blacked out. I don't know. I ran. I had no idea I was carrying the knife and cell phone. I just ran toward the farmer's house. I wasn't wearing shoes, though, so my feet were cold, and I slipped a lot. That must have been when I dropped the knife and phone along the side of the road."

"What do you remember after you got to the farmer's house?"

"Not much. I feel like I woke up in the hospital. Everyone was questioning me. The nurse. The physician. The police. My head was a mess, and I found it difficult to talk—to form words. I couldn't remember anything. There were black spots in my memory, like a bad dream, so I just couldn't provide any details."

Nathan read the next question. "Is that why you didn't tell the Emergency Department staff about Andy?"

"Yes. I honestly couldn't tell if I had dreamed it, or if it had been real. I was so overwhelmed mentally and emotionally that I could barely process where I was."

"And, the next day, all day Sunday when you were still on the Behavioral Health Unit at the hospital, is there a reason you didn't tell them the entire story, as you've shared it with us today?"

"I was so sleepy and traumatized that it wasn't until Monday, when Detectives Breuer and Curfman helped to prompt my memory, that I was able to recall some events and tell them I acted in self-defense."

"Were you and Andy the only two people in his car that day?"

"Yes."

"Why do you think the police found three sets of DNA at the scene?"

"Because I had a bone marrow transplant for cancer treatment. My blood DNA is different than my saliva DNA."

"When did you have the bone marrow transplant?"

"Three-plus years ago."

"Where?"

"In Romania."

"Is that what Dr. Popovich is going to testify about?"

"Yes. He was my doctor."

"All right. Anything else?"

"No. Thank you," Stela said in her sweet voice.

"Any cross-examination by the District Attorney?" Judge O'Brien asked.

Dominique looked like a pointer straining to be let loose in a field of pheasants. "Yes, Your Honor." She rose and went to the podium, facing Stela head-on. "Let's go back to your Romanian past before you came to America. You're a student of chemistry, right?"

"Yes."

"Isn't it true that you buy and sell enriched plutonium and uranium on the black market?"

The jurors' eyes widened, as their gazes volleyed back and forth between the two sparring women.

"Of course not. That's ridiculous." Stela threw her arm in the air, waving away the accusation.

"Approach the witness, Your Honor?" Dominique asked.

"Proceed," he said.

Dominique gave Stela a document, then returned to the podium.

"I've given you what's been marked as exhibit 198, which is a document I obtained from INTERPOL. Can you read the top of the document, please?"

"I object, Your Honor," Stela said from the witness chair, staring up at him.

"What's your objection, Ms. Reiter?" he asked.

"Approach the bench for a conference?" Stela asked.

"Fine," he said. "I'm going to excuse the jury for an early break. "You can remain in the witness box, Ms. Reiter."

After the jury left, Judge O'Brien again asked Stela, "What's your objection?"

"That the prosecutor is attempting to show my criminal record as evidence that I committed the crime for which I'm being tried."

Judge O'Brien wrinkled his pudgy nose then turned to Dominique for an explanation.

"That's not true, Your Honor," Dominique said. "I'm using this document to impeach her testimony. She said she and Andy got together as friends and lovers. This document will help prove that she targeted him because he worked at *Voila!* and had access to nuclear materials."

"Again, Your Honor," Stela said, "the prosecutor is attempting to use my past criminal history to prove I acted a certain way—approaching Andy Nelson—in the commission of intentional homicide. The prejudice of this exhibit far outweighs any probative value."

Judge O'Brien pinched the bridge of his nose closed his eyes. "I agree with the defendant. I'm precluding questions about the defendant's criminal history, even if you're simply trying to impeach her testimony."

Dominique held up the report, which also had a headshot of Stela on it. "Your Honor, it also shows that her name was Mila Golodryga. I should be able to use it to impeach her credibility. She's the one who chose to testify about herself and background."

"That's not true," Stela chimed in. "On direct, I was careful to avoid my background. I didn't open the door to being impeached about my name or criminal record."

"Okay. I've heard the arguments," Judge O'Brien said. "Again, I conclude that the prejudice outweighs the probative value, and the defendant is correct. She didn't open the door on direct. I'm not allowing the prosecution to introduce Ms. Reiter's INTERPOL criminal record."

Dominique worked her jaw, adjusted her lapel, briefly touching the American flag pin, and returned the document to her counsel table.

"Let's bring the jury back," Judge O'Brien said.

Once the jury was seated, Dominique continued. "You testified on direct that you were uncomfortable with Andy's increasingly violent sexual demands, right?"

"Yes," Stela said.

"You told him that you didn't want to see his journal again, right?"

"Yes."

"When he broke out the whip, you told him absolutely not, correct?"

"Yes."

"Then, why didn't you just walk away? Sexual incompatibility is a reason to end a romantic relationship, is it not?"

Stela nodded, giving the impression she had considered the concept of breaking up. "I wanted to, but he had charming characteristics as well. He helped me with my homework, took me out to dinner, and showed me around your lovely city. I thought there was the potential for a long-term relationship, so I didn't want to bail on him just because of some differences in the bedroom."

"From what you described, you were terrified," Dominique said. "Why not walk away?"

"Because he meant more to me than just sex," Stela said, her tone neutral.

Dominique paused for a few seconds, consulting her notes. "Did you purchase enriched plutonium or uranium from Andy Nelson?"

"No," Stela said with unbridled disgust, as though the mere mention was unbelievable.

"We heard from Detectives Breuer and Curfman that they found two lead-lined suitcases in Mr. Nelson's garage. Were you aware of those?"

"No."

"Detective Breuer testified that the Geiger counter detected radioactive materials at Mr. Nelson's house. Were you aware of that?"

"Not until I heard his testimony a few days ago, no."

"So, you had no idea that Andy had radioactive material at his house?"

"Absolutely not. I wouldn't have gone there if I had known."

"Did you ever visit his work?"

"No."

"You testified that you had a bone marrow transplant for cancer treatment."

"That's correct," Stela said.

"Was your cancer from exposure to radioactive materials?"

The cadence of question and answer came to a screeching halt, as Stela paused to consider Dominique's question. Stela frowned and said, "No," but it lacked the credibility and conviction of her previous answers.

"You and Andy were at his house before you drove to the farmer's field?"

"Yes."

"You were familiar with Andy's kitchen block of Trident knives?"

"Yes."

"You took a paring knife from that block, brought it with you in the car, probably hiding it under the seat or somewhere, and stabbed him with it, didn't you?"

"No. I've already explained that *he* brought it."

Dominique moved on. "So, it was only you and Mr. Nelson at the scene? The only reason there are three sets of DNA is because you have two sets, is that your testimony?"

"Yes. It was just the two of us."

"Okay," Dominique flipped a page of notes, letting Stela's answer sit. "Let's talk about when you were in the Behavioral Health Unit at Community Memorial Hospital, and Detectives Matt Breuer and Brock Curfman visited you."

"Okay."

"On their first visit, you told them that you were on your stomach when Andy got on top of you, correct?"

"I don't remember what I said, but I saw that in their reports."

"You told them that Andy attacked you when you were looking for something in the back seat, didn't you?"

"Yes."

"You didn't tell the detectives that Andy blindfolded you, did you?"

"No."

"You didn't tell them that Andy put his palm on the outer aspect of your thigh to mix your blood, did you?"

"No."

"Your testimony is that you wrestled the knife away from Andy with your left hand, correct?"

"Yes."

"And then you stabbed him in the temple, correct?"

"Yes."

"You stabbed him a few times in the genitals when he was in the car with you?"

"Maybe. I don't know."

"You stabbed him the stomach when he was in the car?"

"I think so."

"You stabbed him twice in the back when he was in the car?"

"Yes."

"You sliced him across the neck twice?"

"Yes, but they were clean slices. Not gashes. Those photos from the autopsy show his skin after it fell open."

"Thanks for the clarification," Dominique said. "You're proud of your clean work aren't you?"

Stela stared daggers at Dominique. "I object."

Dominique held up her hand, as she maintained eye contact with Stela, her voice going lower. "I withdraw the question. When you stabbed Andy in the head, how close was he?

"Very close."

"You didn't have your glasses on, but you saw him?"

"Obviously."

"You used your right hand, correct?"

"No."

"So, while wrestling the knife away from him, your testimony is that the blade cut your left palm, and even after that, you used your bloody left hand to stab him in the temple?"

"Yes."

Dominique squinted disbelievingly. "Finally, your testimony is that Andy got out of the car, and you stabbed him in the side when you were both standing in the snow, correct?"

"Yes. Well, not standing, maybe on the ground fighting."

"But he was alive and active. That's your testimony, correct?"

"Yes. You have to be alive to be fighting," Stela sneered.

"Yet, you had already stabbed him several times, correct?"

"Yes."

"It was just Andy and you outside the car, next to the field, correct?"

"Yes."

"Then, you mentioned you got back into the car and blacked out for a while?"

"I think so," Stela said. "I'm not 100 percent sure because it's all a jumbled mess in my mind."

Dominique stared at Stela, seemingly deciding whether to explore the precise details further, then asked, "Andy rose from the ground and attacked you in the car again?"

"Yeah. Maybe. I'm not sure now."

"Not sure that you wrestled in the snow, or that you killed him in the back seat of the car?"

Stela waved her hand nonchalantly, as if the details didn't matter. "Of any of it."

Dominique compressed her lips and nodded, deciding to move on. "Someone else's blood was smeared on the trunk of the car, wasn't it?"

"Yes." Stela stopped and covered her mouth with her hand. "I mean, no. That has to be mine too."

Dominique stared at Stela for a minute, then flipped her notes over and looked at Judge O'Brien. "No further questions, Your Honor."

"Any redirect of yourself, Ms. Reiter," Judge O'Brien asked.

"If I might confer with Mr. Taylor for a minute, please," Stela said.

"You may step out of the witness box and go to counsel table where you can briefly talk with Attorney Taylor," Judge O'Brien said.

Stela quickly returned to counsel table and sat next to Nathan. Keeping her at a distance, Nathan turned his head so he could listen but not make eye contact.

"I'd like you to rehabilitate me with a few questions about self-defense," Stela said.

"What questions?" Nathan asked, playing dumb.

"You know. Ask me about what I was thinking in light of his journal. How terrified I was…Use your lawyering skills."

"I'll try."

Stela gave him a dirty look and returned to the witness chair.

In a monotone, devoid of compassion or enthusiasm, Nathan asked, "When you were in the back seat, pinned by Andy, what were you thinking?"

Stela nodded in approval. "I was terrified that he would act out his fantasies. Since he had already cut me and said it turned him on, I was certain he was going to torture me for his sexual pleasure, then kill me."

"Did you ask him to stop?"

"Yes. Over and over, but he wouldn't."

"Did you try to get away?"

"Yes, but he pinned me down with his weight and held the knife to my throat."

"What did you finally do?"

"I struggled, but I got the knife and stabbed him once. When he wouldn't stop, I had to stab him more and more." She choked up. "And several times more because he kept hitting me and strangling me." Stela's tone suddenly turned deadly. "Until I killed him."

Her portrayal of Andy's evolution from model employee to boyfriend to sadist seemed so farfetched that it would have been laughable if not for his tragic death.

"Is there anything else you'd like to say?" Nathan asked in an exhausted tone.

"No. There's nothing else to say, other than it was him or me."

Nathan pushed back from the microphone, an uncomfortable silence completing Stela's macabre presentation. The jury guardedly watched her leave the witness box and return to counsel table.

Once Stela was seated next to Nathan at counsel table, Judge O'Brien asked her who her next witness was.

"Dr. George Popovich."

"How long will he go?"

"I'm guessing less than an hour," Stela said.

"Okay," Judge O'Brien said, reading the mood in the room, "We're going to take a 15 minute break then return for Dr. Popovich's testimony. All rise."

After the jury left, Judge O'Brien quickly stood and disappeared behind the judicial façade, the squeaky metal door slam signaling he was gone.

"Did we do well?" Stela asked Nathan.

"You did fine."

Stela's gaze left Nathan's and swept the courtroom. When she saw who she was looking for, she burst into a smile and stood.

A man in a suit quickly approached, and they moved to hug, but the deputies stood between them.

"Dr. Popovich," Stela said over the deputy's shoulder.

"Mila," he whispered.

"It's 'Stela' in the courtroom," she said. "This is my lawyer, Nathan Taylor."

"I'm not her lawyer." Nathan didn't offer his hand, as he assessed the physician.

41

After the 15-minute break, everyone took their seats, except for Stela, who hadn't returned from the jail.

Judge O'Brien addressed Nathan. "I thought Ms. Spade would be back by now. Visiting someone in the hospital doesn't take precedence over court."

"I understand, Your Honor. I'm appearing on behalf of Ms. Spade for the entire day."

"Why?"

"Her girlfriend was held hostage by Yuri Zaleski, a known associate of Stela Reiter. Zaleski was attempting to blackmail Attorney Spade. He told Ms. Spade that if Ms. Reiter wasn't acquitted, he was going to kill her girlfriend." Nathan omitted Shelby's name in an attempt to spare her media inquiries.

A look of comprehension crossed Judge O'Brien's expression, as he connected random bits of news. "Did that have anything to do with the police shooting at Antlers' Motel last night?"

"Yes," Nathan said. "The police rescued Ms. Spade's girlfriend and shot and killed Yuri Zaleski, Ms. Reiter's accomplice."

Judge O'Brien stared at Nathan for a second, the gravity of the situation gelling in his mind. He looked at Dominique, silently questioning whether she was aware of the details of the shooting.

She nodded in silent affirmation.

Judge O'Brien returned his attention to Nathan. "Was Ms. Spade's girlfriend shot?"

"No. She required medical attention for some cuts and bruises. Zaleski was pretty rough on her."

"Was he holding Ms. Spade's girlfriend hostage since the inception of this trial?" Judge O'Brien asked, his voice rising in pitch.

"No," Nathan said. "He took her last night."

Judge O'Brien's eyebrows lowered, smoothing the creases in his forehead, and along with them, his incredulity. "The sooner we conclude this trial, the better."

Suddenly, the side door next to Nathan's counsel table opened, and Stela walked in with her deputy escorts, startling everyone. The mood quickly shifted from one of civilized justice to a burning-at-the-stake mentality.

Judge O'Brien barely masked his disdain for Stela, now seeing her in a more premeditated light. The picture was becoming clearer to everyone—she and Zaleski had blown into town to dupe a young man into selling them nuclear materials. A simple plan, ruthlessly deployed by killers.

By unspoken agreement, Nathan, Dominique and Judge O'Brien were united in their responsibility to assure fairness under the law but individually appalled by Stela and Yuri's blatant disregard for human life.

Thus far, Judge O'Brien's rulings had been appellate-proof, and nothing had transpired during the trial that could be overturned. He was determined to stay the course, despite the new, chilling facts.

"Hi," Stela whispered to Nathan. "Did I miss something?"

"No," he lied.

She regarded him closely, intuiting he was withholding information, her flat stare roaming his face. "And, Ms. Spade? You said she had to visit a friend, but that she would return. Where is she?"

"As it turns out, she won't be here today." Nathan used a tone that indicated the topic was none of

Stela's business. He thought it was best for her to proceed under the assumption that her *real* boyfriend was still holding Shelby hostage for leverage. *How ironic*, Nathan thought, *my boyfriend killed yours last night. Welcome to justice in Apple Grove.*

None of them—Judge O'Brien, Dominique, Nathan—was morally, legally or ethically obligated to tell Stela about Yuri's death. Strategically, they knew that the trial record would read better if they didn't speak of it, so they couldn't be accused of colluding to tip the scales of justice in favor of a predetermined guilty verdict. Moreover, they knew it would be much more amusing to watch her operate under the assumption that she held the ace of cards.

Stela faltered, a visible shiver running through her, as she stared suspiciously at Nathan. She seemed to feel the cataclysmic change in energy, her dark eyes darting from Nathan to Judge O'Brien, then to Dominique. Apparently concluding the answer was beyond her immediate grasp, she looked down and flipped open her trial binder to a tab labeled, "Dr. Popovich."

For the sole benefit of Stela, Judge O'Brien looked at her and asked, "Is there anything the parties wish to raise before I bring in the jury?"

"Yes, Your Honor."

"Go ahead, Ms. Reiter."

She adjusted her spectacles. "I would like the record to reflect that Monica Spade is absent again today. I believe my defense is being compromised by this substitution of counsel during the middle of my trial. Ms. Spade and I spent several hours preparing, and this is the heart of my defense. I think due process requires that I have appropriate, continuous, and consistent representation."

Judge O'Brien smoothed his mostly bald head with the palm of his hand. "Are you requesting something specific, Ms. Reiter?"

"That I have Ms. Spade back, Your Honor."

If Judge O'Brien was struck by the hypocrisy, he didn't show it. "We've already been over the law on this topic. It's my understanding that Ms. Spade was called away to an emergency. If you would like to postpone today's testimony until Ms. Spade can return tomorrow, I'd be happy to do that." Judge O'Brien stared down Stela from the bench, calling her bluff.

Stela examined the cuticles of her fingernails, lost in her narcissistic belief that she was negotiating from a position of strength. "No, Your Honor. I choose a speedy trial over rotting in jail. I just question the fairness on the record is all."

"Very well," Judge O'Brien said. "The court notes that the *pro se* defendant was offered, and declined, a postponement for Monica Spade to return tomorrow. In the meantime, Nathan Taylor, a capable trial attorney who is familiar with the proceedings, is sitting by the defendant's side, pursuant to court order. At this time, I request the jury bailiff to bring in the jury."

Isla snapped to attention and went to the jury room to fetch her ducklings. After a few seconds, the jurors waddled in unenthusiastically, having just consumed another box of donuts from a local coffee shop.

Dr. Lisa Gilmore was one of the few who had maintained her curiosity and attention throughout, her intelligent eyes scanning the parties. Mrs. Alina Popa, the Romanian grandmother, consistently bore a pleasant expression under her cinnamon-colored Q-tip hairstyle.

"Welcome back," Judge O'Brien said. "We're going to hear testimony for about an hour, then take a lunch break, then resume again for the afternoon. I hope this will accommodate everyone's schedule." He specifically looked at the young mother who had to pump breast milk, and she nodded.

Judge O'Brien turned to Stela. "The defense may call its next witness."

"I call Dr. Popovich," Stela said.

A pale man in his mid-50s rose and walked forward. He wore a flat gray suit that matched his eyes and the few strands of hair that carelessly swept over his bald head.

He was sworn in and took the stand.

Stela smiled warmly at him. "Please state your full name and where you reside."

"George M. Popovich. I live in Camden, New Jersey."

"What do you do there?"

"I'm an oncologist and hematologist at the MD Anderson Cancer Center in Camden."

"Please tell us your education."

"I went to the University of Toledo College of Medicine in Toledo, Ohio. After that, I did a residency in oncology and hematology at MD Anderson Cancer Center in Houston, Texas. I did my fellowship there as well."

"Are you licensed to practice medicine?"

"Yes."

"Where?"

"In both Texas and New Jersey."

"Are you board certified?"

"Yes."

"In what?"

"Both oncology and hematology."

"Please explain your practice of oncology and hematology."

"As an oncologist, I treat patients with cancer. As a hematologist, I treat patients with blood disorders like hemophilia, or patients with cancers that affect blood, like leukemia."

"Thank you."

"Now, Dr. Popovich, turning to the matter at hand, do we know each other?"

"Yes."

"How?"

"You're my patient."

"When was I your patient?"

"Well, once a patient, always a patient in my practice, but I treated your leukemia with a bone marrow transplant three years and two months ago."

"Did that treatment cure my blood cancer?"

"It's in remission, yes."

"Explain for the jury what a bone marrow transplant is."

"Bone marrow is the spongy tissue inside bones that produces red blood cells, platelets, and white blood cells. Your bone marrow was damaged, so we had to supplement it. We obtained some from a donor who was the correct match for your blood type."

"Please explain what the donor's bone marrow did for me."

"It ramped up production to make new blood cells."

"Does bone marrow contain DNA?"

"Yes."

"What's DNA?"

"*DNA,* or deoxyribonucleic acid, is a molecule that contains your unique genetic code. It's like a recipe book that holds the instructions for making all the proteins in your body. The DNA molecule is shaped like a ladder that's twisted—a double helix." He made a twist with his hand in the air.

"Is my DNA unique to me?"

"Yes. We can identify one human from another by their DNA. Every person differs from another in about 0.1% of their DNA. Scientists have identified 13 places on our DNA that are quite different among each of us. We use those areas to produce profiles that can distinguish one individual from another."

"So, if I receive bone marrow from the donor, do I now have the donor's DNA inside of me?"

"Yes, you do. A bone marrow transplant turns you, the recipient, into a chimera."

"What's a chimera?"

"Chimera is a term derived from Greek mythology. It originally meant a fire-breathing female monster with a lion's head, a goat's body, and a serpent's tail, but now we use it medically to mean a mixture."

Smirks appeared on some jurors' faces.

Nathan openly snorted. *Stela—a fire-breathing monster with a psychopath's head, a librarian's body, and an assassin's soul. How fitting.*

Stela snapped her head at him then turned to Dr. Popovich. She rushed into her next question in an attempt to bury his answer to her last. "What does 'chimera' mean in the context of a bone marrow transplant and the recipient's DNA?"

"In the medical context, it means that the DNA in your blood is different than the DNA in your skin tissue, saliva and hair."

"Please explain."

He turned to the jury with a pleasant look on his face, as if he were talking to a patient's family in his office. "After Stela received new bone marrow, she now has both her own bone marrow and donor bone marrow. This means her blood DNA is a mixture— medically chimeric."

"Just my blood?"

"Yes. Your other cells—saliva, skin tissue and hair —are your original DNA, so their profiles are different than your blood DNA, which is a mixture."

"Turning to the case at hand, have you reviewed the police report regarding three sets of DNA identified in blood samples from the crime scene where Andy Nelson's death took place?"

"Yes."

"What's your conclusion from that report, given that I'm a chimera, meaning I have two sets of DNA inside of me?"

"That there were two people at the scene—you and Andy Nelson. One blood sample matched Mr. Nelson's DNA. The other blood samples represent the two sets of DNA residing inside of you."

"So, three sets of DNA but only two people, right?"

"Yes. Only Mr. Nelson and you." He swallowed hard, shifting his gaze between the jury and Stela, his performance carrying the sheen of deception.

"Thank you Dr. Popovich. No more questions."

Judge O'Brien, a former prosecutor himself, turned to Dominique with fierce intensity, almost begging her to shred Popovich. "Does the prosecution wish to cross?"

"Yes, Your honor." Dominique briefly shook her head, visibly clearing the gossamer web of half-truths spewed forth by the good doctor. "Thank you for teaching us about bone marrow transplants and DNA, Dr. Popovich."

"You're welcome." He straightened in his chair and smiled.

"Going back to the beginning of your testimony —" Dominique uncurled the pages of her yellow legal pad. "You mentioned that a bone marrow transplant was necessary to treat Ms. Reiter's leukemia, correct?"

"Yes."

"Can a person get leukemia from exposure to radioactive materials?"

"Yes. Radiation can cause cells to mutate in a way that can cause leukemia and a variety of other cancers."

"Can exposure to radioactive materials kill bone marrow cells?"

"It can weaken and break up DNA enough to kill bone marrow, yes."

"And the same treatment—a bone marrow transplant—would help that person survive, right?"

"The bone marrow transplant would help the recipient produce new blood cells and platelets, yes."

"Please tell us the reason Ms. Reiter needed a bone marrow transplant."

"She had leukemia."

"From what?"

"She came to me with leukemia, so I treated her."

Dominique squinted at him, questioning his evasive answer, yet she had planted the seed for her closing argument, so she moved on. "Who was Ms. Reiter's donor?"

"Ah," Dr. Popovich scratched his balding head where long wisps of gray hair lay plastered to his smooth scalp. "I don't know if I remember, or if I'm allowed to say. Some donors wish to remain anonymous, and others have the right to their privacy under the law."

"Do you know the identity of the donor without disclosing who it is?" Dominique asked.

He pursed his lips, his eyes darting between Stela and Dominique. "For the life of me, I can't remember."

"Very well." Dominique shrugged him off. "Turning to the homicide scene, let me see if I understand your mapping of the three blood samples to Mr. Nelson and Ms. Reiter's blood and saliva."

He nodded in anticipation.

Dominique rose and walked to an easel with a large, white pad on it. On the left said of the paper, she wrote "Crime Scene Blood," and under it, she drew three boxes in a column, labelling them A, B and C. She turned to Dr. Popovich. "Would you agree with me that these three boxes represent the three samples of blood from the crime scene?"

"Sure."

On the right side of the paper, she wrote the heading "DNA," and under it, "Andy's blood." She connected "Andy's Blood" with a dotted line to Box A. "Do you agree with me that the first blood sample at the crime scene—Box A—matches Andy Nelson's blood DNA?"

"Yes."

On the right side of the paper, she next wrote "Stela Reiter's blood," and connected it with a dotted line to Box B. "Do you agree with me that the second blood sample at the crime scene—Box B—matches Stela Reiter's blood DNA?"

"Yes." Dr. Popovich's beady eyes tracked Dominique's mapping. He'd be a fool not to see where she was going.

"A blood-to-blood match for Box B to Ms. Reiter's blood, correct?"

"Yes."

"And we agree that Stela's blood is a mixture of her own blood and that of her donor, correct?"

"Yes."

"We just learned she's a chimera, correct?"

"Yes."

"This match proves that she was at the homicide scene because she left her own blood behind, correct?"

"Yes."

Dominique turned back to the easel. On the right side of the paper, corresponding to the third box of blood on the left, Box C, Dominique wrote "Stela Reiter's saliva." Rather than connect it with a dotted line to Box C, she instead inserted the equal sign with a red slash through the middle of it, indicating that the two objects were not equal—the third blood sample was not equal to Stela's saliva DNA.

She turned to Dr. Popovich while pointing at the paper with the red marker. "Now, Dr. Popovich, the third sample of blood at the crime scene—Box C—doesn't match Ms. Reiter's saliva sample, does it?"

"Um...I don't know. She has two sets of DNA."

Dominique set down the marker. "We understand that, but let's clarify. We still don't know to whom the third sample of blood from the crime scene belongs, but we know it doesn't match Stela Reiter's blood or saliva, right?"

"Well, since it's blood, it couldn't match her saliva because her blood is different from her saliva, and we've already established that the second blood sample from the crime scene matches her blood," he said authoritatively.

"My point exactly," Dominique said. "And the State Crime Lab report of her saliva DNA indicates it doesn't match the blood from the third sample, Box C, does it?"

"I would have to compare the reports again."

Dominique returned to her counsel table, searched through a few papers, and came up with two reports. "Approach, Your Honor?"

Judge O'Brien eagerly waved her forward.

"I've handed you Exhibits 33 and 34, the State Crime Lab Report of Ms. Reiter's blood and saliva and other samples, and the State Crime Lab Report of the three samples of blood found at the scene," Dominique said. "Do these reports refresh your recollection that Ms. Reiter's saliva DNA does not match the third blood sample at the homicide scene?"

"Let me just study them again." Popovich bent his head, the gray wisps of hair peeling away from his scalp, as he compared the two reports.

"Feel free to look up after you've studied the reports," Dominique said, remaining directly in front of the witness box, hovering over him.

After a few long seconds, he looked up at her.

"The third sample of blood at the crime scene does not match any of Ms. Reiter's DNA, does it?"

"No," he said on a sigh. His eyes traveled past Dominique with a look of sympathy—or was it fear? —at Stela.

Dominique removed both reports from his hands and returned to her counsel table. "Nothing further."

Judge O'Brien gazed long and hard at Dr. Popovich, his own eyes mere slits behind his heavy black frames. He turned to Stela. "Does the defendant wish to conduct a redirect?"

"No, Your Honor," Stela said in a sweet voice.

"The witness may be excused," Judge O'Brien said.

42

Bristling with embarrassment, Dr. Popovich skulked from the courtroom like a frightened porcupine.

"The defendant may proceed with her next witness," Judge O'Brien said.

"I call Dr. Delaney Karpenko," Stela said, as she half-turned to the pew directly behind her.

A tan man with thick, gray hair stood. Wearing a brown tweed jacket over a black turtleneck, he quickly made his way to the court secretary to be sworn in. Along the way, he graciously greeted Judge O'Brien, swung around to nod at Dominique, and made eye contact with practically every juror on his way to the witness box.

"Can you state your full name for the record, please?" Stela asked.

"Delaney Karpenko, M.D.," he said.

"What is your education?"

"I went to Ohio State College, the Cleveland Clinic Lerner College of Medicine, and completed a residency in psychiatry at the Cleveland Clinic."

"Where did you grow up?"

"Ukraine," he said without elaborating.

As the two conversed, their accents flowed together, blending easily, like two people from the same part of the country. Whether that country was Stela's Romania or Dr. Karpenko's Ukraine, only Mrs. Popa stood a chance of knowing.

"Where do you work?" she asked.

"I have my own psychiatric practice in Cleveland, Ohio."

"Have you treated patients with post-traumatic stress disorder in your practice?"

"Many times," he said.

"Please explain for the jury what PTSD is."

"In layperson's terms, it's a disorder in which a person has difficulty recovering psychologically after experiencing or witnessing a terrifying event."

"Thank you," Stela said. "What are the symptoms?"

"That depends on the point in time after the event, whether the person receives treatment for PTSD, and any subsequent triggering events."

"Let's assume a person immediately after the event, before receiving treatment. What are the symptoms at that time?"

"The symptoms are numerous and varied," he said. "They can range from flashbacks to nightmares, panic attacks to eating disorders, and cognitive delays to lowered verbal memory capacity."

"Did you review my medical record from Community Memorial Hospital?" she asked.

"Yes."

"Did you notice the notes that mentioned my limited ability to recall what happened to me on January 4th?"

"Yes."

"Is the inability to recall a traumatic event a symptom of PTSD?"

"Yes."

"Did you notice that my providers documented that I answered with one or two-word phrases without elaborating?"

"Yes."

"Is limited verbal ability a symptom of PTSD?"

"Yes."

"What, if anything, did you notice in my medical record about me disclosing information?"

"You gave more information as each day passed."

"Is it normal for patients with PTSD to recall more details and talk more as they get further and further away from the traumatic event?"

"Yes."

"Did you conduct an exam of me in the Apple Grove jail?"

"Yes."

"What, if anything, is your diagnosis of me from a psychiatric perspective?"

"That you are suffering from PTSD from a traumatic event, specifically being attacked by your boyfriend, Andy Nelson, on January 4th."

"Given that diagnosis, would you be surprised to learn that I told Detectives Breuer and Curfman more information the second time they visited me at the hospital?"

"I wouldn't be surprised to hear that you became more and more comfortable talking about something that terrified you and caused you significant pain and trauma. That type of memory recall—in bits and pieces—along with increased verbal ability, is consistent with PTSD."

"Thank you," Stela said. "I have no further questions."

Judge O'Brien looked at Dominique. "Does the State wish to cross-examine?"

"Yes." Dominique rose and took the podium with a slim little folder in hand. She adjusted her left lapel and faced Dr. Karpenko.

"A woman could experience PTSD symptoms after killing someone, couldn't she?"

"Well, that isn't what I said. Stela was the victim of an attack and experienced dissociative-like symptoms and dysphoria in the aftermath. And, frankly, this trial isn't helping her PTSD—being forced to relive the trauma. The literature and my clinical experience support the profile she exhibited at the hospital, that of inability to recall events or verbalize."

"Thank you for that explanation, doctor, but it wasn't responsive to my question. My question was, 'A woman could experience PTSD symptoms after killing someone, couldn't she?' Please answer yes or no."

Dr. Karpenko glanced up at Judge O'Brien, only to be met with a stern glare.

"I suppose so," Dr. Karpenko said.

Dominique nodded in agreement. "And PTSD doesn't cause a person to lie, does it?"

"Again, the memory sometimes returns in bits and pieces, so a person might appear like she's withholding information, but her reluctance to speak and inability to recall details are both part of the PTSD."

"Doctor, you didn't answer my specific question," Dominique said. "Lying is different than inability to recall. PTSD doesn't cause a person to lie, does it?"

"No," Dr. Karpenko said, flicking back the thick chunk of gray bangs that insisted on covering his forehead.

"Thank you. Turning to your background, Dr. Karpenko, you're originally from Ukraine?"

"Yes."

"What city?"

"Kiev," he said with an accent.

"Do you periodically return to Kiev to visit?" she asked.

"Yes."

"In fact, you visited Kiev last year, didn't you?"

He squinted at her, visibly wondering where she was going with her questioning. "Yes, I did."

"While you were there, you visited your chess club, didn't you?"

"Yes. I enjoy playing chess as a pastime."

"The name of your chess club is 'Kiev Kashtanchek,' isn't it?"

"Yes," he said, the pride of belonging to the club radiating through his guardedness.

"Approach the witness, Your Honor?" Dominique asked.

"Yes," Judge O'Brien said.

Dominique removed a few sheets of paper from her slim folder. She first walked to Stela and handed one to her, then went to Dr. Karpenko at the witness stand and handed one to him.

Stela quickly scanned the document, and her face fell.

Dominique returned to the podium. "I'm showing you what's been marked as exhibit 112. What is the exhibit, Dr. Karpenko?"

"A list of 2019 membership in Kiev Kashtanchek."

"I highlighted two names on that document. Is one of them yours?"

"Yes."

"You're a member of that club, aren't you?"

"Yes."

"You're also listed as a coach, aren't you?"

"Yes."

"You coach other chess players on how to improve their games, don't you?"

"Yes."

"Is Stela Reiter's name on that membership list?" Dominique asked, resting her elbow on the podium and glancing at the jurors, cock sure of the answer.

"No," Dr. Karpenko said.

"Please read the other name highlighted on the list of club members, Dr. Karpenko."

He cleared his throat. "Mila Golodryga."

"The woman sitting at defense table to my left, known in this trial as Stela Reiter, is also known to you, and the chess club, as Mila Golodryga, isn't she?"

His eyes darted to Stela, who said, "Object, Your Honor."

Judge O'Brien looked like he had been asked to take out the garbage during a football game. "What's the basis of your objection?"

"Approach, Your Honor?" Stela asked.

"Of course," Judge O'Brien said.

Stela and Dominique, joined by Nathan, proceeded to the bench.

"Ms. Reiter?" Judge O'Brien asked.

"I object to the prosecutor asking Dr. Karpenko to identify me by a different name based on relevance. Why is it relevant to proving her case? I already admitted that I stabbed Andy. She's attempting to prejudice my reputation, and it outweighs the probative value."

Dominique jumped in. "Their relationship and her name are relevant material to show Dr. Karpenko's bias. They're chess buddies from Ukraine. The jury is entitled to know their cozy relationship in deciding the credibility of his opinions."

"But—" Stela began.

Judge O'Brien cut her off. "Your objection is overruled. The witness can answer the question."

"But, what about—" Stela sputtered.

"Return to your seat, Ms. Reiter," Judge O'Brien said, casting a purposeful glance at the deputy closest to her. He took a step forward, bearing down on her with his thick chest and gut.

Stela turned and sulked back to her table. Nathan followed, cutting a nice silhouette in his expensive suit.

Dominique returned to the podium. "Now, I'll ask you the same question again, Dr. Karpenko. The woman sitting at the defense table to my left, known in this trial as Stela Reiter, is also known to you, and the chess club, as Mila Golodryga, isn't she?" Dominique glanced up at Mrs. Popa. Her arms crossed, she wore a sour look of disapproval on her face, her loyalty to Stela resolute.

"Yes." Dr. Karpenko shrugged at Stela to indicate he had no choice but to confide her real name.

"You met her at Kiev Kashtanchek, didn't you?" Dominique asked.

"Yes."

"You served as her coach, didn't you?"

"Yes."

"No further questions." Dominique made eye contact with the jurors and returned to her table.

"Any redirect by the defense?" Judge O'Brien asked.

"Yes," Stela said, leaning closer to her microphone. "Does the fact that you briefly coached me at chess in Kiev affect the medical opinions you provided today?"

"No."

"Thank you. Nothing further," Stela said.

"The witness may step down," Judge O'Brien said.

Dr. Karpenko left the box, and walked across the arena, his enthusiasm vanquished. He sat in a pew behind Stela.

"All right," Judge O'Brien said, "It's time for the lunch break. After that, does the defense plan to call anyone else?"

"No, Your Honor."

Judge O'Brien turned to Dominique. "Will the State be putting on any rebuttal witnesses?"

"Yes, Your Honor," Dominique said.

"Will they be ready this afternoon?" Judge O'Brien asked.

"Unfortunately, no," Dominique said. "Detective Breuer was called away to something else, and is now completing reports, etcetera. I'm sure he can be ready to testify first thing tomorrow morning."

"That sounds fine," Judge O'Brien said. "Anyone else?"

"No," Dominique said.

"Very well." Judge O'Brien shifted to face the jury, "We're finished for the day. You may take your box lunches with you if you wish. I'm happy to give you the afternoon off to shovel and catch up on your lives. Remember—no watching media about the trial or talking to anyone about it. You may be excused."

Everyone rose while the jurors clamored out, eager to be set free.

After the jury room door slammed, Judge O'Brien asked, "Are both parties ready to give their closing arguments tomorrow morning?"

"Yes," Dominique said at the same time Stela said, "No."

He looked at Stela. "Why not?"

"I'm pulling it together—"

"You have plenty of time," Judge O'Brien said.

She tsked at him and continued, "Now the State is calling Detective Breuer again, and I have no idea what he's going to testify to, so how am I supposed to prepare for his cross-examination?"

Judge O'Brien looked expectantly at Dominique.

"He received a report from the toxic waste disposal plant about nuclear materials found in Andy Nelson's septic system," Dominique said.

"Oh," Stela said, her expression returning to resting chess player face. "I'll be ready for that and my closing tomorrow."

"In that case, court is adjourned," Judge O'Brien said.

Nathan turned his back to Stela to gather his notebook and briefcase.

"Hey," she said to his back. "Meet me at the jail to go over my closing with me."

"I have other business to attend to," he said over his shoulder as he walked away.

She glared at his back and started to move toward Dr. Karpenko, who was loitering by the bar in front of the first pew, but the male deputy stepped between them. "Time for you to return to jail."

Her mouth agape, Stela was suddenly astounded by the lack of hospitality.

43

"Feel better?" Monica caressed Shelby's shoulder, as they woke from a nap.

"Sort of." Shelby rubbed her eyes and shimmied under the covers closer to Monica. "Sleep helped since I didn't really get any last night. I'm still a little disoriented, though."

Monica's phone buzzed on the nightstand. "Just a sec. Let me see what's going on." She scooped it up and read a text from Nathan, then turned to Shelby. "Is it okay if Nathan comes over with a couple of pizzas?"

Shelby nodded, then shook her head vigorously. "Tell him no red sauce. I just can't take red sauce right now. Fucking nightmare. Tell him I want a margherita pizza, and you two can get whatever you want, as long as it doesn't have red sauce."

Monica looked at her quizzically, then made the connection to the motel room. "Got it. I'll text him to get a couple of chicken and pesto or something."

"Perfect." Shelby peeled back the covers and rose, going to her backpack on the floor. Monica watched, as Shelby uncharacteristically dressed in several layers —a sports bra, tank, t-shirt and sweatshirt. She pulled on yoga pants then dug in Monica's drawer for a pair of thick, wool socks.

"Are you cold?" Monica asked. "I can turn up the heat."

"No. I just want to wrap myself in as many layers as possible." Emphasizing her vulnerability, she wrapped her arms around herself.

"Can I help?" Monica asked, getting up and crossing the room to hug her.

Shelby leaned in, still keeping her arms around herself.

"Would you like a cup of tea?" Monica asked.

Shelby's eyes lit up. "In front of the fire?"

"In front of the fire." Monica smiled.

Later, as the wind howled against the windows, they sipped their tea on the loveseat in front of the fire, their legs covered in one of Monica's quilts.

The doorbell rang, and Shelby jumped.

Monica lay her hand on Shelby's leg. "You know it's Nathan, right? He just texted."

"Right. I'm a mess."

"It's okay. You stay here, and I'll bring the pizza to you."

"Thanks."

Monica left the sunporch and walked through the house to the kitchen, where she opened the door to Nathan holding three boxes of small, specialty pizzas.

"Thanks for coming over." Monica took the pizzas from him and set them on the island. "Want a beer?"

"I'd love one," he said. "How's Shelby?"

"Pretty traumatized," Monica said, nodding her head toward the sun porch. "How was court today?"

"A clusterfuck. I'll fill you in while we eat."

They transferred pizza slices onto plates, and, armed with napkins, joined Shelby in front of the fire.

Nathan leaned down and kissed the top of her head. "Hey beautiful. How are you feeling?"

"Better now that I'm home," Shelby said. "Thanks for the pizza."

"My pleasure. I wanted to check on you and give Monica an update."

"Thanks," Shelby said. "Where's Matt?"

"He texted me about an hour ago that he was going to bed," Nathan said. "He has to testify first thing tomorrow."

"What's he testifying to?" Monica asked before biting into a slice.

"He got the report on the nuclear materials in Andy's septic tank. Off-the-charts radioactivity," Nathan said, digging in.

"And Stela still insists she didn't know Andy worked at *Voila!* in the weapons division," Monica said. "Good thing you're not covering for me tomorrow morning, Nathan, or you'd be helping Stela cross-examine Matt again."

He took a swig of beer. "Even though I wouldn't help her do shit at this point, I'm sure Matt wouldn't be thrilled about seeing me sitting next to her."

"I wonder if she's going to attempt to cross him." Monica drank some cranberry juice, now on a mission never to get another bladder infection.

"She probably will," he said, "but who gives a shit? I mean, really, the jurors are going to find her guilty, aren't they?"

"They better," Shelby said. "And thanks for this pizza. I didn't realize how hungry I was." Her plate was empty.

"Would you like me to get you another slice or two?" Monica asked.

"I can get it." She removed the quilt and rose, her energy returning.

Monica observed Shelby leave, noting that her shoulders were still somewhat rounded in defeat.

Following Monica's gaze, Nathan asked, "Are you planning to go to court tomorrow?"

Monica dragged her eyes from Shelby's wake to Nathan. "Yes, but I need to make sure Shelby feels okay first."

"Of course," he said.

Shelby returned with several more slices and a tall glass of water. "I'm starved."

"I'm happy you're eating." Monica situated the quilt over them as soon as Shelby snuggled in next to her.

"Safe and back together again," Nathan said, his eyes bouncing between the two women.

Monica turned to Shelby, and, when she saw the film of fatigue and sadness around her eyes, she almost melted. "It will get better, I promise."

Shelby tried to smile, but the corners of her lips quivered until she cried a little. She set her plate on the coffee table and wiped her eyes with her napkin.

Monica picked up Shelby's hand. "Let's go to counseling together, okay?"

"I'm just so afraid," Shelby said, shaking. "I can't imagine going back to school tomorrow, but I don't want to be here, or my house, alone. What am I going to do?"

"We'll have Todd come over all day," Monica said. "You liked him, right?"

"I think so. I mean, I barely spoke to him, but yeah. I suppose."

Nathan reached across the table and grasped Shelby's hand, careful not to touch her bandaged wrist. "People recover from trauma like this. You will too. Trust me."

"I believe you. I just feel so confused and afraid right now."

"That's normal," Monica said.

"I still can't believe Yuri took you hostage," Nathan said. "This is America. No one gets away with that shit, especially during a trial. What a dumb fuck."

"Well, he did," Shelby said.

"Why yesterday?" Monica asked. "Why did he think he had to leverage me at that particular point in the trial?"

"I know, right?" Nathan said. "Stela was still holding her own in court a few days ago. Why did Yuri hit the panic button?"

Monica angled her head, looking through Nathan, as she reconstructed the events of the last few days. "It's as if something triggered him. As if he saw a turn in the trial, even though he wasn't there."

"Was he sitting in the back, and you just didn't notice him?" Nathan asked.

"Oh no," Monica said. "If he had been there, he would've been arrested. Both the police and Agents McCoy and Scott were looking for him."

They all ate in silence for a few minutes.

Nathan snapped his fingers. "You know, Jim said his electronics guy found a bug in Dominique's office. Did Yuri hear something she said?"

Picturing Yuri eavesdropping on Dominique moved a key piece of the puzzle into place for Monica. "Yuri took Shelby right after Dominique and I were talking about the fake journal entries in court. We never discussed them in her office."

"Do you think he bugged the courtroom?" Nathan asked.

"Let's see," Monica said, retracing her footsteps, attempting to recall the conversation about Andy's journal. "One morning, Dominique came over to me before Stela came in and thanked me for suggesting that Matt go to *Voila!* to get a writing sample of Andy's work notes. She told me that Andy's mother also had noticed the fake handwriting, and had given Dominique the letters that Andy had written to her."

"So, Dominique outed you at counsel table?" Nathan asked and confirmed at the same time.

"Maybe there's a bug in the microphones on the tables."

"That's a possibility," Monica said. "We should have those checked. I'm not sure it could pick up her whispering in my ear though. There would have to be a microphone right next to her mouth—attached to her collar like a TV anchorwoman."

Monica's eyes flashed with revelation, as she pictured the American flag and Wisconsin State lapel pins on Dominique's blazer. "Oh shit!"

"What?" Nathan and Shelby asked.

"Dominique's lapel pins. She has an American flag pin in one blazer and a Wisconsin State pin in another. Those would be the perfect places to plant a microphone to pick up everything she says."

"We better call her!" they said in unison.

"It's kind of silly to call her now and warn her that Yuri put a bug in her lapel pin. He won't be listening to anyone anytime soon," Nathan said, then abruptly turned to Shelby. "Sorry for bringing that up."

Shelby waved her hand in the air while chewing, indicating they could carry on.

"Who knows who else is listening to Dominique's conversations now that Yuri is out of the picture," Monica pointed out.

"His bosses?" Nathan asked.

"Probably Peter and Steven," Monica spat.

"Why don't you like those two?" Nathan asked.

"I'm not convinced they're telling the truth. Yuri told me Peter was CIA, and Peter didn't outright deny it. Put it this way, the CIA has worked with foreign nationals for years to advance a political agenda in a country like Romania or Ukraine."

"Subversive bastards," Shelby said.

Monica and Nathan looked at her, expecting more.

Shelby shrugged and took another bite.

Monica said, "I did some checking into Mila Golodryga, and discovered she has an INTERPOL record in Ukraine."

"Matt and Dominique saw that too," Nathan said. "How did you get access to INTERPOL?"

"Well, Matt did it for me, then when I pestered him for more, he just loaned me his police ID," she said. "Anyway, Mila has quite the arrest record in Ukraine for theft and arms dealing, but the charges were dropped."

"Dropped? Why?" Nathan asked.

"I don't know anything about their judicial system, but she must have friends in high places there," Monica said.

"She probably works for their government," Nathan said.

"Maybe Stela and Yuri were helping Ukraine develop nukes," Monica said.

"I read that a spy satellite recently documented increased activity on the outskirts of Chernobyl, which is in Ukraine," Nathan said.

"And, in true CIA fashion, Peter and Steven might be helping Ukraine secure nuclear materials for the new plant," Monica added.

"Why would they steal from a U.S. company like *Voila!* in the process?" Nathan asked.

Monica's cell phone rang, interrupting their conversation. The screen indicated it was Apple Aerial Advertising.

"I have to take this." Monica stood and wandered to the other end of the sun porch.

"This is Monica."

"This is Cassidy at Triple A," she said in her nasal tone. "You wanted me to call you if Darcy booked another aerial advertisement?"

"Absolutely. Thanks Cassidy. What is Darcy booking?"

"She's back to boycotting the hospital for animal rights abuse."

"What are you charging her?" Monica asked.

"One thousand dollars," Cassidy said. "It would run day after tomorrow."

"Fine. I'll book the spot," Monica said, looking at Shelby and Nathan. "But I don't want the money to go to waste. Here's what I want you to put on a banner." Speaking quietly, so Shelby and Nathan wouldn't overhear, Monica gave Cassidy the phrase she wanted on the banner.

Cassidy repeated it back to Monica and said, "That will cost you $100 to change the banner."

"Done," Monica said.

"We'll fly it day after tomorrow," Cassidy said.

"What time of day will you fly it?"

"Whenever Oscar thinks the conditions are best. Want me to text you when he's wheels up?"

"That would be great," Monica said.

"Deal," Cassidy said. "I'll take your credit card info now."

Monica rolled her eyes at the charming customer service. She opened her phone case and supplied the American Express number to Cassidy.

When she rejoined Shelby and Nathan, at least he had put a smile on Shelby's face about something. Monica was so relieved to see a glimpse of her old Shelby. She plopped herself down next to her, finding Shelby's hand with her own.

"Hey Nathan, how is the Darcy Lemon lawsuit against the hospital going?" Monica asked.

He clicked his fingers. "I knew there was something else I wanted to tell you. Judge Norgaarden dismissed her frivolous suit and awarded the hospital costs." He held up his hand for a high-five.

"Well done, Man!" Monica enthusiastically slapped his hand. "Al Bowman will be thrilled." *That explains why she booked the banner—for revenge.*

"He was," Nathan said. "I already called him."

"Excellent! Thank you so much."

"Wally Leib honestly thought she could bring and maintain a case on behalf of a monkey," Nathan said through a laugh. "Did she even go to law school?"

"Looney," Monica said. "I'm sure she filled Darcy with false expectations too."

"In her screeching crane voice," Nathan imitated. After a few heartbeats, he asked, "Should we call Jim and tell him to have his electronics guy check Dominique's lapel pins and the counsel table microphones?"

"Yeah. I'll put him on speaker." Monica dialed Jim and held out her phone, so he could hear both Nathan and her.

"Hi, Mon," he said. "How's Shelby?"

Shelby smiled immediately.

"She's freaked out but eating dinner with Nathan and me. She's right here, and you're on speaker, Jim."

"Hi, Shelby," he said. "Dom and I were so relieved to hear that Matt found you."

"Thank you," she said.

"Monica was a wreck, you know," Jim said. "It's pretty obvious that she loves you."

"Awww…" Shelby said, leaning into Monica.

"Hey, Jim," Monica said. "Nathan and I figured out something—"

"Well, Monica figured it out," Nathan said.

She rolled her eyes. "Anyway, I think your electronics guy should check Dominique's lapel pins for microphones. She'll know what I'm talking about."

"No kidding!" Jim said. "He told me he picked up a few bugs in her office, but she must have brought the blazers to my place. I'll be goddamned."

"I know," Monica said. "Clever, right?"

"Too clever," he said in disgust.

"Tell him to check the microphones on the counsel tables in the courtroom too," Nathan said.

"Good idea," Monica added.

"Will do," Jim said. "Is there anything else you need tonight?"

Monica looked at Nathan, and he shook his head. "Nope. That should do it."

"Let me know if there's something we can do for Shelby," Jim said.

"About that," Monica said. "I'm going to call the red-bearded Todd to ask him if he can come over tomorrow. Is that okay?"

"Sure," Jim said. "If he can't, I can."

"That's so sweet of you, Jim. Thanks," Shelby said.

"Anytime," he said.

"Okay. Talk to you soon," Monica said.

They rang off.

"Good to know we have options for you, babe," Monica said.

"Jim would be a hoot to spend the day with," Nathan said.

"He would, wouldn't he?" Shelby said, smiling.

"I'm sure he'd be happy to take you anywhere too," Monica said.

"I can see us touring around town," Shelby said with a smile.

"Watch out," Monica said, getting a little jealous, "he's quite the ladies' man."

44

The next morning, Monica entered the buzzing courtroom to Tiffany, who looked glamorous in a short, black dress with red accents.

"Attorney Spade, we missed you yesterday," Tiffany drawled, stepping in front of Monica.

"Thanks Tiffany." Monica shifted her weight from one foot to the other, impatiently waiting for whatever it was that Tiffany had to say.

"Is Shelby okay?" Tiffany rested her hand on Monica's forearm.

"You know I can't comment on anything, and I don't want you guys contacting her, okay?" Monica took a step forward, only to be met by Tiffany's undernourished frame blocking her.

"I'm asking as a friend, not a reporter." Tiffany stuck out her lower lip and rested a hand on her hip.

"In that case, yes, she's feeling better. Thanks for asking."

"Good. That guy deserved what he got."

From her peripheral vision, Monica spied Peter and Steven already seated. She didn't want to disclose anything within earshot to those two mouth breathers, so she said, "How about we talk after the trial?"

"Do you promise to give me an exclusive interview?"

"Absolutely," Monica said.

"Deal." Tiffany stepped out of Monica's way, allowing her to walk to the counsel tables.

Dominique looked up from her chair. "Good morning."

Monica noticed Dominique was wearing her navy suit, and the lapel was conspicuously bare. "Hi. Good to see you aren't wearing the flag or state pin on your lapel."

"They both had microphones in them. I'm so sorry. Yuri obviously heard us collaborating and decided to kidnap Shelby."

Monica removed her laptop from her attaché case. "Thank goodness Matt rescued her."

"I'm so relieved. I hear she's pretty rattled, though," Dominique said.

"She is," Monica said.

"Jim said he was spending the day with her."

Monica opened her laptop and clicked it to life. "Yeah. Todd couldn't make it, so Jim graciously agreed. I think she has a counseling appointment, so he's going to drive her to that."

"That should help her process the trauma," Dominique said. "Don't worry. The entire ordeal will fade in time like a bad dream."

"I hope so. She can hide the scar on her forehead with her hair, and the bruises on her ribs and arm will fade, but those wrist wounds from zip ties are a constant reminder."

"I can only imagine," Dominique said. "I'm so sorry."

"Thanks," Monica said. "Turning to the trial, I understand you're putting on a rebuttal witness this morning."

"Detective Matthew Breuer."

"Did you notify Stela what Matt is going to testify about?"

"Of course." Dominique waved her hand dismissively.

"Just keeping you honest," Monica said.

"I appreciate it." Dominique smiled briefly. "Come closer. I want to tell you something."

Monica rose from her chair and leaned down, her ear next to Dominique. "Yes?"

"I heard from Matt that Agents McCoy and Scott gave him a hard time about killing Yuri."

Monica raised her eyebrows. "How lovely. So, they thought Yuri should just keep Shelby hostage for the remainder of the trial?" She asked rhetorically. She recalled the smug look on Steven's face the night he and Peter came to her house. "I hope Matt told those fuckers off."

"I don't think they wanted Yuri to keep her, but, and I say this confidentially, they wanted Yuri alive. I think there's another layer to their relationship with Stela and Yuri that we don't know."

Monica nodded. "I've thought that all along. Peter told me as much, and Yuri confirmed it. Otherwise, why would they be hanging around the trial? Stela is important to them. Nathan and I were conjecturing that they're probably helping her to steal nuclear materials for Ukraine to start a weapons program outside of Chernobyl."

Dominique looked up at Monica in complete shock. "Wow. My brain didn't go there at all. Why would they steal from *Voila!?*"

"Haven't figured out that piece yet," Monica said.

At that moment, Matt walked in, his large body filling out a navy suit, white shirt and sedate tie. He looked well-rested, his jet black hair held in place with shiny product. Monica was again struck by how handsome he was.

"Hi, Mon," he whispered.

"Thank you for rescuing Shelby," she said.

Their eyes locked, and they both teared up. Unable to hug under the circumstances, they blinked their tears back and tipped up their chins at each other.

The familiar slam of the metal door alerted them that Judge O'Brien had entered the courtroom. He took his chair and scanned his kingdom, immediately registering that Stela wasn't at counsel table yet. He leaned down to the court secretary and mumbled something, to which she nodded and picked up her phone to make a call.

While she did that, Judge O'Brien looked at Monica. "Welcome back, Ms. Spade."

"Thank you, Your Honor."

"I trust all is well?"

"Getting there," she said with a reassuring smile.

The side door squeaked open, and Stela came in with her deputy escorts, who seemed to be hovering closer than they had previously. As soon as Stela sat, Monica scooted her own chair a few inches away. As she did, she glanced behind her, and noticed that Peter and Steven had moved from the back of the courtroom to the pew directly behind Stela and her.

"I understand the State is calling one rebuttal witness this morning?" Judge O'Brien asked.

"Yes. Detective Matthew Breuer," Dominique said.

"I object," Stela said.

"To what?" Judge O'Brien said.

"Lack of advance notice about the details of his testimony."

Judge O'Brien cocked his head. "The State indicated yesterday that Detective Breuer plans to testify about Mr. Nelson's septic tank. If you wish to conduct a cross-examination, then we can take a short break while you prepare."

"That might not be enough time," she said with a hint of haughtiness.

"You had all evening, Ms. Reiter. The court cannot come to a screeching halt while we wait for you to prepare a cross. We have 14 jurors who have already given up their lives and routines to be here. I want to be respectful of their time."

She raised her eyebrows, sensing a monumental shift in tone.

"If there's nothing further, the bailiff can bring in the jury," Judge O'Brien said.

Isla disappeared around the corner, and a moment later, the jurors filed in, looking bright and refreshed from their afternoon off. Dr. Gilmore made eye contact with Monica, and Mrs. Popa looked directly at Stela.

"Welcome back," Judge O'Brien said. "I hope everyone had a nice afternoon off. This morning, the State will call one witness in its rebuttal case, then I anticipate the parties will give their closing arguments. You might get the case for deliberations yet today." Having announced the end in sight with hope and enthusiasm, he turned to Dominique. "DA Bisset?"

"Thank you, Your Honor," Dominique said. "The State calls Detective Matthew Breuer."

Matt rose, was sworn in, then took the witness box.

"Please state your name."

"Matthew Breuer."

"You testified at the beginning of this case, so we heard about your credentials and employment. Just as a reminder, though, what is your current position?"

"I'm a detective with the Apple Grove Police Department."

"Thank you. Did you hear the defendant testify that she left the car during her fight with Andy Nelson, and that he followed her into the snow, so she stabbed him outside the car?"

"Yes."

"In your experience, if someone is stabbed while he's still alive, perhaps fighting in the snow, does he bleed a lot?"

"Yes. The heart pumps out a lot of blood, so there would be evidence of that on the snow, the leaves, the dirt—everywhere."

"More than a few droplets?"

"Pools, like in the back seat of the car."

"And, you found only a few droplets of blood outside the car, didn't you?"

"Yes."

"And, when you found Andy Nelson's body, he was hanging halfway out the back seat, correct?"

"Yes."

"Okay, turning to another topic, while this trial has been pending, did you continue your investigation into Andy Nelson's death?"

"Yes."

"What, specifically, did you investigate?"

"The contents of Andy Nelson's septic tank."

"How did you do that?"

"We hired a biohazard septic system waste disposal company to pump and haul the waste to a center examine it."

"Where is the center located?"

"Milwaukee."

"Did they examine the waste?"

"Yes."

"Did they provide you a report?"

"Yes."

Dominique removed a few sheets of paper from a folder. She handed a copy to Stela, then walked over to give the original to Matt. "Is this the report?"

"Yes."

"Does the report give you a breakdown of what they found in Andy Nelson's septic tank?"

"Yes."

"Please read for the jury the hazardous waste that was found in Mr. Nelson's septic tank."

"Enriched plutonium and uranium pellets."

"Did they assess the radioactivity of those pellets?"

"Yes."

"What does their report say?"

"That their Geiger counter indicated the pellets had more than 1500 CPM of radioactivity."

"Thank you."

"Did they provide a conclusion in the report?"

"Yes."

"Will you read it for the jury?"

"It says, 'We isolated approximately 1.8 kilograms of radioactive material.'"

"In addition to investigating the contents of Andy's septic tank, did you collect blood, saliva and hair samples last night from a suspect to compare to the blood samples at the crime scene?"

"Our lab technicians did, yes."

"And, before I ask you the name of the suspect, what did his blood sample indicate?"

"That it matched the DNA at the crime scene, confirming three people were there."

"And who are those three people?"

"Andy Nelson. Stela Reiter, and Yuri Zaleski."

"Did you arrest Mr. Zaleski?"

"No."

"Why not?"

"He tried to shoot me, so I shot and killed him."

The dramatic effect that Dominique was hoping for transpired instantaneously. Stela opened her mouth to the lonesome wail of a stricken woman, sobbing at the news that Yuri was dead.

Everyone in the courtroom, including each juror, turned in shock to look at her. Stela's breakdown was the best possible outcome for Matt's testimony. Dominique didn't have to ask Stela if she knew Yuri, or if they were working together. Stela's grief-stricken sobs said it all. In contrast to Stela's well-rehearsed, unemotional testimony about Andy's death, her raw display of grief revealed who she really cared about—Yuri, not Andy.

Stela slumped over her arms on the table for a moment, then raised her head and belted out, "Lies! It's all lies!"

Judge O'Brien slammed down his gavel. "We will have order in this courtroom! Bailiff, please remove the defendant."

The bailiffs descended on Stela and scooped her up from her chair like a rag doll. They rushed her to the side door and into the jail beyond.

"We need to take a break," Judge O'Brien said. "Court will resume in 15 minutes. All rise."

Everyone rose while the jury shuffled out.

Judge O'Brien abruptly left too.

Matt came down from the witness box to Dominique's table. "Wow. That was something."

"Pretty much what I expected," Dominique said. "Sometimes trials are better than live theater."

Monica joined them. "You aren't going to mention Shelby by name, are you?"

"No," Dominique said. "I don't want to risk a mistrial. If we start talking too much about what happened last night, Stela will just object as to relevance, and she would be right. I don't need to prove motive, I just need to attack her self-defense argument, and confirming that Yuri was at the scene, too, pretty much eviscerated her case."

"I agree," Monica said, removing her phone from her jacket pocket. "I'm going to check in on Shelby."

"Give her my best," Matt said.

Monica turned and walked over to the other side of the courtroom for privacy while she thumbed to Shelby's number in her contacts.

"Monica? Is everything okay?" Shelby asked.

"Yes. I'm calling to see how you are."

"Good. Jim and I are at the grocery store picking up a few things."

"Thank you. Hey, I just wanted to give you a heads up that Tiffany Rose figured out it was you who was taken hostage based on a conversation that took place in court yesterday."

There was a long silence.

"Shelby? Are you there?"

"Yes. You don't think she'll call me, do you?"

"I asked her not to, but other media might contact you because they've been here too."

"Okay." Shelby's voice grew small.

"It's okay, babe. Just say 'no comment.' In fact, when we hang up, talk to Jim about it."

"This is all new territory for me."

"I know. Jim will give you good advice. This trial will wrap up today, then our lives will return to normal."

"Whatever you say," Shelby said.

"I didn't mean that we'll magically return to normal," Monica amended. "I meant that we'll return to our routines, so we can focus on normalizing—"

"I know. I know." Shelby cut her off, and Monica heard Jim chatting in the background. "I have to go. I'll talk to Jim about it. Love you." Shelby abruptly ended the call.

Monica stared at her phone, a surge of anxiety coursing through her, but she fought it off as an insecurity hangover from the hostage situation.

After she returned to her chair, Judge O'Brien came bustling back to the bench. Within seconds, the side door opened, and a blotchy-faced and cloudy-eyed Stela entered. She had lost her swagger and added a few years to her life, the deep lines around her eyes and mouth a harbinger of how she would age in prison.

The jury returned, and Matt was again in the witness chair.

Judge O'Brien asked Dominique. "Any more direct testimony?"

"Yes," Dominique said. "A few more questions. Detective Breuer, did you investigate Andy Nelson's bank accounts?"

"Yes."

"What did you find?"

"That he had an account in the Cayman Islands with approximately $500,000 in it."

"Did you obtain a statement from the bank?"

"Yes."

"I have what's been marked as Exhibit 35." Dominique walked a copy over to Stela then gave one to Matt. "Is this the statement?"

"Yes."

"Whose name is at the top?"

"Andy Nelson."

"And, it indicates he has $500,000 in his account?"

"Yes."

"When was that money deposited?"

"Over the course of a few months, from October through December of last year."

"Does that time period coincide with his love affair with Ms. Reiter?"

"Yes."

"Thank you. Move to admit Exhibit 35 into evidence, Your Honor."

"Admitted."

"Nothing further for Detective Breuer," Dominique said.

"Does the defendant wish to conduct a cross-examination?" Judge O'Brien asked Stela.

"Yes." Stela cleared the frog from her throat. "I have a few questions."

"Please proceed," Judge O'Brien said.

Stela scooted up to the microphone. "Isn't it true that the septic truck that pumped out Andy's tank tipped over on the road, disgorging most of what it had pumped out?"

"It tipped over, but only a small amount leaked out."

"They cleaned up the spill in the snow and soil, right?"

"Yes."

"Then, they tested what had been spilled, right?"

"They tested both the spillage and the contents still in the truck tank."

"I see," she said. "The report that you read a short time ago. Was that from the tank or the spillage?"

"From the tank."

"How can you be sure it wasn't from the spillage, and that the spillage wasn't contaminated from the surrounding snow and soil?"

"Because the report," he picked up the sheet of paper in front of him, "indicates at the top that they ran the tests on the waste that was in the tank of the truck. The waste that hadn't leaked out."

She took a different tack. "How about Andy's septic system? How can we be sure that it wasn't contaminated from an external source?"

"Also part of the report," Matt said. "The employee who pumped the tank inspected it, and concluded it was a relatively new tank—fully intact. Someone flushed radioactive materials down the toilet."

"You have no evidence to back up that accusation!"

"The report is the evidence," Matt said, holding up his finger and numbering his next points. "In addition, the fact that you admitted to killing Andy Nelson; his employer confirmed missing plutonium and uranium; Mr. Nelson had $20,000 in cash at his house, and an account in Cayman with $500,000 in it; and that Yuri Zaleski's blood was also found at the crime scene. I think it's pretty clear that you seduced Mr. Nelson into a relationship, convinced him to steal nuclear materials, paid him, and when he got scared, he flushed some pellets down the toilet, then got in a fight with you, during which you lost your temper and killed him, then probably called Yuri to help you stage the scene."

Stela immediately realized the error of her ways, quickly saying, "I move that the witness' last response be stricken from the record as nonresponsive to my question."

"Request denied," Judge O'Brien said.

Deflated and defeated, Stela said, "I have no further questions."

A stunned jury watched Matt leave the witness box and walk the length of the courtroom, pushing through the double doors into the hallway.

Judge O'Brien broke the pregnant silence. "Does the State have any more rebuttal witnesses?"

"No, Your Honor."

"Is the State prepared to give its closing argument?"

"Yes, Your Honor."

"Very well. I'll give the jury some instructions, then DA Bisset will sum up her case."

The jury left and Judge O'Brien departed after them.

Monica didn't want to listen to Stela's bullshit, so she went to the ladies' room and then outside for some fresh air. The sun barely warmed the entrance alcove during the current Polar blast of Arctic air.

Peter and Steven joined her.

"Now you know why we're keeping an eye on Stela," Peter said.

Monica regarded him suspiciously. "Not really, but I have a few theories."

"Care to share?"

Monica looked at her feet, considering whether to risk disclosing what she suspected. Was it worth offending them, or worse, coming off as crazy? She decided she no longer cared. "I think you work for the CIA, not the FBI."

When Peter didn't flinch, she continued. "My guess is that you're helping Ukraine build a nuclear arms plant near Chernobyl where the old plant was enclosed in a concrete sarcophagus. Nothing to lose, right? And no one would care about that contaminated ground. First line of defense against Russia and all that."

A small smile formed on Peter's lips. "Why would we steal nukes from an American company?"

"I had to think about that for a while, and the only possibility that came to mind is that you would be helping the U.S. government and *Voila!* by testing their security. Flimsy, maybe, but that's what I deduced."

He tilted his head with plausibility. "What about Stela and Yuri?"

"Well, she told me a few times that you work for the same boss, and you're sitting here waiting for her, so I'm guessing that's true, and that the $520,000 paid to Andy is taxpayer money."

He smiled, his hollow eyes taking on a sinister glow. "You're a clever lawyer, Ms. Spade. You might be surprised to learn that the $520,000 is actually *Voila!*'s money, and that they readily agreed to the scheme to test their security, which failed miserably. Andy Nelson acted rashly—like a guilty man—and went home to flush the remaining pellets. He broke it off with Stela, but she's psycho, so once he threatened to our her or kill her—which I think he did—she professionally disarmed and killed him." He shook his head in disappointment. "I can't always control my assets in the field."

Monica was shocked that Peter had actually confided in her. "Then, she called Yuri to help her stage the scene. They didn't do a very good job, by the way."

"It would have worked in Ukraine, where they're used to doing business," Peter said. "They aren't accustomed to such a rigorous and uncorrupt system of scientific investigation and prosecution. They made some stupid decisions that I couldn't clean up, which brings us to this trial."

"I hope she goes to prison," Monica said. "Your fucked up scheme resulted in the life of an innocent man."

"He willingly stole nuclear materials from *Voila!*" Steven exclaimed then said in a condescending tone, "Not so innocent."

"He was entrapped by Stela," Monica said.

Steven childishly rolled his eyes.

"It must be nice to live in that cheap, sanctimonious suit," Monica threw at him. "Douche bag." She left them and returned to the courtroom.

45

After the break, Dominique took the podium and placed her typed notes before her. She subconsciously adjusted her left lapel, then turned to glance back at Judge O'Brien, nodding at him. She swiveled to Monica and Stela, briefly pinning Stela with a stare, then turned to address the jury.

"May it please the court, counsel, and ladies and gentlemen of the jury, I stand before you today to ask you to find the defendant, Stela Reiter, also known as Mila Golodryga, guilty of first degree homicide."

She turned and pointed at Stela. "Stela Reiter, the woman sitting before you, lied her way into Andy Nelson's life. She brutally killed him by stabbing him 13 times, then lied to the police who drove her to the hospital. She lied to the Emergency Room physician. She lied to the SANE nurse who conducted an exam of her. She lied to Dr. Karey, the psychiatrist who cared for her. She lied to Detectives Breuer and Curfman. And, she lied when she testified in this court before you. She's a liar and a killer."

Dominique shifted her attention from Stela to the jury. "Stela Reiter killed Andy Nelson in cold blood because he wouldn't go along with her nuclear materials theft scheme any longer. We're here to hold her accountable for first degree intentional homicide."

"Let's start at the beginning. Stela applied to Apple Grove University as a Romanian citizen last August. She went to Racy's Coffee Lounge to lay a trap for Andy Nelson. That's where her real boyfriend, Yuri Zaleski, worked as a barista. Why Racy's? Because Andy Nelson got his morning coffee there and liked to hang out there on Saturdays."

"Why Andy? Because he worked in the weapons division at *Voila!*. They needed to buy enriched plutonium and uranium, and he had access to those materials. He was a young, somewhat naïve, man who believed that Stela was interested in him as a boyfriend, not as a means to purchase weapons-grade plutonium and uranium. She seduced him under the watchful eye of Yuri."

"Once she had Andy under her thumb, she manipulated him into selling her $520,000-worth of radioactive materials, some of which were found in his septic system. His boss, Harry Hebl, testified they were missing, and the Septic Company confirmed their presence."

"Mr. Hebl testified that when *Voila!* became suspicious, they questioned everyone in the division. Andy acted rashly. Panicked. Maybe he was angry over being used and flushed the pellets to spite Ms. Reiter. We don't know exactly, and we don't need to know what transpired for her to be guilty of homicide. We do know that Ms. Reiter drove him in his own car—as seen by eyewitnesses—to the farmer's field. She tried to say that Andy took her on a drive in the country that day, but that was a lie. An eye witness testified that he saw her driving. She was the one who drove them to the field that day."

"What happened in the field? Ms. Reiter alleges that Andy brought the knife. Another lie. She brought it. She took it from his kitchen. She tried to paint a picture that he wanted to act out his sexual fantasies, which included harming her. She said his intent was written down in the violent, sexually-explicit journal entries. Another lie. You heard the testimony of Andy's mother, Sharon. That journal wasn't in Andy's handwriting. You saw a letter that Andy wrote to Sharon one year ago. His writing was very different from the cursive in the journal. Someone else wrote those entries to fit Stela's fabricated self-defense."

"Ms. Reiter admitted to killing Andy Nelson, but her defense doesn't make sense. If she were so afraid of him and his fantasies, then why didn't she leave him? She could have walked away at any time, but, when I asked her that during her testimony, she gave a flimsy excuse that he helped her with her homework."

Dominique changed her tone to sarcastic. "She was terrified that he was going to hurt her during sex, but she stayed for homework help? She was a graduate student!"

She lowered her voice again, dropping the sarcasm. "I don't have to tell sensible people like you what's going on here—lying. Stela and her real boyfriend, Yuri, wrote the journal of sadistic fantasies, and Yuri planted them at Andy's house after Stela was arrested."

"Ms. Reiter wasn't scared in the back seat of the car that day. She was determined to kill Andy. The way she described the struggle between them doesn't even make sense. How could she plunge a knife into his right temple if she were pinned down on the seat, him on top of her? How would she have the power to do that with her non-dominant, left hand that was supposedly cut up after she wrestled the knife away from him? It's a lie."

"She testified that he blindfolded her and slowly cut her in the groin and outer thigh, but you heard the testimony from Dr. Tollefson, Dr. Karey and Nurse Brown. They all said those parallel lines were self-inflicted. She's right-handed, and they're all within reach of her right hand. They're all the same depth—very superficial—and they're in a pattern of straight, horizontal lines. That doesn't happen when someone is cutting you, and you're twitching in pain, trying to get away. More lies."

"Ms. Reiter told you in her opening statement, elaborating during her own testimony, that Andy chased her outside of the car during their fight, so she stabbed him while they were fighting next to the car. Yet, there aren't the large pools of blood on the ground to corroborate her story. Moreover, she said she got back in the car and blacked out, then woke up and ran to the farmer's house. That doesn't make sense. Detective Breuer testified that he found Andy's body hanging halfway out the back seat. Did Ms. Reiter sit on Andy's body when she blacked out in the car? Did he miraculously get a second wind after she left and crawl back into the car? There isn't a trail of blood through the snow, so the evidence doesn't support him dying on the ground and crawling back into the car. The evidence supports him dying inside the car. Period. There wasn't a struggle outside the car. More lies by Ms. Reiter."

Dominique walked to her laptop and put up a photo of Stela's clothes, each piece laid out on a white surface. The T-shirt. The sweater. The flannel. All cut perfectly down the middle.

"Do the cuts in these clothes look like the result of a struggle in the back seat of a car or the handiwork of someone laying them out flat on the trunk of a car and cutting them down the middle? The fabric is methodically and perfectly sliced. If Andy were trying to cut her clothes during a struggle, ask yourselves if the lines would have been as straight as they are. Either Stela Reiter, or her friend, Yuri Zaleski, cut them. Slowly. Deliberately. Methodically. After she had killed Andy."

Dominique paused and looked at each juror.

"That's right. Stela cut herself and her clothes *after* she killed Andy. She staged the scene after he was dead. There was a blood smear on the back of the car on the trunk. Not Andy's. Not Stela's. Yuri Zaleski's. Why? Because he stood there cutting Stela's clothes and maybe nicked himself. DNA doesn't lie."

"Ms. Reiter and one of her expert physicians, Dr. George Popovich, testified that there were three sets of DNA at the scene because she had a bone marrow transplant for cancer. During my cross-examination of Dr. Popovich, however, he admitted that one blood sample at the scene matched Andy Nelson's blood. A second sample matched Ms. Reiter's chimeric blood. Then, Detective Breuer confirmed that the third sample matched Yuri Zaleski's blood. Ms. Reiter killed Andy Nelson, and Yuri Zaleski helped her stage the scene."

"Then, we get to Stela running away from the scene with Andy's cell phone and the knife. Why? First, so he couldn't call for help. Second, to get rid of the murder weapon. It didn't work. Detectives Breuer and Curfman found the phone and knife in the ditch between the field and the farmer's house. Stela tried to dump them, but they were there. Both had Stela and Andy's blood on them."

"She ran to the farmer's house and asked him to call an ambulance. He called the police instead. When they picked her up, she said she couldn't remember anything other than she was supposedly sexually assaulted. She lied, not just once, but continuously over the course Saturday and Sunday until Detectives Breuer and Curfman found Andy's body late Sunday afternoon. They confronted her with the facts on Monday morning. It was only after Detective Breuer told her they found Andy that she admitted to being with him in the car that day."

"During this trial, Ms. Reiter brought Dr. Karpenko here, her friend and coach from chess club in Kiev, to testify that she had PTSD. That was her excuse for lying to everyone. When I asked Dr. Karpenko if PTSD made you lie, he said no. Of course it doesn't. Did she have PTSD? Maybe, but Dr. Karpenko also agreed she could have had it from killing Andy. Whether she had PTSD or not is irrelevant. She killed Andy then lied to cover it up."

"She continued to lie to you during this trial. One of the most revealing aspects of this trial was Stela's breakdown when she learned for the first time that her real boyfriend, Yuri, had been shot and killed by Detective Breuer last night. We all watched Stela break down and sob. Sob over her real lover's death— Yuri. She never became that emotional when testifying about Andy, did she?"

Dominique paused to let her words sink in then picked up the verdict form and held it up for the jury to see. "The State requests that you find Stela Reiter guilty of first degree intentional homicide. Check the box here," she pointed to the form. "Thank you for your time and service." She returned to her chair at counsel table.

"Does the defendant wish to take a short break before delivering her closing?" Judge O'Brien asked.

"Yes, Your Honor," Stela said in her small, sweet voice.

"Court will stand in recess for 15 minutes," Judge O'Brien said.

Everyone rose while the jury left the room. Once they were gone, the gallery breathed a collective sigh of relief from the intensity of Dominique's closing. Judge O'Brien stood and left through his door.

Stela turned to Monica. "I think I need to cover three points—"

Monica held up her hand. "I'm not going to help you with your closing."

Stela blanched. "You're my standby counsel."

"You have 15 minutes to prepare your closing," Monica said. "There. I fulfilled my duty to explain what's happening."

"Help me with the points, or else…" Stela's glare turned dark.

Emboldened by her conversation with Peter and tired of the psycho bullshit, Monica leaned in close to Stela, her face only a few inches away. "You and Yuri killed Andy then took my girlfriend hostage. If Matt hadn't killed Yuri, I would have myself." Before Stela could reply, Monica got to her feet and said to the deputies, "She's dangerous. You need to bring her back to the jail during break."

They immediately closed in on Stela and removed her from the courtroom.

Dominique witnessed the exchange and met Monica toe-to-toe in the aisle. "Whoa, cowgirl. You need to cool down. You just told a psychopath that you would've killed her lover if Matt hadn't." Dominique glided her hands through the air to pat it down. "I want Stela in prison as much as you, but don't make it personal, okay?"

Monica was hot with anger and ready to fight. "It became personal when Yuri took Shelby hostage. Fuck impersonal. It's overrated."

Dominique arched a brow. "Be careful, Monica. This isn't a game. Trust the process and let the rest go."

Suddenly, Peter and Steven were hovering by Monica's side. She turned on them. "What do you want?"

They were indifferent to her rudeness. "Stela. We'll be sitting directly behind you, Ms. Spade. Don't get in our way."

"She belongs in prison," Monica hissed.

Peter raised his eyebrows.

"She deserves to be punished for murdering Andy Nelson, and she just threatened me. She shouldn't be allowed around people."

"I made certain promises to powerful people in Ukraine," Peter said.

"Who cares? You and Steven promised to protect Shelby too, but you failed miserably. God, Barney Fife could've done a better job—"

"Okay," Dominique said, looping her hand through Monica's arm and jerking her away from them. "We're taking a break from the courtroom."

"Who's Barney Fife?" Steven asked Peter.

Dominique marched Monica down the aisle and out the door into the hallway, straight to the women's restroom. She pushed Monica through the door ahead of her. Fortunately, the restroom was empty.

Dominique spun Monica around to face her. "Get control of yourself, Mon. You just told off two CIA agents. I get that you're angry over being here, having your practice interrupted and your life turned upside down. But we're in the home stretch now. Trust justice. We'll get a conviction, and she'll go to prison. Peter and Steven are here only in the event Stela gets an acquittal. If that unlikely event happens, they'll take her to Langley, or wherever, so she won't be loose on the street. Done. Over with, and life will return to normal for us."

"She better not be acquitted!"

"It's out of your control, Mon." Dominique rested her hand on Monica's shoulder. "Anyway, did you see the jurors while I was giving my closing? They were 100% on board. Well, except for Mrs. Popa, who's been on Stela's side since the beginning, but we have ways of dealing with her."

Through her fury, Monica tried to focus on what Dominique was saying, but she wasn't confident she was tracking. "Fine. Thanks for helping me regroup. I'll keep my mouth shut from here on out."

"Good girl." Dominique turned and entered a stall to use the toilet.

Monica did the same, using the silence and seclusion to gather herself and her emotions. *I have Shelby back. That's all I need.*

Afterward, as they stood side-by-side washing their hands, Monica looked at Dominique in the mirror and asked, "Do you think I should apologize to Peter and Steven?"

"Personally? I try not to burn bridges," Dominique said.

"This is going to be painful. I can't stand them."

"Stay professional."

Together, they re-entered the courtroom, which was humming with a low level of chatter. Dominique resumed her spot at counsel table, turning to her assistants to talk business, and Monica approached Peter and Steven, who were seated in the front pew, directly behind her counsel table. She leaned over. "I'm sorry for what I said. I haven't been myself since Yuri took Shelby hostage. It won't happen again." She stopped before her face and inflection revealed any insincerity.

"We understand," Peter said. "We're all on the same side, and we're very sorry about Shelby."

Monica took her seat at the table. Swallowing her pride was such a vile affair that it left a metallic taste in her mouth. She took a long drink of water from her thermos and prayed for control in the face of uncertainty.

46

Just as Monica was wondering what stunts Stela would try to pull during her closing, the side door opened and Stela entered the arena, her eyes narrowed to slits, her viperous stare directed at Monica.

Monica registered the unfiltered hate, glanced at Stela's hands to confirm she wasn't holding a sharp object, then shrugged indifferently. When Stela sat, Monica kept her face angled away. She had made an enemy of Stela by telling her off. So be it. Taking Shelby hostage had pushed Monica over the edge of civility.

Surprising Monica, Stela leaned over and whispered, "You think I'm a monster, but you don't realize that I work for the same boss as those two dicks, Peter and Steven. Yuri did too. We all work for the same boss, Ms. Spade. Never forget that. Our goal helps both Ukraine and America."

Fury still flared in Monica. "You were just supposed to buy nukes, Mila, not chop up your source and take my girlfriend hostage."

"Ya!" Stela grunted. "Like you know what you're talking about."

Judge O'Brien entered. "Is the defendant ready to give her closing argument?"

"I am, Your Honor," Stela said, "but I have a request."

"What is it, Ms. Reiter?"

"I request that Attorney Spade not sit at counsel table beside me. She's made it abundantly clear that she isn't on my side, so I request that she sit in a chair directly behind me."

"Ms. Spade, do you have anything to say?" he asked.

"With pleasure, Your Honor." Monica hopped up, grabbed her laptop, and moved two feet behind Stela to the chairs against the railing that separated the court arena from the gallery. She was now within a handbreadth of Peter and Steven, which gave her some comfort in the event Stela went ballistic.

"Are we all set now?" Judge O'Brien asked.

"Yes," Stela said in her sweet voice.

"Isla, please bring in the jury," Judge O'Brien said.

Isla fetched them, and the jurors shuffled in, their gazes quickly roaming the courtroom, taking stock that Monica was now seated behind Stela. To the extent there was an impression to be made, it couldn't have reflected well on Stela.

"The defendant is now going to address you with her closing argument," Judge O'Brien said, gesturing to Stela that she was welcome to take the podium.

She rose, bringing with her a stack of handwritten notes. She used the podium to steady herself, as she looked at the jury, her unwashed hair pulled back in a tight bun. She wore what had become her uniform for the trial—the white, pussy bow blouse and the pink cardigan. If she were dressing for harmless, she had nailed it. Her image might have counteracted the monster Dominique had painted for the jury, but for Stela's eyes. Behind the oversized, horn-rimmed spectacles, her dark eyes bounced from face-to-face like a radar pinging, constantly assessing and calculating, never friendly. Like a snake.

She wrapped her small, scarred hand around the microphone, bending it down to her mouth. "Ladies and gentlemen of the jury," she began in her humble, little-girl voice, "I stand before you to ask that you keep an open mind while I sum up my case."

She turned to Dominique. "Could the District Attorney please display my first slide on the overhead screen?"

Dominique clicked a few buttons on her laptop and a black and white image of a duck's head appeared. Or was it a rabbit? Monica had seen it many times, as the ambiguous illusion had been making the rounds for a hundred years. She was always surprised when seeing it periodically that she consistently saw the duck head first, then had to focus for a second to see the rabbit.

Stela turned to look at the overhead screen, and asked, "When you look at that image, do you see a duck or a rabbit?" She paused a second, allowing the jurors to view it. "I always see a rabbit first, the ears on the left, his nose on the right. If I concentrate, though, I can change my perspective to see a duck beak on the left, and his head on the right. Can you?"

She turned from the image and faced the jury once again.

"I show you this image because it symbolizes what happened in Andy's car when we were parked next to the field. The District Attorney would have you believe that I started the fight with Andy and intentionally killed him. The duck. I'm here to tell you that he sexually assaulted me, ordering me to lie still while he cut me, so I protected myself and stabbed him in self-defense. The rabbit."

"You will have the deciding vote as to whether all the facts you've heard, including our struggle in the back seat of Andy's car, come together as a duck or a rabbit. I simply ask that you give me fair consideration with an open mind."

She took a breath and began in the voice of a storyteller. "As I testified earlier, I came to Apple Grove to study chemical engineering. We have good schools in Romania, but there are classes offered here that I can't get there. That was the only reason I came here."

"I met Andy at Racy's Coffee Lounge. That's true. But he approached me, not the other way around."

"My friend, Yuri, also worked there. We were friends. Good friends. Nothing more. Yes, I cried when I heard Yuri died suddenly. That's normal, isn't it? To cry when you learn a close friend has died? Wouldn't it be more troubling if I hadn't cried? I can't do anything right in the eyes of the prosecutor."

"Object, Your Honor," Dominique said in a dispassionate monotone.

"Approach the bench," Judge O'Brien said.

Dominique, Stela and Monica went to the bench. Judge O'Brien leaned down and whispered to Stela. "The purpose of a closing argument is to sum up the evidence that has been admitted. I'm not going to allow you to personalize an argument against the prosecutor. Do you understand?"

"Yes," Stela said.

He pinned her with a stare, summoning his own look of ferocity. "One more attack, and you're finished."

The women returned to their battle stations.

"As I was saying," Stela continued, "I cried when I heard Yuri died. While that's true, it isn't evidence in this case. It has nothing to do with the fact that Andy sexually assaulted me. I also cried when Andy died, but I was alone. No one was there to see me, so I would ask that you keep my crying in perspective, as you consider the actual evidence before you."

Stela consulted her notes. "The two most important pieces of evidence in this case are the eye witness account and Andy's journal entries. Who is the eye witness? Me. I was there. I was the only person there with Andy, and I barely lived to talk about it. I took an oath and testified, telling you the truth of what happened. Those are the two key pieces of evidence that should decide this case—my account and Andy's journal. Everything else is just smoke and mirrors."

Monica's eyes briefly scanned Dominique, who was making a note on her legal pad.

"Let's revisit Andy's journal entries," Stela said. "May I ask the prosecutor to display the excerpts?"

Dominique brought up the same quotations that Stela had used in her opening statement. Everyone looked at the handwriting on the screen.

Stela argued, "The prosecutor and Andy's mother tried to tell you that these entries weren't in Andy's handwriting. That isn't true. I watched him write in his journal. He showed them to me. What can I say? Maybe his handwriting matured since he last wrote his mother a letter. We all change. Sometimes parents don't notice the changes in their children. Obviously, Andy and I were seeing a lot of each other, yet she didn't know that. He hadn't told his mother about us, so she probably wasn't up-to-date on his other habits either. His dark habits. His sexual preferences."

Stela pushed her glasses up on the bridge of her nose and looked at the screen. She read the lengthy excerpt again in a business-like voice, projecting loudly.

After she finished, she turned back to the jury. "Can you imagine how I felt after reading that? Scared as hell. Terrified, in fact. I told Andy I wasn't into that, and he should stop writing stuff like that. At the time, when we were in his bedroom, he backed off and agreed, so I assumed everything was okay. That's why I didn't leave him. I assumed he respected my wishes. I chose to stay, but that turned out to be the wrong decision."

Monica couldn't believe Stela was still peddling this false bullshit, partly plagiarized from a long-dead playwright.

"When we went for a ride in the car that day, Andy was nervous and sweaty. Before I knew it, he was on top of me. He removed my spectacles, then he blindfolded me with a bandana. I was helpless. Paralyzed."

"When he started getting really rough, I freaked out. I asked him to stop, but he just mumbled that I was beautiful, and he wanted all of me. He pinned my arms above my head. The seat wasn't very long, so our legs were bent, and our feet were crushed against the car door."

"He thrust his knee between my legs, and that's when I felt something sharp cutting my jeans. I lowered my head, but I couldn't see under the bandana. I panicked and screamed."

"He told me to be still, so he wouldn't make a mistake with the knife. I felt unbearable pain and saw white lights, but he put his forearm over my chest and held me down, as he cut through my jeans, making the perfect lines on my inner thigh. I lay frozen in fear. All I could picture was him cutting me up, limb-by-limb, for his own twisted pleasure."

"I screamed at him to stop, so he finally set the knife aside and removed my jeans. He said he was turned on by the blood, so he wanted to cut me some more. He started cutting on my outer thigh, and I screamed again. He wouldn't stop. After a few more cuts, I ripped off the bandana, so I could see what he was doing. When I saw the evil in his eyes, I yelled at him to get off of me."

"He held the knife under my chin and told me that I needed to help him act out his fantasies. He made a tiny cut on his palm. It was no more than a prick, much tinier than the cuts he had made on me. When it began to bleed, he put his palm on my outer thigh, chanting about 'mixing our blood, mixing our blood…'"

Monica glanced at Dominique, who made another note.

"I thought to myself that this was where I was going to die—in the back seat of a car in the dead of winter next to a farmer's field in America. Just like that. Never to be seen or heard from again because my American boyfriend wanted to act out his sadistic fantasies on me. I would never see my family again. So, I knew I had to act to save myself."

"Fear turned to rage, and I went crazy. I found a strength somewhere deep inside of me that I didn't know existed. I reached out to grab the knife with my left hand because Andy was right-handed, and he was holding the knife above me with his right hand. I managed to get the knife from him but not before the blade sliced my palm."

She held up her left palm to the jury, the scabs had fallen off, but the pink scars remained. There were three of them, in perfect parallel lines.

"I killed him in self-defense. I stabbed and stabbed. Anywhere and everywhere. He grabbed my hair, pulling my head with his hand. It was excruciatingly painful. He even pulled out a chunk, which remained on the floor of the car, so I stabbed some more. Blindly. I got out of the car. He chased me, so I stabbed him some more. Finally, finally, he stopped attacking me. After that, everything is a blur… Maybe he crawled back into the car after I left. I don't know."

She looked down at her notes, removed her glasses, dabbed at her eyes with a tissue, put them back on.

"I might have blacked out in the back seat. I don't know. I'm sorry I can't tell you more details. My memory is sketchy."

She wept a little, then gathered herself enough to say, "I can't go on. That's it. That's all I have to say. I did what I had to do to save myself. There was no planning. There was no standing at the back of the car and cutting clothes as the prosecutor would have you believe. It was just a knife fight to the death in the back seat of a car, and somehow, I won. I lived. Now I'm on trial for protecting myself. So much for believing the victim."

"Object, Your Honor," Dominique said in a disapproving tone.

"Sustained," Judge O'Brien said. "The jury will disregard the defendant's last statement."

Stela rested her elbows on the podium, her voice barely audible. "Please return a verdict of not guilty. Don't punish me for Andy's sexual deviancy. I have to live with his death for the rest of my life. That's punishment enough. I'm sorry he died. I apologize to the family, but it was either him or me. I have nothing further."

Stela moped back to her chair, and Dominique shook her head imperceptibly.

Once Stela was seated, Judge O'Brien asked, "Does the prosecution have any rebuttal?"

"One quick thing, Your Honor," Dominique said.

From her chair at counsel table, Dominique displayed the photo of Andy's body on the metal table during autopsy. His lower half was covered with a sheet, his upper half full of stabs and gashes, his palms turned up as they lay next to his body. She used the curser to hover over Andy's palms and magnify them. Each one. She silently moved the curser from one to the other, then, while the left palm was magnified, Dominique said, "There aren't any punctures on either of his palms or fingers. Nothing. Clean. The defendant's story about him cutting himself to mix his blood with hers isn't substantiated by the photos. Another lie."

Knowing full well the impact she was having, Dominique zoomed back out to the image of Andy's upper torso. She remained silent for a second, allowing the jury to see Andy's macabre, disfigured body in repose. Sadness permeated the courtroom, giving proof to his death at the hands of Stela.

Wisely ending on that photo, Dominique said, "Nothing further, Your Honor." She removed the image.

"Very well. The case will now go to the jury after I read the instructions."

Judge O'Brien instructed the jury about how they should approach the evidence in the case and complete the verdict form, then he said, "As you know, there are 14 jurors currently seated, and only 12 will deliberate, so we need to randomly select two jurors who will go home." He gestured to his left where the court secretary's desk was located. "We have a tumbler for the random selection process. All 14 jurors' names are on pieces of paper inside the tumbler."

Everyone watched as the court secretary bent over and lifted the mesh tumbler from the floor. She set it on her desk for all to see, and turned the handle, spinning it around like a hamster wheel filled with slips of paper. When it stopped spinning, she opened the little door and removed two small slips of paper.

She cleared her throat and loudly read the name on each slip. "Mrs. Alina Popa and Mr. Troy Loomis."

Dominique kept a poker face while Stela's face fell.

Mrs. Popa cast a longing glance at Stela, whose upper lip started trembling at the loss of a clear ally.

"If those two jurors could rise, you are excused," Judge O'Brien said. "We thank you for your service, but you won't be needed for deliberations." He waited until they left. "Now, for the rest of you, please start your deliberations by selecting a foreperson. If you have any questions, you can write them down and notify Isla, who will bring them to me."

Judge O'Brien turned to the courtroom, and said, "Court is in recess while the jury deliberates." He slammed his gavel.

Everyone rose while the jurors, then Judge O'Brien, departed.

The deputies hovered over Stela, who turned to Monica. "Rigged. I knew this process would be rigged. It's you and the DA cunt."

"That's bullshit, and you know it!" Monica hissed.

The deputies, still smarting over Yuri shooting Brock, grabbed Stela by the arms and yanked her up and toward the thick metal door. There would be no more delicate treatment of the Romanian, who was probably Ukrainian.

Monica ignored their exodus, instead watching the court secretary clean out the tumbler. She reached into it, grabbed all of the slips, mixed them with the two slips she had removed and read, and dumped all 14 names into the recycle bin. The thought occurred to Monica that the secretary had never shown the two slips with Mrs. Popa or Mr. Loomis's names on them to anyone. Nor had anyone watched over the secretary's shoulder to double check the two names she had read. Moreover, she hadn't separated those two slips of paper to save them anywhere. Instead, they were now mixed with the others.

From her peripheral vision, Monica saw Dominique make eye contact with the court secretary. Dominique tipped up her chin in approval then quickly turned away and focused on closing her laptop and gathering her notes and folders. *So, that was Dominique's plan for neutralizing the Romanian grandmother,* Monica thought. *Well played. Not legal, but probably wise under the circumstances.*

47

Monica shifted in her chair and looked around. *Now, what do I do with myself?* she thought. *I could leave the building and return to the office. I could find Shelby and Jim, and spend the rest of the day with Shelby, but what if the jury returns a verdict in 20 minutes? On the other hand, what if they deliberate for hours?*

She checked her cell phone. No texts from Shelby.

"Are you going to stick around?" Tiffany asked, interrupting Monica's thoughts.

Monica looked up. "Um…I don't know yet. I'm checking with my office right now." A reasonable fib.

"I believe you promised me an interview." Tiffany waggled her finger at Monica.

"Yeah. I suppose so." Monica glanced around. "Where would you like to do that?"

"Can we do it right here?" Tiffany made a circle with her hand where she was standing. "It's a good angle. The judge's bench will be in the background."

"Fine." Monica rose. "Do I look all right?"

Tiffany jumped at the chance to smooth Monica's hair and adjust her collar. "You do now. Do you have any lipstick? The camera washes out your face, you know."

"I think I'll be okay," Monica said, not self-conscious about a pale face or lips.

"Here, stand next to me." Tiffany pulled Monica tight to her side, then raised her microphone.

Her cameraman miraculously apparated, bearing down on them with the device only a few feet from Monica's face. "Go ahead."

"We're in the courtroom of the Boyfriend Killer trial. The prosecution and defense delivered their closing arguments this morning, and the case just went to the jury. With me is Attorney Monica Spade. Welcome."

"Thank you, Tiffany."

"First, I noticed that you moved from counsel table to sitting behind the defendant during her closing argument. Why?"

"She requested it," Monica said, "and I was happy to put some distance between us, because I in no way represent her. She is a *pro se* defendant. I was appointed by the court to explain rulings and process to her. I've observed throughout this trial, however, that she understands judicial process quite well."

"Do you think that's because she's been in the criminal justice system before?"

"It might be that, or more likely, I think Ms. Reiter has some legal education and experience, even though she hasn't told me that."

"Do you think she's guilty?"

Expecting this question, Monica said, "That's for the jury to decide."

"What do you think of the jury? Did they pay attention during the trial?"

"Very much so. They look capable to me."

"What did you think of the Romanian woman being one of the two jurors randomly selected to leave? She indicated during *voir dire* that the defendant reminded her of her granddaughter."

"I remember that. Drawing names from the tumbler is a time-honored method of randomly selecting two jurors to be dismissed. It's fair. Luck of the draw and all that," Monica said, even though she would never forget the secretary's sleight of hand and Dominique's nod of approval.

"What did you think of the defendant's closing argument?" Tiffany asked.

"I think she did the best with the limited arguments she has."

"What did you think of the prosecution's closing?"

"I think DA Bisset did an outstanding job throughout the trial."

"What, specifically, did you like about DA Bisset's closing?"

"The way she patiently walked the jury through the details of the homicide, and the evidence that unequivocally incriminates Stela Reiter."

"Can you explain Detective Breuer's testimony about Stela's friend, Yuri Zaleski, taking someone hostage?"

"I thought Detective Breuer explained the situation quite well."

"Why did Zaleski take someone hostage?"

"To blackmail me."

"Did Zaleski contact you?"

"Yes."

"What did he say?"

"That he was going to kill my friend if Stela wasn't acquitted."

"What did you say?"

"I reported the situation to Detective Breuer, who rescued my friend."

"And shot Zaleski in the process?"

"Yes."

"Are you concerned about Stela Reiter coming after you if she's acquitted?"

Peter and Steven's faces flashed through Monica's mind. "Not in the least."

"How can you be so confident?"

"I trust the judicial system and law enforcement."

"Care to make any predictions about the verdict?"

"I think the jury will return a guilty verdict."

Tiffany didn't raise an eyebrow. "Thank you for your time, Attorney Spade."

"My pleasure."

Tiffany looked directly into the camera. "This is Tiffany Rose reporting from the Boyfriend Killer trial for WQOD."

The camera light turned off, and Tiffany lowered her microphone. "Thanks for the interview. Maybe I'll hit you up after the verdict, okay?"

Monica nodded noncommittally.

"My cameraman and I are going to order some sandwiches. Want to join?"

"Sure," Monica said, not knowing what to do with herself and her stomach growling at the mention of food. "Where should we eat?"

"We have a conference room around the corner."

Monica trailed after Tiffany and her cameraman, and, before she realized it, she was enjoying her time with them over sandwiches that were delivered in mere minutes.

"What do you think the jury is doing?" Tiffany asked.

"Finishing lunch and picking a foreperson," Monica said around a bite.

"Who do you think will be foreperson?"

"My guess is Dr. Gilmore," Monica said.

"Why?"

"She's nice and knowledgeable, and they might want to discuss the DNA evidence, or the PTSD *I-forgot-everything* bullshit explanation. I think Dr. Gilmore could facilitate those two discussions."

"What did you think of Stela's star experts, Drs. Karpenko and Popovich?" Tiffany asked, but they were interrupted by Lori, Dominique's legal assistant.

"The jury is back with a verdict," Lori said.

"What?" Monica asked. "Are you sure they don't just have a question?"

"No. It's a verdict."

"Wow. That was fast," Monica said. "Has 20 minutes even gone by?"

"It's been about 45, believe it or not," said the cameraman.

They quickly balled up their sandwich wrappers and tossed them into the garbage, as they left the room.

Monica took her place in the chair behind Stela's vacant chair, Peter and Steven behind her right shoulder.

Still wearing her pink cardigan and white blouse, Stela entered with her deputy escorts at the same time Judge O'Brien dropped into his chair. Stela immediately registered Peter and Steven's presence but didn't make eye contact with Monica.

Monica remained silent, the tension in her own body building, as everyone took their seats at their desks and tables. Judge O'Brien asked Isla to get the jury.

They filed in like they had many times before, but this time, they appeared equal parts resolute and relieved.

After they were seated, Judge O'Brien asked, "I understand the jury elected a foreperson and arrived at a verdict. Is that true?"

"Yes," Dr. Gilmore said, a folded piece of paper in her hand.

"Are you the foreperson?" Judge O'Brien asked.

"Yes," Dr. Gilmore said.

"Please deliver the verdict."

Dr. Gilmore rose and handed the folded paper to Isla, who walked it over to the bench for Judge O'Brien to review. His eyes traveled over the single sheet of paper, his expression inscrutable. He looked up at Dr. Gilmore, who was still standing.

"Is the verdict unanimous?" he asked.

"Yes," Dr. Gilmore said in a voice certain.

"You may be seated." Judge O'Brien turned to the courtroom more broadly and glanced over the deputies, of which there were now four—two by Stela and two in the aisle between the family and Stela. Satisfied that adequate security was in place, Judge O'Brien said, "I shall now read the verdict."

Stela's thumbs rubbed in a blur over her knuckles

Judge O'Brien announced in his loud baritone, "In the matter of State versus Stela Reiter, the jury finds the defendant *guilty* of first degree intentional homicide."

Monica heard a collective sigh from the gallery behind her, as she turned to look at Stela, who, in slow motion, reached into the right pocket of her cardigan, plucked something out with her fingertips, and popped it into her mouth. She lifted the cup of water on the table before her and drained it in one gulp.

Suddenly, Monica's ears were assaulted by Peter shouting, "She took a pill!"

Before Monica knew what was happening, Peter clamored over the bar railing and attacked Stela, who pressed her hands against him and kept her jaw tightly closed.

"Cough up the pill!" he yelled. "Cough up the pill!" His hands on either side of Stela's jaw, he attempted in vain to open her mouth, pressing into her cheeks, as his thumbs poked into her lips. During their awkward struggle, the chair gave way, and they tumbled to the floor. Peter quickly overpowered Stela, throwing a leg over her abdomen, and straddling her while his hands searched out her face. He again tried to wedge his thumbs between her lips.

"Give it up, you bitch!" he yelled.

Stela stopped trying to push his hands away and instead frantically searched Peter's body for a weapon. He must not have been wearing a holster on his belt, because her fingers moved down the side of his leg. She stuck her hand under the cuff of his pants and deftly removed a knife that he had strapped to his calf. With speed and accuracy, she decisively stabbed Peter in his side, right below his rib cage. He doubled over in pain, going limp on top of her.

"You idiot!" She hissed at him and withdrew the knife, wielding it for another stab. "This one is for Yuri!"

Standing closest to Peter and Stela, acting on instinct, Monica reached down and grabbed Peter by the suit jacket, jerking him into the air, as if she were at CrossFit hoisting a barbell overhead. Whether intentionally or out of sheer panic, Peter momentarily gained his footing and pushed off, propelling himself backward.

One moment he was upright, and the next, his momentum carried him past Monica's shoulder and into Dominique's arms. Dominique caught him like a pro and lowered him to the floor, attending to him.

Less than a minute had passed since Stela had stuffed the pill in her mouth, which Monica assumed was some sort of fast-acting suicide agent. She expected Stela to crumple before their eyes on a swift path to death, but the woman evidently had more fight in her.

In a shockingly quick maneuver, Stela jumped to her feet and slashed at the air. "You're next, you ignorant cunt!" Stela hissed, only a few feet from Monica.

Monica's worst fear had come true. She was now face-to-face with the cold-blooded killer who was as skilled with a knife as any professional assassin.

As Monica stood before Stela, locking eyes in a prelude to battle, Judge O'Brien yelled, "Bailiffs, tase the defendant!"

Monica expected Stela to be electrically shocked into oblivion before her eyes, but nothing happened.

Stela smiled, her eyes piercing Monica now, her mouth parted with saliva foaming at the corners of her lips. She said in a low whisper, "I disabled it. You're mine, Spade!"

Not hearing Stela's threat, the bailiff still pressed the button on his taser for Stela's belt, apparently not registering that it wasn't electrocuting her.

Stela lunged at Monica, angling the knife in a slicing motion toward Monica's chest. Monica did what came naturally, taking evasive action to her right while grabbing Stela's wrist to point the knife down and away.

Their bodies collided in a fierce dual of strength to control the trajectory of the knife. Their arms and hands trembled, as Stela attempted to stab the knife into Monica, and Monica attempted to thrust it away with all of her might.

Monica squeezed her hands around Stela's wrist as tightly as she could, the muscles in her forearms screaming in protest.

"You're stronger than I thought you were," Stela grunted, attempting to pull the knife up and back.

The knife pitched and dove wildly in midair, its direction a reflection of the women's competing forces upon it.

Monica was beginning to wonder whether the pill Stela had swallowed was for added strength or to end her life, because Stela's ferocity seemed to intensify rather than diminish.

For a few critical seconds, Monica held the knife at bay, now pointing it toward the floor, when Stela suddenly went limp, resulting in Monica accidentally jamming the knife into Stela's thigh.

Both women's eyes widened in surprise at the stab, but Stela's eyes quickly rolled back in her head, her chest heaving in final gasps for air, as she fell backward to the floor. Monica stepped back in horror, wondering if her stab was the cause of Stela's limp body, or if that pill had finally taken hold.

"Oh shit..." Monica gasped, not sure what to make of Stela.

Stela's mouth lolled open, and she began seizing, hands and arms shaking first, then her legs and torso convulsing violently. She was a spastic blur until she vomited, choked, then stopped moving altogether, becoming silent and eerily still.

Monica stood a few feet away, now flanked by Dominique and a bailiff. Steven had pushed Dominique out of the way and was now crouched over Peter.

Monica was amped with the adrenaline of battle, her fists clenched so tightly that her short fingernails dug into her palms. She was close to hyperventilating when she felt Dominique's hand squeeze her shoulder. Monica was immediately reassured that the fight was over. The madness had ended as abruptly as it had begun.

"I think she's dead," Dominique said into the stunned silence of the courtroom.

Stela's breath rattled in her chest one last time, then her face turned such a deep shade of blue under her pale skin that Monica had to look away.

"Call 911," Judge O'Brien said calmly to the court secretary.

Monica's first thought was that a 911 call would be in vain. She was certain without taking Stela's pulse that she was dead. Then, she remembered that Peter was lying beside Dominique's counsel table.

Monica's eyes traveled back and forth between Peter, unconscious, and Stela, dead, her mind struggling to make sense of what just took place. She recalled meeting Stela at the jail after Yuri had given her the vial containing a pill. Assuming the pill had been medicine, Monica had delivered it. *Cyanide?*

"Are you all right?" Dominique asked, interrupting Monica's racing thoughts.

"No," Monica muttered.

"Did she cut you?" Dominique grasped Monica's hands where there was a smear of blood on her right hand.

"No. That's Stela's blood from her leg," Monica said, frozen at the sight.

Dominique snatched the tissue box from her counsel table and wiped Monica's hands. Lori, Dominique's assistant, saw what she was doing and opened their cannister of antibacterial wipes. She cleaned Monica's hand like she was prepping her for a surgical procedure.

"What the hell just happened?" Monica asked, stunned.

"Stela obviously took a suicide pill, but she thought she could kill you before she died," Dominique said matter-of-factly, as if this sort of thing transpired every day in the courtroom. She lowered her voice to a whisper. "I can't believe Peter was so reckless that he had a knife strapped to his shin."

"Or, that he made it through the metal detectors," Monica said.

"Just had to show his government ID," Dominique said.

"Oh," Monica said. "Can you believe how fast Stela found it? It's as if she knew it was there."

"Maybe she did." Dominique's usually serene eyes were animated.

Their conversation was interrupted by EMTs entering the courtroom.

"Make room! Make room!" they exclaimed, as they made their way down the crowded aisle to Peter, who was lying in agony on the floor, Steven applying pressure to his stab wound.

Within minutes, the EMTs had Peter on a gurney and were rolling him out of the courtroom, destined for an ambulance at curbside.

A second set of EMTs entered and pronounced Stela dead, then began the grisly task of rolling her into a body bag.

Dominique nudged Monica and said, "Let's get out of here."

Monica spied her laptop under a chair, retrieved it, and followed Dominique through the crowded courtroom. As soon as they entered the hallway, Steven caught up to them.

He grabbed Monica by the arm, twirling her toward him. "Thanks for saving Peter's life."

Sensitive from battle, she shook off his clingy hand. "Um...It was instinct. I just did what anyone would do."

"You acted fast in the face of danger." He cocked his head. "I'm sorry I initially underestimated you. You're one of the smartest women I've met outside of Catholics in Action."

Monica took the backhanded compliment in stride. "Thank you Steven. Give Peter my best at the hospital, will you?"

"I will," he said, then leaned in. "Goes without saying that our earlier conversation is top secret." He briefly glanced at Dominique.

"Of course," Monica said. "Listen, something's been bugging me, and you might not know the answer, but I'm going to ask you anyway."

"Feel free."

"We know that Yuri fabricated Andy's journal entries, but a few lines caught my eye. There are some Eugène Ionesco quotes tossed in there, notably, 'We have not the time to take our time.' Is that a coded message for a call to action?"

Steven's eyes widened with surprise. "I…ah… Hm." He rubbed his eyes, and pulled his phone out. "Say that again?"

She repeated it, as he typed it into his phone.

"There's another one too," she said.

"What's that?" he asked, his thumbs still poised over his phone.

"We can predict our fate only after it has happened," she said.

He typed furiously, as he muttered, "Oh shit."

"I see you're thinking the same thing I am," she said. "Is Ukraine going to launch a nuclear missile attack against Russia?"

His head snapped up. "Keep your voice down, and don't breathe a word of that to anyone." He turned to Dominique. "You either."

"My lips are sealed," Dominique said.

He quickly turned and disappeared into the crowded hallway.

Dominique tipped up her chin at Monica. "Barney Fife, indeed."

Monica shook her head. "Andy, I can't get the bullet out of my pocket." She pretended to be searching for a bullet in her breast pocket.

Dominique smiled. "We should go to my office before we're swarmed by the media. Lori is assembling Andy's family in the conference room for me to address privately in a few minutes."

As the two women walked side-by-side, Monica said, "I can't believe I killed my client after a guilty verdict."

"She wasn't your client, and you didn't kill her. The pill killed her. She was actually trying to kill *you*."

Monica grunted. "Like that's better. My first criminal trial ended with the defendant trying to kill me in open court. Not exactly a ringing endorsement of my legal services."

Dominique chuckled, as she held the door for Monica. "Did you say, 'first criminal trial?'"

Monica whipped around in surprise. "If I did, I didn't mean it. I'm not a trial attorney. If there was ever an experience that convinced me of that, this was it."

"Never say never," Dominique said, as they entered her office. "I think you have a knack for the courtroom."

48

White mares' tails streaked across a brilliant blue sky, allowing plenty of sunshine to counteract the umpteenth day in a row of temps in the deep freeze.

On the final day of the ice fishing tourney, Monica and Shelby, clad in snow pants and parkas, stepped onto the two-foot layer of ice covering Half Moon Lake. The festivities included an ice sculpture contest, a chili cook-off, and the fish weigh-in for the grand prize of a new fishing boat.

"I can't believe Nathan and Matt are ice fishing," Shelby said, as they followed others onto the snow-packed trail to the fishing village of 100-plus ice fishing shacks, some of which were practically three-season homes. The village had become so large that the fisherman had erected street signs for way-finding.

"I wasn't surprised to hear Matt has a shack," Monica said, getting her bearings, for the directions Nathan had given her, "but I can't picture Nathan fishing for longer than 15 minutes."

"Me either," Shelby said. "I hope he has a good book."

"He said he'd be grateful for our company," Monica said, carrying a plastic container of bars they had baked that morning. "Let's see, Matt's shack is on the corner of Bass and Walleye Streets. He said it has brown siding with a red metal roof."

The women walked arm-in-arm, smiling in greeting at others, as they read the makeshift street signs—Crappie Avenue, Muskie Lane, Perch Drive.

Monica was amazed at the creativity of the designs and colors of the shacks.

"You know that Jim has a shack down here, too, right?" Shelby asked.

"I didn't know that, but ice fishing fits his personality," Monica said. "He loves all sports related to lakes. I can picture him with frost on his beard, wearing a pair of overall snow pants and a thick sweater. He could hide from the women in his life and do some thinking."

Shelby giggled. "There seem to be plenty to hide from, that's for sure. He offered to show me his shack yesterday while we were doing errands, but I just didn't have the energy to bundle up and come down here."

"Good call. I'm not sure how I would feel about you spending time with him in such intimate quarters," Monica said, as they crunched through the snow.

Shelby laughed. "You, my dear, having nothing to worry—" Her reassurance was interrupted by their emergence into a garden of ice sculptures, "Oh my God. Look at these!"

The orderly rows of shacks gave way to an ice sculpture competition. As the women walked by, they admired the 12-foot high sculptures of everything from a herd of reindeer to palm trees on a beach tableau. Specialized chain saws whirred, as shapes took form, and sculptors used finer carving tools for the final product.

"I could linger here for a while," Shelby said, tugging on Monica's arm.

"Me too, babe, but let's say hello to Nathan and Matt first, then come back, okay?" Monica tightened her grip on Shelby's hand, who reluctantly followed.

They walked the perimeter of the sculptures, Monica on a mission. A few streets later, they found themselves at the corner of Bass and Walleye. A brown shack had a hand-painted sign over the door with "Breuer" written on it, so Monica knocked.

Nathan opened the door. "Hey, ladies. Welcome!"

Monica noticed he was wearing only a sweater with his snow pants, so he was either impervious to the cold, or Matt's shack was heated. "We brought you some bars."

"Thank you," Nathan said, accepting the container. "Come in. We've been expecting you."

They entered the spacious, well-decorated box filled with sunshine from a skylight and a large window overlooking the village. Nathan hugged both women, then Matt stood from kneeling over a hole in the floor that had two fishing lines disappearing into it. The short rods were resting in some type of apparatus affixed to the floor.

"Impressive setup," Monica said, accepting a big hug from Matt.

"Years of practice," he said. "Come in and have a seat."

There was a built-in bench seat, a table, and two chairs with pads on them. A heater was running in the corner, bringing the temp to a balmy 50 degrees in the wood-paneled shack. The finishing work was so nice that Monica felt like she was in a miniature lake cabin.

Shelby sat on the bench and withdrew a thermos from her bag. "Anyone care for a spiked hot cocoa?"

Nathan's eyebrows shot up. "I'd love some. I have mugs, painted with a fishing motif, of course." He turned to a corner where there was a wall mount of pegs with several mugs hanging on it.

Shelby giggled in delight and handed her thermos to him.

Monica opened the soft-sided cooler they brought. "Would you like a beer, Matt?"

"If you're offering, I wouldn't turn it down."

She handed one to him and opened one for herself. After Nathan poured hot cocoa for Shelby and himself, they all clinked and drank.

"Heard the trial ended with a bang," Matt said, winking at Monica. "Or should I say a stab?"

She rolled her eyes. "It's true. I stabbed a dying woman."

Matt laughed. "Can't blame you if she was trying to kill you."

"Not as easy as it looks on TV," she said in a serious tone.

"You did an outstanding job," he said.

"Did you catch the morning news?" Nathan asked.

"No. We purposefully stayed out of touch this morning," Monica said, squeezing Shelby's arm.

"Oh, then you haven't had time to process this," Nathan said, as he pulled up a news article on his phone. He turned the screen to Monica and Shelby to read. *The New York Times* headline was "Nuclear blast in Moscow from Dirty Bomb."

"No waaay," Monica said on a sharp intake of breath. She grabbed his phone and held it in front of her, so Shelby could read the article too.

Shelby put on her new glasses with the lavender bows, and Monica winked at her. "Sexy as hell, babe."

They read together that a bomb had gone off in downtown Moscow, killing hundreds and spreading radiation for miles in a fiery plume of smoke. Evacuations were underway, but they predicted hundreds of additional casualties from radiation exposure. No one claimed responsibility, but every country had denied involvement. The U.S. President offered both medical and forensic assistance.

When Monica and Shelby looked up, Nathan said, "Looks like you were definitely onto something, Mon."

"I…can't…believe it," Monica said. "Now I'm actually concerned that I shared my theories with Peter and Steven, because they know that I know."

Matt waved her concern away. "I wouldn't worry about it. Your knowledge is a part of history now, and they have bigger problems to worry about."

"But…but… They'll want to cover up what they were doing…and this stupid trial…so that means I'm a liability," Monica said.

"It was a public trial!" Nathan "Don't worry about it."

"You're right," Monica said, finding and squeezing Shelby's hand.

Suddenly, the tip of one of Matt's short fishing rods bent down. He set down his beer. "Looks like we've got a bite."

Monica was grateful for the diversion.

"I hope it's not a tiny perch this time," Nathan said.

"Oh, I can't wait to watch this," Shelby said, pulling out her phone. "Mind if I video?"

"Not at all," Matt said. "Just delete it if it's a perch."

They watched in awe, as he set the hook and reeled patiently, allowing the fish to fight for a few minutes. Finally, they heard the splash of the fish coming to the hole, and Matt expertly raised it up and lay it on the wood floor before it could slither back into the water. "A crappie," he said, removing the hook. "This one is a keeper."

He held it up for a photo then set it in a white bucket in the corner. Monica noticed the bucket wasn't on the wood floor but sitting directly on the ice. "That's an efficient way to keep your fish fresh."

"Flash frozen in a bucket of snow," Matt said.

"Looks like fish fry for dinner tonight," Shelby said.

"You're welcome to join," Matt said. "The more the merrier."

While they watched Matt bait the hook with a minnow, there was a knock on the door. Nathan opened it to Dominique. As per usual, she looked sophisticated in a down parka with a faux-fir trimmed hood. Her platinum hair was perfectly styled, and she was wearing makeup.

"I thought I saw some visitors arrive," she said, a big smile on her face.

"Welcome, Dominique," Nathan said. "Come in."

Dominique entered, a glass of wine in-hand. "Hello, Monica and Shelby. How's the fishing going?"

"Matt's catching some," Monica said. "How about with you?"

"Jim is into it," Dom said, pointing over her shoulder. "See the news today?"

"Unfortunately, yes," Monica said.

"Looks like Barney Fife will have his hands full now." Dominique smiled as she drank.

"Who?" Nathan asked.

"Peter and Steven," Monica said. "We refer to Steven as Barney Fife now."

"Just makes you proud to be an American, doesn't it?" Nathan asked.

Monica checked the time on her iWatch. "Speaking of our great country, we should pop outside for a second to see the ice sculptures."

"But it's so cozy in here," Shelby said. "I just got comfortable."

Monica looked at Nathan for help, as he was in on her secret.

"Oh, there's a special one you'll want to see," he said. "It will only take a second."

Possessing a sixth sense, a look of curiosity crossed Dominique's expression, as she glanced quickly between Nathan and Monica. "I'm in. Just let me set down my glass. The DA can't be seen walking around the fishing village with wine in her hand."

"Good timing," Matt said. "I'll come before I drop this line in the water. Don't want my rod tips to go down while I'm outside." He quickly reeled in the other line and grabbed his beer.

Nathan held the door while they bustled outside the small shack.

Monica took the lead, heading toward the sculpture garden. Her iWatch flashed with a text, and she quickly scanned it, confirming the timing.

"Let me get Jim." On their way, Dominique ducked her head into a substantial shack and signaled for Jim to join.

Monica stepped toward Shelby and looped her hand through her arm, as she heard an airplane in the distance. She scanned the horizon, but she couldn't see it yet.

"I noticed the ice sculptures on the way in, but Monica wouldn't let me stop to look at them," Shelby said, her attention focused on Nathan and Matt.

"There are a few beauties," Nathan said, happily picking up the conversation.

Monica was grateful because she was suddenly too nervous to speak.

As they entered the ice sculpture garden, the familiar sound of the plane grew closer. Monica looked up into the brilliant sky and saw the plane coming into view, on track to fly over the entire fishing village.

Her heart thumped in her chest, and her mouth went dry. She padded her jacket pocket with her hand to confirm she had what she needed.

Nathan slapped Monica on the back and whispered, "Good luck."

As the group assembled around a magnificent sculpture of an eagle, Shelby studying the finer points of feather contouring along the wings, the plane came into full view above the village, trailing a long banner.

Dominique was the first to read it, and she gasped loudly, drawing the attention of Jim.

"Well, look at that," he said, throwing his arm around her shoulders.

"Yeah, look at that banner," Monica said, nudging Shelby, who was the last to tip her head back to gaze up at the sound of the plane overhead.

Centered in the sky above them, in perfect view, the plane trailed a brightly-colored banner that read, "Shelby, will you marry me?"

Returning her own gaze to earth, Monica was enthralled at Shelby's confused, disbelieving expression.

Shelby quickly put on her glasses and mumbled, "What?" her soft, hazel eyes bright with surprise.

Monica pushed her sunglasses up and dropped to a knee. She searched for the black, velvet ring box from her pocket and held it up to Shelby's waist. Her mouth dry and hands shaking, Monica squinted into Shelby's eyes against the brilliant sky, and asked, "Will you marry me?" She opened the lid on the box, revealing a gold braided ring with sapphires.

Shelby's trembling hands flew to her mouth. "Oh my God, Monica. How romantic! Yes. Yes! I'll marry you!"

Dominique squealed with delight, and Jim chortled.

They had managed to garner the attention of others who looked at the banner, looked at Monica on bended knee—now sliding the unique engagement ring onto Shelby's finger—then broke into applause.

Monica didn't understand why she was crying, but tears were streaming down her face, as she stood and pulled Shelby into an urgent embrace.

Nathan clapped. "Well done, Mon!"

Dominique stepped in to relieve Shelby of her mug of spiked cocoa, so she could hug everyone.

"This ring is gorgeous," Shelby said, holding her hand out to admire the sapphires glimmering in the sun.

"If you don't like it, we can exchange it," Monica said. "I got it at Denise's Diamonds. One of her jewelers handcrafted it"

"I love it!" Shelby said. "Did she help you pick it out?"

"Of course," Monica said, her arm around Shelby's waist.

Nathan started snapping photos of them, their heads angled down, admiring the one-of-kind ring, the ice sculpture behind them. "Hey, you two, look at me," he said.

They looked up, grins wide, and he snapped away.

"I believe this calls for a champagne toast," Jim said.

"I didn't bring any," Shelby said, making Monica laugh because Shelby still didn't realize that Monica had planned the occasion.

"We've got you covered, girl," Nathan said, as he snapped more pics.

"How thoughtful," Shelby said. "And romantic." She turned to Monica and lay her hand on her cheek. "Thank you for making this the most memorable engagement ever. I've never been happier."

Before Monica could speak, Shelby planted a kiss on her lips.

As everyone applauded, joy filled Monica's heart. She'd never been happier herself.

***

The End

***

Message from the Author

If you enjoyed *Standby Counsel*, I would be grateful for your review on Amazon and/or Goodreads. I'd also love to hear from you about whether you would like more Monica Spade. Hop over to my website at www.alexivenice.com and use the contact form.

It's not too late to read the original Monica Spade novel, *Conscious Bias*. Available on Kindle Unlimited, look for this cover:

Story Description: Trevor McKnight, a young, white male, is charged with the murder of Abdul Seif, a Saudi Arabian foreign exchange student.

Attorney Monica Spade's physician clients plan to testify at trial that Trevor's punch to Abdul's head killed him. Monica is shocked when her bosses at her all-male law firm warn her not to cross the powerful McKnight family. Facing death threats and career-ending consequences, Monica must decide whether to expose the truth in a bigoted environment.

In her personal life, Monica joins a CrossFit box to work off stress. During class, she meets Shelby St. Claire, a high school art teacher. For the first time in her career, Monica considers coming out of the closet for Shelby.

Available on Amazon and Kindle Unlimited.

If you're looking for a gritty crime drama series with more explicit romance, check out my *San Francisco Mystery Series*. It's a six-book series that explores the nuances and struggles of Dr. Jen Dawson, Detective Tommy Vietti and District Attorney Amanda Hawthorne. Will their unique love triangle survive solving crimes and life together?

Legal and crime drama with a side of romance.

Story Description for *Bourbon Chase, The San Francisco Mystery Series, Book 1:*

Jen Dawson is an emergency room physician in San Francisco who is training for a triathlon. Her boyfriend, Tommy Vietti, is an experienced detective who is loyal to the police force, his Italian family, and Jen.

Amanda Hawthorne is a charismatic District Attorney who prosecutes criminals while fending off attacks from mobsters. As San Francisco's most-eligible lesbian, Amanda has her choice of female companions, so why is she attracted to Jen, who is supposedly straight?

When one of Jen's colleagues becomes a suspect in a murder investigation, Tommy and Amanda invade Jen's professional life. Jen sticks up for her physician colleague, then discovers she has more in common with Amanda than just butting heads. Will Jen stay with Tommy or choose Amanda?

Available now on Amazon and Kindle Unlimited.

Acknowledgements

I'm grateful for the love and support of so many people through the numerous steps from story creation to publication.

My friend and colleague, Erin Skold, continues to serve as a sounding board (and probably "bored") regarding plot and characters. With fond pre-COVID memories, I recall our afternoon chai tea jaunts when we chatted about how Monica would represent a dangerous criminal in the courtroom. Brainstorming with Erin energized me to set the wheels in motion for Monica's standby counsel role, which was a new term to me. I look forward to more chats over tea with Erin, as I write the next Monica Spade book.

Balancing an active career and writing novels is tricky on the home front. I have little time for (or interest in, to be honest) cooking, so I'm blessed with my chef husband, Todd, and his fabulous cooking.

I changed up Reyka's role a bit for this book. Previously volunteering as a proofreader, Reyka instead reviewed the first draft of this book, and I was delighted with her wise feedback.

As always, Rob Bignell provided both editorial and structural commentary to improve upon the second draft.

Laurie generously serves as a legal advisor about criminal defense work and was kind enough to allow me to shadow her to the county jail. I learned so much for this book, but more importantly, I expanded my appreciation for humanity and my community. The experience rekindled compassion where judgment had come to rest after observing a brutal homicide trial. Thank you, Laurie, for teaching me about criminal law on this journey.

As a new member to my team, Andrea read the third draft through the lens of a prosecutor. Her work has served as an inspiration for the *Monica Spade Series*, specifically, the role of Dominique Bisset. Andrea has been generous with her time and expertise, and I'm deeply honored, especially since she has a huge career in addition to a busy family.

Sarah Branham is also new to the team. She's an experienced, top notch editor, so my manuscript definitely married up when it met her. She provided stunning clarity and problem-solving in places where I needed it most. It's an honor to work with someone so smart and talented.

Elizabeth J. Wilson was kind enough to lend me some of her otherwise adventurous time for proofreading. Not only is Elizabeth a speed reader, but she's also incredibly sharp about crime scenes and legal jargon. Curious background, right? I'm fortunate to have made her acquaintance and am grateful for her courtesy.

Robin Elvig took time out of her busy schedule to proofread the final version, and I'm thankful. She brings a background of medicine and writing to the table, which directly aligns with my stories. What a delight! Hope to see her sparkly blues sometime soon.

My dear friend, Mik, came through clutch with some advice at the final, final stages.

About the Author

Amazon bestselling author Alexi Venice writes legal thrillers and crime drama with a side of romance.

Venice's 31-year legal career informs her medical and crime fiction. She is legal counsel under a different name at an international healthcare system, specializing in preparing nurses and physicians to testify in court in both civil and criminal trials. Venice's heart, imagination and life experience inform her romantic drama.

When she isn't writing, Venice can be found on the lake boating with her family. Venice is married and lives in Wisconsin.

Venice says: "One of my favorite characters to write about is DA Amanda Hawthorne in *The San Francisco Mystery Series*. She's heroic and genuinely in love with Dr. Jen, but Amanda struggles with addiction issues, cannot stop herself from personally fighting the bad guys, and engages in self-destructive behavior to blow off stress. She is capable of introspection and love, though, which is why I respect and adore her."

Venice's bestselling *San Francisco Mystery Series* is a crime drama that tests the bonds of love and loyalty among Dr. Jen Dawson, Detective Tommy Vietti and District Attorney Amanda Hawthorne. If you're looking for explicit romantic drama mixed with gritty crime, this series is for you.

Connect with Venice on her website: www.alexivenice.com